Praise for
The Language of Sycamores

"Heartfelt, honest, and entirely entertaining, *The Language of Sycamores* is a novel about the complex ties that bind our families together and the sometimes painful lessons we all need to learn along the way. This poignant story will touch your heart from the first page to the last."
                                                                    —Kristin Hannah

Praise for
Good Hope Road

"*Good Hope Road* is a novel bursting with joy amid crisis. . . . Lisa Wingate is a glorious storyteller. . . . Small-town life is painted with scope and detail in the capable hands of a writer who understands longing, grief, and the landscape of a woman's heart. You will love this story." —Adriana Trigiani, author of the *Big Stone Gap* trilogy

"No storm is ever so far-reaching as the one within the heart. Lisa Wingate has written a beautiful story of family, friendship, overcoming loss, and the courage to rise above destructive forces."
                                     —Lynne Hinton, author of *Forever Friends*

"Wingate has written a genuinely heartwarming story about how a sense of possibility can be awakened in the aftermath of a tragedy to bring a community together and demonstrate the true American spirit."
                                                                         —*Booklist*

continued . . .

Praise for
Tending Roses

"*Tending Roses* is a story at once gentle and powerful about the very old and the very young, about the young woman who loves them all. In Katie, Lisa Wingate has created a wonderful character who listens to the family stories, understands that life is a mystery with family right at its center, lives her own life to the hilt. Richly emotional and spiritual, *Tending Roses* affected me from the first page."
—Luanne Rice, *New York Times* bestselling author of *True Blue*

"Stop what you are doing and experience *Tending Roses* . . . a rich story of family and faith that reminds us of the bittersweet seasons of life and our call to care for each other."
—Lynne Hinton, author of *Forever Friends*

"A heartwarming tale of human compassion and reconciliation. . . . You can't put it down without . . . taking a good look at your own life and how misplaced priorities might have led to missed opportunities. *Tending Roses* is an excellent read for any season, a celebration of the power of love."
—*El Paso Times*

"A touching novel about how an estranged family struggles to reconnect. . . . This novel's strength is its believable characters. . . . Many readers will see themselves in Kate, who is so wrapped up in her own problems that she fails to see the worries of others."
—*American Profile*

"Get your tissues or handkerchief ready. You're going to need them when you read Lisa Wingate's book *Tending Roses*. Your emotions will run the gamut from laughing loudly to shedding tears as you read the story."
—*McAlester News Capital & Democrat* (OK)

"Wingate's touching story of love and faith proves the old adage that we should take time to smell the roses and try to put our modern problems in perspective."
—*Booklist*

Praise for Lisa Wingate's
contemporary romances
Texas Cooking and
Lone Star Café

"Everything a romance should be, yet so much more, *Texas Cooking* is a book that all women, young and old, will remember always."
—Catherine Anderson, *New York Times* bestselling author of *My Sunshine*

"Wingate has cooked up a practically perfect romance: soft, sweet, often uproariously funny, alive with people you'd want to know and places you'd like to be." —*Detroit Free Press*

"Lisa Wingate leaves you feeing like you've danced the two-step across Texas." —Jodi Thomas

"A beautifully written mix of comedy, drama, cooking, and journalism." —*The Dallas Morning News*

"[*Lone Star Café* is] a wonderfully warm story peopled with characters you wish you could meet yet feel you already know."
—*Romantic Times* (4½ stars, Gold, Top Pick)

"A charmingly nostalgic treat. . . . Laura . . . is winning as an ordinary woman faced with conflicting options. Appealingly eccentric secondary characters and beautifully evoked Texas settings further enrich this warmhearted read." —*Publishers Weekly*

"A remarkably talented and innovative writer, with a real feel for human emotions." —Linda Lael Miller

LISA WINGATE

The Language

of

Sycamores

FICTION FOR THE WAY WE LIVE

NAL Accent
Published by New American Library, a division of
Penguin Group (USA) Inc., 375 Hudson Street,
New York, New York 10014, USA
Penguin Group (Canada), 10 Alcorn Avenue, Toronto,
Ontario M4V 3B2, Canada (a division of Pearson Penguin Canada Inc.)
Penguin Books Ltd., 80 Strand, London WC2R 0RL, England
Penguin Ireland, 25 St. Stephen's Green, Dublin 2,
Ireland (a division of Penguin Books Ltd.)
Penguin Group (Australia), 250 Camberwell Road, Camberwell, Victoria 3124,
Australia (a division of Pearson Australia Group Pty. Ltd.)
Penguin Books India Pvt. Ltd., 11 Community Centre, Panchsheel Park,
New Delhi - 110 017, India
Penguin Group (NZ), cnr Airborne and Rosedale Roads, Albany,
Auckland 1310, New Zealand (a division of Pearson New Zealand Ltd.)
Penguin Books (South Africa) (Pty.) Ltd., 24 Sturdee Avenue,
Rosebank, Johannesburg 2196, South Africa

Penguin Books Ltd., Registered Offices:
80 Strand, London WC2R 0RL, England

First published by NAL Accent, an imprint of New American Library,
a division of Penguin Group (USA) Inc.

First Printing, January 2005
10 9 8 7 6 5 4

FICTION FOR THE WAY WE LIVE

REGISTERED TRADEMARK—MARCA REGISTRADA

LIBRARY OF CONGRESS CATALOGING-IN-PUBLICATION DATA:

Wingate, Lisa.
The language of sycamores / Lisa Wingate
p. cm.
"Conversation guide included."
ISBN 0-451-21392-0 (trade pbk.)
1. Downsizing of organizations—Fiction. 2. Loss (Psychology)—Fiction. 3. Cancer in women—Fiction.
4. Ozark Mountains—Fiction. 5. Married women—Fiction. 6. Unemployed—Fiction. 7. Farm life—Fiction.
8. Missouri—Fiction. 9. Children—Fiction. 10. Sisters—Fiction. I. Title.
PS3573.I53165L36 2005
813'.54—dc22   2004014367

Set in Adobe Garamond
Designed by Ginger Legato

Printed in the United States of America

To my teachers
And all teachers,
Who build dreams
By creating the dreamers.

Especially for Mrs. Krackhardt,
My first grade teacher at Peaslee School
Who told me I would become a writer one day.

Acknowledgments

While writing *The Language of Sycamores,* I thought often of my teachers, perhaps because of the children in the story, Sherita, Meleka, and Dell, who so desperately need someone to believe in them. Any words of acknowledgment I would write here would be incomplete if I didn't include the people who inspired me to believe in my dream. My heartfelt thanks to my many wonderful teachers over the years, but particularly to Mrs. Krackhardt, who took the time to notice a shy transfer student writing a book during indoor recess. I still remember the day you stopped by my desk, read my story, and said, "You are a wonderful writer!" From that moment on, I believed I was exactly what you told me I was.

To the principal who sent me to detention for writing stories when I wasn't supposed to, the math teacher who told me that I'd better pay attention in geometry because writing isn't a "real" career, and the graduate teaching assistant who gave me an F on my first essay in freshman composition, I blow a big raspberry at you and say I forgive you completely for trampling on my dream. It is the trampled seed that grows the deepest roots.

My gratitude once again goes out to my writer friends, my constant sources of encouragement (and good reading material), Dusty, Velda, June, Marge, and especially Jessica. Special thanks to my family on both sides, who have peddled books to anyone who will stand still, housed me during book signings, traveled with me to speaking engagements, and read countless rough drafts. You are the reason I write about family bonds. These stories are my feeble attempt to share you with the world. All crazy, quirky, cantankerous and slightly off-plumb characters are, of course, purely fictional.

Thanks beyond measure to the booksellers who have shown such devotion to my previous books, the reviewers and media personnel who have been amazingly kind about giving support and endorsements, and the many readers from all over the country who have sent notes and e-mails about the books. It never fails that, when I'm having a discouraging day at the computer, one of you will send a note that lifts me up. I am blessed to have so many friends so far away. To all of you who read *Tending Roses* and *Good Hope Road* and asked for a sequel, *The Language of Sycamores* is that final chapter. I hope you enjoy discovering it as much as I did.

Thanks, as always, to everyone at New American Library, and especially to my editor, Ellen Edwards. Extreme gratitude also goes to my agent, Claudia Cross, of Sterling Lord Literistic.

Last of all, of course, to my husband and my boys, who inspire me every day and give me a million reasons to live, love, and laugh. What more could a girl ask for than that?

Chapter 1

❧

L ife is like the poster on the wall of the doctor's office—one of those inspirational quotes framed in misty pink flowers.

There are years that ask questions, and years that answer.
—Zora Neale Hurston

It's not easy to be so profound when life actually starts asking questions you can't answer—not just one or two narrow questions, but a barrage of broad, complex, open-ended questions. A flood, my grandma Rose would have called it. "Sometimes life goes by in a trickle, and sometimes life goes by in a flood," she used to say. "It's in those rainy seasons you find out how well you can swim." When she said that, I had no idea what she meant. I never listened much to Grandma Rose. She had an old-fashioned, Bible-thumping, show-me-state Baptist lecture on every subject, and she wasn't shy about dealing them out. I was busy, confident, on top of the world—a modern woman. I didn't have time to listen to what she was trying to tell me. My life was all about things I could program and control—microprocessors and LAN networks and wireless links that move at the speed of light.

I had no experience with realities that couldn't be controlled through data switches and efficiently written code. I knew nothing about surviving a flood because I'd never been in one. I was safely entrenched, or in a rut—it depended on how you looked at it. The problem with ruts is that when it starts to rain, they flood easily.

Things were, all in all, pretty good in my particular rut. Even with the trauma of September 11 and the fact that my husband was an airline pilot, we were fairly content. I had a good career; he had a good career. We had sufficient income for what we wanted. We had friends and activities and, after a few years of living out in California, we were back in Boston, where I grew up and where we met sixteen years ago on an incoming flight. We'd settled into a trendy converted loft in the old Leather District—*the* place to be, if you knew Boston well enough to get past the tourist hype. Sometimes, we both ended up there on the weekend. Together.

The day I read that quote from Zora Neale Hurston was the day everything changed.

I was staring at the misty floral poster in Dr. Conner's office when he told me that my second set of tests hadn't come back normal. I didn't hear him at first—I was thinking that I needed to get back to the Lansing building for the two o'clock management meeting about the newest round of layoffs. If Dr. Conner didn't hurry up, I'd be late. Why didn't doctors realize that everyone else's time was just as valuable as theirs?

"It could be cancer again, Karen," he said.

That one word sliced through my consciousness with the silent swish of an arrow, bisecting everything I was thinking. *Cancer. It could be cancer again, Karen.* My mind rushed back eight years to the first time a doctor told me that. Back to the day I miscarried the tiny baby that was growing inside me, and the doctor, during the D & C that followed, seemed concerned about more than just the miscarriage. He said the same thing then: *It could be cancer.* And it was. A lab test confirmed it.

Surgery removed the spots and a partial hysterectomy took away the chance of ever having children, but it couldn't remove the guilt. It was my own fault for convincing myself that since James and I weren't at the point of planning any children, I could skip the dreaded annual visit to the gynecologist. Eventually, I'd skipped for so many years that I was afraid to go back. Even after I knew I was accidentally pregnant following our romantic seventh-anniversary trip to Fiji, I put off going to the doctor for a week, two, three, until ten weeks into the pregnancy, I started cramping and spotting and I knew something was very wrong.

Now here we sat again, me with my stomach full of the old fear, and Dr. Conner wearing a regretful-but-businesslike mask.

"Karen?" I realized he was talking to me.

"Wh . . . what?" I heard myself say. All I could do was stare at the pink poster on the wall.

"Don't start worrying yet. The biopsy is just a precaution, because the lab detected some inflamed cells on your slide. Seventy-five percent of uterine cancer reoccurrences happen within the first three years, and you've been cancer-free for eight years now. Odds are the tissue sample will come back negative, but we need to go ahead with the biopsy, just to be certain."

"Today?" I muttered. *I have to go to a management meeting. The company's doing a new round of layoffs today—I have to be there to tell my people. . . .*

"No, not today, but let's schedule it soon."

"Sure," I said, standing up and reaching for my purse on the chair, feeling my fingers close numbly over the handle. "I'll schedule it on my way out."

Dr. Conner patted my shoulder, ushering me through the door. "Good. No point spending time wondering and worrying. Let's just do the test, and that'll put the question behind us."

There are years that ask questions. Years . . . "All right." I started down the hall, and I could feel Dr. Conner eyeing me. Slowing as I came near the reception desk, I watched the doctor slip into another exam room. When he was gone, I kept walking, past the desk, through the waiting room door, past the pregnant ladies in the uncomfortable chairs, through the plate glass exit, across the marble lobby where my heels echoed against the silence, and onto the Boston street. I stood there gulping air, leaning against the cool exterior of the building, feeling like I wanted to kick off my shoes and run . . . somewhere.

This is stupid, Karen, I told myself. *You're overreacting because it's already a stressful day, because you're torqued up about the layoffs and the meeting. That's all. This test is nothing. It's nothing. It's routine, just to prove there isn't anything wrong.*

Closing my eyes, I took in a deep breath and let it out slowly, willing away the rush of blood in my ears, the blaring of car horns, the rumble of the subway passing somewhere underneath. I wished the day were over. I wished we were already through the meeting, where we would be given the layoff list, and through the inevitable aftermath of going from cubicle to cubicle, quietly delivering bad news to the unlucky, telling them how sorry we were. Promising letters of reference and handing out severance packages, as if that could make up for the loss of a job you'd put your heart into.

"God, I hate this," I muttered, even though the situation at Lansing Technology had nothing to do with God and everything to do with corporate higher-ups who spent too much, forged earnings reports too often, overextended credit, lined their pockets, and were desperate to save their own six-figure jobs. "This is so wrong." Everything about this day felt wrong.

"I know." A voice echoed faintly against the doorway, breaking through the cacophony, and I jerked away from the wall, opening my eyes. A bag lady was standing there watching me, her silver hair tied in a faded pink scarf like a fortune-teller's. Her eyes were blue and cloudy, folded like two small crystal balls among the dusky wrinkles of her face. She tapped her fingers against the handle of her shopping cart, pointing expectantly to her bucket of flowers. I assumed she was selling them.

"I'm sorry," I said, when she just stood there. "I'm not interested today."

Reaching into her bucket, she pulled out a rose, pink like her scarf, and tried to hand it to me.

I waved her off, repeating, "I'm not interested. I don't need one. I don't . . . have any change today."

Frowning, she moved her lips like she was chewing on a thought. For just an instant, she reminded me of Grandma Rose when she knew

I was tuning out one of her lectures. I felt a pinch of conscience that said I should take the flower and hand the bag lady a few dollars.

I checked my purse. Nothing but fives, tens, and twenties. "I'm sorry. All I have is a . . ."

When I looked up, she was gone, disappearing down the street, probably headed toward Faneuil Hall, where the street preachers and the beggars and the pigeons hung out during the day, competing for tourist dollars and handouts from the lunch crowd. Pushing her cart at an aimless pace, she gazed up into the trees like she hadn't a care in the world. I wondered what it would be like to be her, ambling down the street, studying the spring growth on the maples, no particular place to be.

The alarm beeped on my PalmPilot, snapping me back to the real world where I was going to be late for an important meeting if I didn't hurry the eight blocks back to the office. "Geez, you're a space cadet today, Karen," I muttered to myself. "Get with it."

The pink rose was lying on the steps when I looked up, something soft and living, out of place against the hard concrete. Picking it up, I glanced down the sidewalk, where the bag lady had vanished into the crowd; then I turned and headed the other way toward the office.

By the time I'd walked the eight blocks, I was panting like I'd run a marathon and my mind was fully back to reality. Sweat dripped under my suit jacket, not because it was unusually hot for spring in Boston, but because my mind was in overdrive and my stomach was churning with a mixture of nerves and hunger. No time for a late lunch. Only twenty minutes until the meeting, and I still had to grab the budget spreadsheets from my office and make it back to the war room on the first floor. *Should have skipped the doctor's appointment,* I told myself. *Should have known the appointment would run late.* It seemed like a bad dream, Dr. Conner sitting there telling me about the tests. Abnormal results. Inflamed cells. Biopsy. How could this be happening now?

It had to be an erroneous result—changes in my body brought on by stress, too much caffeine, and guzzling ibuprofen these past few months since the company's financial problems became public knowledge. It was no wonder my body was run-down. After I got through the meeting today, I'd call Dr. Conner's office and schedule the biopsy, get it over with and prove I was O.K. I wouldn't even bother telling James when he got back from his trip tomorrow night. There was no reason to worry him. He tended to overreact to any health issues, because his mother had died of cancer when he was young. *After the biopsy is over and everything's all right, then I'll tell him.*

The war room was already starting to buzz as I passed. Brent Giani from Systems Support was waiting for an elevator. When I turned the corner into the corridor, he glanced up at me with the wry grin of a techie genius who knew *his* job would never be on the line. "Funeral flowers?" He motioned, and I glanced down, realizing I was still carrying the rose.

"A bag lady gave it to me. Could be she knows something I don't know." I held the flower against my chest like a corpse resting in a casket. Black humor, but Brent liked it.

He chuckled, reaching down to hike up his wrinkled khaki pants under a midsection that had spent too many hours eating Bugles in a computer chair. He was missing a button halfway down his shirt. He probably knew it and didn't care. "You're not worried, are you?" he asked.

I thought about that as the elevator whizzed upward. "I wasn't worried on the last round, but if they're going to cut another twenty percent, that's deep. It isn't all going to be clerical help and people in Sales, Marketing, and HR. They're going to get some of *us*. They'll have to. It's the people in tech who make the big salaries."

Brent shrugged, arrogant despite his rumpled pants and the button missing on his shirt. "It's the people in *tech* who keep the systems branch of this company going. Don't worry. They'll do the big cuts other places. They won't cut *our* people."

I nodded, hoping his confidence came from inside information. Brent was always hacking into confidential company files and secret memos. "I hope you're right." The elevator chimed on the seventh floor. "Revenues are down. That's what worries me. It's a hard market these days—less custom installations, more stuff going out canned or using local installers. That has a direct effect on my group, since we *are* custom installations."

The elevator vibrated into place. Brent gave me a wink that said he knew something I didn't, and whispered, "Don't start worrying yet," just before the doors opened and I stepped into my department, where I could feel gazes following me, counting on me to make everything all right.

I hurried to my office, trying to look busy but confident and calm. I didn't want anyone reading disaster in my expression or my actions, which was the reason I hadn't canceled my doctor's appointment. It was easier to be there, reading magazines in the waiting room with the pregnant ladies, than here, walking on eggshells, trying not to watch everyone watching me. Hopefully, right now they were thinking that if I could spend two hours at the doctor's office, there really couldn't be much to worry about back here at Lansing.

I hoped they were thinking that, and I wished I believed it. So far, the only person I'd had to lay off was a kid who'd only been with the company a few months as an installations tech. He decided to go back to college, so there wasn't much harm done. But looking around now, I couldn't imagine who else I would let go. Everyone in my department was good, dedicated, committed—a team, a family. They were all longtimers with the company. Longtimers with kids in private school, braces, college, with retirement funds and families that needed health insurance. People who had given this company, this department, *me* everything they had.

What would I do if I had to cut one, two, maybe even three positions? Who would I pick? How would I tell them?

Reaching for the folder on my desk, I realized I was still holding the bag lady's rose. I opened the desk drawer, setting the flower inside with my purse. It hardly seemed appropriate for the day—a cheerful pink rose, a symbol of friendship and goodwill. A soft, growing thing in this decaying tower of marble and machines.

Closing the drawer, I blocked out the thought, getting focused. A management meeting at Lansing was no place to be sentimental.

I took a minute to look over my budget proposal, getting the figures clear in my head, checking one last time for mistakes, muttering the words just as I would say them in my presentation. With authority, with confidence, just short of a demand—emphasis on all the right points. It was a good budget—a way to cut costs 10 percent without cutting any people. Assuming we picked up a few new accounts this year, we would bring in a solid profit, which was more than could be said for other departments. Besides, it was like Brent said. Tech built the company. They wouldn't cut us.

With that thought in mind, I headed for the door, feeling more like myself, ready to take on whoever and whatever got in my way at the meeting. By the time I reached the war room, I had squelched every last ounce of doubt within me. I didn't know how the rest of the meeting would go, but for my part, I was going to make the brass an offer they couldn't refuse.

I settled into a chair next to Brent and waited. He slid an agenda my way, silently pointing out the fact that Sales, Marketing, Admin, and Training had been scheduled to present first. We nodded at each other, taking that as a hopeful sign. Brent smirked wryly and made a quick throat-cutting gesture. It wasn't very nice, but no one in the room was feeling *nice*. Sales, Marketing, Admin, and Training were clustered on one side of the table, tech on the other, and the brass on the end by the door. Everyone was giving everyone else the look—the one that said, *Hate it for you, but better you than me.* The room had the feeling of a pool full of sharks just waiting for the first drop of blood to hit the water.

Two hours later, it looked like the meeting might not turn into a feeding frenzy, after all. The budget proposals, including mine, had been received fairly calmly. Every department had proposed cuts, and the VPs at the end of the table seemed receptive. In the corner, even the head number cruncher appeared calm, leaning back in his chair, squinting at the rest of us over the top of his Gucci glasses, occasionally jotting details on a notepad.

He barely looked up as Miles Vandever, our interim CEO, rose from his chair, cleared his throat, and braced both hands on the table. "I'm going to be painfully honest," he said, and I realized he was looking at me. "While I compliment all of these efforts at trimming budgets, the fact is that it's not enough. We've got a situation spiraling out of control, and it's going to take drastic measures to keep the company out of bankruptcy."

As if on cue, the head of Accounting stood up, pulled out a stack of red folders, and began handing them around the table. All of a sudden, I and everyone else in the room knew that all the budget talk had been only a formality. The brass had already made their decision.

Vandever went on. "In your hands, you have our plan for restructuring. To survive, we have to narrow the company's focus, get back to the things we've done and done well. It will mean cutting staff, reassigning some management, combining departments where there is overlap. I know it's hard, but these are lean times in the tech world, and this is what it's going to take. After you've looked over the material, please proceed to your departments and notify your people as necessary. In view of corporate security, the layoffs will be effective immediately. All affected parties will be asked to clear their desks. Personal items should be boxed and clearly marked. All boxes should remain unsealed, and may be either carried out today or labeled with an address for shipping. The network will be shut down this afternoon to protect corporate data, and there should be no copying of files from local machines onto magnetic media." He checked his watch like a bombardier counting the seconds until his drop hit the target. "A private security firm should be moving into place about now to see that everything goes smoothly and to safeguard corporate interests. Security officers will be present on all floors and at exits." He paused a moment, surveying the stunned faces, then added, "I'm sorry, everyone," actually managing to look regretful, even though the cuts in the red folder undoubtedly didn't include any vice presidents.

Beside me, Brent was already staring openmouthed at the contents of the folder. He didn't even notice as Vandever and the rest of his cronies left the room. On the other side of the table, Sales and Marketing started to buzz. The director of Admin slammed her folder against the table and stomped out of the room, and the Field Training manager slumped back in his chair like he'd been struck by shrapnel.

Beside me, Brent muttered, "This is crap," then leaned over and held his folder open between us. "They're cutting Tech Support by one-third. There's no way, especially with new installations. . . ." He fell silent, looking first at my face and then at the paper in my hand—my page of the red folder. The one that said my entire department was being cut. Including me.

"That can't be right," he choked out, poking a finger furiously at the paper, then flipping through his copy to see if it said the same thing.

"They're getting out of the custom-networking business," I muttered, as much to myself as to him. "This is it." But even as I said the words, my mind couldn't assimilate the message. It couldn't be. It wasn't possible. I'd been with Lansing for fifteen years, started when it was tiny, worked my way up from a baseline slot as a PC programmer, climbed the ladder as the corporation grew. I'd moved out to California for four years to start a branch office on the West Coast, then moved back without complaint when they decided they couldn't afford a West Coast office.

I'd given the company everything I had, time after time after time. I'd watched it grow from a fledgling business in rented basement offices to a major player in systems, storage, and custom networking, a corporation with a ticker on the NASDAQ and an eight-story marble building in downtown Boston. Every time I walked into the building, I had a heady sense of accomplishment. I had helped build this company. I had a part in it. Lansing Technology was my first love.

All of a sudden, I was realizing that it didn't love me back. I was nothing more than a name on a list. Six months' severance and a lump sum to buy out my retirement fund. Two hours to clean out my desk, and a security officer to escort me off the premises like a criminal.

How could this be happening?

Beside me, Brent was saying that Lansing couldn't possibly be getting out of the custom-networking business. They'd be crying at my door in three months, and I shouldn't worry. The words were meant to be comforting, but they didn't bring solace. My mind spun ahead to the inevitable question—how was someone who made my kind of salary going to find another job, especially in the current economy?

And what about the fifteen people who worked for me? How were they going to find jobs? Glancing at the sheet in my hands, I read the names and severance packages, some as low as only a few weeks' pay. No thank-yous, no apologies. Just a paragraph reminding me that in the short space of two hours, we were supposed to quietly pack our boxes while security officers looked on, and leave for good.

Anger and indignation boiled into my throat, my fingernails biting the chair arms until they throbbed with a dull, rhythmic pain. I wanted to pick up the chair and throw it through the plate glass window, scatter bits and pieces all over the lobby. Everything about this was wrong.

Closing my eyes, I tried to rein in my emotions. I had to keep control, to help my people through this the best way I could. "I've got to get upstairs," I muttered. "I have to tell them before they hear it somewhere else."

"Yeah, me too. I have to ax four software engineers and a documentation specialist." Brent patted me on the shoulder, knowing that my problems went much deeper than his. "I'm sorry, Karen. If I'd caught any word of this buzzing around the network, I would have told you. They definitely kept it under wraps."

I nodded. "I know, Brent. Thanks." Standing unsteadily, I started toward the door, a sense of numbness slowly spreading through me, until I felt detached, as if I were watching the day like a bad movie about corporate greed and underhanded office politics.

I went through the afternoon with a sense of being out of body. I said the right things, called each one of my team members in and delivered the news, discussed severance packages, health insurance, new job possibilities, all with the door open so the grim-faced security officers could listen in. I offered sympathy and regret, anger at the corporation's lack of loyalty to longtime employees. I watched the henchmen checking boxes at the elevator and wondered how anyone could do that for a living.

But even as my coworkers carried out boxes, as one meeting ran into the next, as one hour passed and then another, as I packed my own personal belongings and labeled them so that they could be shipped to my house, I kept thinking that it wasn't true. This couldn't really be happening. I was in a nightmare, struggling to wake up to another normal day.

When it was over, I sat back in my chair, looked around my office, and for the first time in my life, felt completely worthless. What do you do when the thing you've put your time and effort, your heart and soul, into, the thing that is the biggest part of who you are, is gone? Where do you go from there?

The office was empty and silent, yielding no answers. Opening my desk drawer, I reached in for my purse. My fingers closed instead over something soft and damp, alive. Pulling out the bag lady's rose, I gazed at it, remembering that forgotten part of the day, the appointment at Dr. Conner's office, the test results.

The thought made me want to go home and lock the world outside, forget everything. Grabbing my purse, I kicked the drawer shut and headed for the elevator. I didn't stop to see if anyone was still hanging around the cubicles, or to commiserate with the knot of shell-shocked employees in the lobby. I didn't wait to see if the security officer wanted to check my purse or briefcase. I walked right past them and out the door, striding faster and faster, running down the steps to the T, taking in the damp air in huge gulps, trying to leave everything behind. On the train, I sank into a seat, leaned my head against the window, and stared dimly at the increasing rhythm of light and shadow.

A thunderstorm was rumbling on the horizon when I got off at the Leather District. The sound echoed against the old brick warehouses, whipped along by an angry wind laden with dust and the scent of seawater. I didn't stop to listen to the musicians or grab a cup of cappuccino at South Station. I didn't linger by the windows of the art galleries, or stop in J's Deli for a beef and Swiss, or sit on the bench outside and marvel at the enormity of the converted leather tanneries. Instead, I ran blindly up the street, my breath coming in short, quick gasps, tears clouding my eyes so that the storm and the people on the sidewalk were nothing more than a blur. By the time I reached our door on the lower level of a small building that had once housed tannery offices, lightning was crackling sideways across the clouds and the air smelled of saltwater spray. Turning the key in the lock, I slipped into a safe haven and bolted out the wind and the clouds.

The growl of thunder followed. Desperate to drown out the sound, the reality, I sat down at the antique piano in the entry and did something I hadn't done in years.

I began to play music.

Chapter 2

The songs of my childhood flowed through me—songs I thought I had long ago forgotten—recital pieces from Beethoven, Bach, Tchaikovsky, a melody that I'd played for a production of *Hair* in college. I remembered how it sounded in the theater building at U Mass, how the audience burst into spontaneous applause when the dancers finished the number. I relived the joy of being surrounded by a cast of starry-eyed dreamers, still young enough to believe the world would allow us to become artists and musicians and actors. My parents didn't want me wasting my time in the arts department, which made the experience all the more desirable, my one act of rebellion before I settled into a practical mold. An engineering degree. A high-profile job.

Now here I was, fifteen years later, the music rushing out of me like water through a dam left unattended so long that it had finally crumbled. I wished James would come home, hear the music and say, "Where did you learn to play *Hair*?" He didn't know this part of me. By the time we met, I was already settled into my job at Lansing, taken in by the rush of money and success. It was a good substitute for the thrill of art for art's sake.

I didn't yearn for music. The piano in our hallway was just an antique left by the former owners because it was too heavy to move. James's game room upstairs, where we'd decorated the wall behind the wet bar with the old guitars he never found time to play, was just a place to occasionally entertain guests. I'd tried to convince him to sell the guitars before we moved back from California. "Why are we hauling these things around from place to place?" I'd said. "I think we're past our Jim Morrison days."

James just laughed and set the guitars out for the movers to pack. "What will my dad do when he comes to visit if he can't clean and tune the guitar collection?"

"That's true." Every year or two, James's dad came from his farm in Virginia and spent a week tinkering with things in our house that needed fixing, cleaning, or tuning.

"Besides," James added, "the real estate agent just e-mailed from Boston and said they left that old piano in the loft entry—too heavy to move. I told him that was fine. You and I might want to start a mom-and-pop band, take to hanging out in the T and try to make a little extra change."

"With a *piano*?"

"Who knows?" He winked at me and smiled. Both of us were so happy to be moving back to Boston that we wouldn't have cared if the former owners left a four-ton elephant in our loft. California had been hard for us—me working all the time to start the new branch office, and James having to fly out of a new base where he had less seniority and was given less-desirable flight schedules. "Your sister says you're pretty good."

"I don't play anymore," I said flatly. "Maybe we can put hooks on the thing and make sort of an eclectic coat rack."

When we moved into the loft, I stayed away from the piano the way a recovering alcoholic stays away from a drink. But tonight it felt like an old friend. Music was a hiding place where nothing else could enter. Not the realities of the day, not the sound of the storm. Within the music there was only the peace of memory and melody and emotion, slowly strumming forgotten strings.

I knew I should try to catch James on his cell phone while he was between flights, tell him about the layoffs at Lansing, but then the growl of the storm would return and I would have to think about everything. I'd start calculating severance packages, health insurance, mortgage payments, doctor's appointments, more medical tests. It was easier to play melodies I thought I had lost, to let them capture me and take me back.

The phone rang, and I barely heard it at first. I was a million miles away at a grade school talent contest. I was looking into the audience to see if my father had come yet. I missed a note, and one of the kids backstage chuckled. Suddenly, I was glad my father wasn't there. Out of all the notes in that piece, he would have noticed the one that wasn't right.

The phone rang again. Probably someone from work, wanting to hash over the ugly details of the layoffs, hoping I would join them in raging against the machine. It wouldn't be James calling. He wouldn't expect me to be home at six-thirty in the evening. Normally, I would have been at the office with a bag of take-out from the deli down the street.

I played the music louder, faster, until I couldn't make out the answering machine's electronic greeting and someone recording a message. The intonations were familiar, and unconsciously I softened the music, a little more and a little more, until I could hear.

". . . Guess you're not there. Anyway, this is Kate. Remember me? Your sister? Seems like it's been forever. Ben was going to e-mail you guys some pictures of the kids, but I don't know if he ever did. Well . . . anyway . . . listen, James just called and said he'd be coming to the farm Saturday night and staying a couple days while he's on layover in Kansas City." She paused for a moment, seeming unsure of whether to bother leaving the rest of the message. "Well, anyway, remember I told you that after the tornado last year we met those cousins who live over in Poetry, Missouri? We've been trying for a while to get together, and Jenilee called yesterday and said she could come for the weekend. I know it's short notice, but I thought maybe, possibly, since James is going to be here, maybe you could get away and fly down for the weekend—use one of those buddy passes the airlines gives you guys. I know . . ."

I realized the music had stopped and I was across the room with my finger on the answering machine. I pushed the button and picked up the phone. "Hello . . . Kate?" My voice sounded ragged, raspy with tears.

"Karen?" Kate's reply was hesitant. "Is that you? Did I wake you up? Are you at home sick or something?" The sentences ran together, conveying that she was nervous and uncertain. Kate and I didn't talk very often. We didn't know what to say to each other on the phone. Or in person, really.

I cleared my throat, walking into the kitchen for a glass of water. "No. It's just been kind of a tough day."

"Oh . . ." She hesitated, not sure what should come next. "Well . . . is there anything I can do?"

Part of me longed to tell her everything, but part of me wouldn't do it. Part of me was still the big sister who had to know the most and be the best at everything, especially in front of her. "No. But thanks for asking." *You're being stubborn, Karen. You know you're being stubborn. You could use someone to talk to.* I knew Kate would be sympathetic. She would listen. Kate was always a good listener. Kate was good at everything. Disgustingly perfect. Always. "So what's the deal with these long-lost relatives? I didn't catch all of that. I was playing the piano."

"You were . . . I didn't know you played the piano anymore," she said. I had inadvertently clued Kate in to the fact that something was very wrong. Kate had Grandma Rose's nose for trouble. "I didn't even know you had a piano."

"It came with the loft. Antique." I quickly turned the subject back to harmless small talk. "So what's the deal with these cousins? I know you told me before, but I can't even remember how we're related."

Kate exhaled audibly, no doubt frustrated that I hadn't been keeping up with the family genealogy. She'd e-mailed me the details once or twice, even forwarded a note from one of the long-lost cousins. Now that Grandma Rose was gone and Kate was living at the old farm, she had become the official keeper of family memorabilia and lost cousins, and that was fine with me.

She gave me the *Reader's Digest* condensed version of our family history. "Their grandmother Augustine Hope was Grandma Rose's sister. So they're second cousins to us, or something like that. I'm not sure exactly what you'd call it. Anyway, the youngest granddaughter, Jenilee, was going through some things from her grandparents' house, and she found a box of old letters between our grandma Rose and her grandmother, Augustine Hope. She's going to bring those when she comes. It'll be interesting to look at that old stuff."

Long-lost relatives and old letters. Kind of high drama for our family. "Did you ask Dad anything about it? I mean, maybe there was a *reason* Grandma Rose never mentioned these people, Kate." Her name slipped out with just a little too much big-sister tone, and I knew right away that she was going to take offense, so I rushed on. "I'm sorry. I didn't mean to sound critical. It's just been a tough day."

Kate paused a minute, and I was afraid she was going to ask again what was wrong. "That's all right," she said finally. "I admit it sounds strange. Dad doesn't really know anything about Grandma's sisters. He remembers knowing her brothers when he was young, but her sisters were a taboo subject. I thought I'd met one years ago at a family reunion, and seen old pictures, but Dad says those were her cousins. Grandma had no contact with a sister."

An unexpected sense of mystery tickled the back of my mind, and for a moment I forgot everything I had been thinking about. "That's odd, isn't it?"

"I thought so." Kate was pleased that, for a change, we were on the same wavelength. "I know family history isn't really your thing, but I thought maybe . . . well, since James was going to be here this weekend anyway, maybe you'd just get a wild urge to use one of those free airline tickets and fly out for the weekend—or longer, if you can get away. We'd love to have you."

Or longer, if you can get away. Get away. Right now that seemed like exactly what I needed—to get away. "I'm coming," I blurted.

"Oh . . . weh . . . well . . . great," Kate stuttered, surprised nearly speechless, no doubt because in the past two years since Grandma Rose's funeral, I hadn't been back to the farm even once. Kate invited and I made excuses, even to James, who had begun making a habit of taking his layovers in Kansas City so he could drive to the farm and spend time bonding with the piece of land we'd inherited from Grandma.

"I'll throw a suitcase together and get a flight out tonight." Even as I said the words, I couldn't believe I'd actually go through with it.

Kate clearly couldn't either. "Great," she stammered. "Ben can come pick you up."

"No, don't worry about that." I hurried up the iron staircase to the bedroom and started throwing clothes onto the bed in a haphazard pile. "I'll get a rental car. The free passes are standby, so it's hard to tell when I'll get into Kansas City. It could be tomorrow morning, even. I'll just see you when I get there. I'll leave a message on James's cell to let him know I'm coming."

"Great," Kate repeated. I guess she didn't know what else to say. "Well, listen, we'll see you when you get here."

"See you then." Yanking the suitcase out of the closet, I tossed in clothes with the carelessness of someone running away from home.

Kate didn't say good-bye but hung on the line, silent for a moment. Then she sighed and said, "Karen, is everything all right?"

"Yes. Fine. I could just use a few days out of the city." A lie, but a pretty good one.

It seemed to convince Kate. She laughed on the other end of the phone. "Well, we're definitely out of the city. You know, we still barely even have e-mail service out here."

"Well, forget it, then."

Kate took me seriously. "You can check your e-mail at the church office in town," she rushed out.

"Kate, I was kidding." The two of us actually chuckled. Together.

"I knew that," she quipped. "See you tomorrow, then."

"See you tomorrow." I hung up the phone, and all of a sudden I was looking forward to arriving at the one place I never wanted to be. Suddenly, the farm seemed like the music from the old piano—a refuge, a place so far away from my normal life that the problems and the questions couldn't find me there. I could get away for now and put all of it off until Monday. Closing the suitcase, I hurried to the bathroom, threw a few things into the travel bag I kept packed for business trips, and headed for the door.

I was at the airport, slipping into a seat in the tail section of a plane, before it occurred to me that I was acting crazy. A flash of panic bolted through me like lightning from the storm that had vanished over the ocean. Running away wasn't going to solve anything. I needed to go home, make phone calls, formulate plans, look over our finances. Make an appointment at Dr. Conner's office. *I should get off the plane while it's still at the gate.*

But I didn't. Instead, I called James's cell phone and waited, breathless, while it rang. His voice mail picked up, and I was glad. I wasn't ready to talk about the bad news of the day. Talking about it would make it more real.

I left a message for James, trying to sound as if my spur-of-the-moment visit to the farm were a perfectly normal thing. "Hi, honey. Change of plans for the weekend. Kate called and said you were going to layover at the farm, so I decided to catch a flight there for a couple days." As soon as James got the message, he would know something was up. It wasn't like me to suddenly decide to go to the farm. I considered telling him about the Lansing layoffs via voice mail, but then I realized that wasn't a good idea. He would show up at Kate's and want to talk about it, and then everyone would know.

Everyone's going to have to know, Karen. Why did that bother me so much? Why didn't I want anyone to know about the layoffs or the test results at Dr. Conner's office?

Someone sat down in the seat beside me and I glanced away from the window.

Stuffing his backpack under the seat, he smiled. "Hey. How are you?" He was young, probably a college kid, wearing a Les Paul T-shirt, with his light brown hair pulled back in an unkempt ponytail.

"Fine, thanks," I said, turning back to the window. I didn't feel like talking, especially not to some college-aged rebel without a cause.

"So where ya headed?" He fished around in his backpack and came out with a Snickers bar.

"Kansas City."

"Cool." He sounded surprised. "Me too. You visiting someone there?"

"In Hindsville," I replied flatly, still hoping he would get the hint and decide to talk to the guy in the aisle seat instead of me.

"Hey, I know Hindsville." I realized I'd said the wrong thing. Now we had something in common—a reason to chat. "We did a performance there last summer—at the park with the bandstand. You know, the one right downtown on the square?"

It seemed odd to hear "downtown" and "Hindsville" in the same sentence. Curiosity nudged me out my sullen mood, and I found myself asking, "In Hindsville? A performance of what?" I couldn't imagine what this shaggy-haired kid with the loop in one ear would be doing in a conservative Baptist bastion like Hindsville.

"Jumpkids," he answered, as if it were self-explanatory. "Ever heard of it?"

I shook my head. He seemed disappointed, and for some reason, I felt bad. "No, but I don't get to Missouri much."

"Oh, we've got groups all over the country. Our foundation is actually headquartered in New York." He sounded like he was trying to sell me something. "We set up summer mini camps for kids who don't have much to look forward to when school's out—teach them music, art, dance, theater. Give them something to keep them off the streets, something to feel good about, you know? We finish up by doing a musical theater performance. I teach theater and guitar, and last year, baseball, but the music is really my thing. I'm not sure what I'll teach this year or which towns we're going to. Some of the schools are out earlier than usual, so that changed the schedule." He extended his hand to shake mine. "Keiler Bradford, by the way. Nice to meet you."

"Karen Sommerfield," I replied. "That's great about the music program. Sounds like a really good thing." I honestly meant it. There was a sense of enthusiasm, a sparkle in his eyes that was contagious—the diamondlike luster of a true believer with a noble cause. "So is this a full-time job for you, or do you just do this in the summers?"

"Just summers." He paused for a minute, his lips pursed thoughtfully as he glanced out the window, watching the plane shove away from the gate. "This'll be my last year, I guess. I'm a senior at NYU, so after this summer, I'm off to the real world. Unless I decide to go to seminary. I'm really not sure where I go from here. I may just take next winter off—maybe get on at a ski resort, work the lifts by day, play music by night. That kind of thing."

I smiled at the aimless uncertainty of youth. I couldn't remember ever being as lost as Keiler. The very idea of spending years in seminary or summers traveling around spreading music and goodwill was completely foreign to my experience. In my family, everything had to have a purpose, everything had to be part of *the plan*.

"Hey, I'd stay in school," I said, but I couldn't believe I was giving him that advice. How many times had I told summer interns at Lansing the exact opposite? Get your degree, get out, get on-the-job experience, start climbing the ladder. "The real world stinks."

Keiler looked shocked. *The nice lady in seat 21A is a cynic.*

His expression made me chuckle, and I felt a need to apologize. "I'm sorry. It's been a pretty rotten day so far."

"Oh," he said, seeming relieved. Apparently, I didn't look like a cynic.

Our conversation paused while the flight attendant went through the safety procedures. By the time she was finished, the plane was in position on the runway. The attendant sat down, the pilot announced takeoff, and the plane rocketed down the runway and into the darkening evening.

I was on my way to Missouri, and all of a sudden, I panicked again. What in the world was I doing? What would I do when I got to the farm—make small talk for two days, act like nothing was wrong? I didn't want to talk to anybody, much less my sister and a long-lost cousin I'd never even met.

Worse than that, I didn't *want* to go back to the farm. Ever. I hadn't admitted that to anyone. I'd just made excuses every time Kate invited me. When she called about having a family gathering or getting together for a holiday, I told her I was tied up with work or that I had a business trip. She'd say that she understood, but somewhere behind the words there was a wounded sound. Kate had a vision of all of us back together as a family—the kind of family that flew home for holidays and christenings, that sent cards and called for the weekly chitchat. She hated that I wasn't falling in line with her plan. Or maybe she didn't hate it as much as she was *disappointed* by it.

She took it personally, I knew. The truth was that it didn't have a thing to do with her. It didn't have a thing to do with the fact that, at some point in my teenage years, I'd affirmed a growing suspicion that Hindsville was the most boring place on Earth. Compared to the happening scene in Boston, where my parents' involvement in our lives seldom went beyond report-card checks and recital attendance, Grandma Rose's constant scrutiny was agonizing. Her desire to teach us to cook and sew and can vegetables seemed out of step and largely ridiculous, considering that we lived in a posh row house in Boston, where we could walk in Boston Garden, but there wasn't a vegetable patch within ten miles.

My reluctance to return to the farm now had nothing to do with how I'd felt about it in the past. It had to do with me and Grandma Rose and the last time I saw her. The day she passed away.

I hadn't told anyone about that.

That day, she lay silent on the bed in the farmhouse, all of us gathered around her. She opened her eyes just before she passed from this world to the next, and she looked at me, and I swear she said my name. I glanced around the room, and it was obvious that no one else heard it. Then I looked back at Grandma, and she said, *"There's a whisper in the sycamores—can you hear it?"*

I had no idea why she would say that in those last moments of her life—to me and only to me. No one else flinched or looked up or noticed. She'd used the phrase from time to time over the years, when she had a little secret and she wanted to tease us with it. *"I heard a whisper in the sycamores,"* she'd say. *"They told me someone is about to have a birthday. They told me it'll come a snow tomorrow. They told me someone's found a special boy. . . ."*

Whenever Grandma heard a whisper in the sycamores, it meant something was going to change and she knew what it was. As I sat there watching her on her deathbed, I wondered what she'd heard this time, and I knew it was too late to find out.

Oh, God, right then, I wished I had listened before. I wished I'd sat in her kitchen and snapped peas or sliced okra or peeled potatoes all those years I was young and she was full of stories. I wished I'd come to her bedside those last few months, sat with her as Kate did, and listened to her speak in barely a whisper. But I didn't, and that last day, I lowered my face into my hands and wept, because it was too late.

One such realization should be enough to change your focus, but I was always way too much like Grandma Rose. Stubborn. Proud. Set in my ways. I cried like a baby the day we buried her; then I went back home to my normal life. In my mind, she was still at the farm, gathering onions and picking blackberries, baking pies, bread, and banana-nut cookies. She wasn't gone, and she hadn't delivered that silent message to me.

The truth was that I hadn't returned these past two years because I was afraid. That moment at her deathbed had knocked me off my rock-solid foundation, and I didn't like the way it felt. I didn't want things to change. Change was not welcomed. In the business of wires and switches, bits and bytes, uncertainty is the enemy. You must know where every bit of information is coming from, where it's going, and what it means. There can be no nebulous whispers.

Now, sitting on the airplane speeding toward the farm, I wondered if Grandma knew that changes were coming, whether I wanted them or not. Had she been trying to prepare me?

"So, you want to talk about it?" Keiler leaned his head against the headrest, his face sympathetic, soft, filled with the hopeful sense of someone who thought he could save the world and the cynical fortyish lady in seat 21A.

I sighed. "It's a long story."

"I know." He smiled and glanced at his watch. "I've got . . . one hour and forty-seven minutes." He held out the smashed candy bar. "Want a Snickers?"

I couldn't help smiling. Something about his laid-back, raveled-jeans, ponytail-wearing presence was comforting. "You know what? I do."

I took the candy bar, and he pulled another from his bag, and the two of us sat eating Snickers like old friends. I realized I hadn't eaten all day. The knot in my stomach began to work its way out, and all of a sudden, I started talking. I sat there on an airplane headed to the last place I wanted to go, with a stranger who looked like the last person I'd ever want to know, and I told him everything. I started with the doctor's appointment, went through the management meeting, and ended with me wildly playing the piano for the first time in fifteen years.

As the plane was touching down in Kansas City, I finished by telling him about Kate's call. "And you know, my mind was saying no, but the next thing I knew I was telling her I was coming. I don't even know why I said it. I don't know why I'm going. I think I'm having a breakdown."

Keiler smiled. He wasn't a good-looking kid, but there was a serenity, a kindness in him that made him beautiful. "I think we all want to head home when there's trouble," he said with calm assurance. "Sometimes you need that soft place to fall. That's your family, your faith. The stuff that doesn't change when everything else does."

"Yeah, I guess so." It seemed he had a wisdom I lacked. Strange, considering how young he was. "You know, you really ought to think about seminary school. You're good at this."

He squinted like he wasn't quite sure I was serious. "I might. You know, right now I'm just waiting to see. I almost died two years ago during surgery, and I guess that changed how I feel about things. I'm not in such a big hurry to get from one place to another anymore. Once you learn that you can never really plan your destination, you stop worrying so much about being on the map. I figure I'm still here for a reason, and that reason could be anywhere, you know?"

A sense of peace filtered through me as the plane docked at the gate. *Stop worrying about the map,* I thought. "You know what? You're right."

We walked up the gateway together and stood for a moment at the end.

"So what kind of surgery was it?" I asked. The question seemed out of the blue and insensitive, so I added, "I'm sorry. I shouldn't have asked that."

Keiler only grinned. "Brain surgery." He parted his hair, and I saw the large crescent-shaped scar. "I probably shouldn't be giving people advice. I've only got half my marbles."

I laughed, slipped a hand over his shoulder and gave it a squeeze. "I'd say it's the right half. Thanks for listening to me."

He shrugged off my gratitude, letting his hair fall back into place.

"Hey, no problem. If you end up in Missouri this summer, come see our Jumpkids."

"I will," I said, and strangely enough, I meant it.

As I said good-bye to Keiler, I had a feeling that a lot of things about this summer were going to be different.

Chapter 3

As I left the airport and slid into the neon-lit rush of a Kansas City Friday night, I tried not to think of anything but the road, the next mile in front of me. The clock on the rental car dash flashed midnight. Normally, I would have already fallen asleep on the sofa, and around now I'd be waking up and stumbling drowsily off to bed. If James were home, he would wake me up after he watched the late show.

But as I drove out of Kansas City, it didn't feel like midnight. A nervous energy zipped through me, pure adrenaline, preventing my pulse from slowing to a normal rhythm. My mind churned through the events of the day in fast motion, replaying everything that had happened. Everything that was wrong. Without the music of the piano or the comforting closeness of my unusual flight companion, it was hard to block out the disturbing litany of reality.

How am I going to tell everyone? What will I say?

A sense of failure filled me, an odd feeling of shame, as if I had something to hide, some guilty secret I didn't want anyone to know. It didn't make sense, yet it was like a passenger in the car, hissing critical whispers, telling me it was my fault that I'd lost my job. Telling me that when the family heard what had happened, they'd know I was really a failure masquerading all these years as a success.

I could picture my father pointing out that I should have gone into the medical profession, as he and my mother had wanted. He'd remind me that the medical industry is recession proof—*Good times or bad times,* he'd say, *people still get sick.*

Kate would give me *the look*—the sad look that women who have children give to women who choose not to. The look that says, *Oh, you poor thing. All you have is your career, and now look where that has landed you. You'll never be truly happy. You'll always be incomplete.* Even if Kate never said it, even if she didn't do a thing to intimate those words, I would perceive them, and it would be a wedge between us. She would wonder, like she always did, why we weren't closer, why we didn't do the sisterhood thing very well.

And since we didn't do it very well, we would confine ourselves to small talk and job talk. Sometime during the visit, I would put in a plug about how happy James and I were, how Kate's life was right for her and mine was right for me, and it was good that we had both found fulfillment. I would be sure to point out that, for James and me, not having a family was a choice. Obviously, even after the miscarriage and my partial hysterectomy, we could have sought out other ways of building a family, if we had wanted one. We certainly had the money to pursue adoption or surrogacy. The fact that we had never explored those options just proved that our lives were busy and full and complete just as they were.

Only right now, my life was falling apart.

I couldn't admit that to my family. This visit was a mistake. The worst place for me to be right now, when things were definitely not wonderful, was at the farm trying to show everyone how wonderful my life was.

"Oh, God, what was I thinking?" I muttered, raking a hand through my hair, pulling dark shoulder-length strands away from my face. Breath caught in my throat, and my heart hammered painfully against my chest. I shouldn't have come. Coming to Missouri was only going to make things harder.

I pulled into the parking lot of a motel and rolled down the window, trying to think. Tears crowded my eyes and I wiped them away impatiently, taking a deep breath. The air smelled of spring, heavily laden with new grass and the sweet, pungent aroma of blackberry vines blooming nearby. I drank it in like wine, sensing my childhood, wrapping it around me like a blanket sewn from those long-ago summers at the farm—the early ones that I could barely remember. The summers when I looked at the world through the eyes of a little girl, before I reached adolescence and middle school and began to see that I didn't quite measure up to my parents' standards.

At some point around eleven years old, when my body started to change and my awareness began to broaden, I realized that I wasn't particularly brilliant for the daughter of two high-profile doctors. I remember the day it happened: sixth-grade math, an honors class, another C on a test; only this time, Mrs. Klopfliesh didn't tap the paper and say, "I expect better than this from you." She only gave me a sympathetic look and moved on. I realized she no longer expected better. She knew I'd studied, done my homework, and this was what I was capable of. *Average.* Not nearly good enough.

It's funny how a little incident can change your perceptions of everything afterward. My parents hired a tutor, I worked harder, the grade came up, but it didn't alter my new reality—it only helped to hide it from everyone else.

The next summer when I came to the farm, all of Grandma Rose's storytelling and advising and instructing suddenly seemed like criticism. I felt claustrophobic. I couldn't relate to the place or her anymore. Somewhere inside me, there was a vague sense of loss. Childhood's end, perhaps. The drifting away of a time when peace was as simple as the night air floating through the farmhouse windows, the insects lulling me to sleep with their ancient rhythm, while far off in the distance coyotes sang to the moon.

Music was all around me those early summers, before the epiphany of adolescence. Grandma Rose knew I heard the melody of the land and the air and the trees. Sometimes, when she was on the porch at night, I would sneak downstairs and sit with her. We'd rock back and forth on the swing, the cool breeze stroking our faces, and she'd whisper, "Just listen, Karen. Listen to that music." My father didn't like it when she talked about music and whispering sycamores.

To him, there was no music at the farm. There was only the memory of a childhood he was trying to rise above, the constant struggle with Grandma's attempts at manipulation and the pressure of his obligation as her only son.

"I don't hear any music," I'd reply, out of loyalty to my father. Above all else, I wanted him to approve of me.

"Yes, you do," Grandma insisted. "Just listen."

I heard it then, just as I was hearing it now. The sounds of traffic faded away, and there was nothing but the scent of the night and the music of the Ozarks. I couldn't remember the last time I'd been still and just listened. If there was no other reason to go to the farm, there was that one. I needed to reconnect with myself, to drop off the map for a while, to find the little girl who disappeared that eleven-year-old year in Mrs. Klopfliesh's class.

Slipping the car into drive, I left the hotel parking lot and pulled back onto the interstate. The night air rushed in the window, washing over me, filling my senses and quieting my mind as I left the neon-lit city. My thoughts settled like salt sifting to the bottom of a pan as I turned off the interstate onto the two-lane highway, passing the last of the city suburbs. The houses on both sides of the street were silent, lights mostly turned out for the night. Suddenly, I felt exhausted, but I didn't want to stop. I knew if I did, I'd only start trying to think things through again.

Stop worrying about the map. Keiler's words.

Just see what the weekend brings, I told myself. *It's only a couple of days. If nothing else, the rest will do you good.*

If nothing else. But I was hoping for something else. In some hidden part of myself, I could feel it.

By the time I drew near Hindsville, the rhythm of the road and the caress of the breeze had lulled me almost to sleep. I stopped next to Town Square Park and climbed out to stretch, then stood looking around the silent streets, reliving my normal teenage reactions. Too slow, too quiet, no shopping district, no favorite hangouts, no friends. Grandma Rose would fuss constantly about all the dirt we were tracking in and the water we splashed around the bathroom. She'd lay on the guilt trip about how we didn't call often enough, write enough, visit enough. Then she'd complain about how our being there would surely drive up the electric bill, raise her monthly grocery charge at Shorty's Grocery, and put the septic system in danger of overload. She would let us know she was exhausted by all the baking and the cooking and the cleaning up. Yet when we left, she'd stand on the steps and cry.

There was some comfort in the idea that it was nothing new for me to feel lost and confused here. I could almost pretend it was just because I was at the farm, not because I'd lost my job and the doctor was telling me I might have cancer again. I could almost pretend Grandma would be at the house.

Climbing into the car, I drove the six miles out of town, slipping back in time, so that when I pulled into the driveway I had almost forgotten everything. I felt like a little girl again, coming there for a visit. Winding slowly up the gravel drive, I gazed at the old two-story farmhouse, shimmering white on the bluff beneath the low-hanging moon. The windows were dark, and I felt relieved. I'd been worried that even though it was two in the morning, Kate might be up with the baby, waiting for my arrival. I was glad she wasn't. I wasn't ready to talk yet.

Turning off the headlights, I stopped the car behind the garage, by the little cabin that had once been a hired hand's place. In the months before she died, Grandma Rose had moved out there and given the main house to Kate and Ben. I stood looking at it, thinking of her last Christmas, when the family gathered at the farm. Gazing at the darkened windows, I could almost see her sleeping inside. I could feel her close to me—something familiar and solid, unchanging. Grabbing my suitcase, I walked around to the porch of the tiny house and went inside.

I didn't turn on the lights or change clothes. I did nothing to destroy the illusion that she was there. I just walked across the room in the spill of moonlight, lay down on the sofa, and slipped into sleep.

In the morning, I heard someone moving around the kitchen. *Probably Grandma Rose cooking breakfast for all of us,* I thought. I stood up and walked to the kitchen, and she was there, standing at the old gas stove, scooping hot grease over fried eggs, sunny-side up. She glanced at me and smiled. "Good morning, dear one," she said. "Oh, you're finally back! I had some things I wanted to talk to you about. I heard a whisper in the sycamores. . . ."

I stood staring at her, afraid to say anything. Part of me wanted to sit down at the long maple table and talk to her. But in the back of my mind, something was telling me this was wrong, this couldn't be. . . .

My body jerked fitfully, and the vision disappeared like vapor. Opening my eyes, I looked around, and I wasn't in the farmhouse kitchen. I was in the little house on the sofa. I wondered if that was just another layer of the dream—if I was really at home in Boston in my bed.

Closing my eyes, I tried to think, to establish what was true and what was fantasy. The realities of the previous day crept slowly into my mind and I lay there wanting to deny it all. I wanted the dream of Grandma in her kitchen to be real, and the realities of the day before to be a dream.

Gazing around the room, I surveyed objects in the dim light—an empty notepad on the desk, a hairbrush and a string of pearls on the entry table, a white straw purse on the chair by the door, a pair of slippers underneath. Grandma's things, just the way they were when she was staying in the house. For whatever reason, Kate hadn't cleaned out the place, even though it had been two years since Grandma's death. The house smelled musty and unused, as if it had been closed up, left untouched since the days after the funeral.

The distant sound of singing drifted into my thoughts, faint at first, then louder, until finally I let the thoughts fall away and just listened. I couldn't make out the words, but the melody was one of Grandma's old church songs, the title beyond the reach of my memory. The voice was a girl's, not Kate's. It had an ethereal, dreamlike quality, as if it were something from the past, something that wasn't really there.

Walking stiffly into the bedroom, I peered out the window into the dawn gray. The backyard was empty, framed by a wall of fog rising from the river below, the melody drifting from somewhere in the mist. Pushing open the heavy wooden window, I listened as the sound grew faint, then faded like the call of a bird flying away.

When it was gone, I closed the window and sat for a while on the edge of the bed, caught between the need to stay and the irrational urge to jump in the car and leave before anyone saw me. Finally, I opened my suitcase, pulled out a shirt and some slacks, and washed up in the tiny bathroom with its old pedestal sink and half-sized bathtub. I didn't bother to fix my hair, just pulled it back in a hair clip and stood looking at myself as the dark strands around my face slipped free and fell forward.

I looked tired. Old. Weary. The brown eyes, those "Vongortler brown" eyes Grandma always made such a fuss over, were red rimmed, puffy from crying, creased with worry lines at the corners, troubled.

Oh, soul, are you weary and troubled. . . .

A piece of the song came to my mind, a few words to go along with the melody from the mist. Gazing toward the bathroom window, I played the notes in my head, but no words came. I had the strangest urge to pluck out the tune on the old piano in the living room. It had probably been twenty-five years since I'd heard that song, no doubt on some long-ago Sunday at church in Hindsville. I wouldn't have heard it anywhere else. We only attended church under the marshal and scrutiny of Grandma Rose, when all of us dressed up and paraded off to the First Baptist Church of Hindsville, like goslings in a row, with Grandma strutting in front like Mother Goose.

Smiling wanly at the image, I left the bathroom and headed toward the door. The sound of the handle turning stopped me halfway across the small living room, and I paused on the crocheted rug near the piano.

A thin shaft of sunlight crossed the floor and Kate peered through the opening. "Karen?" she whispered. "Is that you in there?"

"It's me," I answered, muted as well. "I'm here."

Kate let the door fall open, but she didn't come into the room. I wondered why. "Hi," she said, and smiled, her dark eyes glittering with joy and what I thought might be tears. Joyful tears, of all things.

I instantly felt guilty for not having come back sooner. "Hi, Kate." I stepped forward, and she stretched out her arms. We hugged, and it felt like the most natural thing in the world. Strange, since it wasn't.

When we let go, she stepped back onto the porch, and we stood there in awkward silence. "When did you get here?" she finally asked. "I didn't mean for you to have to stay out here. You should have come on into the house."

I shrugged, following her out, letting the screen door fall into place. "That's all right. I got in at two in the morning, and I didn't want to wake anyone. Besides, I kind of like it out here."

Kate blinked, surprised, wrapping her arms around herself. "Well, I know it's a mess. I'm sorry. I don't come out here much. I just haven't been ready—you know—to go through Grandma's things. I just haven't been able to clean the place out."

"I understand." I did. I knew that Kate leaving the little house untouched was the same as my not coming back to the farm since Grandma's death. We were both trying to pretend that things hadn't changed, that something as strong and constant as Grandma Rose couldn't possibly be gone. "I'll help you with some of it, if you want." Would I? Was I any more ready than Kate to face it?

"That sounds good." She obviously didn't believe it. Neither did I. We both knew I would come and go and not much would be accomplished.

Kate started with the usual small talk as we walked the stone path to the farmhouse. "I've got Joshua's room upstairs for you and James. Josh's bunking in with baby Rose for a few days. I saved the guest rooms for Jenilee and her boyfriend. I hope you don't mind. Those two rooms at the end of the hall have a separate bathroom. I figured they would be more comfortable there, since . . . well, since we don't really know each other very well."

"That sounds like a good idea." I paused to consider the thought of having a cousin we'd never met coming as overnight company. It was bound to be strange for everyone. We probably wouldn't have much in common other than some family history none of us understood. "But, listen, I'll stay out in the little house. That way Joshua can have his own room—and besides, it's nice out there. It's . . . quiet." I glanced back at the house. "I could use some peace and quiet." The words sounded more wistful than I meant them to.

Kate didn't miss the hidden meaning. "Everything all right?"

I could tell she wanted me to say yes, so I did. Kate had her mind on setting up guest rooms and making beds, entertaining company and discovering the deep, dark family secret, whatever it was. She didn't need to hear my sad story, and I didn't want to tell it. I finished my sentence with a quick excuse as we walked into the kitchen. "It's been a tough week, that's all. Stressful."

Kate nodded. She understood job stress. She'd had a busy career of her own until she moved to Missouri and went the mommy route. I wondered if she missed her life in Chicago, if she ever regretted giving it up. There wasn't any way I could ask. She'd think I was criticizing or comparing. "So, how is life on the farm?" I heard myself say. Kate stiffened, and I realized even that sounded wrong. When I talked to her, I went into sibling mode, whether I meant to or not.

"It's good." Kate switched to a defensive posture. "Busy. I'll tell you, having two kids under age four is a challenge. Seems like I just get one taken care of and the other one needs something." A hint of frustration came through in the words, and she quickly added, "But I wouldn't trade it. The kids are doing so great here. They love being on the farm. Aunt Jeane and Uncle Robert come down from St. Louis every few weeks and do the grandparent thing—spoil the kids rotten, then leave." She smiled at the mention of Aunt Jeane, my father's sister, our family peacemaker. The Pollyanna who gave love so freely that we couldn't help loving her back. It still amazed me that she and my father came from the same family. Kate must have been thinking the same thing. "Dad even comes three or four times a year when he's not busy on consulting jobs. He's still *Dad* in a lot of ways, but you know, he's not too bad at the grandparenting. Joshua's getting big enough to enjoy the yard and trips down to the river to wade and catch minnows. He and Dad take backpacks and go off on these long hikes, looking for fossils and studying plant parts. Joshua loves science, so they've bonded over that. He knows a zillion different kinds of rocks and the scientific terms for all the parts of a flower. It's really a great thing for a little boy, getting to roam and play and discover all the time."

But what about you? I thought. *What do you want?* I didn't say it, of course. I just nodded and smiled. Kate could tell I didn't buy into the whole farm-wife thing. It was hard to believe she could be happy here after living in Chicago and having a career among the movers and shakers.

Then again, I thought, *Kate's kids can't decide to downsize and vote her out of her job.* There were some benefits to having the security of a family.

In the kitchen, Kate poured two cups of coffee and brought the sugar and creamer to the table. We sat down together and fell into silence, like the city mouse and the country mouse trying to decide what to talk about. There wasn't much common ground.

"So," Kate said finally, "tell me about work. Been on any interesting jobs lately?"

I blinked at her, surprised. Either Kate had changed in the last two years, or she was trying very hard to make me feel at home. Normally, she didn't like to talk about my work. There was an unspoken note of sibling rivalry to most of the things we talked about, and work was one of the worst.

I had the urge to tell her the truth—to spill the whole story, as I had to Keiler on the plane. How would it change things between us if I did? "Oh, the usual," I heard myself say, and then I changed the subject. "How's baby Rose? You know, I haven't even seen her yet, except in pictures. How old is she now?"

"Sixteen months." There was glint of maternal love in Kate's eye, and she glanced toward the kitchen doorway, as if she expected the baby to wake up just because we were talking about her. "She's a doll. It's amazing how different she is from Joshua. As a parent, you think it'll be the same with each one. Then they come and you see that they're little individuals, even as babies. It makes you realize that you can't lay all of your personality flaws on your folks—some of them you're just born with."

Kate smiled, and I chuckled. "Well, see, if you don't have children, you never have to face that fact."

We laughed together; then Kate turned serious again. "I hope it won't be like it was with us. I don't want Ben, the kids, and me to just be four people living in a house together, going our separate ways. I want us to be close as Josh and Rose grow up—to eat dinner as a family and sit on the porch in the evenings and talk, really spend time together."

"Well, that's how it's supposed to be," I said quietly. Something pinched just below my ribs, a twinge of some unfamiliar emotion. Jealousy perhaps, or regret.

Kate and I fell silent again. I finished my coffee, and she pushed hers aside half-full, then glanced toward the door again. "Hey, no one's up yet. Want to take a walk down to the river and back? I usually try to walk in the mornings and get some exercise before the kids wake up."

"Sounds good," I said, and meant it. "We haven't done that in years."

Kate and I smiled at each other. She stood up, saying, "Let me grab some tennis shoes," as she disappeared through the utility room door, then came out with a baby monitor and two sets of muddy shoes. She handed one pair to me almost apologetically. "Sorry these are such a mess, but you might want to leave your good sandals here."

I slipped off my sandals and put on the loaner shoes. "Guess I didn't come prepared for country life."

"It takes a little getting used to." Kate hooked the baby monitor on her sweats before we descended the porch steps and walked out the back gate. "Remember how we used to run down that path barefoot?"

"Did we?" I tried to remember as we walked past the blackberry patch, which was in full bloom and just beginning to bear. "Geez, it's all muddy and rocky and there are crawly things down there. I can't believe we ever walked it barefoot."

"We did," Kate assured me. "I guess it's easier when you're young and agile. Dell does it all the time. She hardly ever shows up here with shoes on her feet."

"Dell?" I repeated, pausing to untangle myself from a stray blackberry vine.

Kate glanced over her shoulder, frowning. "The little girl who lives across the river on Mulberry Road?" She was clearly hurt that I hadn't been keeping up with her life. "Remember, she was with us that Christmas before Grandma died, and then when you came down for the funeral in the spring? She and Grandma Rose were really close."

"I remember," I replied, as the path widened and we walked side by side. "Cute little dark-haired girl. Really quiet."

Kate nodded solemnly. "She has a hard time talking to people. She adored Grandma Rose, though. When Grandma was sick, Dell would come over with her schoolbooks and sit for hours reading her homework to Grandma. She kept showing up with her homework even after Grandma was so bad that she was asleep most of the time. I was really worried about how she'd do after Grandma died."

I felt a pang of sadness for the little girl across the river, who had become so dependent on the grandmother all of us took for granted. "How *is* she doing?"

Kate shrugged. "It's hard to say. A little better than last year, I guess."

"That's good," I said, trying to sound upbeat. Clearly there was a lot that Kate wasn't telling me.

"It's better," Kate agreed. "It still isn't good. She likes it when James comes. I'm surprised he hasn't mentioned her to you. He picks up stink bait at Shorty's, and they go fishing at some catfish hole Dell knows of."

I blinked. "Really? He never said anything about that." At least, I thought he hadn't. For the last few years, as Lansing slowly slid downhill, I'd missed a lot of what James had to say, especially about the farm.

I tripped over a rock, losing my footing, and Kate caught my elbow. "Careful. The path isn't very even. It'll surprise you sometimes if you're not watching."

She had no idea how right she was.

The trail opened to the river, and we left off the subject. Kate swept a hand toward the water. "Well, there it is. Hasn't changed much, has it?"

"No, it hasn't," I breathed, the essence of my childhood so strong that in my mind I was ten years old, barefoot and unafraid, and beside me Kate was young. "It's just like it always was. It's beautiful." Closing my eyes, I took a breath, smelling water and earth and the faint scent of spring growth. "It feels good to be here." I wasn't sure if I said the words or just thought them, but it was true. If there was a place on Earth that could quiet my mind, this was it.

Something stirred in the bushes across the river and I glanced at Kate, but she didn't seem to notice. Pulling the baby monitor off her belt, she rolled her eyes apologetically. "The baby's up. Guess I'd better get back to the house, just in case Ben doesn't hear her."

"All right." I wondered if Ben really wouldn't hear the baby, or if that was just Kate feeling the need to make sure the morning feeding and diapering were promptly and correctly handled, her perfectionism coming out.

Across the river, underbrush rustled again, and just before I turned away, I saw the little dark-haired girl, my husband's secret fishing companion, standing in the shadows behind a tangle of vines, watching us.

Chapter 4

Kate went inside to check on baby Rose, and I went to the little house to call James from the phone out there. By now he would have gotten my voice mail message and he'd be wondering why I'd suddenly decided to make a trip to Missouri. When he got to the hotel late last night, he'd probably tried to call me, but my cell phone went dead before I reached Hindsville, and I hadn't bothered to recharge it yet. The reception in this part of the world was so spotty, it was practically nonexistent. He was probably on the way from his hotel back to the airport now, but I might be able to catch him before he got there. It was still only seventy thirty a.m.

The living room seemed close and musty so I opened the old wooden windows, then carried the black rotary phone to the porch, stretching the wall cord through the doorway. Sitting in Grandma's rocking chair, I clasped the phone in my lap, stroking a finger over the dial, trying to think of what to say. How much should I tell James now? I didn't want to get into the whole story as he rushed off to a flight. . . .

Sighing, I dialed the phone, leaned back in the chair and closed my eyes. Why did I feel like this was some sort of secret? Why did it seem natural, easier, to keep it to myself?

I knew the answer, though I didn't want to face it. I hadn't told James how bad things really were at Lansing Tech these past months.

We'd gone along like we normally did—the two of us crossing paths a few days a week, then separating again for his flights and my business trips. As Lansing slipped further and further into the red, my travel grew more frequent and the hours at the office even longer. Because I wasn't going to be home, James took on more flights and spent more layovers in Missouri. The net result was that James and I were never together long enough to do more than skim the surface of each other's lives.

We were drifting, and in a vague way, we both knew it. But we followed our usual pattern of ignoring the problem, letting it work itself out. We'd drifted before—for three months after I insisted we take the job transfer to California and he didn't like living there, for five months when he started counseling a female friend through a divorce and I was afraid she wanted more than just friendship, for six months after September 11 when I begged him to stop flying and he wouldn't, for an entire year after the miscarriage and my mother's death. Like all married couples, we'd gone through our periods of disconnect, but we'd always come back together. We always knew we would.

Why couldn't I imagine coming back now—running to him like shelter in a storm, a soft place to fall? Why did this separation seem so much larger than all the others?

James's cell phone rang, then rang again. I found myself hoping he wouldn't pick up, and was relieved when he didn't. Putting off the inevitable was as easy as leaving another message on his voice mail.

"Hi, James, just calling to let you know I made it to the farm." I paused, rubbing my eyes, unsure of what else to say. "I guess you're probably wondering why I decided to come all of a sudden." Tears choked my throat and my voice started to tremble. I swallowed hard. *Don't fall apart now.* "It was . . . a strange week. Anyway, don't . . . ummm . . . don't worry about anything. I'll tell you about all of it when you get here. Bye."

Setting down the phone, I bent forward, covered my face with my hands, and sobbed in painful gasps so loud I was afraid Kate would hear me from in the house. I didn't want her to find me like this. I didn't want to be like this—a woman somewhere near midlife, suddenly seeing that my existence was a paper tower balanced on one thin card, which had just given way.

I felt someone touch me, smooth my hair back from my face and lay a hand on my shoulder. "Grandma?" I heard myself whisper; then I remembered that it couldn't be her.

The hand fell away, and I wiped my eyes, knowing it must be Kate. I braced myself for the questions that would come next. But when I looked up, the other rocking chair was empty, moving just slightly in the breeze. Through the kitchen window, I could see Kate and Ben in the main house, Kate feeding the baby and Ben helping Joshua pour cereal.

Staring at the empty rocking chair, I touched the warm place on my shoulder, a shiver passing through me. I was imagining things. Trying to pretend that Grandma was comforting me here like a lingering spirit. But that feeling was only an illusion, wishful thinking, because I couldn't bring myself to confide in the living. If Grandma had been sitting in the other rocking chair, she would have said I was too proud.

A movement nearby caught my attention, and I knew suddenly that I wasn't alone. Sitting on the porch railing, legs curled to her chest, was the little dark-haired girl. Resting her chin on her knees, she studied me through wide onyx eyes. She looked curious, her brows drawn together slightly in the center, her head cocked to one side as if she wasn't sure what I was doing.

Was she the one who had touched my shoulder?

Wiping my eyes, I cleared my throat and quietly said, "Hi, there. Are you Dell?" even though I knew who she was. I recognized her from two years before. She'd changed some, her body starting to mature with the first hints of puberty, her eyes set in an oval-shaped face with cinnamon-colored skin and full lips that curved down into a natural pout. She looked like the little Indian doll I'd bought in a souvenir shop at the Grand Canyon when I was ten.

"Hi," she said, seeming noncommittal, perhaps still a little leery at having found me sobbing on the porch. "You're Karen. James talks about you."

"That's right." I don't know why it pleased me that James had mentioned me. I guess it made his secret life here seem a little less secret. "I hear you two go catfishing together sometimes."

She nodded, perfectly impassive, and we fell into silence. I didn't have much experience at making small talk with kids. When James's nieces and nephews came to visit, I never knew what to say to them. Kids didn't want to hear about LAN networks and microprocessors. They were always more interested in James. Flying jet airplanes was something that captured their imaginations.

But for some reason, Kate's little neighbor was sitting there regarding me with obvious interest. I shifted uncomfortably, gazing out at the lawn. "Grandma's rosebushes sure look good this spring. The yellow ones on the trellis are my favorite. I remember when she planted those. I bet I was only about your age. Those bushes were sitting out in front of Shorty's Grocery, marked down on clearance, and they were just about dead. Grandma haggled with poor Shorty until he gave them to her free, just to get her to leave." I chuckled at the memory, forgetting Dell was there. "Kate and I were so embarrassed, we wouldn't even help her load the pots in the car."

I glanced at Dell. She might have been interested. I couldn't tell. We sat silently for a few more minutes, and finally she said, "Grandma Rose let me have one of the yellow ones. She dug some up and I brung the pot home to plant at my granny's house. Uncle Bobby poured out some motor oil and it got killed a while back."

"That's too bad." Hard to say whether losing the rosebush really bothered her or not. She spoke of everything in the emotionless tones of a kid who wasn't used to having her feelings considered. "Well, maybe we can dig up another one for you. Those old-fashioned roses are pretty easy to transplant. You know, women used to carry those on the wagon trains back in the pioneer days, so that they could plant them when they made a new home somewhere." I wasn't sure why I suddenly remembered that story, or where I'd first heard it.

Dell straightened, surprised. "Grandma Rose told me that."

"She did? I guess she probably told me, too. That must be where I learned it. She liked the fact that all of those old-fashioned plants were easy to share around. She had a name for it. I can't remember what she called them."

"Friendship flowers," Dell finished, and I nodded, pointing a finger at her.

"That's right," I said, pleased with our sudden meeting of the minds over Grandma and her flowers. "That is what she called them. Friendship flowers and pass-along plants."

Dell nodded, and we ran out of conversation starters again.

She turned toward the swaying fields of spring wheat below, her eyes fixed on something in the distance. "She tells me about you sometimes."

"She does?" I asked, surprised that Kate would be talking about me to the little girl from across the river. Why would Dell be interested in me?

"Mm-hmm. She said you wouldn't come back for a while." Turning away from the field, she studied her feet, dark against the white railing. I pictured those bare feet dashing up the river path.

"Hmm," I muttered, slightly offended by the idea of Kate and Dell talking about my avoidance of the farm. A prickle of big-sister indignation crept up my spine. "Well, I guess she was right. It has been a while."

Dell brushed a few blades of dried grass from her toes, then watched a ladybug crawl along the porch post, seeming to concentrate more on it than on me. "She said you were comin' because you were sad." She raised her gaze with an intensity that sat me back in my chair. "Are you sad?"

Are you sad? Such a simple question with such a long and complicated answer. "I'm not sure," I whispered, lost in the measureless depths of her dark eyes, surrounded by a tenderness I couldn't explain. "But you know what, it's not something you should worry about, all right?" I couldn't imagine what Kate was thinking, involving this little eleven-, maybe twelve-year-old girl in family business. "Kate shouldn't talk to you about that kind of thing."

Her eyes held mine a moment longer, confused. I had a feeling it was normal for her to be involved in adult business. She had the look of a kid who knew things far beyond her years.

Shrugging, she hopped down from the porch rail, crossed the porch, and started down the steps, her bare feet moving silently over the time-worn wood. "It wasn't Kate that said it. It was Grandma Rose."

"Wh-what?" Breath caught in my throat and the whirling in my mind stilled. I remembered the last moments before Grandma Rose died, when Dell came into the room and lay on the bed, her face only inches from Grandma's. They looked into one another's eyes, and somehow Dell knew that Grandma wanted her flowers brought inside so that she could see them one last time. There wasn't a word spoken between them, but somehow Dell knew.

Shaking off the eerie feeling, I sought a logical explanation. "You mean she talked to you about me those months before she passed away?"

Stopping at the bottom of the steps, Dell frowned over her shoulder. "Maybe," she said simply. "But sometimes I dream about her, too. I think she told me then. She said she heard it in the sycamores." Turning away, she stepped into the early-morning sunshine and skipped to the house with the careless abandon of a twelve-year-old tomboy.

Rubbing the goose bumps on my arms, I watched her go, then sat very still, moving just my eyes as I looked around the porch. "I don't believe in messages from beyond," I whispered, feeling silly. "I don't. I don't. I don't." But suddenly, I wished I'd planned to stay in the main house. If there was anyone, anywhere, stubborn enough to run other people's lives from beyond the grave, it would be Grandma Rose.

Kate called from the main house to tell me that breakfast was ready. Popping up like I'd been shot out of my chair, I hurried down the path, more than ready to return to the company of the living. When I walked in, Kate and Ben were at the table with the kids. Dell was handing Cheerios to Rose, playing peek-a-boo, and acting like a perfectly normal little girl rather than a pint-sized psychic medium.

I began to think I'd imagined our strange conversation.

Ben stood up and pulled an extra chair to the table for me, his usual friendly smile broad beneath his dark hair, which was sporting a bad case of bed head. "I like the do," I joked. "You look like Mel Gibson in *Lethal Weapon.*"

Ben puffed out his chest, grinning. "Yeah, people say that a lot. Me and Mel, we're like this." He held up two intertwined fingers as he sat back down.

Kate handed him a bowl of fruit cocktail. "Here you go, Mel. See if you can get your daughter to eat some fruit."

Ben offered Rose the fruit, then set it on the table when she refused. "She doesn't want any. Karen, glad you could make it to our little meeting of the long-lost relatives." I wondered if, like me, he was a little worried about Kate's plan to bring us together with Jenilee for the weekend.

Kate reintroduced me to Dell as I poured a cup of coffee. "We met outside," I rushed out, hoping that Dell wouldn't say anything about finding me sobbing hysterically on the porch.

"At *Grandma's* house." Dell emphasized the word, almost as if I shouldn't be staying there.

If there was any hidden meaning, Kate didn't catch it. "That's good," she remarked, busy trying to get baby Rose to stop playing patty-cake in her cereal. Irritated, Rose flung her hands into the air and squealed, letting out a very unladylike belch and some suspicious noises on the other end.

Joshua put a hand over his mouth and pointed, hollering, "Rose faw-ted."

"Joshua!" Kate gasped.

Ben chuckled, then boasted in a false baritone, "That's my boy."

Kate slanted a critical glance at him, pulling the cereal bowl away from Rose. "For heaven's sake, Ben, don't encourage him. The other day he told the Sunday school teacher that Kaylee Smith was a p-o-o-p." She spelled out the word and Joshua squinted, trying to decipher his parents' secret code. Kate glanced at me apologetically. "I think all of this has something to do with potty training." She shook a finger at Joshua in a way that was remarkably reminiscent of Grandma Rose. "And you, young man, are *not* to use that word. Remember what we talked about last Sunday, about the word you said about Kaylee Smith in Sunday school? Those are not nice words to say. Do you understand?"

Joshua gave her a confused look, as if he didn't understand why some perfectly good words were not available for everyday use. "Yesh."

Kate tilted her head and gave him *the look*. I recognized it from my mother. "Yes, what?"

He thought for a minute, then added, "Yesh, ma'am." Kate smiled and nodded, and Joshua sat a little straighter in his chair. Grinning proudly back at her, he added, "I'm not supposed to say faw-ted and poop."

"Joshua!" Kate gasped.

Ben lowered his face into his hand and started laughing. Dell twisted around in her chair and hid her grin in her elbow.

"Ben!" Kate scolded, like a mother desperately trying to rein in a situation that was spiraling out of control. She gave me a mortified glance, a woman-to-woman look, and I couldn't help it; I started laughing with the rest of them.

Kate sat there trying to decide between laughing along and taking the hard line.

Ben laughed harder, and Dell bent over like she was picking up something off the floor, all but disappearing under the table.

I snorted coffee up my nose while trying to wash down toast, choked, then tried to get Kate to lighten up on her perfect-mommy-perfect-kid bit. "My gosh, Kate, he's just a little guy."

She delivered a quick blink, the kind of blink that said, *You don't even have kids, so what would you know about it?*

I felt myself bristle instantly, then start to shut down. Why did it always happen like this with us? Why was it always a competition of who had what and who could be the most perfect? "Sorry," I muttered, half-heartedly. "Just my opinion."

Joshua gave me a sudden look of admiration, one that said Aunt Karen was pretty cool. Kate caught it, and for a minute I thought she was going to pop a cork. Suddenly, I wished I hadn't come to the farm at all. I should have stayed home and out of Kate's life. She was only uptight because I was here. She wanted everything to look perfect in front of me, so she could win this year's unspoken contest of Kate versus Karen.

She didn't have any idea how poorly armed the competition was this time. *If you told her, it might actually help things,* a voice said in my head. *Karen's life is falling apart. End of competition . . .*

I bristled again. Old defense mechanisms die hard. For as long as I could remember, every report card, every test grade, every school project had been compared. Kate got straight A's without even trying, moved up a grade, never forgot a homework assignment or made below a ninety on a test, while I worked my tail off to stay on the all-important A-B honor roll. In the back of my mind, there was always that sentence that lay just below the spoken words in our family—*Why can't you be perfect like Kate?* Perfectly smart. Perfectly sweet. Perfectly kind. Perfectly married with children. One boy, one girl. Perfectly Kate.

No matter what we did, there would always be that one problem between us. Kate was exceptional. I was average.

Everything came easily to Kate. I worked hard for what I achieved.

How pathetic was it to still be carrying that around at forty-one years old?

There are, I told myself, *worse problems to have than a little sister who's perfect when you're not.*

And it wasn't like there weren't areas where, growing up, I had excelled above Kate. Music, for one. Music was my one exceptional talent, my solace when it was obvious that I wasn't as academically gifted as my parents thought I should be. I hadn't felt the need for music in years.

"I played the piano last night," I heard myself say. I wasn't sure why I said it—maybe just to break the silence or change the subject.

It took a moment, but Kate softened and we averted the beginning of a new cold war. "That's great. You said something about it on the phone." She paused a minute, meditating on her coffee as she stirred in a spoonful of sugar. "You always had such an amazing talent for music."

On the other side of the table, Dell popped up and appeared interested. Kate turned to her, assuming she was looking for something to eat. "How about toast and some of your blackberry jelly this morning?" Dell gave a noncommittal shrug, and Kate served up the toast platter, butter and jelly, commenting, "Dell and I made blackberry jelly last fall from the berries in the freezer."

I raised a brow. "From scratch?" I couldn't imagine Kate *or* me figuring out the intricacies of canning jelly, even though we'd both watched Grandma Rose dozens of times.

Kate grinned and elbowed Dell. "From scratch, huh, Dell? We boiled the jars and sealed them in Grandma's old white canning kettle and everything."

"Wow," I said and watched Dell cover her toast with something that did, indeed, look like blackberry jelly. "I'm impressed. Where did you learn to do that?"

Dell piped up. "The *Martha Stewart* show reruns."

Kate rolled her eyes. "But somehow when Martha did it, she didn't end up with blackberry juice splattered all over the kitchen."

The three of us chuckled together, then baby Rose started to fuss and Kate paused to take off the bib and offer some bits of toast. "You know, while you're here, you ought to try the old piano in the little house—see if it's any good or if we need to just junk it." She gave Rose a few pieces of cereal. "Why did you quit playing the piano? I can't remember."

I considered the question for a minute. "I don't know. I kept it up the first two years in college, took some theater and dance, but it just got too hard after a while. I needed to buckle down to keep up with the engineering curriculum, and the music had to go." That was exactly what my father had said to me when he saw my sophomore-year report card. *This music business has to go.* "Dad wasn't too nuts about the arts classes on my transcript, either. Waste of money and time. You know the drill."

Kate nodded in silent agreement. She did, indeed, know the drill. When she'd changed her major from medicine to environmental science, my parents had refused to pay for one more credit hour. Kate and Ben almost starved to death, both trying to get through college on part-time jobs. Fortunately, Kate was smart enough to work and pass the classes, so she held to her principles and got the degree she really wanted. Another thing I'd always envied, even though I wouldn't admit that to her. Kate bucked the folks and lived to tell about it. She and Dad apparently had a pretty decent relationship now, these many years later. How she had managed to accomplish that, I couldn't fathom.

Ben clearly sensed an uncomfortable family discussion brewing. Gathering up some dirty plates, he made a quick exit, saying, "Well,

I'm off to get the lawn mowed before the parade of relatives arrive." Bending over, he kissed Rose and then Joshua.

Joshua held out his arms to be picked up. "I wanna go on the lawn mower."

Ben ruffled his hair like he was a puppy. "Not right now, buddy. You stay inside and help Mommy until I get the mowing done, and then I'll hook up the wagon and take you and Rose for a ride."

Joshua sighed and quirked his lips to one side, trying to think of another plan to get what he wanted. Then he finally shrugged and said, "Okeydokey, Dad."

As Ben was heading out the door, Joshua stood up in his chair and hollered after him, "I'm sow-wie I said faw-ted and poop!"

Trying not to laugh, Dell scooped him off the chair and said, "How 'bout we go outside, Joshie," then headed for the door.

Kate slapped a hand over her eyes, shaking her head as she got up and carried her plate to the counter. She had the defeated look of a mom who just wasn't making headway. "Motherhood," she sighed. As soon as the word was out of her mouth, she realized who she was talking to, and she darted a guilty look my way.

I tried to pretend I hadn't noticed it as I carried the remaining dirty dishes to the counter. "Oh, Kate, don't get so worried. He doesn't have to be perfect all the time. He's adorable just the way he is."

Kate nodded, seeming thankful for the reassurance, maybe a little shocked to be getting it from me. "I know," she said quietly as we started rinsing the dishes and putting them in the dishwasher, which was a new addition since the last time I'd been to the farm. "You're right."

We glanced at each other, both surprised to hear those words pass between us. Neither of us knew what to say after that, so we finished the dishes and dried our hands. Outside, the lawn mower roared to life.

That reminded me of what Ben had said. "So what does he mean, parade of relatives? Who all is coming?"

"Oh, Ben's exaggerating." Kate rested against the counter, gazing thoughtfully toward the door. "I thought Aunt Jeane would be able to be here, but Uncle Robert just had a stent put in—minor surgery, but he's supposed to rest a few days. Jenilee's coming, and she's bringing the box of old letters she found. Her boyfriend, Caleb, is joining her. I had asked Jenilee's two brothers, Drew and Nate, and Drew's wife and kids, just because I'd like to meet them, but Nate had a high school baseball tournament this weekend. We'll get together sometime soon, I'm sure."

"Wow," I said. "I didn't know we had so much family around here. Grandma never talked about any of them."

"There's also a cousin of Grandma's living over in Poetry— Eudora . . . something . . . ummm . . . Jaans. Eudora Jaans. We crossed paths briefly after the Poetry tornado, but never really talked. I think she was Jenilee's neighbor growing up. She's a second cousin to Grandma Rose."

"You've really gotten into the family genealogy," I commented, hoping there wasn't going to be a pop quiz later. "I never knew the family tree had so many branches."

Kate took on a mysterious look, her gaze darting around the kitchen as if the walls had ears. "That isn't all of it. I found an old family Bible in the attic, and Grandma Rose had two sisters—Augustine Hope was quite a few years younger, and then there was a sister two years older than Grandma Rose, named Sadie." Leaning close to me, Kate whispered with exaggerated drama, "Her name was *scratched out* of the family Bible. No death record. Just scratched out."

A tingle of mystery sent goose bumps over my arms. "Wonder what that means."

Kate's eyes met mine. "Don't know."

Chapter 5

O̲ur long-lost cousin arrived just before lunch, in the passenger's seat of a pickup driven by a college-aged guy who looked vaguely familiar to me. He smiled and shook Kate's hand in greeting, then Ben's, then mine, saying, "Hi, Karen. Bet you don't remember me." I caught myself staring at his arm, which was red and mottled with old scar tissue, probably from a burn.

I glanced up, embarrassed for staring and for not remembering him. He smiled pleasantly as Kate completed the introductions.

"This is Caleb Baker."

"Brother Baker's grandson?" It didn't seem possible. In my mind, he was still a chubby, freckle-faced kid singing in the choir at Grandma's church in Hindsville. "My gosh . . . I . . . well . . . you're supposed to be about twelve years old." I remembered that he had been in a serious car accident the year that Grandma died. No doubt that was the cause of the scars. The way Grandma had told it, he was lucky to be alive.

Caleb chuckled. "Been a few years, huh? Great to see you again, Karen."

"You too." I shook his hand, purposely not looking at the scars, which seemed to bother me more than they bothered him. I glanced around his shoulder at the petite blonde who had to be Jenilee Lane, our cousin. She was pretty in a natural way that didn't require makeup, like one of the waiflike models in the fashion magazines who could be anywhere between fifteen and twenty-five. Her features were soft, slightly childlike. There was an innate vulnerability in her brown eyes as her gaze darted nervously around. She didn't come forward to greet us, but stood there seeming uncertain.

Caleb sidestepped, slipping his arm behind Jenilee and bringing her closer. "This is Jenilee. Jenilee, Karen. Karen, Jenilee." He smiled encouragement at Jenilee, and I could tell they'd talked about this meeting on the way over. "You already know Kate and Ben, I guess, from when they came to Poetry after the tornado last summer."

Our new cousin extended a hand shyly and fluttered a glance my way. "Good to meet you, Karen." There was a careful pronunciation to her words—one that said she was trying to hide an Ozark accent. She seemed as uncomfortable with all of this long-lost relatives business as I was. I felt sorry for her.

"Nice to meet you, Jenilee." I smiled, trying to look warm and accepting, though those were Kate's usual strong points, not mine. I was known for coming on as slightly overbearing, a trait I inherited from my grandmother. "Did you have a good trip over from Poetry?"

She glanced at Kate, seeming confused, then answered, "Oh, I don't live in Poetry anymore. I started college last fall in St. Louis. Premed."

"That's great." My father would have loved her. Finally, a future doctor in the family. "You know, I think Kate did tell me something about that. . . ." I realized from Kate's expression that she *had* told me all of these details via e-mail, and I hadn't paid attention. "I remember now. Kate said you had a scholarship. That's great. Congratulations."

"It's really more of a work-study." Jenilee seemed embarrassed that our conversation had focused on her.

"Well, it's great, anyway," I said lamely, wishing Kate or Ben would say something. I became acutely aware that I had absolutely nothing in common with this twentyish cousin from a tiny Missouri town, except for some forgotten family history. What in the world would we find to talk about?

Jenilee seemed to be thinking the same thing. She glanced over her shoulder like she wanted to jump in the truck and drive away at high speed. "I've got the box of letters in the car." She glanced at Kate. "You want me to bring them on in now?"

Kate slipped an arm around Jenilee's shoulders like they were old friends. She was determined to make this get-together a success. "We can do that later. You two come on in and have lunch. I know you must be starved after driving all the way from St. Louis. You can tell us all about school and the work-study program. Did you ever get moved into an apartment there?"

Kate started toward the door with Jenilee, and Caleb in tow, and Ben and me trailing behind. As we walked, Kate kept up the barrage of questions and Jenilee answered. Yes, Jenilee was enjoying her first year in college. No, she hadn't found the right apartment yet—she was staying with some girls Caleb knew until she could get into a dorm. Yes, it was a little hard to adjust to life in the big city—she never thought she'd find herself living so far from Poetry. She missed her brothers, who were living in Springfield. Yes, her brothers were doing fine—Nate had finished physical therapy on his leg, which was shattered last summer when the tornado flipped his truck. He was playing baseball this spring at his new high school. Jenilee hoped that would be good for him, as he still had some lasting emotional effects from the *things* (I could tell there was something dark hidden behind that word) that had happened during the tornado.

Caleb jumped in and quickly changed the subject, saying, "Hey, did you know Jenilee's going to make the national news?"

Jenilee huffed an irritated breath and tried to slap him, but he ducked playfully out of the way. "Caleb, will you stop telling everyone about that! It isn't a big deal."

Caleb shoulder butted her off the porch step. I could tell they were more than just casually dating. When they looked at each other, their eyes sparkled with the glow of young lovers. I had a sudden pang of remembering when James and I used to be like that.

"It is too a big deal," Caleb insisted. "It's cool."

Jenilee pursed her lips and wrinkled her nose like she'd just caught a whiff of something awful. "It is like, two minutes, and I sound like one of the Beverly Hillbillies." She glanced at Kate as they crossed the porch. Kate was obviously interested, so Jenilee served up the condensed version. "They were doing a follow-up for *Nightbeat* about the tornadoes in Missouri last summer. They wanted me to talk about what we did in the Poetry armory right after the tornado, where we gathered up all the lost photos and things and hung them so people could get them back. The reporter wanted to know what ever happened to all the stuff—whether the photos got back to the folks they belonged to, that kind of thing. They met me at the Poetry armory, and I walked around and looked at the empty walls and they filmed that. Then they asked some questions about the Poetry tornado and what the town was like afterward. It was all kind of strange, and when they played the tape back for me, I sounded like a hick. I hope they throw it away instead of putting it on the news."

Kate's eyes widened enthusiastically. "When's it going to be on? We'll have to make sure to watch."

I gave Kate a *be quiet* look as we filed into the kitchen, but she didn't catch it. She didn't have any idea she was making Jenilee feel even more self-conscious. "The raw footage always looks bad," I interjected, hoping to reassure her. "Once they've edited it and put together the segment, it's not as bad as you think it's going to be." I sounded like I knew what I was talking about, which was pretty impressive, considering that I'd only been on camera a few times—once when my group had designed a homeland security network for Portland, Oregon; once or twice in PR videos for Lansing; and once when we'd done the first big round of layoffs. I pictured myself standing in front of the Lansing building with other management members, boldly defending the future financial solidity of our company to a pack of voracious reporters. God, what a sickening thought . . .

"Really?" Jenilee said, and my mind snapped back to the present.

"Oh, definitely." I assured her. "Besides, you have to remember that it's natural to hate hearing yourself on tape, but no one else sees it that way. To everyone else, you just sound like you normally do." I launched into a story about my first news appearance—the one about the homeland security communications system. I'd flown home right after filming the interview, certain I'd looked like an idiot, and hoping no one would see me on the news. Of course, everyone I knew saw it. The company president thought it was so good, he played a tape of it the next day for the whole company over the LAN system. "Anyway," I finished, "I was pretty sure I was going to die right there, but, you know, everyone else said it was great. It's never as bad as you think."

Jenilee seemed relieved, and regarded me with a new measure of interest. We'd made a connection—the connection of two people, both obsessed over what everyone else thought. She smiled and said, "I hope you're right," with a cute little accent that made *ri-ight* into a two-syllable word. She did sound a little like Elly May Clampett. But in a good way. Jenilee was adorable. Anyone who saw her on the national news or anywhere else would like her.

"Karen, you want to grab the tea out of the refrigerator and pour the glasses?" Kate interrupted, before the conversation could get going again. I realized I was standing there talking while Kate was busy getting lunch on the table, and she was slightly miffed. My instant reaction was to give her a huffy answer, but the truth was I should have been helping. "Sure," I said, reaching into the refrigerator for the tea pitcher while Ben took down the glasses and started filling them with ice. "Sorry about that. I got caught up in the conversation. What else do you need me to do?"

Kate blinked, surprised. It wasn't like us to make nice, even to impress company. "Take out the potato salad and the pickle tray and pull off the plastic wrap." She went back to putting ham slices on a platter, complete with little pineapple rings and maraschino cherries—red ones and green ones—an arrangement surely worthy of Martha Stewart.

Jenilee beat me to the refrigerator. "I'll get it." She seemed glad to have a job to do. I could tell she was used to taking care of everybody, and having Kate fawn over lunch was making her uncomfortable. The artfully prepared food and the precise table setting with the folded cloth napkins beside the plates gave lunch the feeling of an event. At an event, there are always expectations.

"You've outdone yourself, Kate," I commented, trying to make the moment more relaxed. Kate quirked a brow, so I added, "Everything looks wonderful."

"Sure does," Ben said as he set the glasses on the table. He looked less relaxed than usual. Apparently, even he was feeling the pressure.

"Thanks." Kate fluttered back and forth to the table, putting out little butter spreaders and Grandma's old-fashioned salt wells with tiny silver spoons.

Jenilee gave the salt wells a perplexed look, commenting that the food was too pretty to eat, and Kate shouldn't have gone to so much trouble, and then we fell into silence, unable to think of anything else to say, now that we'd covered the basics. It looked like lunch might be as stiff and formal as Kate's perfectly prepared platters of food.

The hallway door burst open and Joshua bolted through, dragging a toy car tied to a string. Skidding around the curve, the car wrapped around Jenilee's leg, and sent her stumbling sideways just as she took a platter from the refrigerator. Spinning to one side like an off-balance ballerina, she twisted to keep from stepping on Joshua, lost the pickle platter, then caught it just as she collided with the swinging door and fell into the hallway.

The door slapped closed behind her, and we stood staring, shocked for an instant before Joshua dropped the string, straightened his arms at his sides, and let out a wail that probably cleared the woods of wild game for miles.

Kate came to life first, rushing across the kitchen, scooping up Joshua and pushing open the hallway door with a mortified look. The rest of us hurried to the doorway and stood there gaping at Jenilee, who sat against the stairway wall like a hastily discarded rag doll, the toy car still wrapped around her feet.

Dell rushed from the living room, confused, then put her hands over her mouth as she realized what had happened.

For an instant, no one seemed to know how to react, except for Joshua, who was crying and babbling, certain he was in bad trouble.

Jenilee held up the platter, grinning sheepishly. "I saved the pickles."

Instantly, Joshua stopped wailing. "P-pick-wels?" He sniffed, and squirmed down from Kate's arms. "I like pick-wels."

All of us started to laugh. What else was there to do? Our first meal together as a family wasn't going to be perfect, as Kate had planned, but it was going to be memorable.

Ben stepped forward and helped Jenilee to her feet as Joshua advanced on the pickle platter, saying, "I want a pick-wel."

Smiling, Jenilee handed him one, then stepped back. "Oh, my gosh, you look so much like my brother Nate." She blinked and looked again, as if she couldn't believe her eyes, then she turned to us. "If I had one of Nate's baby pictures, you wouldn't believe how much they look alike."

"Really?" Kate seemed politely skeptical. "We've always thought Joshua took after Ben's family."

Jenilee shook her head. "He looks just like Nate. I mean, they could be twins. I'll have to bring one of Nate's baby pictures sometime. You'll be shocked."

We stood dumbfounded, not quite sure how to react to our first case of family resemblance. Something inside me turned a corner. I felt a sense of connection that went beyond words.

"Well, I guess we should go eat." Kate's tone indicated she was glad the excitement was over. On her way through the door, she picked up Joshua's car on a string and said to him, "This is an outside game, Josh. You know that." Then she glanced at Dell, whose dark eyes were slightly downcast. "Honey, please don't help him tie strings on these anymore. The other day he ran past Rose and knocked her off her feet." Dell looked like she was about to cry, and Kate immediately backpedaled. "It's all right, Dell. It was just an accident."

Jenilee quickly chimed in, "It was no big deal, really. It's O.K. I shouldn't have been standing in front of the door."

That seemed to reassure Dell. She and Jenilee stood looking at each other like a couple of shy toddlers, and since I was in the middle, I quickly made the introductions. "Jenilee, this is Kate's neighbor, Dell. Dell, this is our cousin Jenilee."

Dell glanced at me, seeming surprised to be included in the formalities and unsure of how to react. "Hey," she muttered finally, looking at the floor.

Jenilee smiled at Dell and said, "Hi, Dell." Then she leaned closer and whispered, "Don't worry about the toys. My little brother used to do that, too. My mama didn't like it much, either. Moms are funny that way."

Dell fluttered a glance upward, and to my surprise, she smiled back. A kindred look passed between the two of them as we headed into the kitchen.

Lunch went by without any major disasters or pickle-platter incidents. We filled the time with the basic introductory chitchat of getting to know one another. I felt a little sorry for Dell. None of the family business meant much to her. She had the bored look of a kid trapped at a grown-up dinner, but it was pretty obvious that she didn't have anyplace better to go, so she stayed.

When baby Rose woke up halfway through lunch and started babbling over the baby monitor, Dell jumped out of her chair, saying, "I can get her." She waited a moment to see if Kate would say it was all right.

"Thanks, sweetheart," Kate said. "If she has a messy diaper or anything, just call me and I'll come take care of it."

"I can do it," Dell rushed out.

Kate seemed uncertain. "She's pretty wiggly on the changing table these days."

"I'll use the seat belt thingy."

"All right."

"Wo-hoo!" Dell headed for the door, with all of us looking after her, confused.

Ben shook his head. "I wish I got that excited over a messy diaper."

"I wish you did, too." Kate lowered a brow at him playfully, and Ben curled his lip in reply.

"Smart aleck," he said.

Dell's voice came softly over the baby monitor. "Hi, Rosie. Did you have a good nap? Did you see Grandma? I bet she sang you that song, didn't she? Shew, I smell a stinky. Com 'ere—now, hold still. I gotta put on this seat belt thingy. There we go." Then the ripping of diaper tabs, and Dell groaned. Clearly, she wasn't so thrilled about the diaper changing anymore. "Oh, yuck. Gross."

Kate started to get up, then willed herself to leave the situation alone. "She's always trying to earn her way." Her frustration was evident, coupled with a hint of sadness. "It's like she thinks if she doesn't do things for us, we're not going to want her to come over anymore. I don't know how to get across to her that people should love you because of who you are, not because of what you can do for them."

"Sometimes that's a hard thing to understand," Jenilee said quietly, her gaze meeting Caleb's. "Especially if you're used to being around the other kind of people. It's pretty hard to believe that someone could love you just because of who you are." Caleb smiled tenderly, an obvious conversation of hidden meanings going on between them. Jenilee understood where Dell was coming from because she'd been there.

The phone rang and Ben jumped up to answer it. The room had grown uncomfortably silent, so that everyone looked toward the ringing phone with a sense of relief.

Ben answered, then turned to me, saying, "Hi, James. Sure. She's right here. Yeah, I know. She's AWOL, huh? I'll let you talk to her, and she can explain."

My heart went into my throat as I walked to the phone. I'd been so caught up in Kate's preparations and Jenilee's visit that I hadn't thought about Boston in hours. Having James as close as the phone line brought back a crushing sense of reality.

Taking the phone from Ben, I turned a shoulder to the table as the lunchtime conversation resumed. There was nowhere to go for privacy. I stood bound by the curly black plastic wire that brought James's voice through the receiver.

"Karen? Karen, are you there?"

I took a deep breath, trying to sound calm, casual. I didn't want him to ask a bunch of questions. Not now, in front of everyone. "Hi, hon." My voice shook. I wondered if everyone could hear it. Clearing my throat, I went on with something I hoped would sound more normal. "Where are you?"

"Dallas. Karen, what's going on? Why are you in Missouri?"

"It's a long story." Something heavy and leaden pushed the breath out of my lungs. "We can talk when you get here." The words were barely a whisper—a thin, desperate ribbon of sound winding through the phone line to pull him closer.

The line was silent. I sat listening to the low hum in the old receiver. "What's wrong?" he asked finally.

"James, please, we can talk when you get here," I repeated, closing my eyes and rubbing my forehead. I heard the conversation at the table continuing, but it seemed far away. I wondered if Kate was listening, watching me and guessing the truth. James was probably imagining all kinds of things. I swallowed hard, trying to do some damage control. "Kate has a big weekend planned. She has a long-lost cousin of ours here, and we're going to read through some of Grandma's old letters. It seemed like a good time for a visit, you know?"

Surprisingly, James accepted that explanation. "All right. I'm flying my last two legs, Dallas to Denver, and ending up in Kansas City, so that should put me there sometime late tonight." The concern left his voice, and he actually sounded cheerful. "Tomorrow I can take you down the road and show you how our little chunk of land is looking. I've been doing some work out there when I'm in town. It's really shaping up." He went on talking for a minute about eventually building a vacation cabin on the land. I realized that he was so willing to accept my excuse for being here because he didn't *want* anything to be wrong. He wanted everything to be easy and normal and convenient, just like always.

What was he going to say when I told him things weren't going to be *normal* anymore, at least not for a while? Depending on what Dr. Conner found, maybe not anywhere close to normal.

"That sounds good, hon," I heard myself reply in steady, measured words, like a high school actor poorly performing lines.

James didn't even notice. "Yeah, sounds like fun," he agreed. "A little R and R."

"Sure," I said, wounded because he didn't ask again, dig deeper, question one more time, as if he wasn't interested in anything below the surface.

"All right. Well, I'll see you when you get here," I said, the forced enthusiasm so strong, I knew he'd catch it and ask again what was going on. But he didn't, so finally I finished with, "I'm staying out in the little house, so if you get here after everyone's asleep, just come in there." I thought about not having to sleep alone tonight, and the image was comforting. I wanted to curl up and cry like a baby. I hadn't done that in years—since the miscarriage, when they told me I'd lost the baby and they thought I had cancer. Later that night, we received the news that my mother had been in a car wreck on the way to the airport. One minute she was on her way to Boston to comfort me. The next minute, she was dead. After that, everything went numb.

I wondered if James was even aware that, in a way, we'd been drifting for longer than just the past two years, and there was more to it than my obsession with saving Lansing. We kept ourselves busy and distracted for a reason. Standing in my sister's kitchen, I realized that we'd been numbing the pain for years now—with jobs, with vacations, with possessions. Ever since the miscarriage, we'd maintained a hum of activity that kept us from having to talk about the questions that accidental pregnancy and the loss of it brought into our lives.

But now, here at the farm, everything was silent. I could hear it all—the pain I felt at the loss of that baby, the grief he didn't seem to share or recognize, his focus on the cancer, his fear that I might die like his mother, his unwillingness to talk about the baby, or whether we wanted children in the future.

As I hung up the phone, I felt all the unanswered questions returning like the dull roar of a jet far off in the distance.

What would the sound be like when it finally touched down?

Chapter 6

After lunch, Ben offered to take everyone on a tour of the farm. The idea of driving by the family cemetery on the hill overlooking the back of the farm, of seeing my mother's grave and Grandma Rose's, was more than I could face, so I told them I was tired after getting in so late last night and I wanted to rest before going through the old letters Jenilee had brought.

I stood on the porch of the little house, watching as they climbed into the old flatbed farm truck by the barn. Dell said something to Kate, then headed across the newly planted cornfield toward the river, toward home, I supposed. Did anyone at home keep track of her at all? She'd been at Kate's the entire day, and no one had called to check on her or to see whether she was staying over for lunch.

What would that be like? Kate and I had always had someone monitoring our activities, making sure we had meals to eat, clean clothes to wear, homework done. There was always someone looking after us, even if it was a hired someone. Our days were scheduled and tutored. We were always safe. We were never like Dell, running unbridled in the woods and the hills, passing the unplanned hours of the day, searching for somewhere to be. I thought about it, watching her disappear into the lacy undergrowth at the edge of the pasture. In a way, I was like her now. Suddenly, all the normal underpinnings were gone, and I was drifting in a world that seemed vast and un-predictable.

The noise in my head started growing again, so I went inside, sat down at the piano, and began to play. My fingers wandered through a long, slow melody, and peace washed over me like the warm river water in summer. I abandoned myself to the sound of the music and the smooth feel of old ivory beneath my fingers. My thoughts went back to some long-ago afternoon, when I sat with Grandma Rose at the old piano. It was in the main house back then, the strings perfectly tuned, not slightly off-key as they were now.

Grandma Rose loved to hear me play, but she seldom took time from her household chores to sit down and listen. That day, she sat on the bench beside me, closed her eyes, and lost herself in the music. When the song was over, her cheeks were damp with tears. I asked why she was crying, and she told me the music reminded her of someone, but she wouldn't say whom.

"I could stop playing," I said.

She kissed my hair gently. "No." Tears trembled in her voice. "It's a good memory."

"If it's a good memory, why are you crying?" I asked, unable, as usual, to figure her out.

She let out a long, slow breath. "Because it's a memory of some-one"—pausing for a long time, she gazed out the window, seeming to forget I was there—"who is gone." She asked me to play the song again, so I did.

Now, all these years later, I could feel tears damp on the keys again. Her tears, my tears . . .

A sound in the room interrupted my thoughts, and I looked up. Dell was perched in the chair by the doorway with her knees curled to her chest, watching me through thoughtful, dark eyes.

Wiping my face on my sleeve, I turned to her. "You're back." I couldn't think of what else to say.

"I just went home to see if Uncle Bobby come by. Granny was sleepin', so I left her be."

"Oh," I said. "Well, maybe he'll come later."

She didn't seem excited by the prospect. "Maybe," she said flatly.

We sat silent for a moment, Dell studying me while I absently tested the piano keys, one by one, listening to how far out of tune the notes were. "You might be able to catch up with Kate and the rest of the group."

"I don't like to go to the graveyard." She wrapped her arms tighter around her knees.

"Me either," I admitted, and the conversation ran out again. I tested some more of the piano keys, then played a few notes of a soft, slow melody. I couldn't remember the name.

"I know that song," Dell piped up, sitting a little straighter in her chair and watching the keys with interest. "The one you were playin' just now. I know that song. Grandma Rose used to sing it."

"Really?" I asked. I hadn't been thinking about what I was playing, or why. "I'm not even sure what that song is called. It's just been running through my head all day."

" 'Turn Your Eyes on Jesus,' " she informed me. Lowering her feet soundlessly to the floor, she crossed the entryway and sat down beside me. "We sing it in church some, when I get to go. Grandma Rose used to sing it, too, out in the flowers. I learnt it from her."

I tapped out the first notes of the melody, and the words played in my mind. *Oh, soul, are you weary and troubled. . . . No light in the darkness you see. . . .*

The same words I'd heard floating up from the riverbank that morning. "Was that you singing this morning? I heard someone singing down by the river. I thought maybe I was imagining it."

Dell watched my fingers intently as I replayed the beginning of the melody. "Grandma sung that song while I was sleepin', and when I got up, I thought about it. I sung it while I was walking over."

Gooseflesh prickled on my arms. All this talk about her seeing Grandma Rose in her dreams was too much mumbo-jumbo for me. It probably wasn't something to encourage, either, so I changed the subject. "You have a beautiful voice. Do you sing in the choir at school?"

She knitted her brows as if she thought I was making fun of her, as if I couldn't possibly mean it. "Huh-uh. Choir's after school. I gotta get home after school to help Granny change her oxygen and stuff."

"Oh," I said, again getting a glimpse of her life. "Well, really, it's a shame to have such a beautiful voice and not do something with it. I could talk to Kate. Maybe she could help you get back and forth to after-school practice."

For a split second, Dell seemed to entertain the thought, even be excited by it. Then she refocused on the piano keys, shaking her head. "Kate's busy. She's got a lot to do all the time with Josh and Rose."

"Yeah, I know." I'd already noticed that, as much as Kate and Ben seemed to care for Dell, she was mostly a shadow on the fringes of all the baby activity. "That has to be kind of disappointing sometimes, huh?" Some strange urge compelled me to reach over and brush her hair away from her face. "It's not always fun being an older"—I realized that I'd been about to say "sister," but Dell wasn't Josh and Rose's sister—"being older. But it's nice that you're around to help Kate and Ben. I know they like it when you're here."

She didn't reply, but instead motioned to my hand on the piano keys and changed the subject. "I can do that."

"Hmm?" I wasn't sure what she meant. "Do what?"

Sliding her hand over, she studied the keys for a minute, tentatively pressed the first one, then tapped out two bars of the melody with one finger—every note perfect.

I sat looking at her, amazed. "I didn't know you played the piano."

"I don't know how, but I can hear the way it sounds," she said simply.

"You mean you memorize the notes?" I asked. "You saw which keys I was pushing and you remembered the order?"

She shook her head impatiently. "No. I hear it in my head, like this"—she tapped out the first few bars to "How Great Thou Art"—"and I *know* which ones to push."

"That's fantastic." Something that my old piano teacher had said ran through my mind. *Great musicians don't learn the music—the music is already inside and they only learn to bring it forth.* "What else can you play?" My pulse sped up with an anticipation that surprised me. I felt like I'd just unearthed a hidden treasure.

"I dunno. I do it on the church piano sometimes when no one's there." She shrugged, then started tapping out the melodies to song after song—hymns, pop songs, and finally, the theme to *The Brady Bunch*.

"Wow!" I gasped. "You're amazing."

She drew back at the compliment, then slowly broke into a wide, slow grin that lifted her face and made her eyes sparkle. I had a feeling no one had ever said that to her before.

"How about if I teach you a few things?" I tasted a sweet sense of purpose that pushed away the lingering salt of my tears. "You should learn to play with all of your fingers. If you can do that . . . well, there's no telling what you'll be able to play."

" 'K," she agreed, seeming a little uncertain. "What if I can't do it?"

"I think you can." I didn't wait for her to change her mind or decide to turn shy again. Taking her hands, I gently laid them over the keys, and we began.

We spent the next hour working together—an unlikely student, an unlikely teacher, finding perfect harmony at the keys of an out-of-tune piano. It was as my old piano instructor had told me—the music was already inside her, and it was only a matter of coaxing it forth.

When Kate and Ben came back with the group, we were doing a duet on the piano—Dell playing melody and I the harmony chords. Dell was singing the words to "Over the Rainbow," which she said she had learned from Grandma Rose. She didn't notice that we had an audience at the door.

I winked at Kate and gave a shrug toward Dell. Kate widened her eyes, then mouthed, "Wow," and just kept shaking her head in shock.

Joshua finally squealed and started to clap, and Dell realized they were watching. She blushed and stopped singing.

"Hey, how about that!" Ben cheered. "When did you learn to play the piano?"

"Karen taught me just now," Dell replied matter-of-factly, as if everyone learned to play the piano in less than an hour.

I stood up, raising my hands helplessly. "Don't ask me. She's a quick study."

"Karen's a really good teacher," Dell bubbled, and she gave me an exuberant hug.

Kate blinked in surprise. There was, I thought, a hint of jealousy in her look, though she was trying hard to hide it.

Dell didn't notice Kate's expression. She hurried to the door and scooped up Joshua, looking happier than I'd seen her since I arrived. "It was fun! Want me to teach you the piano, Joshie?"

Joshua said yes, and I stood up so the two of them could have the piano bench. Dell began carefully explaining the notes to him, and of course, he quickly frustrated her efforts by banging on the keys so loudly that it drove the audience onto the porch.

Ben screwed one eye shut, shaking his head. "Sounds like the piano needs tuning."

The rest of us laughed, because we knew the piano wasn't the problem.

Kate leaned in the door and told Dell we were going to sit on the porch of the main house, and she and Joshua could come join us when they were done.

" 'K," Dell chirped, and went back to trying to teach Joshua the theme song to *Sesame Street*. "No, push this one, then that one, Josh. You gotta hear the music in your head, like this. See? No, don't push those four all at once. Ja-osh!"

The rest of us started across the lawn. Jenilee and Caleb stopped by their truck to get the box of letters, and Ben veered off toward the back door to take baby Rose in for a diaper change.

Kate and I walked slowly past Grandma's rose garden. "I don't think I've ever seen Dell that excited about anything," she commented.

"I know." It sounded like I was boasting that I had outdone Kate's efforts with Dell, so I quickly added, "It's the piano. She's amazing with it. I've never seen anyone pick up the notes that fast. Has she ever had any kind of music lessons?"

Kate frowned thoughtfully. "I doubt it. They took music classes out of the elementary school a few years ago because of the budget crunch. I think they have some kind of extracurricular vocal music program after school, but that's about it."

"She should have music lessons. It's almost a crime if she doesn't get to develop that talent. She's amazingly gifted." My mind rushed ahead, trying to work out the details of how Dell could continue playing piano after I left. "Who's the pianist at the church these days? Is it still Shorty's daughter? Does she give lessons? Maybe Dell could go after school, or something. I'll . . ." I stopped short. One look at Kate told me I was stepping all over her toes.

"Karen, you don't understand a thing about Dell," she snapped in a way that caused me to back off. Kate stopped walking, and so did I. "In the first place, she can hardly even bring herself to talk to people she knows. There's no way she'll want to go take music lessons from a stranger. In the second place, it's almost impossible to get her anywhere on a regular basis. We can't even get her to church on Sunday, and I can't tell you how many times Ben's gone by to give her a ride to school, and she's wandering around the woods or gone to some medical appointment on the dial-a-ride van with her grandmother. The last couple weeks, every time I turn around she's off somewhere with this Uncle Bobby, whoever he is. I don't have a clue what's going on there, and Dell won't tell me."

"She doesn't want to bother you, Kate," I heard myself say. What was I doing getting in the middle of Kate's family business? "She's afraid to *be* a bother to you. She sees that you're busy and you're stressed, and she's afraid to pile on more."

"I know that," Kate bit out under her breath. "But I can't change the way she thinks. I've talked, and I've tried. I've loved her all I can, but you know what? I can't work miracles."

My mind went silent, then I whispered, "There's your miracle." I pointed toward the little house, toward the sound of the piano drifting through the still air. Dell was playing again. "Right there. There's your miracle. There's her chance to be extraordinary, her special gift. The one thing about her that isn't like anybody else. She hears music in her head." Kate's eyes met mine with an expression of sudden understanding, and I whispered, "If that isn't a miraculous gift, what is?"

Kate seemed surprised to hear me, of all people, asking that question. "I don't know," she admitted quietly. "I just don't want her to end up worse off than she already is. She has such a hard time in school and with the other kids. It's all she can do to keep up now, and she's getting to the age where she's starting to change physically. I just don't think she can handle any more pressure, any more activities."

"Kate, I wouldn't have made it through school if it *hadn't* been for music." I couldn't believe I was admitting this to her after all these years. *News flash: Karen isn't brilliant.* I'd never even admitted that to James. Perhaps because he, like Kate, was brilliant and gifted. "You don't know what it's like to struggle, to not have everything come easily, to have to hang around the classroom after school so you can get the teacher to explain calculus equations one more time." Kate's eyes widened, and she blinked like she was seeing me for the first time. I didn't care. "All that time, the one thing I knew I was really good at was my music. I knew that made me special, even though I wasn't the brilliant, gifted, and talented student that you were. My music was enough to keep me going, and it could be that way for Dell. It could be better than that for Dell. I was good at music, but she's extraordinary. She's remarkable. She started to see that today, and it lit her up. There has to be a way to keep that flame burning."

Kate didn't answer—just nodded, then finally choked out, "O.K."

Jenilee and Caleb were coming up the path behind us, walking arm in arm and gazing at each other in a moonstruck way that made me miss the days of young infatuation. He leaned down to kiss her, and they stopped near the rose trellis, forgetting there was anyone else in the world. I smiled, seeing myself and James the weekend we first met. He was deadheading on a flight to Boston so that he could spend a couple of days at the summer music festival in Tanglewood. I was flying home after working on one of the first big network jobs for Lansing. I had some of the programming code in my head already, and when the plane landed, I planned to go straight to the office, input the code, and test it. Then James sat down beside me, said hi as he tucked a carry-on under the seat, and all of a sudden, I couldn't have programmed my way out of a cardboard box.

We talked for an hour and a half on the flight, shared cheap airline food, and compared his childhood on a small farm in Virginia to mine in Boston. I teased him about being a farm boy, but he didn't really seem like one. He was sophisticated, intelligent, secure in himself, and just arrogant enough to be successful. He had beautiful hazel eyes, gorgeous light brown hair, and a countenance that made him seem mature, despite that he was only twenty-seven, just two years older than me. He liked music, everything from classical to James Taylor, but he wasn't one of the starry-eyed dreamers I'd dated in college. He had an actual, practical college degree and a career path, a plan for the future. He loved flying planes, and he was on track to eventually move from first officer to captain. I couldn't help thinking that even my parents would like him. By the time the flight was over, there was nothing I wanted to do more than go to Tanglewood with him, wander around the grand old Berkshires estate together and listen to the Boston Symphony. I knew, even at that point, that it wouldn't really matter who played that weekend. All I could see was him.

It was like that every time we were together, from the moment he flew into town until the moment he left. After two months, he surprised me with a weekend trip to Nantucket and a proposal at the top of Sankaty Lighthouse, overlooking the massive cranberry bogs. We bought a ring at one of the little art shops in town and married at a little chapel right there on the island. It was, he confessed, one of the few impulsive steps he'd ever taken. I loved him even more because of that, but as time went by, it was one of the things that frustrated our relationship. For James, life was a flow chart, carefully mapped out on the squares of invisible graph paper. Lines all over the place, no reason to talk about anything that deviated from the flight plan . . .

Kate nudged me as Jenilee and Caleb broke off the kiss and turned toward us. Kate wiped her eyes, and my thoughts flipped back to our conversation about Dell. Kate and I had deviated from our usual flight plan, gotten emotional and honest for a moment, and now it seemed uncomfortable. I'd said too much, revealed too much of myself.

All of the habitual self-defense mechanisms went up. By the time we sat down on the porch with Jenilee and Caleb, both Kate and I were back to our unsentimental selves. Jenilee set the box of mystery letters on the wicker table between our chairs, and we regarded it like a welcome distraction.

"I haven't read them," Jenilee told us. "There was so much to do after the tornado last spring. Drew, Nate, and I worked for nearly a week cleaning out what was left of my grandparents' old house. Daddy had junk stored there for years, and I didn't even know some of my grandparents' things were in there until the tornado scattered their papers everywhere. We boxed everything up after the tornado, and I didn't start going through it until a couple weeks ago." She lifted the lid, and the musty scent of aged paper drifted from the box. "It seemed like the right thing would be for all of us to go through these together. I never even knew my grandmother had a sister."

"There were three sisters," Kate interjected, her voice taking on an air of mystery. "I found an old family Bible in the attic, and there are three sisters listed—my grandmother Rose, your grandmother Augustine Hope, and Sadie, who would have been two years older than my grandma Rose. Her name was scratched out of the family Bible, but there's no explanation."

"That's weird." Jenilee's reaction was much like mine had been. "I wonder why."

Kate shrugged. "I don't know. I'm hoping we'll learn something from the letters." She tentatively touched the letters, and a crow called in the garden like some mystical omen. Our circle suddenly had the feeling of a séance.

No one said anything until finally I suggested, "Why don't we each start reading individually? If one of us finds something interesting, we can read that part out loud."

A sudden breeze slid along the porch, and across from me, Jenilee shivered. "That sounds good. Let's do that."

Each of us reached into the box and took out a letter.

Chapter 7

The three of us read as the afternoon shadows lengthened. Slowly, one word, one page, one letter at a time, we began slipping into the lives of our grandmothers. The things they chose to write about, the words they used, the styles of handwriting told us who they were. Rose's pen was quick, angular, practical, to the point. She talked about the weather, the price of crops, the children, the household work, the birth of young animals in the spring, and the weaning in the fall. Her relationship with her younger sister was parental; her letters were often filled with advice and tips on cooking, canning, housekeeping, and marriage. She didn't sign her letters *With Love,* but simply *Your Sister,* as if no more needed to be said.

Augustine Hope's hand was precise, contemplative, the lines gently curving and artistic, the words carefully thought out even when she was describing the most ordinary events. She did not address my grandmother as Rose, the nickname my grandfather had given her after their marriage, but just by her initial "B," short for Bernice.

> *Dear B,*
> *Today I put up jars and jars of the peaches gathered from our secret tree in the wood near Mulberry Creek. How good to go back after all these years and find that our enchanted glen*

remains! Our sister trees still stand in the center of the glen, side by side, as they were when we played there, each of us claiming one lofty sycamore as our imaginary castle. Such good memories those are.

As I finished the canning today, I sat looking at the fine golden jars of peaches and wondering—who planted the peach tree in such an unlikely place, deep in a glen of sycamores where no one would find it? I suppose we will never know. Perhaps no one planted it there at all. Perhaps the seed fell from the basket of young lovers on a picnic, or dropped from the pack of a wandering tinker looking for work. Perhaps it fell from the mouth of a bird or floated down the river from some fine plantation far away. Or perhaps it was planted by the wood fairies. Remember how we could see them hiding among the cowbells and Queen Anne's lace, wearing their little skirts of hollyhock petals? I have not seen one in years. But then, I have forgotten to look.

We never told their secret, did we? Not even on that horrible day when we trotted home with our little bucket of peaches, a surprise for Mama's birthday. She was certain we'd stolen them from someone's orchard, and she came after us with a switch. You wrapped your body over ours and whispered, "Don't tell. Don't tell. Don't tell." You didn't want Mama to find our secret place. We kept silent, and when Mama wasn't looking we went back to the sister sycamores to hide away. We could hide from everything there. Nobody knew.

Do you ever think about that place? Do you remember how many trees stood in the glen? There were three.

In my mind, I see them yet.

Your Beloved Sister,
Augustine Hope

Jenilee looked up with questions in her eyes when she finished reading, and for just an instant, I saw my grandmother the moment before she died, when she was trying to tell me something, but time had run out.

My mind replayed that silent good-bye. What did she want to tell me? What was she thinking at that moment?

Dimly, I heard Kate talking about the letter—saying something about my grandmother's mysterious older sister. "I think I have the letter that answers that one," she said to Jenilee. "I didn't understand it until you read yours."

I tuned in to the conversation again, but in the corner of my mind, I was still thinking about Grandma Rose just before she passed from this world to the next.

Kate picked up a letter to read, just as the front door opened and Caleb poked his head out. He and Jenilee smiled at each other, and I had another pang of missing James. How long had it been since we'd smiled at each other that way?

"Need anything?" he asked. "Need any help?"

Jenilee glanced around our circle, then answered, "I guess not."

Kate winked at him. "It's kind of a girl party out here. What are you guys doing in there?"

"Watching a ball game. Ben put the baby down for a nap." The TV got louder, and he glanced over his shoulder. "Josh is having a blast, but I don't think Dell's too into it."

Kate chuckled. "Tell her to come out here with the girls. This is much more interesting than baseball."

"All right. I'll tell her." Caleb smiled at Jenilee one more time, then closed the door.

Kate was getting ready to read again when Dell peeked out the door. Pausing, Kate motioned for her to join us. "We're reading through some old letters. Trying to solve a family mystery."

"Cool," Dell said, but she didn't seem overly enthused. Crossing the porch, she stood by me. "I taught Joshie to play a C chord on the piano." She waited expectantly for my approval.

"That's great." The words conveyed a rush of pride in my unlikely pupil. "Just had your first lesson, and you're teaching piano already."

She tried not to look too pleased with my comment. "Can we play some more later?"

"Sure." I noticed Kate watching our conversation with interest. Deep inside me there was just the slightest bit of gloat, like we were kids again, vying for the same playmate. I knew that was the wrong way to feel. "Aren't your fingers getting sore by now, though?"

Dell quickly shook her head. "Huh-uh."

"All right, then, in a little while, after we go through some more of these letters," I said. "Kate was about to read us a letter that Grandma Rose wrote to her sister when she was young, probably not too long after she got married and came here to the farm."

Dell glanced at the letter with mild curiosity as she sat on the porch floor and crossed her long, sun-browned legs. I watched her, wondering what she was thinking.

Kate started reading the letter.

> *Dear Augustine,*
> *I suppose it is all the emotions of coming motherhood that make you go on so about the sister trees, but do you think it wise, when you are heavily in a family way, to go walking so far back in the wood, so deep into the past? I do not think of the sycamores any longer. I do not think of her. When I was younger, I dreamed of that place, but now I have banished it even from my dreams.*
>
> *It is only a fading picture left too long in the summer sun. I will not dwell there any longer, and neither should you. What good, now, is all her talk of castles and fairies? What good was it ever?*
>
> *Augustine, you must not walk in the past. Finally, after these many years of wanting, you are to be a mother. Rest, Augustine. Take good care. When it is closer to your time, I'll leave my little ones here with their father and come to be with you. Don't argue. They can do without me for a little*

while, and you will need a woman nearby to help care for
you and the babe those first days. I would not be anywhere
else but with my only sister.

Your Sister

"But Augustine wasn't her only sister. We know that from the entry Kate found in the family Bible," I said as Kate finished the letter. "The third person they're talking about is probably the other sister."

Jenilee shrugged in a way that said *Maybe so*, and Kate frowned thoughtfully. "We don't have any way to know for sure, I guess. I wish I could have asked Grandma about Sadie."

A breeze slipped across the porch, and on the horizon the amber sun disappeared behind a bank of clouds, dimming the afternoon light as Kate spoke the name of the mysterious long-lost sister. I'd never been a believer in spirits and séances and messages from beyond, but goose-flesh rose on my skin.

Kate whistled the theme song to *Scooby-Doo*, lightening the moment.

"She didn't like to talk about Sadie," Dell muttered so quietly the words were almost part of the breeze. If I hadn't been sitting so close, I wouldn't have heard her at all. I glanced sideways, and she was sitting cross-legged, lazily drawing lines in the sand with a blue jay feather.

"What?"

"She didn't like to talk about Sadie," Dell repeated, loudly enough for everyone to hear.

Kate stopped in the middle of folding the letter into an envelope. "Did Grandma talk to you about Sadie?"

Dell nodded, seeming more focused on drawing in the sand than on us. "Sometimes she dreamed about when her and Sadie and Augustine was little girls. Sadie had red hair, and Grandma had brown hair, and Augustine had blond hair. Everybody thought that was pretty funny and maybe they didn't have the same daddy, like with me and my baby brother. He's got yellow hair and pretty skin and blue eyes. Uncle Bobby says that's because he didn't have a nigger daddy, like me."

I jerked upright at how easily that word rolled off her tongue.

Kate closed her eyes, clearly trying to hold back an emotional reaction. "Dell, I told you that's not a nice word."

Dell shrugged and went back to drawing in the dirt. The lines were slowly becoming a portrait of one of the climbing roses blooming on the porch railing. "Uncle Bobby says it."

Kate grimaced, her hands clasped tightly over the letter, her expression frustrated and helpless. I could tell this was an issue she'd been dealing with for a while. "He shouldn't say it, either, and he shouldn't say it to you. If you want, I'll talk to your granny about it."

"Huh-uh." Dell quickly shook her head. "I won't say it anymore. It's no big deal."

The porch fell silent. Jenilee leaned forward and studied Dell's picture in the sand. "You know, Dell, sometimes people in your family do things that aren't right just because they don't know any different. It doesn't make you a bad person, but it doesn't mean you should do the same wrong things, either."

A look of understanding passed between them, and Dell answered, "That's what Grandma Rose said."

Jenilee smiled. "It sounds like she was a pretty smart lady. You know, I never really got to know my grandmother. She and my grandfather both died when I was still little. I think that's why I like reading her letters. It lets me know her a little bit."

Dell nodded. "Grandma Rose said Augustine was kind of quiet-like." Dell might have been uncomfortable talking to the rest of us, but she seemed perfectly at home with Jenilee. "Sadie was really, really pretty, and folks used to talk about it, how pretty she was and all. She didn't have to do any work because when she was little, she'd have spells and faint dead out. Their mama was always afraid she was gonna just up and die one of those times. Grandma Rose used to have to do all the work because Augustine was too young and Sadie fainted. Grandma didn't think that was real fair. Sadie was a good singer, and everybody made a big deal about that, too, and Grandma Rose used to get jealous of her. It's not a good thing to be jealous of other people's gifts—Grandma Rose told me that. God gives everybody different stuff."

Kate and I both sat transfixed, wondering how Dell could possibly know the secret history of Grandma Rose's childhood, a childhood she had kept from her children and grandchildren, a life of poverty and neglect. Why had she been so willing to share all of this with Dell and not with us? Did she think we wouldn't be able to relate because we had been brought up in a privileged Boston home? But then, I'd never asked her. I'd never taken the time to talk to Grandma Rose about those old times or the family history. I'd barely even listened when she told stories of way back when. Now I wished I'd paid attention.

"Grandma felt awful sorry about Augustine and Sadie." Dell's words broke into my thoughts.

"You mean because they passed away?" Kate interpreted.

Dell squinted, her lips twisted to one side, as if we should already know the answer. "Because they had a fight. Grandma said being mad at people for a long time is like leaving the bread dough out too long. It just gets bigger and bigger until it's so huge you can't do anything with it." The corners of her lips tugged upward. "Me and Grandma saw it on *I Love Lucy*, and that's what made her think about it. Lucy's bread dough got way too big and it went all over the kitchen. Grandma said that's how it is when you put a mad on and keep it for a long time, like she did with her sisters."

Kate quirked a brow.

"So why were Grandma and her sisters mad at each other?" I asked.

Dell shrugged. "She never did tell me that."

Jenilee reached into the box and thumbed through the letters. "I don't think we're going to find the answer in here—the ones we just read have the most recent postmarks. I do know that my grandmother's baby died not long after birth. There was another letter I found earlier on, blowing around in the grass after the tornado. In that letter, my grandmother was writing to her baby daughter—you know, sort of a note for the baby to read someday when she grew up. She was writing about how heartbroken she was after her baby's death and how a woman came to them with a baby girl, and my grandmother took the baby in. I thought that baby was my mother, but now I'm not sure. My mother was an only child, but her birth certificate doesn't say she was adopted, so maybe they ended up giving that baby back to her mother, and later on they had my mother. Mama never said anything about it, even after she came down with cancer and we were trying to trace family medical histories and that kind of thing. And also I look a lot like my grandmother, and . . . well, when I came here and saw how much Josh looks like my brother Nate . . . well . . . we have to be blood relations. There's no way my mother could have been adopted."

"Hmmm," I muttered, turning to Kate. "Are you sure Dad and Aunt Jeane don't know anything about this?"

Kate shook her head and laid her stack of letters in the box. "They both said they didn't know anything except that Grandma Rose had a falling-out with her family and it was a forbidden subject around the house."

"Mrs. Gibson might know something," Jenilee mused. "She's our neighbor down the road from Daddy's place. She was cousins with Rose and Augustine. I've always had a feeling she knew some things about my family she didn't want to tell me. I can stop and ask her on the way back to St. Louis."

"Well, maybe she can tell us something." Kate climbed stiffly to her feet and stretched. "In the meantime, my stomach's telling me it's time to get some supper going. Rose ought to be waking up any minute."

Dell stood up with her legs still crossed. "I'll go get Rosie. She likes it when I wake her up." She didn't wait for an answer, just turned and hurried through the door.

"She sure loves the kids," I observed.

Kate's forehead wrinkled with concern. "That worries me a little. I mean, it's great that she has fun with the kids, but she's already starting to talk about when she has one of her own. Her granny seems to think it's fine for her to talk that way. Her mother was fifteen when she got pregnant, and Dell's set to fall into that same trap. She doesn't have much at home, the kids are hard on her at school, and she's looking for a way out."

Jenilee nodded like she knew exactly what Kate was talking about.

"Music could be her way out," I blurted, not thinking of whether I was stepping on Kate's toes. In my mind, I could hear Dell coaxing melodies from the old piano, singing in a clear, sweet soprano. "I know

I keep pushing, but she's incredibly talented. You only have to look at her to know that she needs to be incredible at *something* right now."

Kate sighed. "I'll try to work it out—I promise. Maybe one of the older guys who do the picking and grinning downtown on Saturday nights would be willing to get her started on guitar or violin, something like that. James plays guitar with them when he's here on layover, and he's taken Dell along a couple of times."

"James?" I repeated incredulously. *"My* James?" I hadn't heard him play a guitar in years. Now Kate was telling me he hung out at the pickin' and grinnin' on Saturday nights in Hindsville?

"Sure." Kate cocked her head to one side, confused. "He goes down there quite a bit. They even ask about him at the domino table when I go into Shorty's for groceries. He's taken Dell along a couple of times when she was bored around here."

"You're kidding." Suddenly, I felt like my husband had a secret life I knew nothing about. He played guitar on Saturday nights, he and Dell spent time fishing and at the weekly jamboree, and he'd never said a word about it. Had he? Had he tried to tell me, and I wasn't willing to listen? Every time he talked about the farm or his work on the land we'd inherited from Grandma Rose, I took it as pressure to come to Missouri for a visit. It was a discussion that started fights, an issue I didn't have time for, with everything that was going on at Lansing. We'd finally quit talking about it.

"Guess you guys need to converse more." Kate was joking, but she was so close to the truth that the comment stung.

I quickly turned the conversation back to Dell. "Do any of them play piano? Maybe one of them would come out here and start Dell on some lessons, or maybe they could use the church piano."

"I'll try to set something up," Kate repeated. "But you know how Dell is about new things and new people. There's a good chance she won't be willing to go."

"What if I came back in a week or two and got her started?" I heard myself ask. "I'm going to have some time off . . ." I suddenly realized what I was saying, and my pulse rocketed, sending blood into my cheeks. Now Kate would ask why I was having time off.

The phone rang somewhere beyond the screen door of the little house, and I was never so glad for a distraction in my life. "I'd better get that. It's probably James." I hurried off the porch without waiting for an answer, feeling completely unlike myself. It wasn't normal for me to run away from my little sister, or from reality.

Reality, it turned out, was waiting on the other end of the phone line. James had landed in Kansas City, and he was going to be at the farm in a couple of hours. With the pressure of flying out of the way, he was now fully zeroed in on the fact that something was wrong.

"Karen, you want to tell me what's going on?" he said when all of the normal trip talk was out of the way. "You know my mind's not all here when I'm in the middle of a trip, but the radar's going off now. What's up, and why this sudden junket to the farm?"

I closed my eyes, determined not to get into it over the phone. "Let's just talk when you get here, all right? I need to help Kate get supper on." He didn't answer right away, so I added, "Don't worry. It's not life or death or anything." *It could be,* a voice whispered in my head. "Just job stuff and . . . I thought a weekend at the farm would help me get some perspective."

He waited before agreeing. "All right. I'll see you in a couple of hours."

"O.K." Suddenly, I felt tired, uncertain, as if I were in a movie and had just forgotten which character I was supposed to be. "James?"

"Yeah?"

"Why didn't you tell me you've been playing guitar down at Shorty's?"

Another pause, a hesitation during which I wondered what he was thinking. "Guess you didn't ask."

"Guess I didn't," I whispered. And then we said good-bye.

The little cabin suddenly felt too empty, too quiet, so I returned to the main house. Kate, Jenilee, Caleb, and Dell were in the kitchen working on supper while baby Rose played with Tupperware containers, babbling gleefully and shaking measuring cups in the air.

"Hi there, Rose." I squatted down to talk to her. "Did you have a good nap?"

Rose gurgled, then popped the pacifier from her mouth and tried to put it in mine. I probably looked like I needed it. "She's so cute," I said over my shoulder as I smoothed the faint curls on Rose's mostly bald head. "My gosh, Kate, do you think she's going to have red hair?"

Kate stopped in the middle of chopping a bell pepper and pointed the paring knife at me thoughtfully. "You know, I've been wondering about that. She had light brown peach fuzz when she was born, and then that fell out, and now it seems like her hair is turning kind of reddish. But none of us have red hair, so I don't know."

"My mom had red hair," Jenilee pointed out.

"And Sadie had red hair," Dell added.

Kate nodded and went back to cutting up the pepper. "I guess that's true. I guess it's a family trait we just never knew about." She paused for a moment, seeming to think about something, then went on, "Speaking of family traits and things like that, Jenilee and I have come up with a plan." Clearly, she had something she wanted to ask me, but she was worried about how I would respond. "Jenilee and I thought maybe we'd try to get everyone together for Memorial Day—our family and Jenilee's family, and this cousin of Grandma Rose's who lived down the road from Jenilee. Sort of have a mini family reunion." She stopped and stood there with her back turned to me, stiff with anticipation.

"And maybe see if we can piece together the mystery of the three sisters and whether or not my mother was adopted," Jenilee added quickly.

"You could teach me some more piano." Dell threw her comment awkwardly into the mix like bait into a rat trap.

It was clear that I was the rat. They had been talking about me in my absence, and all of them were worried that I wouldn't go for the idea of a family gathering—probably because a family gathering would be likely to include my father.

I resisted the urge to respond out of habit, instinct, and old sibling rivalry. Kate had obviously portrayed me as the family stick in the mud. What I really wanted to do was tell her I didn't appreciate it. Of course, if I did, everyone would know she was right. *Kate is the sweet one, and*

Karen is the snotty one with the attitude and a chip on her shoulder the size of Nebraska. Those were pretty much the roles we'd always portrayed in the past.

Don't answer yet, I told myself. *Count to ten first,* which for me was an unusual measure of reserve.

"Sure," I said finally. The word sounded almost natural. "A family reunion sounds great, and it just so happens that I'm free on Memorial Day."

Chapter 8

After supper, Jenilee, Caleb, Kate, and Ben decided to take the kids down to the river. Dell and I went to the little house to play piano. Dell was filled with enthusiasm at the prospect of a lesson, but my mind was elsewhere. I was thinking of James driving in from the airport. What was I going to say when he arrived?

My stomach had tightened into a knot. I wasn't sure why. James was never reactionary about anything. He would take the news about the layoffs calmly. His engineering mind would begin analyzing the house payments, car payments, severance, résumés, job prospects, adding me to his insurance policy—all of the practical issues.

Maybe that's what I was afraid of. Maybe I was afraid that he wouldn't see, that he wouldn't realize how I *felt* about being betrayed by the company I'd helped build. Maybe I was afraid he would react the way he did when we lost the baby and found out we'd never have another.

"We'll get through this," he said as he sat by my hospital bed. *"We'll go ahead with the trip to Bali next month, the way we planned. That'll take your mind off things. . . . Come on, honey, it'll be all right. This just wasn't meant to be right now."*

Right now? I thought. What he meant was *ever*. This wasn't meant to be, ever. The truth was that no matter how much he hedged, or danced around the subject, or tried to be supportive about our accidental pregnancy and then the loss of it, he didn't want a baby. Not then, probably never. He'd helped his father raise the three younger children after his mother died of cancer, and the idea of taking on parental responsibilities again didn't appeal to him, not at thirty-five anyway. *"Maybe in a few years we can explore our options for having a family,"* he'd said.

Options? I didn't want to explore options. I didn't want to move on or get through. I didn't want to talk about whether we would someday replace the baby. I wanted to grieve for the loss, to fall into James's arms and cry until I didn't ache anymore. I wanted him to understand the sense of loss. Even though it wasn't planned, this baby, this child, was part of us. Our child. I had begun to imagine that tiny new life as a person, a son or daughter. Blue eyes, brown eyes, blond hair, brown hair, short, tall, shy, outgoing, straight toes like mine, curly toes like his . . .

James didn't want to talk about that. He wanted to move on to the next logical step. To keep things on an even keel, to put off the decision of whether we would ever slow down our lives and make the sacrifices necessary for a family. It wouldn't help to dwell on what had happened, to try to reason it out, he said. We just had to let time pass and get back to normal. It wasn't like we didn't have a good life, just the two of us. . . .

Finally, I gave up and did what he wanted. I moved on. By silent mutual agreement, we never talked about the miscarriage or the partial hysterectomy that followed it. We didn't talk about my mother's sudden death in a car accident that same day, or how I suddenly felt like an orphan in the world. James went on his way and I went on my way, and occasionally we slipped off together for a romantic weekend, where we could crowd our senses with the sights and sounds and tastes of an exotic location, so as not to notice that there were things we'd never talked about. Only now I needed someone to talk to. I needed him. . . .

Dell stopped playing "Eagle Summit" on the piano and turned toward me. "What's wrong?" she asked quietly. I realized I'd been off in my own little world and hadn't been listening.

"Nothing," I said. "It's just kind of a strange weekend for me."

"Want me to quit?" She motioned to the piano. "I don't sound very good."

"Oh, no, it's not you," I rushed. "You sound wonderful, and I love hearing you play. It's just that I have some things on my mind. . . . It's a little hard to explain."

She focused on the keys, her face solemn, one slim brown finger wiping a piece of lint off middle C. "Granny doesn't like me to bug her sometimes. Maybe I hadn't ought to bug you right now, huh?"

"It's all right. Really." Slipping an arm around her, I hugged her against me. It didn't feel the least bit stiff or strange, and she didn't pull away. "When we sit here and play together, I feel great."

"Are you sick?" The question seemed to come out of the blue. "My granny's been sick."

I shook my head. "No. I'm fine." *I hope.* "What's wrong with your grandmother?"

Dell shrugged noncommittally, her chin still tipped downward, as if she were conversing with the piano rather than me. "Sometimes she has a spell for a day or two, then she's all right."

In spite of the quick answer, she was obviously worried. It was hard to imagine being only twelve years old and having to deal with those issues. "Is there anything we can do? Maybe pick up some medicine for her or send over a meal?"

"No," she said quickly. Too quickly, I thought. "It's O.K. Anyway, she's got Uncle Bobby to help her out. He don't have an apartment no more, so he's been stayin' at Granny's, unless he's got a girlfriend."

I paused, unsure of what to say next.

Dell didn't wait for an answer. Instead, she started picking out the melody to the hymn I'd heard her singing in the woods earlier.

"You have a beautiful voice."

Spitting a puff of air, she rolled her eyes. "Ppfff. Yeah, right."

"You do," I said, elbowing her playfully.

Cocking her head to one side, she gave me an almost smile. "You sound like Grandma Rose."

I reached up and tweaked the end of her nose. "Well, Grandma Rose was right. You know, she was *never* wrong about *anything*." I performed a fairly good imitation of Grandma Rose. It won a giggle from Dell.

"Grandma used to sing this song." Giggling, she began singing in a facsimile of Grandma's high, squeaky old-lady voice.

Laying my fingers on the keys, I played chords to her melody, and together we managed a fair duet, all the while laughing and singing in our best old-lady voices. By the time we finished, both of us were red faced and breathless. We collapsed against each other, laughing. It felt good. I couldn't remember the last time I'd let loose like that.

The sound of a truck coming up the drive put an end to our merriment. Dell stiffened against me, turning an ear toward the door. Outside, someone laid on the horn, the sound rattling the evening stillness.

I stood up and started toward the door with Dell, suddenly somber and quiet, following me. We rounded the corner of the house just as an old primer-spotted pickup with a rebel flag decal rattled to a stop near our garage. A strange disquiet tickled my senses as the driver stepped out. Dressed in torn jeans, a grease-stained denim shirt, and a dirty ball cap with long, stringy hair hanging out the back, he looked more like a criminal than a neighbor.

I hurried to beat Dell to the yard gate. "Can I help you?" I said, blocking the opening.

Pulling off his baseball cap, the stranger combed dampened strings of salt-and-pepper brown hair out of his face, then replaced the cap, staggering backward a step. He had the look of someone who'd spent forty-some-odd years the hard way, on beer, cigarettes, and probably various kinds of drugs. His clothes had a sweet smell, suspiciously like marijuana, and his breath, even from three feet away, reeked of beer. "I come to pick up Dell," he said. "Her granny said she'd be here." Without waiting for an answer from me, he motioned to Dell, who had stopped a few feet away. "C'mon, don't act all shy on me. I ain't got time for that," he said to the top of her head, looking her up and down in a way that was anything but parental.

" 'K," she muttered, her chin still tucked.

He moved forward, then took a step back when I didn't vacate the gateway. "Well, let's go, girl. I gotta go to town and get some hamburger meat for your granny. I'll buy ya an ice cream."

"I just ate," she said, crossing her arms over herself, darting a nervous glance toward him.

"I can give her a ride home," I interjected, a prickle crawling up my spine. Dell didn't want to go, and I didn't want her to go. I wished Kate were here, instead of down at the river with everyone else. I had no idea whether it was normal for Dell to go with this man, but it didn't feel right.

Think, Karen. Think of something. "I want her to take home a plate of cookies for her grandmother," I blurted. "I was just going to get them ready. I can give Dell a ride home in a minute, if you want."

He returned a narrow-eyed look that was hard to read. "No need. She can come with me." He waved a hand irritably at Dell. "Go git yer stuff, girl. I ain't got all day." Without waiting for an answer, he turned and staggered back to his truck, climbing impatiently into the driver's seat.

I started toward the main house with Dell beside me. "You don't have to go if you don't want to," I said when we were safely in the kitchen. "I'll give you a ride, or we can go down to the river and get Kate so she can take you." I wanted her to say yes, even though I knew I might be getting her into trouble with Uncle Bobby. He clearly didn't want to take no for an answer.

"It's O.K. I better go on now," she muttered emotionlessly. "Granny might get mad. She doesn't really like it when people come around."

I caught her gaze as I opened the cookie jar and quickly filled a paper plate. "Are you sure it's all right? Dell, if there's anything you need . . . if there's a problem, I can help."

"No, ma'am," she said and hid herself behind a curtain of dark hair. "I gotta go or Granny'll be mad. I'll see ya tomorrow. Are you gonna go to church with Kate and Ben?"

"Oh . . . I . . ." The last time I'd been to that church was the day of Grandma's funeral. I didn't want to go back, but the expectant look in Dell's eyes made me say, "Sure. Of course I am. I'll see you in the morning."

She smiled as I covered the cookies with plastic wrap. "See you in the morning." Taking the plate, she turned and scurried out the door as the truck horn blared, demanding action. I followed her out, crossing the yard and standing uncertainly at the gate. Uncle Bobby leaned over and opened the passenger's side door for Dell.

"So how's my little nigger girl?" I heard him say as she climbed in with her plate of cookies. "What you been doin' over here again, hangin' out with the white folks. . . ." The rest was drowned out by the sputter of the engine as the vehicle pulled away.

Standing at the gate, I hugged my arms around myself, feeling sick.

Kate came up the river path carrying Rose just as the truck was disappearing down the driveway. "We heard someone honking up here." She stopped beside me, giving me a questioning glance as I watched the vehicle disappear. "Who was that?"

"Uncle Bobby," I said. A shiver traveled up and down my arms, even though it wasn't cold. "What a jerk. Is it all right to let her go with him?"

Kate sighed, wrapping her hand around the gate and tapping her ring impatiently against the metal pipe. "I hope so. I've asked her, but she won't say much. I'd go talk to her grandmother, but every time I try to get involved, her grandmother quits letting her come over here. She doesn't like people interfering. When the school started pushing her about Dell's attendance, she threatened to pack up their stuff and move to another county. If she does that, we won't have a clue where to find Dell."

"What a mess," I muttered.

"I know." Kate let out a long sigh. "I just keep trying to have faith that there's a plan here—somehow it's all going to work out."

I glanced sideways at Kate, surprised. She was starting to sound like Grandma Rose. "I hope so," I muttered, wishing I had Kate's confidence. "It seems like there ought to be . . ." I caught myself about to say *something we could do.* I knew Kate would take that as criticism, so I finished with, ". . . some solution."

Kate sighed, looking tired, like she'd already been up and down this road a dozen times. Shaking her head, she pushed the gate open and started toward the house, saying, "I'd better go change Rose's diaper."

I knew she'd taken my comment as criticism, maybe because in the past we had criticized each other so much. I wasn't the one to be giving her advice.

When she came back out with Rose I was sitting on the porch of the little house. "Want to come back down to the river with us?" she asked.

"No, I think I'd better wait here for James." I waved at Rose, who was fanning her chubby hand furiously and hollering, "Ba-ba, ba-ba, ba-ba," which was baby language for *Let's get back to the river right away.*

I chuckled at her. "I think Rose is ready to go. Bye-bye, Rose."

Rose responded with another furious round of "ba-ba, ba-ba, ba-ba" and nearly wiggled out of her mother's arms.

"Looks like she's another river baby," I said. "A future mermaid." That was what Grandma Rose had called Kate and me, because we spent so much time at the river.

Kate laughed at the old term. "Guess we'd better get going." Bending over, she turned Rose upside down so that Rose squealed with delight. "You silly girl, are you a mermaid?" Kate cooed, placing noisy kisses on Rose's bare stomach when her shirt flipped up. There was a look of pure joy on their faces, and I felt a pang that I couldn't describe, deep in some forgotten part of myself. When Kate stood up, she gave me a guilty look, as if she saw that pain in me. "Guess we'd better go," she repeated, seeming apologetic for engaging in a moment of mother love where I could see it. "When James gets here, y'all come on down to the river with the rest of us, O.K.?"

I blinked at my educated, Boston-raised sister and repeated, "*Y'all come on down?* You're starting to sound like Grandma Rose."

Kate grinned sheepishly. "Oh, Lord."

"*Oh La-wd?*" I repeated in my best Southern accent. "That *really* sounds like her."

"You hush!" Kate stomped a foot impatiently, starting to laugh.

I pointed a finger at her. "See, that's Grandma Rose all over the place. We're going to have to do an exorcism on you."

The two of us laughed together. "Go on," I said finally. "Y'all git on down to the ree-ver."

Shaking her head, Kate walked out the gate with Rose still waving furiously at me, hollering, "Ba-ba, ba-ba, ba-ba!"

I waved until she was out of sight, then settled back in my chair. Closing my eyes, I drifted slowly, my thoughts floating into the summer evening, into the soft sound of the spring lilies strumming the old iron fence, and the muted whisper of the trees overhead. Their voices were familiar, and in my mind I was a little girl again, walking by the river with Grandma Rose on a warm summer day when I was eight. All around me, I could hear music—the gurgle of the water and the hush of the breeze, the faint crackle of broad sycamore leaves fanning the afternoon air, the low groans of the branches, heavily laden with summer growth. If you listened, it sounded almost like murmurs, like the whispering of something old and wise.

I knew Grandma heard it. When I turned to her, she was gazing into the canopy of leaves, her face damp with tears, her mind far away. "Sadie Marie, you come down from there," she whispered, and I wondered what she was talking about.

I tugged her hand, but she didn't seem to notice. "Grandma, who are you talking to?"

She startled, her mind coming back to the present. "Oh, no one, Sweet," she said, giving my hand a squeeze. "I was just listening to the sycamores. Each type of tree has a sound all its own. Have you ever noticed? Sadie used to say that was the fairies running through the leaves."

"Who's Sadie?" I asked.

"No one you know," she replied in the stern voice she used when we weren't to question.

"I don't believe in fairies," I told her, trying to sound very mature. "They're a myth. They don't exist."

Grandma raised a brow, the pleated line of her mouth lifting. "My, so grown-up this year." Lightly, she cupped my chin in her hand. "Is this the same girl who thought she could wish upon a star and get a pony last year?"

I huffed, "I'm *eight* now."

"Oh, I see."

"I don't believe in *Santa Claus,* either."

"Well, that's a shame. I'll tell him not to be leaving things for you under the tree this year."

"He's a myth."

"If you say so."

"Isn't he?"

She smiled and bent down in front of me, her face aged and leathery from years in the fields, her eyes the twinkling blue of a little girl's. "Don't be so quick to let go. Some things, when you send them away, never come back again." Sighing, she straightened and turned away. I wandered down the riverbank, searching for fossils and throwing in stones. When I checked back, Grandma was gazing into the sycamores, listening again. . . .

The wind went silent, and my memory faded as the trees grew still. My mind returned to the present with an elastic snap that threw me into a grown-up body and a modern world, with all its modern problems. I jerked upright in my chair, wishing I could go back. I hadn't thought about those old times with my grandmother in years. I probably never would have if the sound of the leaves hadn't taken me back. Strange how a memory could be tied to such an insignificant thing.

If only I had asked more about Sadie. Would Grandma have told me of the secret glen and the sister trees? Would she have remembered her sisters and decided to make contact with them before it was too late? Did she ever try in the years that followed, or did she carry her resentments to the grave?

I didn't want it to be that way with Kate and me. I wanted us to be sisters, the way sisters were supposed to be. What point was there now in hanging on to whatever was wrong between us in the past?

The sound of a car coming up the drive punctuated the question. Standing up, I walked around the corner of the house just as James was parking his rental and climbing out.

I met him at the gate and opened it so he could get through with his suitcase. He looked good in his pilot's uniform—tall, dignified with his thick hair prematurely gray at the temples. "Hi, hon," I said, and gave him a quick kiss. The usual greeting, a comfortable hello. As if nothing were out of the ordinary. "Good trip?"

"Not bad," he replied, his hazel eyes a weary brown in the afternoon light. "Rough weather around Denver. Made for a bumpy landing, but that was about it."

"Oh." I led him around to the little house and opened the door. "We're staying out here. Kate wanted to boot Joshua out of his room, and I told her not to."

"Anything's fine with me." He groaned, stretching his neck side to side. "I just need a place to lie down, and a little chow. I don't think I'll be very good company this evening. I'm wiped out."

I wondered if that was his way of telling me he didn't want to talk tonight. The idea of waiting, of just having a nice time together at the farm, was tempting.

He sat down on the couch. "So, anyway, what's up? How's the visit going?"

I knew he was giving me the opportunity to say whatever I needed to say. "It's been a good visit," I said, glancing at the piano as I sat down next to him. "The most amazing thing happened. I mean, it was just like in the movies. You know Kate's little neighbor Dell?"

"Sure. She's my catfishing partner," he said, and I was once again struck by the fact that James had a whole life here I knew nothing about.

"Well, she wanted me to teach her some things on the piano, so I started showing her a few notes, and then a few more notes, and then she started picking out tunes on her own—things she'd heard on TV and so forth. I'm telling you, it was amazing. No one would have believed it without seeing it. . . ." I went on telling him about Dell and our lessons, and what an amazing musical talent she possessed. I recounted my discussion with Kate about piano lessons, and the disconcerting appearance of Uncle Bobby. "But seeing her at the piano was amazing, and oh, God, what a feeling to experience it," I finished, reliving the rush of excitement I'd had when Dell and I were at the piano. "It was like . . . she was filled with music, and I was the one who came along and unlocked the door." I couldn't believe I was telling him all of this, and even more, I couldn't believe he was interested.

"That *is* amazing." He watched me as if I were someone he'd never seen before and he liked what he saw. "You know, a couple of months ago, I took her to the pickin' and grinnin', because Kate and the kids were sick, and Dell was just sitting out on the porch with nothing to do. Every time I come now, she hints around about going to the guitar playing, but I just thought it was because she was bored. I had no idea she was interested in music."

"I don't think anybody did," I told him. "That's what makes it so incredible. I don't think she has any idea that it's unusual to have a talent like that. She just thinks it's something everyone can do." I laughed, remembering her and Joshua at the piano. "She can't understand why she can't teach Josh to play in an hour like I taught her."

James laughed with me, and for a minute it felt like we were on one of those comfortable vacations, where both of us were loosened up and we'd left the work worries at home. "She's a good kid. Doesn't say much, but she's a good kid," he said.

"Why didn't you tell me you'd been . . . well, I don't know . . . mentoring her, or whatever?"

He drew back, surprised by the word. "Well, it's not a big deal. She's just bored a lot of the time, you know. Kate and Ben are tied up with the kids, and Dell's hanging around looking for something to do. When I'm here, I have time. I like to fish. She knows where the fish are. I wish I'd known she had all that musical talent. I'd have had her teach me some new guitar licks, because the old guys at Shorty's pretty well put me to shame."

"That's another thing." I felt a pang of separation, a reminder of his hidden life. "Why didn't you tell me about that? I haven't seen you pick up a guitar in years—well, except to dust the ones on the rec room wall."

He shrugged, embarrassed. "Geez, you act like I've been keeping secrets or something. It's just something to do for entertainment when I'm here. I play sometimes when I'm home—it's just that you're usually gone."

The comment hit me like a sudden slap, a reminder that we were living mutually exclusive lives.

He seemed to sense it, too, and leaned forward, bracing his elbows on his knees, letting out a long sigh. "So, why don't you tell me what's going on, Karen? Why the sudden visit to the farm?"

Chapter 9

I sat staring out the window for a moment. James rubbed his hands together nervously as he watched me. His arms were tan from some layover near a beach.

My heart raced into my throat and fluttered there as I measured out words in my head. Why did I feel like losing my job was some sort of personal failure? Why was it so hard for me to admit to failure? *Pride,* my grandmother would have said, *too much pride.* But it was more than that. There was also the fact that I hadn't told James anything about the problems at work these past months. I wasn't sure why, except that by the time I came home from work each day, I was exhausted, with nothing left to give. His thoughts were focused on the airline's recent financial problems and the resulting layoffs and difficulties with flight schedules. When we were together, we were content to wander around the house in decompression mode.

Outside the screen door, a breeze whispered through the sycamores, and my mind wanted to go back to childhood, to forget. . . .

"Karen." James's voice cut into my thoughts, his tone impatient, demanding, authoritative, like he was talking to one of his flight crews. *No time for fooling around. Let's get this bird off the ground.* "Tell me what's going on. Why are you at the farm? I asked Kate, and she didn't seem to know. She said you'd been acting strange ever since she talked to you on the phone Friday night."

"You talked to *Kate* about me?" I spat out, picturing them on the phone trading theories about what was wrong with Karen. No doubt they hadn't come up with job layoff and possible cancer. "Great, James. Thanks."

He waited a moment before answering, trying to keep his cool. James didn't like to fight. He preferred that everything remain on an even keel, at a constant altitude, steady airspeed, no turbulence. "I called this morning to talk to you, and I got Kate. We spoke a minute. It wasn't any kind of conspiracy. I was worried. That's all." His hazel eyes turned slowly my direction, his gaze steady and pointed. "Let's get back on the subject, shall we?"

I nodded, regretting the fact that I'd gone off. A fight wasn't what we needed right now. "Something happened Friday at Lansing," I said slowly. "I found out in the management meeting that they're closing down the custom-networking business." I turned to him, searching for his reaction.

He didn't move and his expression remained guarded, as if he sensed that I was testing his reactions. "What . . . does that mean for your department, exactly?"

"Laid off."

"And for you?"

"Same thing."

He exhaled a long puff of air, looking down at his fingers. "This is kind of sudden, isn't it? Last thing I heard you had that big homeland security contract in Portland. What happened to that?"

"James, that was over a year ago," I snapped, even though it was as much my fault as his that we were out of touch. I took a deep breath, reining in my temper. It wasn't him I was mad at; it was the management at Lansing, and the slow economy, and some nebulous sense of persecution I couldn't put a name to. "We've been having problems at Lansing for a while now. Six months ago, the earnings reports didn't add up, and when that became public knowledge, the stock tanked, Patterson resigned, and Vandever moved in as interim president. Three

months ago, they cut twenty percent in the administrative departments, and then Friday they cut again."

James blinked at me like I was an alien from another planet. "Why
didn't you tell me any of this?"

"I don't know. I thought things would work out. With all the stuff
going on at the airlines lately . . . it didn't seem like you needed anything else to think about."

He nodded, his eyes darting back and forth, putting together the
pieces of a puzzle. "So that's why you've been so edgy these past few
months."

"Edgy?" I repeated, trying to think back.

"Oh, come on, Karen, you've been a basket case." No supporting
statements needed. *Karen's been a basket case.*

"You never said anything."

He threw his hands up, standing and pacing the floor in front of the
piano. "For heaven's sake, Karen, I thought if you needed something
you'd tell me."

"Sometimes I *need* you to ask." It was beginning to sound like an
old argument that went back almost as far as our marriage. I wanted
him to care enough to ask what was going on in my life, and he wanted
to go on the assumption that if I had something to tell him I would
bring it up while he watched me with one eye and *The Late Show* with
the other.

"Let's not go back to that old crap." Obviously, this conversation
was pushing his buttons. His skin was starting to redden along the
patch of salt-and-pepper gray that had developed in his sideburns these
last few years. It made him look dignified, mature, more in command
than ever. "If you want to talk to me about something, all you have to
do is tell me." He threw his hands into the air. "Just because I don't go
around emoting all over the place doesn't mean I'm not here. I certainly
didn't think you'd let something this big go on and never say a word.
How long have you known about this?"

I winced. If anyone was in the wrong here, it was me. I was dredging up all of our old issues as a smoke screen, and I wasn't sure why. "Six
months, maybe a little more. I never thought it would lead to the com-

pany going almost bankrupt and me being laid off. No one saw that coming. Even Brent didn't see it."

"Oh, well, if *Brent* didn't see it coming . . ." James said sarcastically.

I rolled my eyes. If it hadn't been such a serious conversation, I might have laughed. James's latent resentment of Brent was more than ridiculous. It was a reaction to evenings James spent home alone while Brent and I were at the office eating take-out pizza and running late-night beta tests. "All right, now you've gone too far." In spite of everything, the corners of my lips twitched upward. The idea of James being jealous of the world's biggest techno nerd was more than funny.

"I don't know." James suddenly clued in to what he'd said, and in spite of the ongoing argument, his eyes started to twinkle. "We all know you love a guy in uniform. I think seeing him in his full Trekkie outfit might have pushed you over the edge."

I slapped a hand over my eyes, laughing and groaning. We were doing what we always did—using humor to bridge the gap so we wouldn't fight anymore. "Shut up," I muttered.

He didn't, of course. "Hard to resist a guy with such a big . . . bag of Bugles."

"James, cut it out." But I was laughing even as I said it. "I'm trying to be serious here."

He sighed, his rare moment of angst obviously over. "All right, then, seriously. You should have told me about Lansing, but you didn't. I didn't ask, you didn't tell. It's done, so we move on and figure out the logical next step."

The logical next step. Exactly what I knew he would say. "No." I groaned, keeping my hand over my eyes. "I know you'd like to, but I'm not ready to plot out the next logical step, O.K.? I don't want to pick myself up by my bootstraps and dust myself off and march onward. I want to wallow in self-pity, and hate all my bosses, and obsess over the fact that this is unfair, and make board-of-directors voodoo dolls and stick pins in them. That's what I want to do right now, all right?" I let my hand fall into my lap and hoped he would understand. This wasn't a mature reaction to the situation, but it was *my* reaction. I hadn't been this pitiful in . . . well . . . ever, probably. My eyes started to fill with tears and my lips trembled.

He nodded, his mouth a straight, somber line, so that I couldn't tell how he felt about my sudden descent into dysfunctionality. Leaning back on the couch, he reached across the space between us, and I fell into his arms, glad not to be alone.

You should tell him the rest. You should tell him about the doctor's appointment. Even though I knew it was the right thing to do, I couldn't force myself to go through with it. Telling James, bringing it into the open, would make it as real as the job layoff—another disaster waiting to crumble our lives. This one would be harder for him. It would remind him of losing his mother. Even though he'd never admitted it to me when I had my first cancer scare, I knew that when he saw me in that hospital bed, he thought of his mother and her five-year battle with lung cancer. He thought of losing her, and his father's depression afterward, and the years of trying to keep the family emotionally and financially together while his younger brothers and sister grew up. If I told him about the news at Dr. Conner's office, it would bring all of that back. He wouldn't react calmly or try to interject humor or agree with putting off the biopsy for a little while, until I could handle it.

If I told him, I would have to schedule the biopsy immediately, as soon as we returned. What if the test came back positive? I couldn't face that and the disaster at Lansing at the same time. Surely, a few weeks, maybe a month, wouldn't make any difference. In a few weeks, I'd have my feet under me again. If the test did come back positive, I'd be ready to handle it.

For now, it was enough just to be together, here in this quiet place, where the evening breeze swished through Grandma's flower beds, and the long, slanted sunbeams were fine and golden. In a strange way, I was relieved that the situation at Lansing was finally over. I felt as if I'd been clinging to a lifeline for months, and James had just stepped in and grabbed the other end. It was good to be together, hanging on against a storm. If there is any reason to be grateful for a storm, that must be it: It reminds you of who you can rely on.

James drew a contemplative breath, his chin resting on my head. I wondered if he was thinking the same thing—that it felt good to lean on each other, to need and feel needed.

"I have a question," he said softly, his breath brushing my hair.

"Yes?" I muttered, the anxiety draining from my body.

"Do I get a Trekkie voodoo doll?"

I laughed, then smacked him in the stomach, and he let out a loud *Ooof!*

"No, you do not."

"Well, can I at least stick some pins in the board-of-directors dolls?"

"Sure." I gave a rueful snort. "But don't bother sticking them in the wallet. They're pretty well padded there."

"I'll bet," he muttered, and we sat there, united in a moment of mutual rage against the machine. It felt really . . . good.

Voices drifted through the screen—the sound of Kate and the rest of the family coming through the blackberry patch, reminding us that we weren't alone.

"I don't want to tell Kate." I knew how that sounded. "I mean, I don't want to tell anyone yet. I don't want to spoil the weekend, all right?"

James squinted one hazel eye, then shrugged and said, "All right," before both of us stood up and went to the yard to greet the family. James patted me on the shoulder as we walked out the door. "Don't worry, hon. It'll be all right."

I hope so, I thought. *I hope it will.*

We sat in the kitchen over a late dessert, talking about James's flight, Jenilee's first year in premed, Ben's work developing drafting software, and Caleb's upcoming summer internship with the county hospice program. We talked about Kate's volunteer work at church, Rose learning to walk, and Joshua starting preschool.

We talked about everyone's work but mine. Kate thought that was odd. She kept glancing at me, waiting for me to bring up whatever big, new megajob my team was into. James caught the look a couple of times. He knew what she was thinking. *Something's wrong. Karen's not bragging about her job.* By the time dessert was over, I was ready to get out of there.

Ben suggested that we head down to Shorty's to see if the Saturday night pickin' and grinnin' crew was still playing on the porch. "It's only eight thirty, and they usually go until nine thirty or ten," he remarked.

Kate frowned doubtfully at baby Rose, who was already starting to yawn and rub her eyes.

"Sounds interesting," I said, a little too quickly, and Kate clearly sensed an evasive action. She wasn't used to such blind enthusiasm from my side of the table.

"You gonna do Elvis if we go down there?" Caleb asked James.

James shrugged, a bit reticent. "Don't know. I might embarrass my wife."

"You do *Elvis?*" I said.

"He does a great Elvis," Kate replied with an imitation grin that looked more like a grimace of pain.

Ben elbowed me in the side. "Come on, Karen, let James do Elvis for us."

"Ya, Aunt Ka-wen, let James do Elvis," Joshua chimed in. "Pweeese."

I realized that everyone was looking at me, and they really thought I might say no—Karen the killjoy. The family stick-in-the-mud. The realization hurt my feelings. Was that what I had become—the one who went around dredging up the past, hauling out old resentments, and bragging about how successful and perfect my life was? Did they really think I couldn't laugh at James's Elvis impersonation?

But then, that was the persona I had created. A straightlaced, impatient, demanding caricature that worked to my advantage in my career—no-nonsense, always on top of things, not too social, tough, slightly superhuman. The only problem being that the mask had become who I *was*. Until now. Now I didn't know who to be.

I started to say something, but James beat me to it. "Well, as much as I'd like to do Elvis tonight, little man," he said to Joshua, "it's been a long trip and I'm wiped out. How about we do a little Elvis in the morning before church?" The look on James's face spoke volumes. He wasn't tired; he was worried about things, about us and our future. He didn't feel like socializing. He wanted to go off by himself and brood.

Joshua frowned. "Al-wite. Can we play pilot?" He held out his arms and James scooped him up, flying him expertly around the room. I realized again that James had a routine here that I knew nothing about. I was jealous of his comfort level. Even more than that, I was jealous that everyone liked having him around. He was part of the family. Seeing him with Joshua hurt, and I knew why. I wanted that too—I wanted to be part of something that no failing economy or crumbling corporate structure could take away. I wanted to love something that could love me back.

How do I get myself to feel that? I thought. *How do I let go of all the baggage and the jealousy and just feel the good stuff? How do I love instead of compete?* Competition came naturally to me and blind love did not. I'd learned from my father that love had strings. It had requirements. To be loved, you had to prove yourself. How could I banish that idea from my life?

James patted Joshua on the back, then set him down. "You know what? I think I'm just going to get a shower and maybe turn in early, if nobody minds."

Kate glanced from James to me and back, her expression acute, suspicious, slightly worried. She could tell something was going on. "Sure, James." She shifted Rose from one hip to the other, pointing to the downstairs bathroom. "You two really are welcome to stay in here."

"No, that's all right," I rushed.

"It's fine out there," James echoed. "Thanks, Kate."

"Sure," Kate said, studying both of us one more time. *Something is going on between Karen and James, and it doesn't look good.* That's what her face said. "Just let me know if you need anything." She handed Rose to Ben. "If you'll take her to bed, I'll finish the dishes."

Ben quickly took her up on the offer, grabbing Rose, giving her a sloppy kiss, and winning a giggle.

"I'll help with the dishes," I offered, because I didn't want to go to the little house with James and either watch him brood or be forced to talk about the next logical step.

"Good night, all." James waved over his shoulder, then started out the door, looking like he had a hundred pounds strapped to each shoulder.

Jenilee stood up and started to carry dishes to the counter, but Kate took them out of her hands. "Karen and I can do this. Why don't you two go out and enjoy the stars? It's such a nice night, and you said yourselves you don't get out of St. Louis much."

Jenilee and Caleb exchanged moon-eyed smiles and quickly agreed, then walked out the door holding hands. Kate sent Joshua upstairs to his dad, and with that final exit she had managed to clear the kitchen of everyone but her and me. That, no doubt, wasn't an accident.

I could tell there was something she wanted to discuss as we cleared the dishes and made small talk about meeting Jenilee and reading Grandma Rose's old letters to Augustine.

"I never knew Grandma was such a writer," I said. "I guess I just never pictured her as the poetic type." Even as I said it, I knew that wasn't exactly true. While Augustine spoke of fairies and dreamlike secret places in the wood, Grandma saw the poetry in ordinary things. She mused on the meaning of life while her hands were busy with everyday chores. Anything else would have been far too impractical to suit her.

Kate put a stack of dishes in the cabinet and turned to face me, resting her hands casually on the countertop. "She didn't have time for nonsense. I think that made it seem like she didn't care about things when actually she did. It made her seem harder than she was. You know, she regretted that in the end. She wished she had been a little more open with people instead of being so stoic all the time." I wondered if she was talking about Grandma or about me. "Did you ever read her journal—the one with the stories she wrote before she died? Remember, I sent it to you for your birthday last year?"

I pretended to think about it, but in reality I knew exactly what book she meant. It had arrived with a birthday card, last summer, and an invitation to come to the farm for a visit. It was waiting in the mail the day I came home from a big job overseas. I'd glanced at the card, then flipped through the book, my eyes skimming writing that trembled, running downward across pages. I could feel the end of my grandmother's life, her slow decline in those pages, in the changes of the handwriting as the book progressed. When I looked at it, I saw her on her deathbed, watching me with that silent message in her eyes.

I couldn't bear to read the book, so I put it away where I would be guaranteed not to stumble across it. In the piano bench under the old sheet music.

"I didn't read it, Kate." I realized I had stopped wiping the table, and there were tears pricking behind my eyes. "I just didn't . . ." There was so much more I should have said, that I should have explained to my sister. I should have told her that I appreciated the thought, but it was too hard to look at something Grandma had written so close to her death. Instead, I said, "I just didn't have time right when it came, and you know, after that I forgot it was there." I knew Kate would be disappointed in that answer. I knew it even before I turned around and saw her looking wounded. Why was it so hard for me to admit my weaknesses to her?

"Well, just don't lose it," she snapped, then seemed to catch herself and softened. "I mean, I think she would have wanted you to read it. I learned a lot from that book. It was such a tough time for us when we came here—new baby, job problems, Joshua's heart surgery, and Ben and I were having problems with each other. Grandma was watching all of that, and she wrote the stories down as advice, I think. She wanted me to see what things really matter when you're ninety years old, looking back on your life. I'm not sure if I would have ever figured it out without her."

Kate's eyes met mine, and for a moment, all of the barricades fell away. "You're lucky, Kate," I said quietly. "You're really lucky you had that time with her."

"She wanted you to be here, too, you know. She understood why you weren't, but she wanted you to be." Kate looked down at her hands. Something about the curve of her cheek in that moment reminded me of the past. She was my little sister again—my sweet, perfect, brilliant little sister, who had figured out algebra, calculus, physics, and now the meaning of life before I did.

How could I let anyone know that?

"You're just more forgiving than I am, Kate. I'm sorry." I felt my defenses going up brick by brick. The old chip was weighing heavily on my shoulder. "You do the family thing much better than I do. You know, to this day, I still can't stand to be around Dad. He knows *everything,* and *nothing* is ever good enough."

Kate smiled slightly. "So what?"

So what? I thought. *What kind of an answer is that?* "It doesn't matter how hard you try, Kate. You're never going to get what you need from him."

She shrugged again, regarding me very directly when she replied, "Life isn't all about getting what you need from people. Sometimes you're put with someone because you have what they need."

I crossed my arms over myself. It all sounded very philosophical, but not very much like Kate, not very much like our family. We had always been every man for himself. "So your theory is just be nice and keep taking whatever he dishes out." It sounded more bitter than I meant it to.

She shook her head, which surprised me. In the past, the one thing that Kate and I always had in common was resentment of our workaholic parents. We could count on that to bind us together, in a twisted sort of way. "No, my theory is to move on. What other people do is out of my control. I only have control over what I do."

I wasn't sure what to say. "Did you learn all of that from Grandma's journal?"

"Some of it. I'm still working on getting it right, but I know that I don't want to end up ninety years old, alone in this house for years on end because I've driven everyone away." She held her hands in the air between us, pleading. "Karen, Grandma Rose had so many regrets. She wanted us to do better. The one thing she wanted before she died was to piece this family back together."

I sighed, feeling Grandma in the room with us, standing at the old Hoosier cabinet, listening while she measured out the ingredients for bread. "I know. I know she did."

"It's possible," Kate whispered into the still air. "Anything's possible."

"You're such a positive thinker, Kate." Even as I said it, I wondered if she might be right. Inside, I felt a growing need that hadn't been there before—a need for this place, these people, a family. This family.

With everything else in my life spinning out of control, I needed something solid to cling to. When things around you change—where you are, where you're going—the one fact that remains constant, the one anchor that holds fast, is where you have been.

Chapter 10

In the morning, Kate was up early fixing breakfast, so that we could eat together before heading off to church. By the time I got to the kitchen, she had already fried bacon and eggs and was putting biscuits on the table. She sent Joshua to gather the family, and we ate a quick breakfast, during which Kate and Ben shot questioning glances at James and me. Even Jenilee and Caleb seemed aware that there was an undercurrent at the table. Caleb rescued us by filling the conversational gaps with various news from town. Because his grandfather was the Baptist preacher, he knew who had died and who'd had a baby, who'd built a house or started a new business or gotten a divorce.

When breakfast was over, I went out to the little house to finish packing my suitcases so I could head for the airport after church and Sunday dinner at the café. My mind hadn't quite settled on the idea of returning to the corporate jungle, but I knew I didn't have any choice. The world would start turning again on Monday, and I had to jump on or be left behind. No more time for wallowing in self-pity. I had to get out there and circulate résumés before the job pool filled up with Lansing's castoffs. It was the logical next step, and I knew I needed to face it.

"I can trade out the rest of my trip and go back with you," James said as he came into the bedroom.

I realized that I was sitting on the bed beside my suitcase, silently crying. "No, it's fine." Feeling stupid, I wiped my eyes. James was supposed to be in Kansas City until Tuesday morning, then fly several legs before coming home. "Go ahead and finish the rest of your trip. You'll be home Wednesday." I knew that was what he wanted to hear.

Stopping in the bathroom doorway, he studied me with obvious concern. For just an instant, I could tell he was wondering, *Karen, is something else wrong? Is there something more?*

I didn't give him the chance to ask. "Guess we should go." Closing my suitcase, I stood up and dabbed at my eyes. "Sounds like everyone's out in the yard already."

"Let me get my wallet," he said, and by silent mutual agreement we dropped the subject.

"Aunt Ka-wen . . . Aunt Ka-wen," Joshua called from the porch, and then the screen door squeaked as he peered inside.

"Who's out there?" I peeked into the living room, then walked through the door, wheeling my suitcase behind me.

Joshua gave the wheelie suitcase a look of fascination. "I can pull it."

"All right." I slipped the handle into his tiny fingers, holding open the screen door so he and the suitcase could get through. "Sure it's not too heavy?"

"Nope," he replied confidently, as the suitcase bounced down the porch steps sideways, dragging him with it. He and the suitcase landed in a pile at the bottom, and he scrambled quickly to his feet, laboring to roll the suitcase back onto its wheels. "I can do it. It's not hebby."

"I can see that." I ruffled his hair as we started down the path, Joshua walking backward with both hands on the handle, lugging my suitcase over the uneven stones, determined to be my helper no matter what. I was suddenly filled with a rush of affection for him. "Hey, big man, you gonna miss me?"

He nodded, his big blue eyes soft with the unashamed love of a child. "I'm gonna mi-iiiss you!" he said, dropped the suitcase, and threw his arms around my knees. Suddenly, I wanted to cry again, which, of course, was silly.

"Next time I come, we'll do something fun," I promised.

"Okeydokey." He punctuated that with a curt nod and hugged me again as James came out of the little house, then walked with us to the gate.

Dell appeared on the river path as we met up with the rest of the family by the yard gate. She dashed across the gravel driveway barefoot, wearing a wrinkled blue cotton dress and a choker of blue plastic beads. We waited while she pulled a pair of shoes out of a Wal-Mart sack and chewed off the tags.

Kate gave the shoes a double take, and Dell glanced up as she slipped into one of the stringy sandals with three-inch stiletto heels. "Uncle Bobby brung me some new shoes. These kind make your legs look long."

Kate frowned at the footwear and then at me, obviously thinking the same thing I was. *Who would buy leopard-print stilettos for a little girl?*

Buckling the sandals, Dell stumbled around on the gravel, trying to get her balance. "These are kinda hard to walk in."

"They're awfully high," Kate said, then bit her lip to keep from adding that the shoes weren't at all appropriate for a twelve-year-old girl, who shouldn't have been worrying about whether her legs looked long.

Jenilee stepped from behind the gate and held her own foot up next to Dell's. "I think we wear about the same size. Want to trade me? Mine are flats."

Thinking over Jenilee's offer, Dell tried a few more steps in the high-heeled shoes. Finally, she took the shoes off and set them on the post by the gate. "I think I'll just go get my flip-flops." Without waiting for an answer, she turned and dashed to the porch, then came back wearing red plastic flip-flops that didn't match her dress, but were still an improvement.

"I guess we should get going." Kate glanced at her watch.

Caleb and Jenilee headed for Caleb's truck. "I went ahead and loaded our stuff," Caleb told Kate as he passed. "My granddad's going to have a fit if we don't stay at his place tonight. Jenilee wants to do some visiting in Poetry tomorrow, too."

Kate finished buckling Rose into her car seat, then stood up and stretched her back. "I wish you two could stay longer, but I understand. We have to share you with everyone else. We get to have you over Memorial Day weekend, though, right?"

"Sure." Jenilee paused to smooth a stray wisp of blond hair back into her hair clip. "I hope all my family being here doesn't drive you too nuts," she added self-consciously.

Kate glanced at her watch again. "No, it'll be great. We'd better go. There's probably some special penalty for making the preacher's grandson late for church."

Caleb chuckled. "Well, when I was young, he'd make me do the opening prayer. It didn't matter if I walked in thirty seconds late or five minutes late—he'd stop me wherever I was, and say, 'Caleb, would you open us in prayer?' There I'd be, halfway in the door, and all the old ladies would turn around and give me *the look*. If that doesn't break a kid of diddling around in the Sunday school rooms, looking for leftover doughnuts, nothing will."

The rest of us laughed, then turned around and headed for our cars, because we weren't entirely sure Brother Baker wouldn't do the same thing to us. He had been known to put latecomers on the spot.

"I'm gonna ride with James and Karen," I heard Dell say behind me. She didn't wait for an answer, but caught up with James and me and started talking about music. "Can we come home and play the piano after lunch?"

I felt something twisting inside me. More than anything, I wanted to be able to say yes. "I can't," I admitted. "I have to head for Kansas City after lunch so I can catch a flight home."

"You're goin' already?" she asked, the sparkle of excitement fading.

"Yes." I turned to her as we reached the car. "But I'll be back in a couple weeks for Memorial Day. James is going to be here until Tuesday. Maybe he could show you a few things on the guitar. I bet you'll be just as good at that as you are at piano." James gave me a distracted look. All morning he'd been brooding, mentally adding up the emergency fund and seeing how long it would carry us if I didn't get another job right away.

"You think I could play the guitar?" Dell asked, turning to him with her heart on her sleeve. I hoped he would wake up and pay attention. "Is it hard?"

"Not as hard as piano," he answered, shifting out of brooding mode and starting to look interested. "I think you could do it. Let me see your hands."

Dell's eyes lit up with instant adoration, and she held up her hands.

James chuckled, raising his hand next to hers, measuring the size. "I think you need something with a smaller neck. See, my fingers are quite a bit longer than yours. It'd be tough for you to manage my guitar, I think." Pulling the car door open, he ushered her in. "Tell you what. We'll try a few things on the guitar that I have here, and if you decide you like it, I've got an old youth-sized guitar at home in the attic. I'll bring it next time I'm down. Comes complete with *The Partridge Family* logo and the whole deal. It's pretty rad, man."

"Cool!" Dell bounced to the middle of the backseat and sat leaning through the front console so she could talk to us. "What color is it?"

Sliding into the driver's seat, James closed his door. "All colors. Haven't you ever seen the big bad Partridge bus on TV? It's like that."

"Cool," Dell said again.

"Oh, it's way cool." James chuckled. "Now slide back there and put your seat belt on, all right?"

Dell shrugged, still leaning through the console. "Uncle Bobby says I don't need one."

James started the engine, glancing over his shoulder with an obvious fondness. "Well, Uncle James says you do, so put on your seat belt. If we have a wreck, I don't want you to end up as a little greasy spot on the dashboard."

Dell huffed an irritated puff of air, disappointed that she wouldn't be able to hang over the console and talk to us on the drive to church. "All *right*."

"Because then," James finished, "who would show me all the best catfish holes?"

In the backseat, Dell giggled and said, "O.K.," again, more pleasantly this time, as the seat belt clicked into place.

By the time we reached Hindsville, Dell and James had shared an entire conversation about playing the guitar, and how the notes were created on a stringed instrument. They talked about the chords and how they compared to the chords on a piano, and why some guitars had six strings and some had twelve, and bass guitars had only four. Dell was fascinated, just as she had been when we sat together at the piano. It was as if someone had turned on a switch, and she was so filled with enthusiasm, she forgot to be shy.

My mind drifted as we wound through the back roads of town, heading for the church parking lot. I thought of the weekend and everything that had happened since that horrible Friday night when the storm blew through and I sat playing the piano, trying to drown out the clatter of life. Friday seemed a lifetime ago now, and Boston a million miles away.

I tried to snap back to reality as we pulled into the church parking lot and walked into the chapel with the rest of the family. It felt strange to be there again after so long, but stranger still to be there without Grandma Rose at the head of our procession, shaking hands and kissing babies, making sure everyone saw that the granddaughters had finally come to visit.

Inside the chapel, the organist started the instrumental meditation as we slid into the usual pew, three rows from the front on the left. That much hadn't changed. Grandma's pew was still unofficially reserved. She had made certain of that at some time in the past, making a donation and having a plaque affixed to the end of the pew, which she insisted meant it was her spot.

My mind drifted between the past and the present as the music stopped and the service began moving slowly through the same timeless routine—greeting, hymn, prayer, offering, and finally Brother Baker's sermon. He paused to smile at Caleb as he climbed to the podium. "So good to see my grandson Caleb here with his little girlfriend, Jenilee," he said. Caleb did the parade wave, and Jenilee ducked her head as everyone turned to look at them.

Brother Baker went on. "And nice to have Karen and James Sommerfield visiting from out of town. We see James around here from time to time playing guitar on Shorty's porch, but haven't had the pleasure of Karen's company in quite a long while." He smiled at me, and I'm sure I turned ten shades of red. I was tempted to stand up and defend myself—*Yes, I haven't been here in a while, but we do go to church at home.* Which would have been a lie. Brother Baker knew that. It isn't good to lie in church, so I waved like a visiting celebrity, wishing I could sink into the seat and disappear.

Fortunately, Brother Baker moved on to the sermon. "Yes, it's so good to have Caleb here today. I'm constantly reminded of how much he's grown up. I asked him the other day if I could talk about him during service, and he didn't even hesitate; he just said, 'Sure, Grandpa.' Wasn't that long ago, as a teenager, he wanted me to pretend I didn't know him." The congregation laughed, and Brother Baker chuckled with them, then turned serious again. "I have to tell you that seeing him sitting out there now, a young man, through his last year of college and about to start medical school, I want to fall down on my knees with gratitude. I think back to that awful day two and a half years ago, when we got the call that Caleb had been in a car wreck, and he was lying in a hospital in critical condition with internal injuries and serious burns. Most of you remember that. I stood here on the podium and wept, asking all of you to pray for him as I left for the hospital. It was a low time, a time when I questioned God's reason for things." He pointed a finger at the audience. "We all have times like that, times when we stumble in our faith. Anyone who tells you they don't isn't being honest with you or himself. It's the lowest point in your life when it happens—the one time when you're really, truly alone. I'll raise my hand right here and tell you that I stood in Caleb's hospital room alone that day. I looked at that bed. . . ." He paused, taking off his bifocals and wiping his eyes.

When he spoke again, the words were choked with tears. "I looked at that bed and there was the boy who had played linebacker on the football team, who made good grades and earned a scholarship to college. Who never disappointed his parents a day in his life, a perfect son, a perfect grandson—everything we ever hoped for. And now the doctors were telling us he wasn't going to be *perfect* anymore. If he recovered, he was going to have scars on his arms and legs from the burns."

Brother Baker looked at Caleb, his eyes filled with love and remembered anguish. Around us, the room was silent except for the hush of breathing. "And I asked God *why*. Why would you take this young, good-looking, beautiful boy and leave him the rest of his life with scars?"

He paused, looking up toward the heavens and then down at the pulpit. "And you know, God doesn't always answer our questions right away. Sometimes he leaves us to think and ponder, to find our way back on our own. Sometimes the answers are so ordinary, you could walk right by without even noticing." He paused and reached behind the pulpit, pulling out something that clattered like metal on metal. Everyone leaned forward in their seats, and I realized I was stretching upward, trying to see. As we watched, Brother Baker lined up several old containers—a rusted tin bucket, a dented flowerpot, an old saucepan, a partially smashed coffee can, and a new child's beach pail—in a row along the railing. The members of the congregation began to murmur, theorizing on the purpose of the unusual display.

Dell leaned close to me and whispered, "What's he doing?"

A memory flashed through my mind, of me asking my grandmother the same question on some long-ago Sunday. "I don't know," I whispered, just as Grandma Rose had whispered to me. "Watch."

Brother Baker waited, allowing the suspense to build before he took the pulpit again, one hand in his pocket, the other leaning casually on the podium as he gazed at the pots. "The other day, I was out in the back lot behind the church, back there near that hill where the kids play in the sand sometimes." He chuckled, looking at all the rapt faces in the audience. "It's a funny thing about kids—you can make them all the clean sandboxes in the world, and they'll still prefer an old hill of real, one hundred percent dirt."

The congregation chuckled in response, the tension easing as Brother Baker went on. "It's been kind of a dry spring so far, so we haven't had to do much mowing out in the back lot, but we finally had some rain a few weeks ago, praise the Lord. So I went out to mow, and I saw all of these old buckets, pots, and pans the kids had left sitting around near their dirt pile. And you know, as I looked around, I noticed something. The perfect ones had caught rainwater and held it until it became stagnant and black. All the grass around them was dead. The containers that were dented or cracked or had holes had probably caught rainwater as well, but they had poured the water out through the holes. There was no stagnant water in them, and all the grass around them was growing."

Brother Baker paused, moving his gaze slowly from the buckets to the congregation, holding the parishioners riveted. "It is the same with people. It's those little nicks and dents and imperfections of spirit that allow us to flow out into a thirsty world. It's our scars that allow us to relate to the scars of others, our suffering that connects us to others who suffer." Holding out his arms, he turned his hands over slowly, studying them, then looking again at his grandson. "I don't know why God put scars on my beautiful grandson, but I do know that when he becomes a doctor, when he reaches out to those who are wounded and hurting, they're going to realize he's been there. He's going to understand his patients in a way that many doctors never will, and just by virtue of those scars on his arms, he's going show them that life goes on. He's going to be able to flow out into other people in a way that would have been impossible if God had left his life perfect."

Leaving the pulpit, Brother Baker walked to the railing and picked up the new plastic bucket and the dented coffee can. "Consider for yourselves which life you'd rather have, which vessel you'd rather be. Perfect?" He tipped the plastic bucket toward the audience so that we could see the inside, which was blackened with the mold and algae left by stagnant water. "Or imperfect?" Tipping the coffee can toward the audience, he displayed the inside, washed clean by the rainwater passing through. His gaze slowly swept the congregation, stopping when it came to me. I felt myself move forward in my seat, forgetting there was anyone else in the room. "Ready to hold in everything that comes your way, or ready to pour out and be refilled with each new rain? Closed to the world . . . or open to the possibilities . . ."

I'm ready, I thought. *I'm ready.* I realized there were tears streaming down my face.

Chapter 11

By the time the service was over, I was emotionally exhausted. I had cried during the sermon, wiped my tears, then cried again during the closing hymns. No doubt, James thought I was having a breakdown. I was glad I was at the end of the pew with Dell and James was sitting between me and everyone else, so the rest of them couldn't see.

Dabbing at my mascara, I tried to get myself in order as Brother Baker made the closing announcements. "Have a wonderful day with your families. You young parents, get the kids out and enjoy the beautiful weather. I have it on good authority that the swimming hole down at Boggie Bend is warm enough for taking a dip, and the perch are biting on the river, just below the old bridge. Church council will meet tonight at five o'clock, prior to the evening service. The mission women would like donations of scrap material to make lap quilts for the nursing home, and don't forget, starting next week, we'll be hosting the summer day camp, so we'll need some strong men and older boys to stay after service tonight and move furniture.

"The volunteer instructors will be arriving on Monday morning to spend two weeks helping kids prepare a musical theater performance, which will be presented Saturday after next. If you missed the program last year, be sure to come this time. Eighty-seven kids from all over the county have been accepted, so it should be a full house. I think they're doing an adaptation of *The Lion King* this year, to be presented at the end of camp, on Memorial weekend. If you've never worked with the Jumpkids team, I urge you to come down and volunteer.

"That's all I have for today. Come help this evening if you can. If you can't, please keep our Jumpkids program in prayer these next two weeks."

Jumpkids . . . the word wound into my thoughts. Where had I heard that before? The college kid on the plane, Keiler . . . something . . . Bradford . . . Keiler Bradford. Jumpkids was the summer program he was working with in Kansas City. He had mentioned something about coming to Hindsville last year to put on a performance. Was he one of the counselors coming this year?

Thinking back to the plane ride, I remembered the way his eyes sparkled when he talked about Jumpkids, the way he was almost bubbling over with exuberance. That luster of a true believer was an awesome thing to witness. I could only imagine what it would be like to see him in action, when he was actually working with kids.

You won't be here to find out, Karen, I reminded myself. *You're going home today.* The realization came with an inexplicable disappointment, and I found myself calculating the passage of days. If I returned a little early for Memorial Day weekend, I could be back in time to see the last of Jumpkids camp. Maybe catch a small dose of Keiler's zest for a life unplanned, spend some time with Kate and the kids, commune with nature, pick blackberries, work with Dell on the piano . . .

Dell . . .

I hit on an idea. "Excuse me a minute," I whispered to James and slid out to catch Brother Baker before he was surrounded by the usual crowd of old after-church hand shakers.

"Brother Baker," I said, as he was picking up the pots from the railing.

He paused, seeming surprised that I'd left the security of the family pew. "Karen." He extended a hand, toppling the old coffee can off the railing. "So good to see you here this morning."

I caught the coffee can as it landed in the altar flowers. "It was good to be here." Turning the coffee can over, I watched bits of light shine through the holes in the bottom. "It was a good message."

Brother Baker smiled that warm, benevolent, slightly reproachful smile I remembered from my childhood. "It's a good thing to remember, isn't it? We don't have to be perfect vessels—just useful ones." He finished stacking the containers, motioning to the one in my hands. "Want to keep that one?" The twinkle in his eye told me he knew what I was thinking. He knew I was looking at that battered container with the light shining through the holes and considering my own life.

I laughed softly and handed him the coffee can. "No, thanks, but I did want to ask you about something."

"What's that?" He put the can on the stack. "How can I help?"

How can I help? It seemed like an odd thing to say, considering that I hadn't asked him for anything. Could he tell just by looking that I needed help? Was it that obvious? For a split second I had the urge to pour out the corners of my soul right there at the altar as people filed out of church. How would it feel to unburden myself of it all and be free?

I shook my head, trying to get my bearings. "Actually, I was wondering about the Jumpkids program."

Brother Baker set down his pots and clasped his hands together, seeming pleased. "Are you going to be here through the week? We still need more help, and as I recall, you were quite the musician." His bushy gray eyebrows rose hopefully at the chance to get me into church for an entire week. Brother Baker hated it when one of the flock strayed. These days, he was probably pretty happy with Kate, but I was still living the big, bad, secular city life. *Ignoring the spirit,* he would have said.

"I wish I could." Surprisingly enough, that was true. Helping kids develop a summer musical sounded fun, something like a return to my college days in the university theater. Unfortunately, then as now, practical matters got in the way. "I have to fly back to Boston today, but I was wondering, is registration still open for the Jumpkids day camp? Can kids still sign up?"

Brother Baker frowned, now thoroughly confused. "Well, I don't exactly know. The applications had to be turned in several months ago. The kids were selected on the basis of financial need, recommendations from teachers and social workers, and a two-page essay about why they wanted to attend the camp. It was quite a long process." He must have noticed the disappointment on my face, because he stopped and said, "Why?"

"I was thinking of Dell," I replied. Why in the world, if there was a program like this available in Hindsville, hadn't someone made sure she got in? "I've been teaching her some piano the last few days, and she is very, very talented. I've never seen anyone pick it up the way that she did, and she has a beautiful singing voice, as well. She's very interested in learning more."

Sighing, he set down the stack of buckets. "I'll be honest with you, Karen," he said quietly, checking that Dell was out of earshot. "I thought about her when it was time to do the applications. I even sent one home with her, but nothing ever came of it. Generally, she isn't willing to put herself in new situations. I consider it a small gift of grace that, before your grandmother passed, she got Dell to attend church on Sunday mornings. We have tried to involve her in other activities, but for the most part she is reluctant, or her grandmother is reluctant, or both. Her grandmother is something of a recluse and very suspicious of any and all interventions."

I shifted impatiently from one foot to the other. I'd already gotten the speech from Kate, and it wasn't the answer I wanted. Music wasn't just another activity for Dell, not just something to do or something new to learn. It was a passion she was born with and it was awakening in her like a sleeping tiger. "What if I can talk her into it?"

"There's still the matter of the application, and—"

"What if I can get the application approved?" How in the world was I going to do that? Just because I'd talked to one Jumpkids intern on a two-hour plane ride didn't mean I could get Dell a free pass.

". . . and permission of a parent or guardian," he finished. "It isn't like church activities, where we can let her participate and take our chances, knowing that we don't have any signed permission slip for her. The Jumpkids program has an official form that has to be filled out and signed by a guardian. Dell's grandmother doesn't allow anyone into the house. Typically, she's reluctant to sign any forms regarding Dell, because they've been investigated by social services numerous times over the years. In her mind, any interest in Dell is a plot to remove her from the home."

I scratched my head, trying to think. Maybe Brother Baker was right. Maybe I was asking for the impossible. Maybe it would be better for Dell and everyone else if I just tried to find someone who could give her piano lessons.

But at the same time, something inside me was screaming, *No. For once in your life, do the right thing instead of what everyone else thinks you should do.* "Well, let me at least give it a try," I said finally. "Nothing ventured, nothing gained."

Brother Baker shook his head with a rueful smile. "Spoken like a true descendant of Rose Vongortler."

In the past, that comparison would have bothered me, but now it seemed like a vote of confidence. Grandma Rose knew how to manipulate things into the shape she wanted them to have. "You don't happen to have any of the application forms around, do you?" Exactly how was I going to get an application filled out and signed by Dell's grandmother? I was supposed to be heading for the airport after lunch.

"I think I have some in the office. How about if I bring one by the café in a few minutes?" He glanced toward the pews, which were empty except for my family, standing a polite distance away, watching me with curious expressions. I could only imagine the questions they were going to ask. They probably thought I'd gotten the Holy Ghost.

"That sounds good," I said. "If I can get her in, could you arrange a ride back and forth for her, at least some of the time? I know Kate would do it, but she's so busy with the kids."

"I think I can take care of that. We'll be transporting some students in the church vans. We can put her on the list."

"O.K. I'm going to do my best, and I'll let you know," I said, trying not to wonder what I'd gotten myself into. From the piano vestibule, the theme from *Gilligan's Island* tinkled into the silent air. Brother Baker turned in surprise, shaking his head and smiling as he watched Dell patiently trying to instruct Joshua.

"I think she's one of your holy buckets," I whispered.

Dropping his sermon notes into the old paint can, he winked at me just before he exited the altar. "I think she's not the only one."

I knew he meant me, and as I watched him walk away dangling the paint can with the light shining through the holes, I couldn't help feeling good. How long had it been since I'd taken the time to do something completely unselfish?

When I turned around, the rest of the family was waiting in the aisle. Kate and Ben eyed me quizzically as I joined them, and we started toward the door. James leaned close, muttering, "What in the world was that all about?"

"Long story. I'll tell you later, all right?"

He studied me a moment longer, then shrugged and said, "All right."

Ben rounded up Dell and Joshua, and together we headed for the café across the square. My thoughts were spinning as we walked, plotting ways to get Dell into the Jumpkids day camp. If I did get her in, how would I convince her to give it a try? Brother Baker was right that the idea of being surrounded by kids and counselors would be terrifying to her. But if she knew there would be a chance to learn more music, she would try to overcome her shyness, wouldn't she?

I watched her in her wrinkled dress and red flip-flops as we walked around the square. She moved like a shadow, head down, shoulders slumped forward, dark hair hanging over her face. She'd taken out the ponytail holder sometime during church, as if not having the curtain of hair made her uncomfortable. She moved so as not to be seen, as if she wasn't worthy of being noticed, and she knew it. She had no idea how special she was.

Please, God, let this work out. The voice in my head surprised me. A prayer, for the first time in years. *She needs this to work out, and so do I. Please.*

The café entryway was crowded with "those Methodists," as Grandma Rose would have called them, who were known for finishing up Sunday service a half hour early and getting to the café ahead of everyone else. Kate, Ben, and the kids sat on the bench out front to wait for a table. I suggested to Dell that she and I walk over to the gazebo and back. The first part of my plan, I had decided, was to convince her to try camp, if I could get her in.

"So I was thinking about something," I said when we were out of earshot. "I had an idea to get you some free music lessons for the next few weeks."

"Really?" she asked, lighting up, then narrowing her dark eyes suspiciously. "Well . . . umm . . . how? Are you gonna stay longer?"

"No." *Why not? Why not stay?* "I have to go home." *To what?* "But did you hear Brother Baker talking about the Jumpkids camp the next two weeks? It's going to be right here in Hindsville at the church."

She shrugged. "Yeah. They were here last year. They did, like, a play and some songs at the gazebo. It was cool, I guess."

My hopes crept up. "Well, I was wondering . . . if we can get you enrolled for the camp, do you think you'd want to go? I hear it's a fantastic program. You'd learn some new songs, have a chance to work with some people who love music just as much as you do. I talked to one of their counselors on the plane coming here. It sounds like a great time."

Dell stopped walking and crossed her arms, jutting out one hip and looking at me like I was the stupidest person in the world. "I can't go to that. It's for *smart* kids."

"Dell!" I gasped, sounding more stern than I meant to. "You are smart. Stop that."

Shrugging, she backed off the aggressive posture, looking down at her red flip-flops, wiggling her toes up and down. "Anyway, Sherita and Meleka Hall are gonna be in that Jumpkids thing, and if I show up, they'll knock my lights out."

"No, they won't." *Did she mean that, or was she making excuses?*

"Yes, they will."

"Nobody is going to knock your lights out at a *church* camp."

Growling under her breath, she threw her hands up, looking more animated than usual. "*Yes,* they *will.* They don't like me, and nobody there'll like me. I'll be all by myself and everyone will make fun of me. I don't wanna go, all right?" She glanced toward the café, ready to get away from me and Jumpkids as quickly as possible. "Everyone's goin' in. Can we go eat?"

I realized my chance was slipping away. If I didn't do something now, I'd never convince her to try the camp. She'd build it up in her mind into something terrifying. I had to pull out some desperate measures to stop her from shutting down. "I'll tell you what. Assuming that I can get you into the camp, what if I stay a little longer, and we go to the first couple days together? That way you won't be by yourself, and if Sherita and Meleka want to knock your lights out, it'll be two on two."

Her eyes widened and her mouth hung open; then she snapped it shut. "Sherita's bigger than you. She's a big, *big* girl."

I did my best imitation of a jive-talkin' street girl and said, "I can handle it."

A puff of laughter burst past Dell's lips.

"What?" I did the chin bob the break-dancers used down at Faneuil Hall in Boston. "Where's Sherita? Bring 'er on."

Giggling, Dell slapped her hand over her mouth. "You look majorly lame when you do that."

We laughed together for a minute, and then I closed the deal. "So do we have a bargain? If I can get you in, we'll do the first few days together."

" 'K," she answered tentatively.

" 'K," I replied, and we headed to the café for lunch.

Kate was definitely curious about what was going on between Dell and me, especially after Brother Baker joined us for lunch. He handed me an envelope with the Jumpkids forms in it, said, "Here's what you asked for," and then glanced at Dell, so that it was obvious the contents of the envelope had something to do with her.

Jenilee and Caleb didn't notice, but Kate and Ben were more interested in the contents of the envelope than they were in the lunchtime conversation. James seemed fairly oblivious to all of it, off in his own world, probably thinking about my job and our finances and our return trips home.

My mind wasn't in that world at all, even though it should have been. I was right there in Hindsville, and Boston felt far away and insignificant. All of the things I would normally have been doing Monday morning—getting up, going to the office, gathering my team for our Monday staff meeting, looking ahead to the next job or the next business trip, working to debug our newest installations—seemed like some old, uninteresting, nearly forgotten routine. I'd done those same tasks for fifteen years now, and one week was pretty much the same as the next. These next few days in Hindsville would be something completely different, an adventure. A big jump off the map.

What was James going to say when I told him I might not go home this afternoon—that I might stay a few days and help college volunteers teach underprivileged children to sing and dance? Would he think it was some sort of acute avoidance reaction? My excuse for not facing the realities of our life?

Was it?

I watched Dell helping Joshua color a Farm Bureau paper the waitress had brought him. Was I suddenly so interested in her because I couldn't face going home?

No, I told myself. *Don't second-guess this.* I was trying to do something nice, something that would be good for Dell, and in the process good for me. In a way, this would prove I still had a function in the world, that there was more to me than just my job at Lansing.

As lunch progressed, I listened absently to Jenilee and Caleb telling Brother Baker about Caleb's enrollment in medical school and Jenilee's first year in premed. It was pretty obvious that Brother Baker was fishing around, trying to see how serious the relationship was. He was playing the role of both grandfather and pastor, making sure that way up there in the big city, no hanky-panky was going on.

Kate took pity on the young couple and led Brother Baker astray, asking him questions about the upcoming Jumpkids camp. I tuned in to the conversation, gathering that the church facilities would be rearranged right after tonight's service. The Jumpkids counselors would be arriving from Kansas City early in the morning and would be staying with local families. Kate offered the guest rooms in the farmhouse, if they needed more space, but Brother Baker said they had found places for all ten counselors to stay.

By the time lunch was over, I had a pretty clear picture of the Jump-

126 · LISA WINGATE

kids setup, and I was more determined than ever to get Dell in. Ten counselors, some church volunteers, eighty-seven kids, ten days of music, dance, theater, set design, and outdoor recreation, a performance of *The Lion King* at the end. It sounded perfect. I was going to get Dell in and get the forms signed, no matter what it took.

Excusing myself from the table as Ben and James were arguing about the check, I walked back to the bathroom to use my cell phone. My hands started trembling as I fished Keiler Bradford's card out of my change purse and set it on the vanity, then dialed the number and waited for the phone to connect. What if he couldn't help get Dell in? What if he wasn't one of the counselors coming to Hindsville? What if he didn't even remember who I was? What if . . .

"Hel- . . . shoot . . . hello?" A voice stuttered on the other end of the phone. I recognized it immediately, even before he added, "This is Keiler."

"Hello . . . Keiler?" I paused to clear the knot from my throat. I hadn't been so nervous on the phone since I was in middle school, calling boys. "Uhh . . . you may not remember me. This is Karen . . . from the plane the other day . . . Karen Sommerfield?"

He didn't answer right away. I heard a crash in the background, then someone hollering. He moved away from the noise to someplace quiet. "Karen?" He repeated my name as if I were an old friend, as if he'd expected to hear from me. "Hi there. How's the trip off the map?"

I chuckled. "Pretty far off. But in a good way."

"I had a feeling it would be. Good, I mean. Did you get to meet the new cousin and spend some time with your sister?"

"I did." I smiled at my reflection in the mirror, at the brown-eyed woman in the expensive suit and the fashionable, neatly highlighted hair—not at all the person Keiler had met on the plane the other day. It felt good to know he remembered me. In some inexplicable way, there was a connection between us. Once again, I felt like I could tell him anything. "Actually, something really amazing happened while I was here, and that's what I'm calling about. Are you coming to Hindsville this week with the Jumpkids program?"

"I am," he answered hesitantly. "That is, if we ever get there. We just lost our director, and things are a little nuts right now. If you can believe it, I've been elected temporary director. I'm the only counselor over twenty-one, so that makes me qualified. I hope we can get the soundstage packed up so we can be on time tomorrow morning. Shirley—the director—usually takes care of all this, but we'll figure it out." He paused and covered the phone to talk to someone, then came back. "I hear we have a good-sized group of kids waiting on us down there in Hindsville."

"You do. Eighty-seven, Brother Baker said. That's what I was calling about, actually. I'd like to make it eighty-eight." Crossing my fingers, I plunged in. "If I knew of an extraordinarily talented kid who had missed signing up for the program, do you think you could get her in? I know there's an application process, but do you think it would be possible?" He didn't answer right away, and my hopes slid downward. I was probably putting him in a difficult position. Now he'd have to tell me that rules were rules and so on. "I'm sorry to ask, Keiler, but you just can't imagine. She's my sister's twelve-year-old neighbor. I sat down with her at the piano, and in an hour she was playing things most people can't learn in a year. She can pick out the melody to almost any TV theme song. She has a beautiful singing voice. Keiler, please, she really deserves this chance. Is there anything you can do?"

"Well . . ." he said slowly, contemplatively. "Ordinarily, I'd say probably not . . . but . . . right now . . . it's the monkeys running the zoo around here with Shirley gone. If you bring me this girl's application and I put it in the stack, who'll know the difference? Just don't say anything to anyone. You know how people can be sometimes."

I let out a long, slow sigh of relief. "I won't say a word. Thank you, Keiler. I promise you won't be sorry. We'll see you Monday morning."

"All right. See you Monday," he replied, and then we said good-bye.

Dropping my cell phone into my purse, I yanked open the door just as a gigantic squeal started somewhere in my stomach, whizzed like a rocket up my windpipe, and burst from my mouth in a gigantic "Yes! Yes! Yes!"

Kate and Joshua were standing outside the door. They stared at me with their mouths open.

"Long story," I said, sliding past them, smiling ear to ear and trying to suppress a giddy giggle.

Kate glanced after me, then started into the bathroom with Joshua, who asked, "Did Aunt Ka-wen make a poo-poo in the potty?"

No doubt, the only reason he could imagine for such exuberance while exiting the bathroom.

Chapter 12

As we were gathering our things to leave the café, I started thinking about getting the signature on Dell's Jumpkids permission form. If Brother Baker was so downbeat about the possibility, this was going to be a difficult job. Brother Baker was usually an optimist.

Following Kate and the kids out the door, I waited on the sidewalk as Joshua and Dell took Jenilee to see the historical marker in the park.

"So I guess you're heading back to the airport," Kate said, sounding a little down. This visit hadn't been all she'd hoped for. She glanced at the envelope in my hands with an expression that said, *What could Brother Baker possibly be giving to Karen?*

I pretended to be occupied with watching the kids, but in reality I was trying to decide what to tell Kate. I wasn't up for another round of discouraging stories about Dell's grandmother, and then there was the whole issue of why I wasn't heading off to the airport as planned, and why I didn't have to rush back to work on Monday.

"Actually, I'm not heading home just yet," I said, noticing that she drew back in mild astonishment. "There's a little . . . project I'm working on . . . with Brother Baker. It may keep me here a day or two."

My sister looked pleased, then confused. "Don't you have to get back to work?"

"No." I was struck again by how wrong it was that I hadn't told Kate about my job. She could see that something was going on. "I can spare some time." Actually, as of last week, I had nothing but time.

Kate cocked her head to one side, smiling. Shifting Rose to her other hip, she looked at the envelope. "So what's this project? Not that we're not glad to have you stay, because we are, but nothing's ever convinced you to stick around Hindsville for a couple extra days."

I chuckled at her observation. In the past, I would have taken it as Kate pointing out that she was much more connected to our home-place than I. Now it didn't seem to matter. I felt a connection here, too. "I'm trying to get Dell into the Jumpkids camp." I held up a hand, in case she was going to start on the nay-saying. "Please don't rattle off all Brother Baker's reasons why it isn't a good idea." I felt surprisingly sure of myself. Considering that I'd been on uneven ground all weekend, it was a pleasant sensation, a little like being the old Karen who knew what she wanted and how to get it. "It *is* a good idea. The program is made for kids like her, and you can bet that not one kid there will be more talented than she is."

Kate shot a glance toward the children, who had paused in a dandelion patch at the edge of the park. "Did you ask *her*, because I've tried to get her interested in things like this before, and she absolutely refused. I signed her up for a 4-H pet show with her dog last spring, and she almost had a panic attack. She wouldn't go, no matter how I tried to convince her, and she really loves that dog. I know she *wanted* to show him at the pet show, but the idea of getting up in front of people was too terrifying."

"I already asked her about the Jumpkids camp." Obviously, Kate thought that as usual, I was trying to bulldoze my way through. "It took some convincing to get her to say yes. I promised I'd stay around and go with her the first few days."

"I can do it," Kate offered quickly, too quickly, because it came out sounding like she didn't want me to stay. "I'm sorry." She paused for a minute to disentangle Rose's pacifier from her purse strap. "I think it's great that you and Dell have found this thing in common, I really do. . . . But I'm a little worried that, in her mind, you're going to stay here and be her piano teacher forever. I'm afraid that when you go home, she'll be crushed the way she was when we lost Grandma Rose. Dell kept insisting that Grandma Rose wasn't going to die. She had this fantasy that Grandma was going to get better, even after she was really sick, and when Grandma died, Dell couldn't deal with it. Two years later, she's still walking around convinced that she's getting beyond-the-grave messages from Grandma."

"I'm not going to die, Kate." The words fell to the pit of my stomach like a chunk of lead. *What if?* What if Dr. Conner did find cancer? What if it was something really serious this time?

Kate drew back, surprised. "I know that. But you have a busy life and you're going back to it, and Dell doesn't want to face that. Last night she tried to tell me that you weren't *going* back to work."

Fortunately, Kate was occupied with untwisting Rose's pacifier, so she didn't catch my reaction to that statement. Had Dell somehow figured things out? "I really think it'll be all right." Why was I keeping up this masquerade with Kate? Why didn't I tell her? "Let's just take things one step at a time, all right? First of all, I have to get her grandmother to sign the permission form."

Kate grimaced. "That's not going to be easy. Do you want me to try?"

Smoothing my fingers along the edge of the envelope, I tried to decide which method was most likely to work. Some divine whispering inside me said that I would have a better chance. "No, let me. Brother Baker was worried that her grandmother might get suspicious of someone coming around with forms to be signed. I wouldn't want her to get suspicious of you and quit letting Dell come over."

Kate nodded, visibly relieved. "I hate to sound like a wimp, but when I've talked to Dell's grandmother, things have not gone well. She's very paranoid that we're trying to take Dell away from her, so I've tried to play it low-key."

"Low-key it is, then. I'll soft pitch my proposal as much as I can."

Kate smiled at me as the guys finished up in the café and the kids came back across the street with Jenilee. "Good luck."

"Thanks," I replied. "I'll probably need it."

Twenty minutes later, as Dell and I turned onto Mulberry Road, I wondered if luck was going to do it. Driving through Dell's neck of the woods, I felt like I needed more than luck—maybe a bodyguard and a shotgun. On both sides of the road, the ditches were littered with trash, old furniture, and the forgotten carcasses of rotting mattresses. Tiny houses and decaying trailers squatted here and there, the yards strewn with rusted cars, old school buses, broken lawn chairs, cast-off toys, and bits of trash. Dogs, chained to turned-over barrels, barked as we passed, and their owners eyed us suspiciously from decaying front-porch sofas. The shiny rental car looked out of place as it passed through what had once been a small community of sharecroppers and farm laborers. It didn't look like there was much ongoing labor in Mulberry these days. There was only a sense of quiet disinterest in life.

Gazing at the roadsides, I tried to reconcile the place with the little girl beside me. It was hard to believe that only a mile or so upriver, on the opposite shore, lay Grandma Rose's farm, where the fences were always neatly painted and the flower beds manicured. Even the wild-flowers seemed to have given up on Mulberry Road, leaving behind only tall stands of last year's fescue sagging over the road like funeral palls, so that even in the middle of the day, the place was gray with shadow.

I glanced at Dell, sitting in the seat beside me with her bare feet braced on the dashboard, her dark eyes only skimming the landscape, her body not reacting as the dogs jumped at their chains, snarling as the car passed. All of this seemed perfectly normal to her. She didn't feel the need to be appalled by it or to rail against it. This was life. This was all she could expect.

I had a sudden sense of gratitude for my own life, for my worka-holic parents, the upscale school where success was life and death, for my father and his thinly veiled criticism, my perfect little sister to whom everything came easily. There were worse problems to have. My family may have been disconnected, stressed, busy, but we knew where our next meal was coming from. We lived in a house that was large and airy, where the bills were always paid and the cupboards were magically restocked each week. We played in Boston Garden, and roller-skated on paved sidewalks, and rode our bikes down clean streets, where there were no growling pit bulls on chains, threatening to break free.

It was that very life, that easy life, that taught us to believe we should have more, that we *deserved* more, that we should have *it all*. Perfect home, perfect parents, perfect family. *Enough* of everything. At least enough, and maybe a little more than enough. Without it, life was wrong; it was not everything we had a right to expect.

Dell couldn't even imagine such an expectation. To her, this was fine. It was all she had a right to. There was nothing better, no sense of *perfect* right around the corner, waiting to be grabbed. No belief that things would ever, could ever, get better.

The idea filled me with sadness, but more than that, with determination to help her see a broader possibility for herself. My soul expanded with the idea, and I felt lighter, more filled with energy than I had been in years. How long since I'd done something strictly for someone else, fought for a cause just because it was right?

She pointed to a house ahead, nearly hidden behind a fence made of loosely wired wooden pallets and chain-link. "It's that one. Right before the bend."

"All right," I said as we rounded the corner and the driveway came into view.

"Uncle Bobby's here." She pointed to his truck. Almost before I'd stopped the car, she opened the door and held out her hand. "I can take the paper inside and ask Granny."

"That's all right. I'll go in with you." I put the car in park and killed the engine, noticing someone working on the truck in the driveway. It looked like I'd have to go through Uncle Bobby to get to Dell's grandmother.

"I can do it," Dell protested as I grabbed the envelope and opened my door.

"Don't worry," I said, even though I was worried. Did the skills you learned in Dale Carnegie class work in places like this? "I'm good at talking people into things. That's what I do for a living back in Boston."

She tipped her head to one side, eyeing me quizzically as we walked to the yard fence. "What kind of stuff do you talk people into?"

"Well, mostly into buying computer systems."

Dell sagged. "Well, Granny don't know anything about computers."

Laying a hand on her hair, I guided her through the yard gate before me. "People are people, and sales is sales. It really doesn't matter what you're trying to persuade people to do. The principles are all the same. Don't worry."

" 'K," she said doubtfully, jerking sideways as the dog barked, straining against his chain beside the house.

Uncle Bobby glanced up from beneath the truck hood, pointing at the dog. "You better make sure that damned dog of yours don't get off his chain. It comes after me again, I'm gonna shoot it."

Dell's face washed white with sudden panic, and she turned quickly, scolding the dog. "Rowdy, hush."

Rowdy barked once more, then obediently lay down and rested his head on his paws, eyes following us intently as we moved toward the door. I found myself reluctantly agreeing with Uncle Bobby. I hoped the dog didn't get off his chain. He looked like he was part German shepherd and part God knows what, wolfhound or something else capable of quickly tackling and eating ladies in pumps and church clothes.

Uncle Bobby set down his wrench and crossed to the driveway side of the fence, eyeing me narrowly as he wiped his hands on a grease rag, then smoothed stray strands of sweaty salt-and-pepper brown hair into his ponytail. "You want somethin'?" I was glad to see that in contrast to our last meeting, he seemed relatively sober this time. Sober, but not friendly.

I realized how strange I must have looked, standing there in an expensive silk suit. "I stopped by to talk to Dell's grandmother." I tried to sound casual and at ease, in spite of the fact that I was way out of my element. "It'll only take a minute. I know she's not feeling too well."

He scoffed, curling his lip to reveal an uneven row of lower teeth peppered with dark bits of chewing tobacco. "She's had one too many of them Darvocet pills, if that's what you mean. She ain't feelin' nothin' right now. She's smooth out on the couch." Bracing his elbows on the top of the fence, he grinned and leaned closer to me, probably just to see if I would back up, which I didn't. "Guess you gotta talk to me." Glancing at Dell, he reached into his pocket, pulled out a pack of Life Savers and tossed them to her. "You been makin' a pain in the butt of yourself again?"

Dell shook her head, looking down at the Life Savers, not at him. "Huh-uh." Unwrapping a piece of candy, she popped it into her mouth.

Uncle Bobby returned his attention to me. "You a Jehovah's Witness or somethin'?"

I smiled with my best sales smile and said, "No. Did you want me to be?"

The joke actually won a bit of a laugh, and he relaxed his posture, bracing one boot on an overturned log by the fence. "You're a funny lady." Pulling a tobacco can from his jeans pocket, he took a pinch and crammed it in his lower lip. "You with the welfare?"

"You know those government people don't work on Sunday."

"Ain't that the truth?" He liked me better already. We were, as we say in sales, building a rapport. "What was it you said you come for?"

I rested one hand on the fence, standing close enough to smell a mixture of tobacco, grease, sweat, and stale beer. "To get a permission form signed for Dell. There's a kids' day camp in town next week, and I was hoping she could come."

"It cost anything?"

"No." My hopes crept up. He was leaning forward, nodding—all the signs of a client about to take the bait. "It's not a big deal or anything. Just kids from around the area and some volunteer teachers. They'll learn some songs and dances for a couple weeks, then do a performance at the end."

Scoffing, he wiped a stray drop of tobacco. "Sounds like one of them ignorant do-gooder things. What good is singin' and dancin' gonna do kids out here? Kids around here got plenty of work to do." He pointed at Dell. "She needs to get her butt in there and clean up all them dirty dishes."

Dell squirmed and took a step toward the house, and Uncle Bobby straightened away from the fence. I could feel the rapport breaking down. So could Dell. She looked ready to give up and go wash dishes.

"I can help her do that," I heard myself say. "Maybe by the time we're done, her grandmother will wake up, and I can ask her about day camp."

I took a step backward, starting toward the door with Dell, wondering what Uncle Bobby's reaction would be. He didn't seem to want me going into the house. He vacillated a moment, then stuck his hand across the fence so quickly that I drew back out of reflex. "Give me the thing and I'll sign it."

I didn't ask whether he was legally able to sign Dell's form; I just handed it to him and smiled. "Great, thanks. You've really helped me out a bunch."

Snatching the paper, he flipped through the pages, then searched his pockets for a pen. I handed him one from my purse, and he found the signature line, talking to Dell as he signed. "What about you, girl? You really want to spend two weeks at kiddie camp, singin' and dancin' with a bunch of little butt-heads from town?"

Dell didn't answer, just stared at her toes. For a mortifying instant, I thought that here in this dingy yard, under the scrutiny of Uncle Bobby, she was going to say no. Her cheeks went flush as he glanced up from the paper and pulled his pen away. "I asked you a question, little girl. You wanna go sing and dance with the white folks, or don't ya?"

"Uh-huh." Her voice was little more than a whisper, a choked sound she could barely force from her throat. She was afraid to say yes.

"Fine by me," he muttered, then finished signing the paper and handed it to me. "There ya go. She's all yours." He slanted a narrow look at Dell. "Now, tell your friend good-bye and git your butt in there and wash them dishes. There ain't any clean plates left." The log on which his foot was braced tumbled over, and he kicked it irritably, ready for me to leave.

I followed Dell a few steps to the dirt path, which would take her to the front porch and me to the yard gate. Her into this world, and me back to mine. "Are you going to be O.K.?" I asked quietly, turning my back to Uncle Bobby, still very aware that he was watching.

"Mm-hmm." She squinted past me, watching him. "So am I gonna go to Jumpkids tomorrow morning?"

"You betcha," I answered, unable to contain my enthusiasm, even here in this place. "I'll come by for you first thing in the morning. Seven forty-five. Camp check-in starts at eight thirty."

Her brows drew together as she glanced around my shoulder. I wondered what she was looking at. "I'll just come over to your place. 'K?"

"O.K. I'll be . . ."

A crash and a string of curse words brought me up short. Dell jumped back, her eyes widening, and I spun around just in time to see Uncle Bobby drop his pants right there in the driveway. Wildly batting his skin and spitting out obscenities, he ran for the water hose, grabbed the squirter and sprayed his pale, thin, hairy legs, then rinsed territory I didn't even want to think about underneath his faded purple underwear.

The dog bounded to the end of his chain, yipping gleefully, ready for a game of chase.

Dell turned her back, biting her lip, desperately trying not to laugh. "Guess there was red ants in that log."

"Guess so." A puff of laughter slipped past my lips as Uncle Bobby ran around the corner of the house, still dragging the hose and spraying water into his underwear. When he was gone, Dell and I burst into laughter, collapsing against each other as the dog dashed back and forth on the end of his chain, trying to see what had become of Uncle Bobby.

"Rowdy, h-hush," Dell called. I was struck by how good it felt to see her really let loose and laugh. "Row-deee!"

The dog ignored her command, and just kept yapping. Somewhere in the distance, Uncle Bobby hollered another string of obscenities, and Dell sobered. "I better go get my dog." She sighed, seeming sorry, but not surprised, that the moment was over. In her world, joy was fleeting.

"All right. I'll see you in the morning, bright and early." I couldn't keep the excitement from my voice. She might have been hesitant about what tomorrow would bring, but I couldn't wait. I had a sense of something wonderful just around the corner.

The dog quieted to a series of low yips and playful growls, and Dell walked with me to the yard gate, not ready to say good-bye. Pausing just outside the fence, I waited to see if she wanted to ask something.

"Is everything all right?" A dozen questions rushed into my mind, but I knew if I pushed, she would back away. "Here . . . I mean. Do you want me to stay? I could help you get the dishes done."

Twisting her lips to one side, she glanced toward the house, then back at me, taking in my silk suit. "No. It's all right. You'd get dirty."

"Are you sure? I don't mind." Was it just the sadness of that place she didn't want me to see, or did things happen in there that she didn't want anyone to know about? What secrets was she hiding?

"Granny wouldn't like it. She don't like people coming around."

"O.K." It seemed anything but O.K. I felt like I was tossing something precious into a landfill and hoping it would still be there when I came back. "I'll see you in the morning."

She shifted from one foot to the other and crossed her arms over herself, but didn't leave. "You're gonna go with me in the morning, right? You aren't gonna leave?"

"Yes. I'm going to be there with you. Wouldn't miss it." Remembering what Kate had said earlier, I leaned closer, stroking a hand over her hair. "But listen. In a couple of days, I'll have to head back to Boston. Kate told me you said something about me staying the whole time, and as much as I'd like to do that, I can't. We're sort of . . . in a tough time at home right now. I have to get back."

Her dark eyes searched my face, reflecting the afternoon sky like mirrors. She had a wise look, the tranquil expression of a very old soul. "Grandma Rose told me you'd stay awhile." She presented it like a fact, as if she knew more about my life than I did.

I tucked her hair behind her ear, gazing into that shy, quiet face; not quite a child, not yet a woman, filled with so many secrets. "Honey, Grandma Rose is gone. Kate is worried about the fact that you think she can still talk to you."

"She *does* talk to me," she said, her gaze earnest, tender, a million miles deep, her voice little more than a hush of breeze.

"Dell, she's gone," I whispered, my heart aching for both of us. "She isn't here anymore."

Dell only smiled the slight, trusting smile of a child who still believed in things she could not see. "She's with God," she replied, turning away from me. "And God is everywhere."

Chapter 13

I took the long way home from Dell's house, went around the mountain, as my grandmother liked to call it. When we drove home from town during our summer visits, she would sometimes say, "Well, my fine ladies, shall we go the direct way, or shall we go round the mountain?" It was an unusual bit of whimsy for a woman who usually didn't believe in wasting time or gasoline.

Kate would always pipe up quickly and vote for the most direct route. Sometimes I would, as well. Even at a young age, I knew that the trip around the mountain would give Grandma thirty minutes of uninterrupted time during which she would tell the stories of her Depression-era girlhood. The stories were, of course, intended to point out how spoiled and overindulged we modern children were. It was a lecture Kate and I learned to hate, and one of the things that eventually drove us away from her. We did not feel spoiled and overindulged; we felt ignored and invisible. It hardly seemed like we deserved a lecture for that.

But sometimes, even though I knew Kate would groan and sneer at me, or maybe *because* I knew it would goad my little sister, I'd say, "Yes, let's go around the mountain." Grandma would nod, turn the Oldsmobile off the main road, take a deep breath, and we'd be off—on the journey and on the lecture.

Perhaps it was the artist in me, or just the fact that I could tune out Grandma's lectures, but I loved those trips around the mountain. The gravel roads were narrow and ancient, curving slowly up mountainsides, plunging deep into shaded valleys, where crystal streams wandered over beds of multicolored river rock, worn smooth over time. Those places had the feel of being old and untouched, magical. Even now, the unlikely network of roads, the distinguishing features of each valley, were ingrained in my memory. I could recall the two places we always stopped. The first was in a valley where an old wooden bridge crossed the river. We climbed from the car, slipped through the rusted barbed wire fence, and picked wildflowers in a valley where a waterfall tumbled over smooth gray shale into a deep pool.

We stayed there long enough to play mermaid princess and hunt for shiny stones, or carve our initials into the chunks of brown sandstone beside the water, where long ago other young people had carved their own childhood marks. When we climbed out to dry, Grandma left us sunning on the rock shelf and wandered upstream to pick wildflowers. On the way home, we stopped at the family graveyard on the back side of our farm, where we placed the flowers on the grave of my grandfather, who was little more than a shadow in the farthest corners of our memories.

My mind swept back in time, clearing away the dust on those memories until the essence of my childhood was so strong that I could feel it all around me. I knew that I would find the old wooden bridge and the mermaid pool in the next valley.

They're probably gone by now. That was a long time ago. . . . But I found myself hoping, the way we all hope that our childhood places will be eternal, a sort of proof that time can be stopped, after all.

I held my breath as I topped the hill, and the car wound slowly downward, sliding silently beneath the thick canopy of overhanging branches, moving in a rhythm of sunlight and shadow. I stretched to see ahead, a little farther past the trees, around the next bend, until finally I caught a glimpse of something. Something metal and new, glistening in the patchy sunlight. My eyes took in the reality that my heart had refused to frame. The old wooden bridge was gone. Time had moved on and everything had changed. On the far side of the river, someone had cleared the overgrowth of cedars, put in a culvert, a driveway, and a new metal gate. The rusted wire fence that once hung in loose and broken strands, allowing Kate, Grandma, and me to slip easily into our magical spot, had been replaced by a new woven wire fence, silver and clean, unwelcoming like the bridge. A new gate lay beside the fence, not yet placed on its hinges but ready to soon bar trespassers from the place. The wildflowers, at least around the gateway, had succumbed to the bulldozer, as well.

It's gone, I thought, tasting the salt of raw emotion in my throat. Even though it shouldn't have mattered that much, I stopped the car on the bridge, gazed down the river toward the bend, and started to cry. I wondered if even the mermaid pool was gone, dozed away like the wildflowers and the old fence. Did I even want to look? If the pool was gone, as well, it would be proof that there was nothing left here but memory.

Things are changing. I didn't want things to change. I didn't want my life to change. I didn't want to lose my job, or face having cancer again, or go back and investigate the reasons why James and I never talked about the baby we lost. I didn't want to relive the pain of the miscarriage or consider how I had gotten from there to here. I wanted to just go along, day in, day out, in my rut. Busy. Comfortable. Passing time. Mindless of life or its meanings.

Pulling the car to the roadside, I stepped out, moving slowly through the gate, my steps directed by memory and a need I couldn't put into words. The old paths were no longer visible. The way was always hard to find, but Grandma Rose knew it intuitively. She went through the meadow, into the trees, as if she belonged there. Ahead, I could see her now, disappearing into the undergrowth, passing through a tangle of brambles that seemed impenetrable.

I followed the memory, slipping through the entwined branches. The thorns snagged my suit, but nothing seemed to matter. I followed the path, seeking the way to the water's edge, drawn by the sound of the river. As I moved, it grew louder—not the soft, quiet whisper of water trickling smoothly among rocks, but the low roar of it tumbling over the rock shelf into the pool below. My hopes leapt up, and I pushed through the last of the underbrush, emerging onto the river-bank, rushing downstream to that old place.

"It's here. It's still here," I heard myself whisper as I stood above the falls, breathing in the scent of water and damp sandstone. Silk suit and pumps forgotten, I picked my way down the uneven tangle of boulders to the pool. Beneath me, the bare, brown legs of a ten-year-old girl traveled easily over the rocks, moving from memory, finding every foothold, every bit of space large enough to anchor a hand.

A sound slipped from my throat as I reached the bottom—something between a laugh and a sob. I stood gazing up at the water-fall, a mist of droplets touching my face. It felt good to be there. Oh, it felt good! A sense of joy lifted my heart, the same joy I felt when I sat at the piano and found music again. This was another part, I realized, another bit of my authentic self. Somewhere inside was the little girl who wasn't afraid to dream impractical dreams, who believed she could be a mermaid, a princess, an actress, a classical pianist.

I sidestepped along the narrow shelf near the falls, sliding my hands carefully along the rough, damp sandstone, searching for the letters we had carved into the rocks so long ago. One more step and I could see our initials. KEV, Karen Elaine Vongortler. KAV, Kate Allison Von-gortler. Above each name was a tiny etching that looked like a crown—a symbol we had learned from the older carvings on the rock. A symbol that Grandma told us was the mark of the mermaid queens.

Taking another step, I felt for the other initials, remembering the day that Kate and I had found them there. We were surprised that others had been to our secret spot before us. *Who?* we asked Grandma. *Who had been there?*

She gazed at the rock and then at us, her eyes a mixture of melancholy and contemplation. "The mermaid queens," she said finally. "But they were gone a long time ago." Turning away, she walked up the bank to the Queen Anne's lace. We knew better than to ask any more questions.

I looked at the initials now, running my hands along the tiny crowns we had tried so hard to imitate, then tracing the letters. All at once, I understood the identity of the mermaid queens, and the reason

Grandma wouldn't tell us more about them. BEG, Bernice Ella Gray; SMG, Sadie Marie Gray; AHG, Augustine Hope Gray.

My grandmother and her sisters were the first to come to this place. For reasons we might never know, they left it and they left each other. In her letter to Augustine, Grandma said she had erased this place from her memory, but that wasn't true. She brought us here because she had not forgotten this place or her sisters. She hadn't ceased to need it, even though she was too stubborn to admit to that longing.

I thought of Kate and me. I had been drifting away from Kate for years, even these last few years, when she was trying so hard to pull me back. I had been telling myself I didn't need this place, this family, my sister—that my life was complete as it was. It was a deception I practiced until I had it down perfectly. The truth was that part of me needed all of those things. It was the weakest part, I had always thought. My father had taught me that to need anyone, to not be self-contained and self-sufficient, was weakness. But now I understood that this need was not my weakness; it was my humanity.

I pushed away from the rock, stretching my arms outward as I did when I was a child, embracing sky and sunlight and water, letting myself fall backward—just fall and fall and fall and fall, until the water caught me. I sank into the pool and the cool water surrounded me, washing away . . . everything.

When I came to the surface, I felt new. I felt as if I'd been burning with a fever for thirty years, since that eleven-year-old winter when I let go of my childhood. The fever was finally gone, every thirst suddenly quenched. I lay in the water, gazing upward at the sycamores, listening.

I don't know how long I lay there, my ears just below the current, enveloped in the silence beneath the surface. An object floated by, touched my cheek, and I brushed it away, then reached for it again, my hands closing over something round and wet. I held it up. A tiny peach, still hard and green. Not yet ripe, but somehow cut loose from the tree. What would it be doing here, out in the woods?

Who planted the peach tree in such an unlikely place, deep in a glen of sycamores where no one would find it? Perhaps the seeds floated down the river from some fine plantation far away. . . .

I remembered the words from Augustine's letter to Rose. Their secret place had to be nearby. That was why their initials were carved in the rocks. This was where they came to hide from their mother, to hide from the world. Somewhere nearby were the sister trees.

Swimming to the edge of the pool, I stood up unsteadily, stumbling on the loose river stones, dimly aware of my wet clothes and shoes. Letting myself fall into the water in my dress clothes should have seemed foolish and ridiculous, but at that moment it seemed like a bold adventure. I wanted to find my grandmother's secret place, to add one more piece to the puzzle of my family's past.

The river led me through a tunnel of overhanging branches and into the clearing beyond, where the banks became less steep, the slopes rising gently into thick stands of primrose and wild huckleberry. A pair of deer startled as I rounded the bend. Raising their heads, they stood frozen in place, fanning their tails and snorting warily. I stopped, enjoying the exhilaration of being so near something wild and beautiful.

Finally, the deer turned slowly and disappeared down a trail through the underbrush. I followed, slipping quietly past the primrose and low-growing huckleberry, just beginning to fill with tiny wild blueberries.

Beyond the stand of berries, the way began to clear and the trail became more visible, passing through the deep magenta of wild sweet pea and the puffy white of blooming clover. Ahead, the trail led through a grove of twisted trees, some only now surrendering the final blossoms of spring and forming tiny green fruit.

I followed the trail through the peach trees, imagining three little girls there picking sweet amber fruit, inviting one another to imaginary playhouses for tea. I could hear their voices somewhere just beyond view as I continued to the clearing's edge, where the grove opened into a tiny meadow. The glen was carpeted with new spring grass, shady and serene beneath the thick, far-reaching branches of three ancient sycamores, their limbs rising like castles toward the sky. The sister trees. I stood beneath them, looking into the broad, waving leaves, connected to the past in a way I couldn't explain.

A dove called somewhere off in the distance, its low, mournful sound making me aware that it was already late afternoon. Kate and James would be wondering where I was. I had no idea how long it had been since I pulled the car off the road and stumbled out. An hour? Maybe longer?

A cool breeze stirred as I made my way back to the road. The air carried the scent of a storm coming, and somewhere far away thunder rumbled. I shivered as I climbed into the car, the seat pressing my wet clothes against my skin. A glance in the rearview mirror brought back reality. My makeup was gone and my hair clung to my face in damp, dark strands. How would I explain this to everyone at the farm?

Worry replaced peace as I drove home. I was suddenly aware of what an irrational act it had been—tromping down to the river in a silk suit and pumps, climbing down the rocks, plunging into the water. It wasn't like me to do something so careless, so pointless and impulsive.

So free.

That was how I felt when I fell into the water. Free from everything. Lighter than air. Every logical impulse was telling me it was foolish, yet I wanted to turn the car around, go back, and dive in again.

The thought scared me. Maybe I was having a breakdown, some kind of temporary insanity brought on by stress. Where would it end? How far would it go? How far would I go? How long would I keep up this illogical search for myself? Maybe it was time to go back to Boston. Maybe things would be more normal there. I could wrap myself up in the job search and filling out unemployment paperwork. Practical things. Predictable things . . .

Everyone was in the yard when I reached the farm. As I stepped out of the car, they hurried to the fence, then stopped and stared in shock.

James surveyed me from head to toe, his mouth open. "Karen, what the . . . ?"

"What happened?" Kate finished for him, gaping like she was looking at a space alien. "Where have you been? What happened to your clothes?"

Only Ben came closer. He slipped past Kate in the gateway, frantically giving the car and me a once-over. "Are you all right? Did you have a wreck or something?"

My stomach rolled over. They all thought I was a mental case, and it probably seemed that way. "I'm fine." I tried to look as composed as was possible in a wet suit, muddy pumps, and bedraggled hair. This was very unfamiliar territory for all of us. I never even left the bathroom without makeup on, hair fixed, clothes pressed. "Everyone calm down. I went round the mountain coming home from Dell's. It . . . took a little longer than I thought, that's all."

Joshua squeezed past Kate and stood beside his dad, his little arms stiff at his sides, fists clenched, face turned up toward me. "Aunt Kawen, did you go swimmin'?"

I could tell by the body language that what he meant was, *Did you go swimming without me?* "Yes, I did," I admitted, and he narrowed his eyes, quickly producing a pout lip. "But I didn't mean to. I was down by the river, and I slipped." Not exactly true.

Everyone seemed relieved. Karen was making some measure of sense, which was what we were all accustomed to.

Joshua thought about it as he studied the evidence of my plunge into Mulberry Creek. "You shoulda put on your play clothes and old shoes." He braced his hands on his hips, shaking his head, doing a fair imitation of his mother. "Them clothes are *chu-ch* clothes."

Right then, I could have picked him up and kissed him for stating the obvious in such a perfectly adorable way. Everyone chuckled, and the tension was broken.

"Joshua!" Kate giggled. "Stop bossing Aunt Karen around. And it's *those* clothes, not *them* clothes."

Joshua screwed his lips to one side, giving us an exasperated look, because, of course, he was serious.

I pointed at him, trying to look like I was having a eureka moment. "You are absolutely right. Next time I will put on my play clothes. But this time I just couldn't resist. I went looking for an old place your mommy and I used to swim, and do you know what? I found it. I even found the very spot where your mommy and I carved our initials into the rocks."

Joshua gave me a confused look, but Kate gasped. "Oh, my gosh, I haven't thought about that place in years. You found the mermaid pool?"

"I did." All of a sudden, I didn't care if my clothes were wet or if I looked foolish in front of everyone. The luster in Kate's eyes was worth all of it. She remembered, and so did I. We felt the bond of common experience, too seldom shared. "And that wasn't all I found. I found the sister trees. They're just down the river from where Grandma Rose used to take us swimming. That's why she went there, and that's why she'd always walk around the bend without us after we got out to dry. She wasn't going there to pick special flowers. She was going there to remember her sisters. What she said to Augustine in the letter wasn't true. She never stopped thinking about them, even all those years later."

Kate sighed, her eyes misty. "I wish we knew what happened."

"I don't know if we ever will," I admitted.

"Maybe not."

I nodded, and the strange thing was that I understood exactly what she meant. Just a few days before, I couldn't imagine why Kate was so determined to dredge up all the old family history—why she cared. Now I wanted to know, too. This was not just her history, it was *our* history, and with the future so uncertain, the past seemed important.

That evening before we left for church, Kate showed me the Gray family Bible she'd found hidden in the attic. We stood together looking at the page with Sadie's name scratched out, then we closed the Bible with the sense that Sadie might forever remain a mystery.

After the church service, I ended up in a Sunday school room with Jenilee and several other church ladies, moving tables and rearranging chairs, then laying out mats borrowed from the school gym to produce a practice area for our young dancers.

"Kate said you're going to stick around and help with the Jumpkids camp tomorrow," Jenilee said as the two of us labored to drag the heavy foam rubber squares into place and lock the tongue-and-groove joints to form a huge square.

"For a day or two. I wanted to help Dell get started, at least."

Jenilee shrugged back dampened strands of blond hair while working to secure the joints on one of the mats. It was hard to tell which was more difficult for her—hauling the mats around or carrying on the conversation. "That's really nice of you."

"Actually, I'm looking forward to it." I didn't know why I felt the need to tell her that.

She glanced over at me with a genuine, affectionate smile, one that said she was glad I wasn't the grouch Kate sometimes made me out to be. "I think the camp sounds great. The kids are going to have such a good time. Gosh, if I would have gotten to do something like this when I was a kid, I would have . . ." She left the sentence unfinished, pretending to focus on the work. "Well, anyway, when things at home aren't so great, it means a lot to have something positive to do. It'll mean a lot to Dell."

"Thanks," I said as we finished locking the last joint and sat in the center of the mat. "And by the way, you're still a kid. Don't let the pressures of premed and work and everything else take that away from you. Enjoy being twenty-two. You only get to do it once." I gazed into her brown eyes and remembered my grandmother saying that to me the first time I came to visit from college. I told her I didn't play the piano anymore because I didn't have time for it.

Jenilee nodded, seeming to understand. "That's what Mrs. Jaans told me. You'd like her. I hope she can come over when we all get together for Memorial Day."

A spark of interest lit somewhere inside me. "I'd like to meet her. When you talk to her, will you be sure and ask her if she knows anything about Sadie and what happened between Grandma and Augustine? E-mail me in Boston if you find out anything."

"All right." Jenilee seemed surprised by my interest.

"I guess we'd better get on with the rest of the work." I climbed to my feet, already feeling stiff and sore. Jenilee followed, and together we helped with the last of the preparations for the Jumpkids camp. When the group was finished, we stood together in the sanctuary and prayed for the success of the camp.

As we finished the prayer and parted ways, Jenilee and Caleb said good-bye and headed off to Brother Baker's house. James and I waited by the door while Kate and Ben gathered the kids from the nursery. James gave me the same worried look that he'd sent my way several times since I came home wet and dirty in my Sunday suit. I wasn't acting like myself, and he didn't know what to think.

"Everything all right?" he said finally, focusing on the heavy arched ceiling timbers.

"Yes." Just then, I felt all right. It felt good to be tired from actually doing something rather than just from stress and artificial exercise workouts.

Looking at the altar, now transformed into a Jumpkids practice stage, I thought about Brother Baker and his menagerie of rusty pots. Had that only been this morning?

Tonight, I felt like one of those relics—worn-out, cracked, and imperfect. Useful, for the first time in a long time.

Chapter 14

I awoke early on the first morning of Jumpkids camp, filled with an excitement that both surprised and invigorated me. I couldn't remember the last time I had been so filled with curiosity about what the day would bring. The last few years at Lansing had become so routine as the company declined and the corporate culture grew stagnant that the days lacked any sense of possibility. But today seemed to be filled with endless potential for new and interesting experiences, and I couldn't wait for it to begin.

I made coffee and dressed, then stood on the porch and waited for the sun to rise. In the quiet gray morning hush, I walked among Grandma's flowers, some already in bloom, and some just beginning to push from the damp soil. How many times I had seen her out there on her knees planting and pruning, handling tiny seedlings with a gentleness she seldom showed to people? *We're never really gone*, she told me as we worked in the garden one day. *We survive in the things we leave behind.*

She survived in this flower bed, in the gardens of other people to whom she had given tiny seedlings, starts, and bulbs. All over the county there were people who remembered getting friendship flowers from Grandma Rose. There were neighbors to whom she had taken bouquets and casseroles when they were sick, babies for whom she had knitted afghans, and children she'd taught to make pies and quilts in 4-H class.

Everywhere I looked, there were things she had left behind, things that put her life in stark contrast to mine. What had I left behind that anyone would remember?

The yard gate squealed on its hinges and I turned to look, letting the question go unanswered as Dell came up the path. She was wearing denim shorts and a red T-shirt, her feet bare and her long, dark hair swinging back and forth. She raised her hand and waved, dangling a Wal-Mart sack that probably contained her shoes.

I was filled with a rush of love that surprised me. She must have seen it, because she smiled, her teeth white against her tanned skin, her eyes glittering.

"I couldn't sleep," she whispered, as if she didn't want to wake anyone else, so that this morning could be just for the two of us. "I'm nervous."

"Me too, but I'm really excited. This is going to be so much fun. I couldn't sleep, either. I've been up since four a.m."

Giggling, she jittered in place, something I had never seen her do before. "Me too," she echoed, then threw her arms out and slapped them around my waist in a hug so tight it pushed the air from my lungs in a soft *Ooof.*

I laughed, slipping my arms around her slim shoulders and resting my chin on top of her head. "We're quite a pair."

"Yeah."

James was standing on the porch of the little house, watching us and smiling, his expression filled with a fondness that I knew wasn't just for me. He pointed at Dell, winked, and gave me a silent thumbs-up.

As spontaneously as the hug began, it was over, and Dell stood looking around the yard, not sure what to do next.

I glanced at my watch. "It's six a.m. The Jumpkids people should be getting to the church about now. How about we head out now, stop by the café and get some doughnuts, and go help them get their things set up at church?"

Dell looked uncertain at first, then excited, then uncertain again. " 'K," she said finally.

James gave us a quizzical look as we walked to the little house, and I trotted up the steps to get my purse and briefcase. "We're going into town to help set up for the day camp. Neither of us can wait." I gave him a quick kiss, which seemed to surprise him. Lately, when we parted ways in the morning, we said good-bye from three rooms away while we were both busy doing other things.

He frowned as I walked past him and started down the steps. "You're going to town at six a.m.?" It was impossible to miss the undertones in his voice. He had something on his mind this morning. "I thought maybe we'd better take a minute to talk about . . . things."

"Things?" I repeated.

Stroking his bottom lip thoughtfully, he nodded. "Things. Like . . . flights. Are you planning to catch one this evening? Do you want to drive back to the airport with me tomorrow? I'm just trying to get the schedule in my head."

Ah, the schedule. Morse code for *the plan.* I'd strayed from the plan by staying for the first day of Jumpkids camp, and in the cool light of morning, James was worried. This wasn't normal. It wasn't like me.

"I don't know," I admitted. "I thought I'd play it by ear."

James raised an eyebrow.

"I'm just excited," I explained. "It's hard to picture exactly how the day's going to unfold, so I thought I'd leave my options open." It sounded like I was making excuses for my erratic behavior.

If Dell hadn't been standing there, James probably would have gotten down to brass tacks, but as it was, he glanced at her fondly. "How about you, Shorty? Are you ready for this? All charged up for a big day?"

Dell nodded, and I smiled at her, glad to shift the focus. "James, you're going to have to quit calling her Shorty. She's almost as tall as I am." Spanning a hand across, I measured the difference between us—probably five or six inches.

James nodded in agreement, as if he were seeing her for the first time. "Yeah, in a year or so, she'll be all girly. Too big to go fishing," he joked. "She won't want to touch a can of stink bait, and she'll be scared of the fish, and—"

"Huh-uh!" Dell squealed. "You're the one who's scared of the fish."

James coughed indignantly. "Yeah, just remember who caught the whoppin' big specimen down at Sand Barge Hole last time."

"*I* had to unhook it."

"Because I was busy wrestling that monster to shore," James defended, and I had a mental image of him as the Crocodile Hunter, battling a giant catfish.

Dell giggled, motioning to his guitar, which was balanced on one of the rocking chairs. "Are you gonna come to camp with us today?"

Stroking a hand through his tousled hair, he scratched the back of his head contemplatively. "You know, I think I might do that." He seemed glad to be asked, and I wished I'd thought to include him. "I'll try to come by later. I have to meet a man this morning about building a tractor barn on the land Grandma left us. Can't have our tractor sitting outside all winter."

"Our tractor?" I quirked a brow. "I didn't know we had a tractor. When did we get a tractor?"

James stiffened. Of course, he thought I was being critical. "I told you about that, Karen. I was here on layover when they auctioned off the Tompsey place down the road, and I bought the old tractor, remember? About six months ago."

"Oh." I nodded, but he could tell I didn't remember. He'd probably said it in passing, and I'd been focused on something else and it was just another missed connection between us. Now I was doing it again. I was focusing on Dell and Jumpkids when I should have been taking time to talk to him. I was tromping through the woods, trying to find myself, when I should have been trying to find *us*.

"I guess we'll see you later, then," I said, feeling a twinge when he didn't answer right away.

Dell swiveled back and forth between us, trying to read the situation. "Hey, maybe after Jumpkids we can all go on a tractor ride." James and I both looked at her simultaneously, and she raised her eyebrows hopefully, adding, "That would be cool."

I found myself nodding in agreement. "You know what? That *would* be cool." If James and I were to make contact again, what better way than on our land with his new tractor? If that didn't show him I was interested, really interested, in reconnecting, what would?

"Cool," Dell said.

"Cool," James agreed; then he winked at her and smiled slightly at me. "Guess I'd better get the tractor shined up." Looking pleased, he leaned against the porch post.

"See you after a while, then," I said. "If you can come by in time for lunch, we're having potluck, courtesy of the church ladies. It should be good."

He looked tempted. "I'll try."

We said good-bye; then Dell and I climbed into the car, driving to town without really talking, both of us trying to picture the day ahead. In my vision, it was a perfect day—a day in which Dell found out how special and talented she was, a day in which I shared the music I had kept bottled up for so long, a day in which James came by and together we did a little good work in this unlikely place before going to see his tractor and discovering our land. It would be a day that ended differently than it began.

But when we arrived at the church, things looked anything but idyllic. The parking lot was filled with stacks of sound equipment, boxes of costumes, bits and pieces of what looked like a stage, and nine confused volunteer college kids. A pack of stray dogs was running through the middle of things, searching for discarded food and playing tug-of-war with someone's duffel bag.

Dell and I came with our doughnuts just in time. We climbed out of the car, and I did exactly what Grandma Rose would have done if she had been there. I assessed the situation and took charge. The college kids quickly gathered around me, attracted by the doughnut box. "Where's Keiler Bradford?" I asked. "I thought he was supposed to be heading things up."

A tall, clean-cut kid in a basketball jersey traded an answer for a doughnut. "He had to go back to pick up the speaker cables and the music folders. We accidentally left them behind when we packed up the stuff. He oughta be here pretty soon"—he grimaced, looking worried, then finished meekly—"I think."

I chewed the side of my lip, glancing at my watch. Six thirty. In two hours, the parking lot would be filled with cars dropping off eighty-seven children in need of structured activity. The group in front of me seemed anything but structured. They were . . . well . . . ragtag. Everything from a basketball player with a baby face to an African-American kid with a *Mod Squad* Afro, a boy with buzzed hair and a stringy goatee, a leggy high-society blonde with a ponytail, two fairly normal-looking girls in jeans and T-shirts, a young man with horn-rimmed glasses who must have shopped for clothes in Mr. Rogers' neighborhood, and a girl with a tie-dyed peace sign on her shirt and an earring in her nose.

"Where's Brother Baker?" I asked.

The basketball player winced again and reached for another doughnut, looking defeated. "He left a note that he had to go hunt down the plumber. The bathroom's flooded, so the water's turned off."

Oh, no. This did not look good. "Well . . . we'll just accomplish what we can until they get back." The college kids gave me hopeful nods. Finally, someone was going to take charge. "Does anyone have *any* idea where this stuff goes?"

They stared at me like I was speaking in a foreign language.

"No, ma'am," said the girl with the peace sign on her shirt, smiling in a way that was sweet in spite of the nose ring. "None of us have done this before. We all just came in for the summer term, and the director had to quit last Friday. She went into premature labor, and her doctor put her on bed rest. She wasn't going to come back after she had her baby in the fall, anyway, but she was supposed to stay through the summer. We don't really know what we're supposed to do. Keiler's the only one who was even *here* last summer."

"Oh." My hopes sank. I had been counting on so much from this camp, but this motley crew of young people hardly looked like miracle workers. "Well . . . that's all right." *It is?* "We're going to get this figured out." *We are?* "Let me show you the rooms we set up last night, then we'll move things in. If something ends up in the wrong place, we'll just move it again later. One way or another, we'll be ready before the children arrive." My voice rose with convincing enthusiasm, and I punctuated the statement with a little "Hoo-rah" hand motion that was worthy of Bear Bryant or General Patton.

The troops started nodding in unison, bolstered by the pep talk. They returned a chorus of "O.K," "All right," "Sure," and "Cool." The girl with the nose ring said, "Radrat." I wasn't even sure what that meant, but she looked willing.

With a military-style pivot, I started toward the building, Dell and the doughnut box trailing behind me. Halfway to the church, I realized that the doughnut eaters were not following. They were standing in a circle with their hands joined, praying, which didn't seem like a bad idea. We were definitely in need of some divine intervention. When they finished, they grabbed their backpacks from a psychedelic minibus with JUMPKIDS FOUNDATION printed on the side. I pulled my cell phone out and called Kate. What we needed now were reinforcements.

She answered with a rushed hello, covered the phone, and said, "Ooohhh, Joshua, wait a minute, I'll pour the milk!" Then she came back and said, "I'm sorry. Hello?" Something crashed in the background and she groaned.

"Kate?" I suddenly felt bad for even calling her.

"Karen? Is everything all right? You didn't even stay for breakfast this morning."

"We picked up some doughnuts." The kids were headed my way, so I hurried to get to the point. "But we need some help down here. Is James or Ben around?"

"No." My hopes tanked. "James headed out to talk to some guy about a barn, and Ben had some meetings at the office in Springfield today. He just left."

"Shoot." Amazing how easy it was for me to forget that the rest of the world had jobs to go to. I hadn't even thought about the fact that it was Monday and I wasn't headed to Lansing Tech. The realization was surprisingly freeing. I felt like I was back in college with the cast of *Hair*. No jobs, no real schedules to keep—just thousands of pounds of equipment to move, and nine young people who appeared to believe we could do it.

"I'll come," Kate said quickly, and I heard the rattle of dishes going into the sink.

"Oh . . . Kate, you've got your hands full." I felt both guilty and grateful. The last thing Kate needed was one more job to do, but she was willing to drop everything at a moment's notice to help.

"That's all right—Joshua, stop that—I'll call Verna and see if I can take the kids to her house for a few hours . . . Come here, baby girl. Oh, did you pour milk in your hair? . . . I'll be there. I'll see if I can get in touch with Jenilee and Caleb over at Brother Baker's house. They'd probably come down and help for a few hours before they head over to Poetry. There should be some other church volunteers showing up there pretty soon, too. I'll call around, maybe see if I can rustle up a little more help."

"Kate, you don't have to do this." I pictured how much trouble it would be to get two toddlers cleaned up, diaper bags packed, in the car, delivered to someone's house. Kate hadn't mentioned all of that. She'd just said she was coming, and she'd dropped whatever was on her agenda for the day. I couldn't think of one person back in Boston who would do that for me. But Kate would.

I started to tear up.

The college kids gave me nervous glances.

"It's all right," I said, wiping my eyes. "I'm always emotional." That couldn't have been further from the truth. "Help is on the way. Let's get to work."

So we did. We toured the church, then started bringing in everything from huge rolling mirrors and dance bars to boxes of instruments and baseball equipment for the recreation class. About halfway through the process, Jenilee and Caleb showed up, and then Kate. Brother Baker arrived with the plumber and they disappeared into the back of the building. The work out front took on the air of a well-oiled machine, and I had the adrenaline rush of a job that was falling into place. This wasn't so different from moving my Lansing team to a new customer site. We came in, we assessed how to make the facilities work for us, we established our various bases of operations, and we got down to business.

By the time Keiler Bradford came squealing up in another multicolored Jumpkids minibus, the work was practically done, which was a good thing, because we were a half hour from the arrival of the children.

Keiler hurried to the door, carrying a huge wad of stereo cables and power cords. Skidding to a halt beside me, he looked not nearly as chilled out as he had been Friday on the plane. He glanced frantically around the parking lot, strands of flyaway hair sticking out in all directions like an electric halo. "I'm scared to ask—where is everything?"

"Set up, for the most part." I found myself grinning like a parent on Christmas morning, waiting for the kid to find Santa's toys. "We have the orchestra center in the practice choir room—there were two pianos in there, anyway—the dance center in a large Sunday school room, the art and set design in the old kindergarten area, the theater in the sanctuary, complete with the expanded bilevel stage you brought, and the recreation's out back on the baseball field." He stood gaping at me so I added, "That's pretty much everything, isn't it?"

"I . . . I think so." Pulling a handwritten list from his pocket, he checked the items, then handed it to me. "I think that's about . . . everything. See what you think."

I scanned the piece of yellow notebook paper, reading the former director's hastily written instructions on how to set up camp, and concluding that we had done a pretty good job. "Registration table . . ." I muttered when I got to the bottom of the second sheet. "We didn't do this one. Where are these file boxes with the files on each of the kids?"

Keiler thumped his forehead with the palm of his hand. "Back in Kansas City. I didn't even think about bringing those." Bracing his hands on the droopy waist of his camp shorts, he heaved a sigh, looking defeated. "We're never gonna pull this off without Shirley here. We've never even tried to do a camp without our director."

I felt an almost motherly urge to comfort him. He looked completely despondent. "Oh yes, we *are* going to pull this off," I said, the same way I would have told my team we *would* have a network up in six days, when they were telling me it would take ten. "We've got a good start this morning, and there are church volunteers showing up to help. We'll just keep putting it together one brick at a time, all right?"

He nodded, still crestfallen. "I'm sorry. It's not supposed to be this big of a mess. Shirley usually has everything in order and has prep sheets for everybody so they'll know what to do. Everyone assumes that I know what's going on, but last year all I did was coach baseball and teach a few guitar lessons. I don't have any idea about running all the other stuff. The doctors told Shirley no stress, so I can't call her either, and . . ."

I laid a hand on his shoulder. "Hey, where's the guy who was looking for a trip off the map?"

Keiler managed a feeble laugh. "Very funny."

"Oh, come on, remember him?" I teased. "*My reason for being could be anywhere. . . . Stop worrying about the map. . . .* Remember all that stuff? What happened to that guy?"

Rubbing his eyebrows with his fingers, he shook his head back and forth. "He doesn't like being in charge."

I chuckled as we started down the hallway. "Well, I'm sure he'll do just fine. Let me show you how we have things set up."

"All right," he agreed, and together did the tour, plugging in power cords and stereo cables as we went. When we were finished, we had fifteen minutes to slap a registration table out front, hang the Jumpkids banner on the portico of the church, and plunk down a set of recycled church file folders in a Cheetos box so we could do some sort of record keeping.

Keiler and I and Mindy, the girl with the nose ring, slid into chairs behind the table, and Dell was our first customer. She handed Keiler her application, complete with a two-page essay, neatly handwritten on wrinkled spiral notebook paper. I glanced at the first few lines as he made a folder with her name on it. *Why I Want to Go to Jumpkids Camp,* it said as a title, and then in the first line, *I want to go to Jumpkids Camp because Karen told me I would learn more about music. I love music, and I am good at it. It isn't like most things. . . .*

I swallowed the lump in my throat. In that one moment, every bit of the work was worth it.

"Hello, Dell." Keiler greeted her as he tucked her application into the folder. "Thanks for being such a big help this morning. I don't think we could have done it without you."

Dell smiled shyly and muttered, "Thanks."

"I have her permission form in my briefcase. I'll go get it in a little while," I said as Keiler leafed through the papers, then closed the folder.

Keiler nodded. "I hope the rest of the kids show up with their Jumpkids packets. It should have a copy of their applications and essays in it. We need those for camp." He gave the empty file box a look of concern. "Our copies are back in Kansas City in the file box. Without the files, we don't know if a kid is really registered or not."

"Oh, let's just let them all in," I said, and Keiler went pale.

Mindy let her head fall into her hand. "That means we don't have the name tags. The name tags were in the file box."

"Ohhh, man," Keiler groaned.

I turned around to see if Kate was still in the sanctuary. "Kate, do you think there are some name tags around or big stickers we can write on?" I asked. "And some permanent markers?"

"I think so," she called back. "Just a minute."

She returned as the first kids were showing up, and she apologetically offered a stack of tooth-shaped stickers left behind by the local dentist.

KEEP YOUR SMILE, they said at the top, which, considering the way the day had started, seemed . . . perfect.

Chapter 15

By nine o'clock we had ninety-five children registered, and Keiler was worried. "We're only supposed to have eighty-seven," he whispered as another car raced up to the curb. A heavyset woman in a flowered housedress climbed out, gruffly hustling two tall, slender African-American girls, probably about fifteen and twelve years old, toward the registration table. They did not appear happy to be joining us.

Keiler looked like he was about to panic. Leafing through the file box, he shook his head. "All the ones we've registered have paperwork, but Shirley said there were only supposed to be eighty-seven." He stopped talking as the woman plunked down yet another set of paperwork, which appeared to be in order.

I read the names on their application—Sherita and Meleka Hall, the ones Dell was afraid would knock her lights out. Great. Just what we needed: eight extra kids, and now two more who, judging from their body language, were ready to start a brawl. "You're their foster parent?" I asked, thumbing through the foster care forms attached to the paperwork.

"Yeah," the woman said, then glanced toward the car, where a toddler in a diaper was climbing out the driver's-side window. "Git back in there, Myrone!" she hollered, and I had visions of the squirming child accidentally kicking the car into gear.

The foster mother did not appear worried. She turned back toward the table to converse with me, while I glanced around her, wondering if I should do something.

"Myrone, cut that out!" she hollered, obviously more for my benefit than for his, because she didn't turn around and check on him. Heaving a sigh, she rolled her eyes at me, as if I should sympathize with how much trouble this was for her. "So we supposed to pick the kids up, or the church van gonna bring them home?"

"The van can bring them home." I glanced toward the car, where little Myrone had turned on the flashers and was looking for something else to play with. He decided to shinny out the window again, headfirst. "He's going to fall," I said, and stood up.

The foster mother didn't even bother to look. "Naw, he's fine. That one's just like a little monkey. He climbs everywhere." She leaned over to sign the transportation form that Keiler had laid on the table.

Slipping one leg out the window, Myrone called to his sister. "Shawita. Sha-wita . . ."

The older girl glanced at the foster mother, then huffed and walked down the sidewalk, hollering, "Myrone, you get your butt back in the car or I'm gonna whip it for ya."

Myrone scurried back through the window with amazing dexterity. He didn't stop until he was in the backseat. Reaching in through the window, Sherita buckled him into his car seat, then threatened him again, making a few hand motions to show him the whipping he'd get if he caused any more trouble. Then she leaned in through the window and kissed him on the forehead.

I liked her immediately, despite her apparent threat to Dell.

By the time she returned to the table, she was once again wearing the in-your-face scowl. Keiler welcomed her to camp, and she sneered at him, crossing her arms over her chest, letting us know she did *not* want to be there, we were all idiots, Jumpkids camp was a stupid idea, and she hated her foster mother.

The foster mother returned a narrow-eyed glare that said pretty much the same thing, then told me, "They give you any trouble, call me. I'll come thump heads." She turned and started toward the car, where Myrone was once again trying to wiggle out of his seat.

"Honky ho," Sherita muttered, then returned her attention to us, crossing her arms tighter and jutting her slim hips to one side.

Keiler received the performance like he'd seen it all before. Pushing a few fallen strands of brown hair out of his face, he leaned back in his chair and asked, "So, Sherita, what do you like to do? Sing, dance, do artwork, play an instrument? Everyone will get to do a little bit of everything, but we try to put kids in a group that's going to concentrate most on their main deal." He gave her another welcoming smile, which went unrequited. "So what's your thing?"

She lifted her lashes slowly, delivering a dark, murderous glare and a threatening head bob. "Nothing. I don't wanna do nothing."

Keiler nodded and made a mark on her tooth name tag, then handed it to her. "That's fine. There. I've got you marked down to do nothing. If anyone asks you to participate, just show them your name tag, and you'll be all right. I try to put a few nothing people in each group. It gives the rest of the kids an audience to work to. As long as you're chillin' and not bothering anybody, we'll know that you're happy in the nothing group and we'll leave you alone. If at any point you start talking to the performers or making comments or moving around during the rehearsals, we'll know you're tired of being nothing, and you're ready to try something. It's entirely up to you. Fair enough?"

Sherita was completely baffled. Quite clearly, she had no idea how to respond to that. Her arms fell to her sides as she tried to think up a negative answer. Then she crossed them again, huffed, and shrugged.

Keiler turned to her younger sister, who was probably about Dell's age. "So how about you, Meleka? What do you like to do?"

"Dance," the girl said quickly. Obviously, she'd figured out what came from saying nothing.

"Hmmm, a dancer," Keiler said, sounding impressed as he marked her name tag and handed it to her. "All right, there you go. You're a dancer."

We stood up and ushered the dancer and the nothing inside, where the rest of the kids were in the chapel, waiting for the opening ceremony.

"That was very well done," I muttered to Keiler as we walked through the door.

He gave a sly sideways grin. "The kids I can handle. It's the organizational side that's not my thing."

"Not your *deal*, huh?" I joked.

He chuckled. "Not. So I guess you and Brother Baker better stick around and run things." He pointed Sherita and Meleka to a pair of seats along the aisle. "Looks like this is about all that's open," he said to Sherita, who was already sneering at the other kids nearby. "You two can either sit here or stand in the back with the teachers. Your choice."

Sherita didn't answer, just slipped past him and plunked into the seat with a loud thud. Her sister slid in beside her and they sat with their arms bolted across their chests, dealing out dirty looks to kids, counselors, and church volunteers.

Dell glanced nervously across the aisle. Sherita and Meleka glared at her in unison, and Dell shrunk back in her seat. Sherita raised her chin triumphantly, pleased to have finally intimidated someone.

I moved to the back with the teachers as Keiler grabbed his guitar, jogged to the stage, and bounded up the steps to the microphone. "It's showtime!" he hollered so loudly that the sleepy crowd of kids bolted upright in their seats. "Are we gonna do some jammin' today?" he asked, as the Jumpkids theme song came up in the background, the sound rising until I was sure it would rattle the old building off its foundation.

"Yeah!" the kids screamed, throwing their hands in the air and starting to clap in unison with Keiler.

"A-a-all right!" he cheered. "I see some familiar faces out there. How many of you were with us at a Jumpkids camp last year?"

About half of the kids raised their hands into the air, vibrating up and down in their seats.

"All right, then, you're gonna know this song!" The lyrics came up on the screen behind him, and he started playing his guitar along with the music. "Let's get the rest of the Jumpkids mentors to come up and help with the hand motions, O.K.?"

"O.K.!" the kids cheered, and the counselors deserted me as Keiler announced their names like they were celebrities taking the stage.

"We've got Too-Tall Paul!" he said as the basketball player bounded forward. "You'll be seeing him at the baseball field out back." He pointed to the clean-cut kid in the button-down shirt. "And Marvelous Marvin! Don't let the look fool you. He's a wild man, and he knows his way around a box of crayons. You'll be seeing him in the art and set-design room!" Pausing while the kids cheered, he motioned to the counselor with the Afro. "And Mojo Joe, you'll see him in the dance studio, along with Lim-ber Linda!" He indicated to the leggy blonde with the ponytail, then waited while she took the stage and the kids cheered again. The girl with the nose ring headed up, along with the boy with the buzzed hair. "And Magnificent Mindy and Dynamic Dillon, your acting coaches!" The children bounced up and down in their chairs, screaming like they'd just seen the Backstreet Boys. Keiler motioned to the last two counselors, and they jogged up the aisle. "And Harmonious Heather and Tune-Time Tina, your vocal music instructors—that's singing, in case you didn't know!" Keiler swept his arms toward the crew on both sides, motioning for the cheers to continue, then suddenly slicing his hands back and forth to cut off the noise. The kids cooperated, as if they knew the routine, and the room filled with little voices whispering *Ssshhhh, ssshhh, ssshhh!*

Keiler lowered his voice, sounding serious, "And of course, we have Jammin' Jason on sound, and Way-Cool Keiler, in instrumental music." He motioned to himself, then pointed to the audience. "And for a special limited engagement, Crazy Karen, queen of the ivories!"

I noticed that he was pointing at me.

Kate and Jenilee turned around in the front pew, gaping. My young cousin gave me the thumbs-up, and my sister mouthed, "Woo-hoo!"

I didn't know what to do but shrug helplessly and wave to the legion of cheering fans.

"Come on up, Karen, let's do the Jumpkids song!" Keiler motioned for me to join the rest of the crew on stage.

Dell threw her hands into the air, cheering wildly and standing halfway out of her seat. All of a sudden, her piano teacher was a minor celebrity.

Sinking against the wall, I shook my head. I couldn't think of anything more mortifying than trying to sing and dance onstage with a bunch of college kids. Imagine what the people at Lansing would think if they could see that. *Karen's lost her mind.* . . .

Keiler gave a big, exaggerated frown that made him look like a long-haired clown. Motioning for the sound engineer to pause the music, he surveyed the crowd. "She's a little shy," he lamented, and the kids started to moan and groan as he pointed a finger at them. "Are we supposed to be shy at Jumpkids camp?"

"No-ooooo!" the kids squealed.

"Right!" Keiler cheered. "Should she be afraid to get up here and sing the Jumpkids song?"

"No-ooooo!" The crowd sounded ready to riot.

"Does it matter if we mess up?"

"No-ooooo!"

"Does it matter if we're not perfect?"

"No-ooooo!" All of a sudden, I sensed what Keiler was up to. I was being used as an example, or a guinea pig, depending on how you looked at it.

He waved a hand in the air. "It only matters that we"—then he pointed at the crowd, and they hollered—"Try!"

"That's right! Let's help Karen out. Let's give her some encouragement!"

As if on cue, the college kids, the very same kids whose rears I had pulled out of the noose earlier that day, mutinied on me and started chanting my name. Before I knew it, the entire crowd, including my sister and cousin, were chanting, "Ka-ren, Ka-ren, Ka-ren!"

There was nothing to do but either go forward or make a run for the door, so I dragged myself off the wall, making an exaggerated display of how much trouble it was. The kids went wild, squealing, cheering, clapping, screaming my name.

Dell was on her feet, clapping and cheering, "Go Karen!" as if this were some sort of sporting event.

I walked to the front, giving the college kids an evil look, which only served to pump them up. They were having a good time making a patsy of the old lady.

When I reached the stage, the crowd started chanting my name even louder, and Keiler whipped it up, presenting me like a sacrificial goat and saying, "Let's have a big hand for Mi-i-iss Karen!"

The next thing I knew, I was grinning from ear to ear and taking a bow. I'd never felt so popular in my life. It was good, euphoric in spite of the fact that I didn't know the song and was about to make a fool of myself.

Keiler spied Brother Baker at the back door showing the plumber out. "Hey, look, everybody, there's our host, Bad-out Brrrother Ba-ker! I think he ought to help us with the Jumpkids theme song, too, don't you?"

The kids went absolutely out of their minds. Three of them latched on to Brother Baker, dragging him toward the front as he shook his head and good-naturedly put up a fight. When they deposited him on stage, he tried to escape. The front row stood up and herded him back, like a mosh pit of munchkins.

I laughed so hard that my stomach ached and I doubled over, out of breath, tears of pure exuberance streaming down my face. In the front row, Kate had mascara running down her cheeks, and Jenilee was rocking back and forth, holding her ribs. They waved when they saw me looking and I waved back, then held my hands up helplessly as the theme song started again.

"The grown-ups have left the building!" Keiler cheered. "There's no one here but Jumpkids! So let's do the Jumpkids song! Are you ready?"

"Yeeessss!" the kids screamed.

Caught up in the enthusiasm of the crowd, I felt ready to do the Jumpkids song. The lyrics began, and I started right along with the rest of the counselors, singing, "Jump, jump, jump, Jumpkids! Jump, jump, jump, Jumpkids!" bending lower and lower on the first three "jumps," then throwing my hands up and bounding into the air on "Jumpkids!" After the first round, I figured out that slacks and heels were not the right attire for a Jumpkid, so I kicked off my shoes and went barefoot. I glanced over at Brother Baker, squatting lower and lower, his ample stomach hanging out one end and his wide behind hanging out the other, wiggling a little just before he bounded into the air on the second round of "Jump, jump, jump, Jumpkids!"

So far, we weren't doing too badly. Even the audience seemed impressed.

The song went into the first verse, and the rhythm changed, gaining a backbeat that sounded like rap music. The college kids began a series of hand motions and spins that looked like a combination of rap movements and contortionism. Mojo Joe and Limber Linda fell on the floor and started spinning on their backs, and Mindy did the splits, then popped back up with amazing speed. Brother Baker and I just stood there looking at each other, doing a poor job of mouthing the words "When you're afraid to start a new day, you gotta reach inside you all the way. It ain't hard, when you know who you are. You're no ordinary Joe. You're a star. . . ."

Suddenly, Brother Baker gave up on the rap movements and started doing, of all things, the chicken dance, in perfect time to the rap beat. The kids in the audience stopped following Keiler's hand movements, pointed at Brother Baker, squealed, and started flapping their wings and shaking their chicken feet right along with him. The next thing I knew, I was doing the chicken dance, too.

The back door opened, and James stepped in, carrying his guitar case, then just stood gaping at Brother Baker and me doing the chicken dance together. I could only imagine what was going through his mind. Of all the ways to survive my first day out of work, he probably never pictured me doing the chicken dance, barefoot, with the Baptist preacher, in front of a room of screaming children, with nine gyrating college kids.

I couldn't remember when I'd ever had so much fun on a Monday.

By the time the theme song was over, the room was a giant chicken coop and the crowd was sufficiently energized. If some of the kids had been afraid of trying something new or worried about looking foolish in front of a group, they were now completely cured. Even Sherita and Meleka were on their feet, at least until the music died and Sherita realized she was participating. Looking around to see if anyone had noticed, she quickly replaced her scowl and plunked back into her seat as Keiler began to talk. Meleka sat down beside her as the other kids wiggled into their seats, anxious to see what kind of entertainment Keiler would offer next.

He stepped up to the microphone. The hum of little voices and the rustle of bodies stopped. "All right!" Keiler mopped his forehead and caught his breath, as psyched as the kids. "I can tell this is going to be an outstanding Jumpkids camp. Everyone out there looks ready to get started, so I'm going to tell you what you need to do. It's really easy, so don't anyone panic out there, all right?"

"All right!" the kids answered enthusiastically. Keiler and the chicken dance had clearly won their minds and hearts. He was the pied piper, and they would have followed him anywhere.

Never ever in my life had I seen anyone work a crowd quite like that. The same charisma that had caused me to tell him my life story on the plane was now holding the room spellbound. I made a mental note that when we had a quiet moment, I would encourage him toward seminary school. He had a special talent with people, a rare gift. It would be a shame to waste it bumming around ski resorts. Whatever the purpose of his life, it had to be something much greater than wandering musician. If there was a plan for any of us, there had to be a plan for someone like him.

I watched him as he directed the kids to move to different parts of the room, grouping them according to their name tags. Our bunch moved to one corner, with Caleb acting as temporary roundup leader.

Keiler carefully reintroduced each group to their leaders, then looked thoughtfully at Sherita and a few other nothings who were still sulking in their chairs. He assigned two to each group, and Sherita wound up in vocal music with Harmonious Heather and Tune-Time Tina. Unfortunately, Dell was in that group, as well.

Dell hurried over to us as the others headed for the vocal music room down the hall. "I wanna be in your group." It was more of a plea than a complaint. There wasn't an ounce of petulance, just fear.

Keiler smiled and patted her on the arm, then glanced at his watch. "You will be in about an hour and fifteen minutes. We'll be rotating, and the vocal music kids will be coming to us, to see if anyone can play and sing at the same time." By "anyone," I could tell he meant her.

She knew it, too, and she started shaking her head. "I don't like to sing."

Keiler scratched behind his ear skeptically. "Well, hmmm, I heard you singing earlier when you were helping with the speaker cables, and I thought, *Now, there's a girl who really has a voice. She must sing all the time.*"

Dell was flattered. A blush crept into her dark cheeks, but she fought the urge to smile. "I don't like to sing in *front* of people."

"Oh, now, that's no problem." Keiler was luring her in like a fish. "Heather and Tina have a little magic trick to help people get over that. Never fails. It's a Jumpkids trade secret, so you can't tell anybody, all right?"

"All . . . right." Dell knitted her eyebrows doubtfully. On one hand, now she wanted to know the magic Jumpkids secret. On the other hand, she didn't want to go with the vocal music group, who were just about to head out the door. Turning to me, she shrugged in their direction. "Sherita's gonna make fun of me, and then she'll knock my lights out."

"No, she's not," I promised, but I glanced at Heather and Tina, who were busy chatting at the front of their line, and I wasn't inspired with great confidence. What if they didn't supervise closely enough and something happened to Dell? What if the delicate thread of confidence that had brought her here was broken? I was the one who convinced her to come. . . .

I chewed my lip, leaning close to Keiler. "Maybe . . ."

He pretended not to hear. Handing me his guitar, he slipped an arm over Dell's shoulders. "Now don't forget," he said, loudly enough that Sherita, who was trailing at the end of the vocal music line, could hear. "Being in a Jumpkids group is like being part of a family. Your job is to do your own personal best, but it's also your job to help the other family members. If you see one of the singers not singing, you might need to slip in there and sing their part, so they can hear how it sounds when someone else does it. If you see someone not listening when your counselor is giving instructions, you might need to listen and repeat the instructions to them. In your group, you also have a couple of audience members—you'll know them because of the big *N* on their name tags. If you see one of them frowning, or making fun, or moving around, or making noise, you might need to take their job and sit down while they get up and sing your part. That's the way a Jumpkids family works together. We don't criticize each other—if we see someone not doing what they should, we get in there and set a better example. If we can't do any better or if we don't want to switch places with someone, then we keep our mouths shut. That make sense?"

Dell nodded, and he deposited her at the back of the line. In front of her, Sherita didn't even turn around. She just marched off like a little soldier. A sullen soldier, but a soldier. Part of the Jumpkids family, whether she wanted to be or not.

James crossed the room and stood beside me, smiling. "Boy, he's good." He nodded in Keiler's direction. "Normally, when Dell gets that look on her face, she's about to make some excuse and head for the hills."

I nodded. "Keiler really seems to have a magic way with kids."

"With adults, too." James grinned. "He got you to do the chicken dance." Then he turned around and introduced himself to Keiler.

Keiler shook James's hand, taking in the guitar case. "That really a Martin?"

Laying the case down, James popped it open. "Nineteen seventy-five anniversary model."

Keiler drew a breath, running a hand reverently over the smoothly polished surface. "Man, an antique."

James and I winced in unison, realizing the guitar was born before Keiler. If it was an antique, then we were ancient artifacts.

"What a *boss* instrument," Keiler remarked. "Those Martin strings?"

"Of course," James replied. "Is there any other kind?"

"Nope," Keiler replied. "You here for the day? Because I'd really like to get my hands on this old baby."

James answered in the affirmative, and within moments, he had been elected honorary Jumpkids counselor, which wasn't really fair because he never had to do the chicken dance.

Chapter 16

By noon, Jumpkids camp was moving along without a hitch. No one, including the bevy of silver-haired church ladies who showed up to serve lunch, would have guessed that the morning had started out with confused counselors and a septic system meltdown.

When we arrived in the fellowship hall for our sandwich lunch, the counselors were psyched and the children were chattering about everything they had done that morning in their primary classes. After lunch, they would rotate through several other stations.

"On the last three days of camp, we concentrate on putting the whole production together," Keiler told me as we moved to a table where James was already unwrapping his sandwich. "By then, the kids have been in camp a week and a half, and they know their individual parts pretty well. Then it's just a matter of showing them how to work together as a group. Last year we did an adaptation of *Cats*, and this year, of course, it's *The Lion King*. The Jumpkids Foundation is head-quartered in New York, so they usually try to do things that are big on Broadway. It's better publicity, and the kids like it."

"You make it sound so simple." I tried to imagine how they were going to turn so many squirming bodies into a musical theater group. "*The Lion King* is a pretty complicated production for a bunch of kids."

"It'll be tough without Shirley," Keiler admitted. "She knew how to put a production together. She's been doing it for—I don't know—twelve years or something. She's amazing. She runs the Jumpkids after-school arts program at Kansas City schools during the school year, and then in the summer, the Jumpkids camps."

"That *is* amazing," I agreed, trying to imagine maintaining this level of activity all the time. It was only eleven thirty, and I felt like I'd been run over by a bus. "And she's been trying to do this while she was pregnant?"

Keiler nodded. "Yeah, but the doctors said she had to quit. Too much stress and her blood pressure's up."

Mindy set down her tray at our table and interjected into the conversation, "She's, like, over forty and pregnant with twins."

James and I both winced. Glancing at me privately, James gave Mindy a playful sneer, mouthing, "Over forty, naa, naa, naa."

Keiler caught it and felt the need to bridge the generation gap. "Forty's not that old."

Mindy glanced up, embarrassed. "Oh, man, I didn't mean . . . I mean, you guys don't *seem* so old."

Resting his chin on his hand, James watched Mindy dig the hole deeper. "I mean, like, you're"—she searched for a word, and came up with—"cool. You're not over forty. My parents are *over forty*." She said it like there was some kind of terrible dividing line between her parents' generation and the rest of the world. "How old *are* you, anyway?"

I refused to answer, and James raised an eyebrow, saying, "I remember the Beatles."

Mindy's face dropped, and she breathed, "Whoa," in amazement. Then, "Radrat. Really?"

James was clearly amused, so he laid on a little more ancient trivia. "Yeah, and believe it or not, Karen here was once in a college production of *Hair*."

"James!" I gasped, blushing. "How did you know that?" *Hair* was long before I met James. By the time we met, I was already a junior exec at Lansing—straightlaced, business suit, no sign of the girl who once put on a tie-dyed halter top and bell-bottoms and performed barefoot in *Hair*.

James winked suggestively. "I know all your dirty little secrets."

Keiler and Mindy stopped eating and leaned forward, waiting for more dirt. Fortunately, Dell and Harmonious Heather arrived at our table and interrupted the *Jerry Springer* session of marital secrets revealed.

Heather gave us an apologetic look, nodding toward Dell. "I know she's supposed to sit with the class, but she really wanted to sit over here with y'all. Is that O.K.?"

"Sure." I scooted sideways, and James brought a chair over for Dell. Heather grabbed Dell's ponytail, giving it a playful tug. "You have to come back after lunch, though." Winking at us, she whispered, "Dell's my best student, but don't tell everyone else I said so."

Dell blushed and looked at the floor.

"I don't doubt that," I said, feeling a burst of parental pride, even though Dell wasn't mine. "I heard her singing when we walked by the classroom. She sounded great."

Heather nodded. "She's a natural. She has a vocal range over three octaves, at least, and that's really unusual, even for an adult. Especially when she's never had any voice training."

"You should see her on the piano," I bragged. I couldn't help it. I felt like I might burst.

Dell secreted a little smile beneath the curtain of hair, then slid onto the seat between James and me.

"Are you having a good time?" I asked.

Her smile broadened until she couldn't hide it anymore. "It's *fun*." Leaning across the table toward Keiler, she proudly whispered, "Heather told me the Jumpkids secret."

Keiler winked, a knowing twinkle in his eyes. "It worked, didn't it?"

Dell nodded.

"Don't tell anyone," Keiler said.

"I won't," she replied, snickering.

I was jealous. I wanted to know the Jumpkids secret.

We talked for a while about Dell's morning, and how things were going with the vocal music group. A little boy named Edwardo had been selected for the role of the young Lion King, and Heather was still trying to find some older boys and girls to play the grown-up lions and lionesses. Heather was trying to talk Dell into auditioning for the role of Nala, which would include a solo and a speaking part. Dell, on the other hand, didn't want a solo or a speaking part. Playing an instrument in the orchestra pit sounded "easier," she said, which meant that playing an instrument didn't require getting up in front of people.

Pointing at her behind her back, Heather mouthed, "Nala," winking and nodding at us. I had a feeling she would eventually talk Dell into it.

Heather left to join the vocal music students at another table. Sherita was still trailing the group, dangling a couple of scripts at her side, looking like she wanted to throw them at somebody. At the dance table, Meleka was talking to Mojo Joe. From their hand motions, it was clear they were discussing some of the dance moves the class had studied that morning. I couldn't hear the words, just the hum of their conversation mixed with the other voices in the room. Meleka must have finally understood what he was explaining, because she stood up, looked around for a clear space, and proceeded to do a hitch kick, three-quarter turn, a perfect stride leap to a crouch, then a cartwheel that almost landed her on the condiments table.

She didn't even notice. Her entire group were on their feet, giving her affirmations and a standing ovation. She broke into a grin so big that there was hardly any little girl left—just a shining row of white teeth.

"Good for her," I said, realizing I was halfway out of my chair, applauding.

"It is good for her." Keiler pushed his hair out of his face and started eating lunch, as if these moments of pint-sized personal triumph were an everyday occurrence. "You wouldn't know by looking at her right now that she's been in four foster homes already and held back twice in school." Glancing at Dell, he seemed to realize he shouldn't have said that in front of her. "That shouldn't be repeated, all right?"

Dell nodded, and she actually gave Meleka a sympathetic look. "All right."

I turned back around and said quietly to Dell, "So how are things going with Sherita?"

Dell shrugged. "Fine. She doesn't wanna do anyone else's part, so she's not sayin' a word to anybody. She's just sittin' in the corner reading the script is all. It looks pretty boring. I don't know why she wants to do that."

"She'll figure it out." Keiler stopped eating and butted Dell good-naturedly in the shoulder. "And let's remember, you can't help somebody by being critical."

Taking a bite of her sandwich, Dell thought about that. "Grandma Rose says, 'Hard words can't turn a heart.' "

James and I smiled at each other, and Keiler gave Dell a look of respect. "That's a good way of putting it. I like that."

The first buzzer went off, telling us that in five minutes our lunchtime would be over. We hurried to finish our meal, then threw away our trash. In the doorway, we passed Kate and Jenilee coming in for lunch with the art group. Both of them were wearing painting smocks, and Jenilee had blue paint on her hands and in her hair.

"This stuff is supposed to wash out," she said when she noticed us looking. "I'm not much of an artist. I told Caleb he should have done art and let me go outside and do baseball. I know baseball. My brothers played for years. I don't know one bloomin' thing about making a theater set."

"It's time to learn." Kate nudged her playfully, and I could tell that surviving in the art room was a bonding experience for them. "You are *not* leaving me alone in there with Mad Marvin and his seventeen little Picassos. Your artwork looks just fine."

Jenilee giggled, shaking her head, her brown eyes glittering. "There's no telling how this set's going to turn out. The trees look like celery stalks and the rocks look like giant cow pies."

"Well, that's a picture." James laughed.

Jenilee rubbed the back of a blue hand across her forehead, leaving a streak of war paint. "You have no idea. There's paint *everywhere*."

Kate nodded. "I hope Brother Baker doesn't come in there. He'll have a fit. It's just a good thing we draped plastic all over the room yesterday, because there is no way you can turn seventeen kids loose with paint and butcher paper and end up with a clean room."

"Sounds like a challenge." I had a feeling that was hard to describe—a sense of camaraderie, of family. No matter how much fingerpaint was involved or how tired we were, it felt right for us to be here together, doing something good as a family.

"I'm glad we're all here today." My voice was choked with emotion.

Kate's eyes welled up and she blinked hard, her lips trembling. Jenilee gave us a tender look, and the next thing I knew, we were sharing a group sister hug. The guys stood on the fringes and added a chorus of "Awww."

Men.

We spent the afternoon rotating kids through the various stations, then finished the day outside with a disorganized baseball game as we waited for parents to pick up kids. James, who had been a small-town Virginia baseball star in high school, was the star of the show. The kids were awed by his fast pitch and amazed at how far he could hit a ball.

Kate and I stood at the fence, watching. "He's pretty good," she commented, rolling her head wearily from side to side and rubbing the back of her neck.

"I think he's enjoying all of this."

Kate gave me a thoughtful sideways glance. "He's not the only one. You look like you're having a blast. Jenilee and I were lucky to have *survived* the day, but you're actually . . . well . . . good at this." She waved a hand vaguely toward the organized chaos on the field.

I chuckled, noticing for the first time that Kate looked haggard, paint covered, and exhausted. "Yeah, who'd have thought?"

"I would have. You're always good at everything. My gosh, Karen, you've never failed at a thing in your life."

"Me?" I gaped at Kate, wondering if she really meant that. It was exactly what I'd always thought about her. "You've got to be kidding. You're the math whiz, the science genius, the president of the physics club, and now you're Martha Stewart and Grandma Rose all rolled into one. I can't even begin to compete with that. Let me tell you, it's not easy always being shown up by your little sister." It was a surprisingly honest admission, one I'd kept to myself all these years. Right now, I couldn't imagine why.

Kate was speechless. Her surprise slowly melted into a sardonic smirk. "You're just trying to make me feel better because I look like such a basket case right now, and you're"—she threw a hand up and let it slap against her leg—"well, you haven't got a hair out of place. You've got the nice highlights and the snappy little shoulder-length bob. You look like a darned fashion model. You're the one who's impossible to keep up with."

A puff of air stole past my lips, and I stood shaking my head, fully understanding in that one strange moment the paradox of our relationship. We'd never been able to stop competing long enough to just love each other. "You know what, Kate? I'm not just saying that. I really do mean it. You're incredible. You've always been incredible, and now here you are, raising two wonderful kids, doing a great job of keeping up the farm, volunteering at church, and cooking big meals in Grandma Rose's kitchen to boot. If I've ever made you feel like you're less than incredible, I'm sorry. I'm no one to compete with. As of last Friday, I'm unemployed, for heaven's sake." As soon as I said it, I wished I could swallow the words back down my throat.

Kate's eyes flew wide, and she clung to the chain-link fence, blinking at me. "What?"

"I'm unemployed. Laid off. Jobless," I admitted. "Lansing's in financial trouble. Last Friday they cut my department and they cut me."

"Karen," Kate breathed, as if someone had just died. In a way, someone had—her imaginary big sister with the perfect life. "Oh, my gosh, I'm sor—I mean, you've been at Lansing forev—" She laid a hand on my shoulder. "I don't know what to say. I know this must be really hard."

The sympathy was completely genuine, her horror over my situation absolutely heartfelt. I knew what she was thinking. *What will Karen do without Lansing Tech? It's her life. How can she survive without the bonuses and the promotions, the high-powered meetings and the big, fancy incentive trips?*

She was reacting exactly as I'd thought she would. The strange thing was that I didn't feel the way I thought I'd feel. I wasn't embarrassed or ashamed or worried that Kate finally knew. I was relieved. For the first time in . . . well . . . ever, I didn't feel like I had to build myself up into something I wasn't. I could just be who I was.

Kate was doing a little mental algebra. "That's why you sounded so strange when I called Friday night. Geez, Karen, you should have said something. We could have talked."

"I wasn't ready to talk about it."

Kate nodded, her brown eyes filled with understanding but also a hint of disappointment. She obviously wished we could have sat down and shared a good girl cry. "But if you need somebody . . ."

"I know," I said quietly, and then the strangest thing happened. I felt as if Kate were not just my sister, but my friend. "I'm sure I'll get to that point, but for now I just want to hibernate."

"And that's why you finally came back to the farm? To hibernate?"

I searched Kate's face, wondering how to tell her that this trip had been so much more than that. "I just wanted to feel . . . grounded."

"O.K.," Kate said quietly, and slipped her arm around my shoulders. "You're officially grounded. Anything else I can do?"

"No." Stepping closer, I rested my head against hers. "Lay off the perfection thing a little, O.K.? I can't take the competition right now."

"I will if you will."

"Deal," I whispered, and we stood there leaning on each other, basking in the biggest epiphany of our lives as sisters. Both of us turned back to the game, because there wasn't much more to say.

On the field, James was pitching a no-hitter. Suddenly, Sherita stood up from where she'd been sulking and marched past the dugout. Yanking a bat away from Edwardo, our chubby little future lion cub, she walked to the plate.

In the parking lot, the church van started honking and Brother Baker called for the bus kids to load up so he could take them home.

Meleka grabbed her stuff and hollered, "C'mon, Sherita, we gotta go!"

Sherita never looked away from the pitcher, just narrowed her hazel-gray eyes and said, "This won't take long."

"Oh-ho!" James coughed, then said to the outfield, "Back up, boys. We've got a hitter!"

Pursing her lips, Sherita gave him a sneer. After a whole day of sitting around being nothing, she wasn't in the best mood. "Gimme a pitch."

James lobbed a ball across the plate, and she swung. The bat connected with a metallic ping, and the ball sailed over the heads of the outfielders, who hollered, "Woah!" and "Awesome! She's good!"

Sherita didn't even flinch, just gave a little head jerk and challenged, "Gimme a *real* pitch."

He did, and she sent that ball to the outfield, too.

"Not bad." James braced his hands on his hips.

Sherita tried not to seem pleased by the comment. Tossing the bat by the fence, she gathered her things, then glanced back at James. "You gonna be here tomorrow?"

James paused. I could tell he wanted to say yes, but he knew he would be heading to Kansas City in the late morning for his next trip. "No. I have to leave tomorrow."

"Figures," she said flatly and headed for the van without looking back. There was a world of anger and disappointment and dropped expectations in that one little word.

James watched her go as Kate helped herd the remaining kids into the van. "Guess I wish we didn't have to head out tomorrow," he said as we stood by the fence.

I didn't miss the *we*. "I was thinking I'd stay through the day tomorrow, at least." Bracing my hands on my hips, I stretched my back. Kate may have thought I didn't have a hair out of place, but every muscle in my body was aching.

He reacted exactly as I thought he would, with a look of concern that said I ought to be getting back home and back to business. "You sure you're up for another day?"

"Yeah." The truth was that I felt good. Exhausted, but good. It had been years since I'd ended the day with such a profound sense of accomplishment. I thought about all the kids who'd filed through our class, learning to play simple string and percussion instruments. Occasionally, they tried a smattering of piano or guitar. Some, like Dell, pushed for more and more and more until the class time was over.

What would those kids have been doing if they hadn't been at

Jumpkids camp—watching TV, playing video games, wandering idly around town, sitting in foster homes wondering how long it would be before someone came for them? Instead, they'd had a day that was completely out of the ordinary. Off the map. Music, dance, art—but it was more than that. It was a chance to express themselves, to accomplish something, to be special. Who could say where that might lead?

Who would have ever guessed that part of me would be secretly glad I'd been laid off, so that I could spend the day a thousand miles from home at a camp for kids? Who knew I'd cross a major bridge with my sister while standing on the sidelines of a baseball game? Some things defy logic. . . .

"You're in another world." James was waving a hand in front of my face, and I hadn't even noticed.

"I was just thinking." I had the strangest urge to tell him what was on my mind. *Maybe it's time for a change.* What would he say?

Keiler caught up with us from behind, and the moment was lost. "It was a good day."

Both James and I nodded, and James said, "It was good—a little tiring for the over-forty crowd."

Keiler slapped James on the shoulder. "Too bad you're not going to be here tomorrow. We could use you in recreation. You sure made some points with Sherita."

"She's a good ballplayer."

Keiler nodded. "She's good at a lot of things. You should see the essay she wrote to get into camp. It's ten pages long, and she wanted to try everything—singing, dancing, playing an instrument, you name it."

"Then why isn't she doing it?"

Keiler sighed, shaking his head slowly. "She changed foster homes since she wrote that essay. That's hard, especially in your teenage years. You start thinking nobody's ever going to want you for good."

Something in his voice told me he was speaking from experience. That surprised me. I had pictured Keiler as an Ivy League kid from a good family who nursed him through brain surgery, who loved and encouraged him despite the long hair and rumpled clothes. "You sound like you know what you're talking about," I said carefully.

"I was a foster kid from the time I was ten." The words were matter-of-fact—like "I have brown eyes" or "I'm five foot eleven." "When I was fifteen, I got lucky. I found someone who wanted to keep me." He grinned. "Of course, they didn't know they were going to end up paying for an NYU education and brain surgery, but hey, by the time that happened, they were already attached."

The three of us chuckled together, and even though Keiler was making light of his past, I felt a new level of admiration for him. "I guess that's why you're so good with these kids."

Pointing a finger at me, he turned to head into the church. "Better watch out, Karen. You're starting to sound like a true believer."

James gave me a thoughtful frown as we stood alone on the curb, waiting for Dell to carry an armload of baseball equipment into the building. "He's right, you know. You haven't exactly been sounding like yourself these last couple of days."

I stared into the trees at the edge of the parking lot, thinking. "I guess I've been having sort of an identity crisis since last Friday." How could I explain what I didn't understand myself? "I feel like I've lost some parts of myself these last few years, like I've just been getting up and going through the same routine because . . ." Because why? Because we couldn't talk about losing the baby? Because it was easier to just let time pass? "Because I didn't know what else to do, I guess," I finished lamely. Dell was coming out of the building with Jenilee and Caleb. Now wasn't the time to talk.

James seemed reluctant to leave our conversation unfinished. He was about to say something when the others walked up.

Jenilee gave us a questioning look, noticing that they had walked in on something. Slipping her hand into Caleb's, she gave a little tug toward his truck. "Well, we're going to go on over to Poetry to stay overnight and do some visiting before we head back to St. Louis. I promised Kate I'd ask Mrs. Jaans if she knows anything about your grandma and my grandma and the other sister, Sadie, but I think if she knew anything, she would have told me by now."

"It's worth a try." My mind wasn't on the past. It was on the present, and the conversation James and I had left unfinished. Were there things he wanted to tell me as well? What if he wasn't happy with our life, either?

Jenilee shifted uncomfortably. "Oh . . . Kate said to tell you she had to rush off to go get the kids, and she'd see you at the farm whenever."

Dell piped up before I had a chance to answer. "We're goin' on a tractor ride out at Karen and James's land."

"That sounds fun." Laying a hand on Dell's shoulder, Jenilee leaned down a little so that they were face-to-face. "I guess I won't see you again until Memorial weekend. You sounded great on the piano today. I think your only problem is going to be deciding which part to do in the show. You'd be good at all of them."

Embarrassed, Dell threaded her arms together. "You're gonna be back for the Jumpkids show?"

"Oh, you bet we are," Jenilee promised, her face filled with a tender affection that made me think she would be a very good doctor. She knew how to connect with people. "I'm trying to get my whole family to come for Memorial weekend so that we can all see your show."

Dell looked terrified by the idea, but halfheartedly said, "Cool."

We hugged good-bye, then Jenilee and Caleb left. James, Dell, and I decided to leave my rental car at the church overnight and drive home in his. We slid wearily into the seats.

"Buckle your seat belt back there," James said as we pulled out of the parking lot. Dell was too tired to argue. Buckling her belt, she yawned and sighed, resting her head against the seat and closing her eyes. By the time we reached the edge of town, she was drifting off to sleep, her face turned toward the breeze from the window.

"Been a big day," James said quietly, glancing at her in the rearview mirror.

"Yeah, it has," I agreed, laying my head against the headrest. "James, we need to talk."

"You're right, Karen." His words seemed flat, calculated. "We do."

Chapter 17

M y heart skipped, then jolted back into action as we rattled over a row of potholes, leaving the blacktop for a gravel back road that would take us around the far side of the mountain. The car began to hum to the rhythm of the old road. I wanted to lose myself in the song, just close my eyes and drift away. . . .

"Karen?" Why, now that James wanted to talk, was I so afraid?

The car went silent, passing over a short stretch of pavement on a bridge. In that one soundless instant, I understood the source of my fear. Our lives were comfortable—filled with a steady white noise, like the car on the gravel road. It was easy to be lulled into complacency. Friday the white noise had stopped, and I was alone in a quiet I hadn't experienced in years. The hush of my own soul.

Out of that silence came my first question to him. The hardest one of all. "James, are you happy?"

"What?" He lowered his brows, blindsided.

"Are you happy?" I repeated. "With our life, with the way things are. Do you feel"—I searched for the word, and ended with—"stagnant? Like maybe you're just going through the motions, and the years are passing, and you're experiencing life through a layer of insulation?" He didn't answer, just stared straight ahead. I went on, trying to put words to something I didn't really understand. "Because that's how I feel. It's like I just get up every day and I go through the routine, making sure I do all the right things, stay busy, get a lot accomplished. I feel like I've been gorging on job promotions and big corporate deals the last few years, only to wake up and realize I'm starving to death." Tears stung as I felt that hungry part of myself come so close to the surface—the emotional, vulnerable part that needed family, love, a life with meaning beyond just satisfying worldly desires.

James sighed, stroking a hand roughly through his hair, combing the smattering of premature gray at the temples. When he said we needed to talk, he undoubtedly hadn't anticipated anything like this. "Are you talking about us, or are you talking about your job?" As usual, he was going to dissect the situation, whittle it down to a manageable size.

"Both," I said.

He glanced in the rearview mirror at Dell's sleeping form. "I'm not sure now's the time—"

"It's never the time," I rushed out. Outside, the dappled shadows of oaks and sycamores slid silently by, slipping over the car, seeming in no hurry at all. "It's never the time. We've been through eight years of not the time, ever since"—I forced out the last words—"ever since we lost the baby."

His hazel eyes took on a fog of confusion, and he craned to look at me. "I don't see what that has to do with the way things are now."

"It has everything to do with the way things are now." Didn't he see it? Didn't he realize that was the day we stopped discussing the future and started marching blindly through our routines? "Don't you ever wonder why we never talked about losing the baby, or what we wanted from life after that?"

He shifted uncomfortably in his seat. "I thought we decided that."

"When?" I shot back. Dell stirred in the backseat, and I lowered my voice. "When did we *decide* anything? We just let time go by and let life happen."

He thought for a minute, measuring his words. "That's pretty much the same thing, isn't it?" There was something just below the surface. A truth he didn't want to say out loud.

"No, it isn't the same thing. It's a coward's way out," I bit out, trying to bait him. "I'm not saying that we made the wrong choices. I'm saying that we never *made* a choice. I'm saying that I wanted to talk about it—to talk about how you were feeling and how I was feeling. What we wanted in the future, whether we wanted a family or not. Every time I've brought it up over the years, you've changed the subject. I guess I just kept thinking you weren't ready yet, that at some point there would be a perfect time for us to talk about the baby we lost and the future. I thought we'd grieve together and then move on. Now it's like I woke up and realized eight years have passed, and we're still stuck with this huge taboo subject between us."

Exhaling through pursed lips, he shook his head slowly, as if he had known for a long time that this moment would finally come. "I didn't have all the feelings you wanted me to have, all right? How was I supposed to tell you that? How was I supposed to tell you that when you miscarried, when the doctors found the cancer and said they could operate to remove it, all I felt was relief. We hadn't planned the pregnancy. We both knew we weren't ready for a baby at that point. It just seemed . . . like things happened the way they were meant to, I guess. All I could think about was what would have happened if you hadn't lost the baby. What if the pregnancy had gone on five more months? The doctor said it was probably the change in hormones that prompted the cancer to develop. What would have happened in six more months? How far would it have spread?" He sighed again, the shadows passing over his face. "I'm sorry, Karen. I suppose I thought that if we avoided the issue, over time it would just . . . fade away. I thought it would be better that way."

The past and the present swirled through my mind in a tempest of emotions—grief over the loss of the baby, anger at the doctors for performing the surgery that meant we'd never have one, anger at God for letting cancer grow inside of me when I was only in my thirties, anger at James for not grieving with me. How could he sit here now and say it was best that things happened this way? How could that be his excuse for not grieving the loss I still felt so intensely? "There's no way to know if . . ."

"If the cancer would have spread?" He finished the thought, his lips set in a hard, determined line. "There's no way to know that it wouldn't have." I felt the car slow, come almost to a stop as we wound through a valley of overhanging pecan trees. He turned to me, his look intense. "How could I tell you that every time you wanted to talk about your grief over the baby, all I could think of was what if the baby had survived and you hadn't? I know the baby was real to you. You felt it. You imagined the person it would become, but to me it was still just a thought, an idea, something I hadn't planned on in my life. I was willing to give up that idea for you to be healthy and here with me. I knew you wouldn't be able to understand that. I knew if I told you, you'd look at me just the way you're looking at me now."

I stared at him, tasting the salt of tears, feeling betrayed. "I would have . . . understood. I would have figured out how to understand."

"No, Karen, you wouldn't have." He focused on the road as we wound up a hill into the afternoon sunshine. "You haven't even forgiven me for not *talking* about grieving for the baby. How would things have been if I'd told you I wasn't grieving—I was relieved that you were going to be all right? I helped my father raise three kids after my mother died of cancer, Karen. I watched how it consumed him. It exhausted him. I know it may be selfish of me, but I didn't want that kind of life."

I wiped my eyes, then let my hands fall into my lap as a new rush of tears came. Outside the window, yellowbonnet flowers swept by like an ocean. "That's why you never wanted to talk about losing the baby, about possibly having a family through some other means—because you were afraid I might not be around long enough to raise a child?" I muttered, dumbfounded.

Nausea spiraled through me, and I rested my head against the seat belt, gulping in the thick, pollen-scented breeze. What would he say if he knew about the tests last week in Dr. Conner's office?

"I don't know," he admitted, sounding weary, confused, scrubbing his forehead as if to wipe away the thoughts. "It was never anything that clear-cut. I never put it into those terms in my mind. It was just easier to let time go by."

I nodded, understanding. *Easier to let time go by.* Hadn't I thought the same thing myself? Only now I was waking up and realizing that sleepwalking through life, never facing the risks and the realities of human existence, wasn't a solution. The time that had drifted by was lost, like water down a river. My fears were still with me. I was older and still afraid. Living, really living, was about stepping out in spite of fear, about taking a leap of faith.

"We've done this too long," I said softly. "We've spent too many years just making a living, but not really making a life—with your family and my family, with each other. We go on a vacation every once in a while. We see your dad, your brothers and sister and nieces and nephews every couple years. Until you started coming to the farm, we never saw Kate and Ben. We're not really making a life, making real human connections. I had a sense of it on September 11, but I didn't grab on. I knew those weren't your flight numbers on the news, but when you finally called me and told me you were on the ground in Denver, I was so relieved. I thought, *When he gets home, we're going to take a long vacation. We'll just get in the car, and we'll go see all the places we always wanted to see. We'll go visit the family instead of sending Christmas cards, and not just for a day or two. This time we'll really stay.* Shaking my head, I wiped my eyes again. Two years ago, I'd had a wake-up call, and I'd let it slip away. "By the time you got home, I was already back at work, figuring out how Lansing could get into the homeland-security business." A rueful laugh pressed my throat. "A lot of good that did me. I should have taken the time to be with you, to figure out what was right for us."

He nodded, but he didn't answer. Stroking a thumb back and forth on the steering wheel, he scanned the horizon slowly, thoughtfully. We turned from one road onto another. I recognized this one. It was the old road that led around the mountain and past the back side of the farm.

"So is that what's behind this sudden interest in Jumpkids camp and teaching piano lessons?" he asked. "A latent sense of needing to do something meaningful with your life?"

I thought carefully about the answer. It was hard to tell from the question how he felt about it. "I don't know," I admitted finally. "That could be some of it, but there's more." How could I explain to him? How could I show him this part of me that he never knew, the part that was locked up in the attic, in an old trunk with various recital costumes, old sheet music, and a stack of ribbons from teenage music competitions?

Taking a breath, I plunged into a reality I had yet to explore to myself. "When I sat down at the piano the night I was laid off . . . when I started to play, it was like a door had been thrown open inside me and the music came rushing out. I remembered how much I loved it, how much I lived for it. I remembered how I gave it up when I got to college, when I was struggling to get through the engineering degree. And I thought, *Why did I do that? Why did I do that to myself? Just because my parents thought music and theater were a waste of time, or because my professors told me I needed to devote myself to the engineering curriculum? Why was I so afraid to be who I was?*" I glanced at Dell, sleeping in the backseat, so unaware of the tempest traveling in the car with her. "And then when Dell came along, I saw how the music brought her out of herself. I realized how special her talent was, and all she needed was someone to tell her that. And while I was telling her, she was telling me the same thing."

Looking at Dell, I suddenly understood the connection between us. "I realized that the parts of me she admired are the very parts I had decided didn't matter. These kids don't like me because I have a six-figure job and a big title. They like me because I can play the piano and do a bad chicken dance. It's a powerful thing to realize that someone can like you for who you are—not who someone else wants you to be or tells you to be. I don't want to give that up."

Craning his neck at me, he drew back a little. "So what are you saying, exactly?"

"I'm not sure," I admitted. I felt like I was groping through a dark, unfamiliar place, trying to find the light. "I don't want to go home and just blindly soldier on, type up a résumé, beat the pavement until I find another job with another Lansing Tech. I want to take some time to . . . to really think about . . . life."

He started to talk, to analyze my plan, and I held up a hand to stop him. "I know you're going to say that doesn't make sense." He nodded almost imperceptibly, and I went on. "But everything doesn't have to be logical. It's not the end of the world if things don't make sense. Some things you just feel and you don't know why. All I know for sure is that I haven't been this exhilarated at the end of a day in years. It's like I'm operating on pure oxygen, like I can breathe all the way to the bottom of my lungs."

He scratched his head, torn, I could tell, between being supportive and telling me what he really thought. "So, you're saying that you want to spend the rest of your life giving music lessons to underprivileged kids?" His hazel eyes took on a slightly scolding, mildly parental expression. "That isn't very lucrative, Karen."

"I realize that," I snapped, feeling eighteen years old, like my father was telling me that taking theater and music classes wasn't productive. "I'm not talking about forever. I'm just saying that I don't want to make any permanent decisions right now. I"—the truth came to me in a rush of self-discovery that sat me upright in my seat—"want to stay here through Memorial Day and finish out the Jumpkids camp. *Stay here? For two weeks?* I tried to make the idea sound less radical than it was. "Kate has the whole family coming for the holiday weekend. I can help her get things ready, spend some time with Josh and Rose, reconnect. Kate and I haven't spent more than an hour or two alone, without the family, since I left for college."

"That's because you haven't wanted to," he reminded me in a flat, slightly reproachful tone. He was so much like my father—logical, analytical, careful. Safe. Always. "Karen, I've tried to get you to come down here dozens of times these past two years, and you were completely against it. Now you're telling me you want to spend two weeks communing with Kate and the kids? That doesn't make much sense. It sounds like a knee-jerk reaction to what happened Friday at Lansing. Are you sure this isn't just an excuse, a way of running away?"

No. "Yes." I knew that wasn't completely true. I probably was reacting to losing my job and the news from Dr. Conner. "But does it really matter? Am I not entitled, for once in my life, to be a little off plumb? I've been floating right on level for years. Is it the end of the world if I have a little . . . breakdown for a few weeks?" I waved a hand toward the brush passing on the side of the car. "I mean, you're out here on your layovers buying tractors, plowing over cedar trees, and building barns on land we'll never use. How logical is that? But it makes you feel good. It helps you relax and reconnect with growing up on a farm. That's what I need—a little time to relax."

Raising one brow and lowering the other he delivered a comical look that told me we were going to move from arguing to joking again. That was, thankfully, the one way he differed from my father. James could see the humor in things. "You're going to relax with ninety-seven Jumpkids banging on percussion instruments, a bunch of daffy college students, Sherita skulking around like an axe murderer, and the plumbing backed up in the church?"

"Exactly." I knew I'd won the argument, and at that moment, I loved him so much for accepting feelings that were still so nebulous. "Sounds great, doesn't it?"

"No."

I prodded him playfully in the shoulder. "Oh, come on. You're great with the kids. They love you. You're the baseball king."

He chuckled, and I felt the oppressive emotions fly out the window. "Yeah, well, it's good in small doses, but I'll tell you, I'm not sorry to be getting on a plane tomorrow."

"Wimp," I joked.

"Nutcase," he retorted, and we laughed together. I felt like a thousand pounds had been lifted from my shoulders. There was only one gigantic weight remaining. The news from Dr. Conner's office. I needed to tell James, but if I did, he'd insist that I go right home for the biopsy. And he'd be right. There was no logical argument to combat that—except that I wasn't ready to go home yet. That didn't qualify as an excuse, and I knew it.

I could schedule it here, I told myself, trying to absolve a measure of the guilt. *I could schedule it here with Grandma's old doctor . . . what was his name? Schmidt. Dr. Schmidt. By the time James comes back, I'll know the answer.*

I looked up and realized we were passing through the valley where the old wooden bridge used to be, where I had found the mermaid pool and the sister trees. "Oh." I pointed as we crossed over the new bridge. "Stop. I want to show—"

James pulled into the newly cleared driveway.

"James, what are . . . ?" I looked around for an explanation. How could he know about this place?

In the backseat, Dell stirred and stretched, then put her hands on the window frame. "Are we there yet?" she muttered sleepily.

"This is the place," James answered. "Just had the new fence put in last week, and I put the gate up this morning."

My mouth dropped open. "This is . . . We have . . . I didn't . . ." I babbled, still trying to process the idea that this was our property. When we'd inherited land from Grandma Rose, I had assumed that it was actually attached to the farm, not down the county road. "This is the piece of property Grandma Rose willed to us?"

He quirked a brow at me as Dell hopped out to open the gate. "Yes. I've told you about it, remember? It was originally a three-hundred-acre piece your grandparents bought sometime after World War II. The hundred acres on this side of the creek are ours, and the hundred on the other side are your aunt Jeane's. Your father has the hundred on the north side of ours."

All of that was familiar. I remembered it from the reading of the will, but in all the times Grandma had taken us here, she never mentioned that our family owned the property. "I knew about the division of the property, but I didn't realize it was located here. James, this is the place I was talking about—where I stopped yesterday to find the swimming hole Grandma Rose used to take us to. This is the place. The waterfall where Kate and I played is right down there, just down the path a bit, and Grandma Rose's special place—the sycamore grove that she and Augustine talked about in their letters—it's just a short walk down the creek." My mind filled with memories, and I saw Kate moving down the path, trotting ahead of the car, like Dell was now, Queen Anne's lace skimming her bare brown legs, long dark hair swinging back and forth in the sun. I could feel the past all around me. "I just can't believe it's ours."

"It's ours." There was a twinkle of satisfaction in his eye, a pride of ownership. But more than that, he was happy that I was finally taking an interest. This place was special to him, and now it was special to me, as well. I was filled with a sense of something meant to be. James smiled as if he felt it, too.

I wondered if Grandma Rose had planned it this way. If she knew that I would someday come back here to remember the history I shared with my sister, and to learn about the history she had shared with hers. Could she possibly have known that when my world was spinning out of control, I would come here to feel grounded?

James drove to the end of the new gravel driveway, which extended perhaps fifty feet into the property, and stopped beneath a grove of trees where a pad had been cleared. "The barn's going to go there." He pointed to some orange construction flags nearby. "Nothing fancy— just a small workshop and a place to keep the tractor for now, until we decide what to do with the place in the long run."

"We'll never sell it," I rushed out, gazing at the flower-laden mead- ows below, the low sweet peas stretching their blossoms sunward in the dappled, lacy shade. Overhead, the sycamores whispered in a language I remembered and understood. I watched Dell disappear among them. "It's too beautiful to ever let it go."

James nodded, seeming pleased. "It's a beautiful place." He pointed up the bluff. "There's a fantastic spot up there for a weekend house. The other day I found an old rock chimney, and the foundation of a log cabin."

"Amazing," I whispered, stepping from the car, anxious to explore all the secrets of this magical place. Our place.

James walked to where an old green tractor sat parked, and I fol- lowed. "There she is." He gave the tractor an affectionate pat that made me smile.

"She's a peach." I took in the rusty paint job and the big dent in the front-end loader, recalling James's sister telling me that when he was young, all he ever wanted to do was drive the tractor and other farm machinery. That love for all things mechanical had led him to eventu- ally become a pilot. "What a cream puff."

He squinted, sensing that I might be making fun of his baby. "Fifty-seven John Deere." He introduced me to the tractor as I walked slowly around it. A tractor was pretty much a tractor to me, but James, of course, knew his sweetheart inch by inch. "She's a good old girl. Three-point hitch, live PTO, mint condition, still has good compression and plenty of power."

"Wow." I batted my eyes, pretending to be impressed. "What a babe. I think I'm jealous."

James turned and gave me a slow, flirtatious grin. "You two might have to fight over me." He was so handsome when he smiled like that—slightly mischievous, slightly wild. Not the straightlaced, sophisticated airline captain. "But you'd better watch out. She can mow over a two-inch cedar tree in nothing flat. She's tough."

"I'm tough." I cut a suggestive glance at him. It felt good to flirt again, to be like we used to be.

"Oh, really?" He grinned over the hood of the tractor. "Show me."

Raising my arm, I made a muscle to be silly, then ducked away just as he was about to test it. He came after me, and I turned and ran through the field, laughing, as he hollered, "So that's how it's going to be?"

He caught me halfway across the field, his arm snaking around my waist and spinning me around midstride, pulling me into the air. He drew me close, and we fell into the tangle of lacy sweet peas, hidden from the world like young lovers. Closing my eyes, I drank in the scent, the feel of the moment, the sound of the breeze, the touch of his lips on mine, the warmth of his body, the exhilarating press of his weight holding me close to the damp earth. I remembered everything I loved about him, and everything I treasured about this place.

I felt young again, and in love with the world.

Chapter 18

By the time we went home, James and I had explored what seemed like every inch of our land. *Our land.* I loved the way it sounded.

I showed him the initials in the rocks while Dell waded in the creek, then we took a tractor ride around the perimeter and stopped near the sister trees. James and I stood admiring the gigantic sycamores, while Dell discovered that, even all these years later, they were still easy to climb. Watching her, I painted the glen as it must have been years ago—the three sycamores much smaller, the peach grove only a single tree, grown from a mysterious seed perhaps dropped by lovers or planted by woodland fairies. I saw three girls in plain cotton dresses and bare feet—beautiful Sadie with her long, red hair, quiet Augustine with soft golden curls the color of the evening light, and my grandmother, the middle girl, her brown curls falling around her shoulders in wild disarray. I imagined them there, escaping from the world, still able to believe in things they could not see.

The evening light felt warm on my face and James's hand was firm and solid in mine as I closed my eyes, turning my face upward toward those ancient branches, thinking, *I want to believe. I want to believe in things I can't see.* I yearned to be as fearless and free as those little girls, as Dell when she climbed high into the branches, never looking back to see where she had been.

"I guess we should go," I heard James say.

I nodded reluctantly. The day was over, but I didn't want it to end. Tomorrow morning, James would be leaving. It seemed as if this new magic between us would leave with him, that it would evaporate bit by bit, and when he came back things would be as they had always been.

Why did I feel that way? Why was I so afraid to grasp this new happiness? Why did I feel as if James's leaving was the beginning of the end?

We drove Dell home in silence. When we turned onto Mulberry Road, James studied the decaying cracker box houses, the ditches littered with rotting furniture, the snarling dogs on chains. His face held a silent expression of horror and disgust that spoke volumes. Obviously, in all of their fishing trips together, he had never taken Dell home. For a moment, I thought he'd say something, then he just glanced at Dell in the rearview mirror, privately gave me a sad look, and slowly shook his head. If he had any illusions about what her life was really like, they were swept away when we pulled up to her house.

He sighed, taking in the ramshackle dwelling, the yard strewn with broken household items and trash the dog had chewed up, the driveway littered with tools and parts from Uncle Bobby's pickup, now jacked up with one wheel off.

I didn't want Dell to go, but I knew there wasn't a choice. Our day of *Let's pretend* was over. "I'm sorry we kept you out so long," I said. "Maybe I should come in and explain it to your grandmother."

"No," she replied, quickly gathering her papers from Jumpkids camp and the flowers she'd picked by the creek. "Nobody cares." A simple fact of life.

Biting my lip, I closed my eyes for a second. James noticed it. "All right, then, I'll see you in the morning." My voice held a false cheerfulness. "Do you want me to pick you up, or are you coming over to the farm?"

"I'll come over." She climbed out, then stopped at the driver's-side window and frowned at James. "Are you leavin' tomorrow?"

He nodded, turning his gaze from the house to her, then back and forth again, like he was having trouble assimilating the two. "Yeah, I'll be leaving in the morning," he said finally, reluctantly. "But I should be back sometime next week, and when I come, I'll bring the *Partridge Family* guitar. I'll even bring some new strings and show you how to put them on. Maybe we can take it down to the river and see if the catfish like guitar music."

She giggled. " 'K." Her eyes lit up and she jittered in place. Reaching through the window, flowers and all, she gave him a quick, awkward hug. "Thanks!" Then she pulled away.

On the porch, Uncle Bobby was watching. He staggered a step backward and held the door open as she crossed the yard, stopping to pet Rowdy on the way.

"Hey, how's my little brown girl?" His slightly slurred words drifted across the yard as she continued to the house, the dog following behind her. "You have a good day with the white folks?" He glared toward the car, and James jerked forward in his seat.

I laid a hand on his arm. "Leave it alone." I thought of all the warnings Kate and Brother Baker had given. If James started a confrontation now, tomorrow her grandmother would keep her locked away and there would be no more Jumpkids camp for her.

Uncle Bobby waited, still talking while Dell went in the door. "Got you some new clothes at the Wal-Mart over in Springfield. Thought you'd like that . . ." The screen door fell closed, and the dog lay down outside, head on his paws, nosing through a hole in the corner of the screen, as if he shared our misgivings about sending her in there.

Uncle Bobby came back to the door and kicked at the dog, then stared at us.

"We'd better go," I said, my hand still on James's arm. "We might get her in trouble."

Nodding reluctantly, James backed the car onto the street. "Someone ought to report that." He nodded toward the house.

I sighed, laying my head back against the seat as we drove away. James was accustomed to a world where he was in command, a world that was right and level and clean. "Kate says it's been reported in the past. Brother Baker told me that every time someone gets involved, the grandmother starts keeping Dell home and away from other people, which will only make her situation worse." I could tell he wasn't satisfied with that answer, that he still thought he ought to be able to fix the problem. He was looking for logic where there wasn't any. Why would God give Dell a talent like that and put her in a place like this?

"It's wrong," he grated out, his hands kneading the steering wheel, his level of emotion surprising. I couldn't remember the last time I'd seen James red faced and tight jawed, teetering on the edge of control. It wasn't like him at all.

"It sure seems that way," I agreed, caught between sharing his anger and wanting to calm him down.

Glancing narrowly in the rearview mirror, he slowed the car, his face a mask of frustration. Was he thinking about going back and doing something rash?

"James, we have to just let it be." I pried his hand off the steering wheel, threading my fingers through his. "Kate and Brother Baker know a lot more about the situation than we do. They have Dell's best interests at heart, too."

"Guess so." He looked out the window, watching the dumping grounds of Mulberry Road pass by. He seemed disappointed—in the situation, in me, in himself for not going back after Dell? I wasn't sure which.

We drove back to the farm in silence. A heavy feeling settled over the car, wrapping around me like the weighty lead cloak they use for X-rays at the dentist's office. Where I had been filled with joy as we explored the mermaid pool and the sycamore grove, now there was a fear that something was about to go wrong.

"James," I said quietly, as we parked the car in the driveway and got out.

"Hmmm?"

"Be careful this trip, all right?"

He frowned as we walked through the gate. "I'm always careful," he said, then kissed me on the top of the head, slipping his arm around my shoulders. Resting against him, I took a deep breath, trying to shake the sense of foreboding.

Perhaps, I told myself, it was only guilt talking—a nagging whisper reminding me that I shouldn't be keeping my medical tests secret. . . .

That off-balance feeling stayed with me through the evening and into the night. In the morning, the phone jolted us awake before daylight. James answered, said, "Yes," then turned on the bedside lamp and began jotting down numbers on a piece of paper. I knew what it meant. His trip had changed, and he would be leaving even earlier than expected.

"Gotta go," he said, setting down the phone and leaning over to kiss me. "Guess you're on your own to get to town this morning. I have to head for the airport."

"All right," I whispered, still hoarse from sleep. Sitting up, I slipped my arms around him and held him tight. "I love you." How long had it been since I'd told him?

He grinned suggestively. "I've got a minute."

"A minute won't do any good," I teased.

"I've got"—he twisted his head so that he could see the windup clock on the nightstand—"twenty minutes."

"That might do it. . . ."

Turning off the lamp, he slipped back into bed and I felt an electricity that had been missing between us for too long. I surrendered myself to it, losing all sense of time and place. There was only him and me. His hands, his body, the soft sounds of passion. In my mind we were in the field among the lacy sweet pea vines, wrapped in the grass and the flowers and each other, a perfect circle. . . .

When he finally slipped from the bed, I didn't want him to leave. "Don't go." I reached for him, unwilling to let the moment end.

He chuckled, a deep, warm, resonant sound. "I'll see you next week."

I heard him moving around the room in the dusky predawn light, hurriedly gathering his things. "Be careful," I said again.

"I will." Then the sound of a suitcase zipping. The last thing he always did before he walked out the door. He stopped to lean over the bed and kiss me, his hand softly cupping the side of my face, then threading into my hair. Closing my eyes, I rested my cheek on his arm. "You be careful, too. Watch out for Sherita. She's good with a baseball bat."

"You're so bad," I chided, lightening the moment.

"You like me when I'm bad," he breathed against my cheek, then kissed me again and headed out the door.

I lay in the empty bed for a long time, watching the first rays of morning slowly creep in around the windows. I felt lost and lonely.

From somewhere outside I heard singing.

"Oh, soul, are you weary and troubled? No light in the darkness you see. . . ." Dell's voice.

Pushing open the window, I spotted her coming up the path, little more than a shadow against the gray morning, the big dog following behind her.

Slipping into my sweats, I waited until she rounded the blackberry patch. "Hey, there," I whispered through the window. Even though we were too far from the main house to worry about waking anyone, it seemed a shame to disturb the morning hush.

She stopped just beyond the blackberry bushes and looked up quizzically. "What are you doing?"

"Still sitting in bed. It's early yet." Hadn't she noticed it was barely light outside? Why wasn't she afraid to cross the creek and walk through the woods in the dark? Did anyone at home even notice when she got up and left at this hour of the morning?

"Did James go already?" She checked the driveway, sounding disappointed. I realized why she'd come so early. She wanted to tell him good-bye.

"Yeah." The melancholy was obvious in my voice. "Want to come in?"

" 'K," she said, and in a minute she was on the porch. I heard her leave the door open, closing only the screen. Outside, Rowdy gave a low whine.

Propping the pillows, I sat in bed with my bare feet tucked under the covers.

Dell came in carrying a handful of ripe huckleberries. "Want some?" She plopped on the other side of the bed, testing the old mattress for bounce before crossing her legs.

"Sure." I took a few of the tiny blue berries, and for a few minutes, we sat savoring the wild delicacies, not speaking. When the berries were gone, we lay back against the pillows and talked about the day and what would happen at Jumpkids camp. Finally, the light grew bright outside the windows, and I climbed out of bed to shower and get ready. Dell started practicing *Lion King* dance steps, muttering to herself as if she were the teacher talking, and occasionally singing a line or two of the song. When I was finished showering and dressing, she came into the bathroom and sat on the edge of the tub, watching me put on makeup, then timidly experimenting on herself. I swept her long hair into a high twist, and we did a cramped version of beauty shop, draping each other with old costume jewelry from Grandma's vanity drawer. We stood laughing at the results, sharing a girl moment before she washed off most of the makeup and became herself again, so that we could go in and eat breakfast with Kate and Ben.

All week long, we followed that same routine. Dell arrived at daybreak, we ate huckleberries, we talked about the day, tried on makeup, had breakfast with Kate and Ben, then headed off to Jumpkids camp.

By the following Monday, we had our routine down pat. There was a lot to talk about that day. It was to be the first partial onstage rehearsal of the Jumpkids production. The set, complete with movable clouds, ten-foot trees, and gigantic boulders, was almost finished. The dancers had learned the steps, the singers knew the songs, the actors knew their lines, and the percussion orchestra didn't sound too bad when they played along with the sound track.

All in all, it was an impressive feat, and the kids were excited about the idea of practicing onstage. Dell was set to play Nala, the female lead. The part included one solo and one duet with Edwardo, the Lion King cub. Dell would also play several songs on the piano before the first act, while the audience was being seated.

She and I had been at the church off and on all weekend practicing the piano numbers, but on Monday morning the pressure was getting to her. She came in the door with no huckleberries, complaining that she was probably getting sick.

I didn't hear her at first. My mind was on the fact that I was supposed to go by Dr. Schmidt's office that afternoon for my biopsy—just a minor in-office procedure in which he would take a few small tissue samples to send to the lab in Springfield. Painless. Quick. Terrifying. Secret from everyone. I didn't want to think about that. I wanted to focus instead on the Jumpkids production and Dell.

"You are not getting sick." I patted the bed beside me, and Dell flopped down with drama worthy of an actress. "You're just nervous. Don't worry. You'll be fine. You know all of it by heart."

She huffed, falling back against the pillows, her dark hair tumbling around her. "I stink at it."

"You do not stink at it." Lying next to her, I tried not to smile.

"Sherita says I stink at it."

"What does Sherita know? And besides, last I heard, she wasn't supposed to be talking." Sherita had been sulking around all week, still determined to do nothing. Now that James wasn't there to pitch during baseball, she didn't even want to participate in that.

Dell rubbed her eyes, red and swollen. She looked like she'd been crying or hadn't slept much. "She said I stunk at it, and Tina made Sherita get up and do my part. She knew it all perfect, even the dance at the waterfall, and she was better at it than me. Tina said she could be my understudy, and Sherita said she didn't want to. I hate her. She's so mean all the time, and she makes fun of me, and then I forget what I'm supposed to do."

"Just ignore her." I turned onto my side and smoothed the hair from her face with one finger. "Try to cut Sherita some slack, O.K.? She and her brother and sister are going through a really hard time right now." It seemed strange to be telling Dell that someone else had it even worse than she did. "She's not mad at you. She's mad at the world."

"That's what Keiler said." Her eyes drifted closed and she yawned.

"Well, Keiler's pretty smart."

"Grandma Rose said it, too." She burrowed deeper into the pillow. "She talked to me last night."

"You mean you dreamed about her?" Goose bumps prickled over my skin.

"She was telling me about Sadie Walker." Her words stretched out lazily, with spaces between, as she drifted into sleep. It was still early, so

I didn't try to wake her up. It was nice talking to her when she was un-guarded like this.

"Who's Sadie Walker?"

"You know—Sadie."

"Oh, Sadie." I wondered how she knew the last name. That was the only piece of information Jenilee had been able to come up with when she talked to my grandmother's cousin. The last anyone had heard, Sadie had married and changed her last name to Walker, but that was fifty years ago. "What did she say about Sadie?"

Sighing, Dell smacked her lips, tasting the edges of a dream. "That Sadie liked to sing and dance, like me."

"Oh," I said, feeling a connection with my grandmother's long-lost sister. The music that was in her was also in me, a shared inheritance of sorts.

"Do you think Sadie Walker was—" Dell sighed, a long, slow, ex-hausted sound. I wondered again why she was so tired this morning. The dim light showed deep, hollow circles under her eyes. "Somebody famous?" She blinked her heavy lashes to look at me, and quickly they pulled closed again.

"I don't know." My mind wasn't on Sadie Walker. My mind was on the little girl lying on top of my covers, exhausted on what should have been a very exciting day for her. "Dell, is everything all right at home?"

"Um-hmm." She let an arm fall across her eyes, as if to block out my questions.

"You seem really tired."

"Granny had a bad night. I had to . . . help her with her medicine and her . . . oxygen tank."

I sat up, frustrated, wanting to wake her up and demand answers, but I knew I should let her sleep for an hour or so until it was time to go. "Where was your uncle Bobby?" As if I even needed to ask. Proba-bly drunk and passed out on the sofa.

"He's gone." That, at least, was good news. Rolling away from me, she hugged the pillow, trying to end the conversation.

"Where did he go?"

"Ohhh-kla-homa," she sighed, her words garbled and little more than a whisper, like the speech of a sleepwalker. "He wanted to take me . . . Graaah-ny said no, 'cuz she needs me . . . heee-er. They had . . . a big . . . fight."

A note of panic went through me at the idea of her going anywhere with Uncle Bobby. "You wouldn't go anywhere without telling me or Kate first, right?" I pictured them forcing her into a truck like kidnappers, not giving her a choice. The uneasy feeling I had been trying to put to rest all week came speeding back like a freight train.

"Huh . . . uh."

"Is your granny all right? Do you need help at home?"

"Huh . . . uh." She smacked her lips, unaware of the roller coaster of emotions I was riding. "She's sleepin'."

"All right," I said, pulling up the quilt to cover her. "You get some sleep, now. I'll wake you up when it's time to go." I laid a hand on the quilt where it rested over her slim shoulder. "Dell, if you ever need anything, you know you can tell me or Kate."

She didn't answer, and I sat there hugging my knees while she slept. I tried to imagine what the night had been like in that tumbledown house on Mulberry Creek, but I couldn't. I couldn't imagine what the real truth was, and she wasn't going to tell me.

Outside, the farmhouse door slapped. Probably Ben leaving for a big meeting in St. Louis—something about bidding on a contract for the structural steel design on a big, new industrial complex. The project would keep him away for the rest of the week, so it would be just Kate and me and the kids at the farm for a few days. Suddenly, I wished he wasn't going. I felt uneasy and insecure. I wished James were back, just in case Uncle Bobby decided to come around looking for Dell.

Disturbed by the images in my head, I got up and went to the bathroom, showered, slipped on jeans and a T-shirt, then stood staring into the foggy mirror, thinking that I looked like my mother—dark eyes, dark hair, same slightly narrow lips that made my face look serious, responsible. My mother would never have sneaked off for a biopsy without telling anyone. . . .

Combing my hair back impatiently, I fished through my makeup bag for a clip, fastening it at the nape of my neck. Staring at myself in the mirror, I yanked the clip out and let my hair fall damp around my shoulders. Nothing seemed quite right. The clear spot in the mirror grew smaller, and I reached for the door handle, pulling it open to let cool air into the room. Dell was waiting on the other side, sitting on the edge of the bed with her hands folded between her knees. She came into the bathroom and took her spot on the edge of the tub, but this time she wasn't interested in trying on makeup. "When's James coming back?"

I wondered if she had read my thoughts, if she knew that I was feeling worried and lonesome and guilty. "The end of the week. Friday, it looks like." That seemed too far away. I wanted him to be here, strong and steadfast. I wanted him to analyze the queasy whirlpool of fear in my stomach and tell me there was no reason for it. If I told him about the biopsy, would he be that rational?

Beside me, Dell picked at her fingernails, looking worried. "He said he was gonna be back tomorrow."

I was surprised she remembered that. It was the reason I'd originally told Dr. Schmidt I'd come in on Monday—to get the procedure over with before James came back. Then it would only be a matter of waiting a few days for the lab results. "I know, but he had to take some trips from another pilot who was sick, so that changed his schedule this week. So far, he hasn't even been able to get back to Boston to check on the loft. He said to tell you that no matter what, he'll be here Friday for dress rehearsal night, and if he isn't able to bring the guitar for you, he'll mail it as soon as he gets back home."

" 'K." She seemed disappointed. I couldn't tell if it was about the guitar or about James not coming yet.

"Let's go in and have some breakfast with Kate," I suggested, trying to lighten the mood. "It's just us girls this morning."

"And Joshua," she reminded me as we left the bathroom.

"And Joshua." I chuckled. We walked out, and Dell trotted ahead to the farmhouse. I took my time, strolling the long way through Grandma's flower beds, enjoying the menagerie of blooming iris and early roses. Grandma would have been pleased with Kate's upkeep of the flower beds.

207 · *The Language of Sycamores*

I thought about Dell's claim that Grandma Rose had mentioned Sadie Walker in a dream. *Do you think Sadie Walker was somebody famous?* Why would Dell ask that? What in the world would give her that idea?

What if Sadie *was* famous?

An idea lit in my mind, and I hurried to the house, calling out to Kate as I rushed in the door. "Kate, do you have Internet service out here yet?"

Kate frowned apologetically as she set cereal and milk on the table. "Well . . . yes and no. It's a really slow, sort of . . . Stone Age Internet service, but Ben keeps his old computer up in the pink bedroom. If he has anything serious to do, though, he logs on at the church office or at his office in Springfield."

"That's all right." Grabbing an English muffin, I headed for the stairs. "This won't take a high-powered computer."

Chapter 19

I sat down at Ben's computer and clicked the icon to log on, drumming my fingers impatiently on Joshua's Barney stickers beside the keyboard. When the computer finally made a connection, I punched up a search engine, typed in *Sadie Walker singer,* then waited, holding my breath for what seemed like forever.

The page timed out and then the computer promptly logged off the Internet with a cheerful "Good-bye."

"Darn," I grumbled, glancing at my watch. Time to go. Logging on again, I reentered Sadie's name into the search page, then sat there while the computer was hung up, a tiny electric hourglass flowing endlessly in the center of the screen. Finally, I gave up and hurried down the stairs.

"I left the computer searching for something," I said, as I whizzed through the kitchen, gathering Dell and a cup of coffee. "It probably won't find a match. I think it's hung up. Remind me later—I might be able to adjust the software to help that problem."

"That would be great." Kate stopped to hand Rose her sippy cup. "Sometimes it sits like that for five minutes, then either logs off or goes on just fine. Ben said it could be software, but hasn't had time to tinker. I'll check later and see if anything came up."

Rose waved her arms and said, "Mmm-mmm-mmm," then smiled

at me with oatmeal running down her chin. "Ba-ba, ba-ba, ba-ba!" She waved enthusiastically. Over the past week, she had come to know who I was, and every time I came into a room, she made me feel like a queen.

"Bye-bye, pretty girl," I said, and she smiled wider, cereal oozing between her baby teeth as she raised her hands and covered her eyes.

"Oh, where's Rose?" I lamented. "She disappeared. Where did she go?"

Rose giggled, squealing hysterically, but didn't come out of hiding.

"I can hear her, but I can't see her." I stomped closer, my feet echoing on the wooden floor, so that it sounded like the Jolly Green Giant was coming. "Where is she?" Leaning close to her, I smelled baby powder and oatmeal. Sweet, soft smells.

Letting out a gleeful, ear-piercing screech, Rose threw out her arms and slapped cereal-covered hands on my cheeks.

Kate and Dell burst out laughing.

Joshua squealed and pointed. "She got you! Wose got Aunt Ka-wen."

"A-a-a-ahhhh!" I screamed like a crazy lady, touching my face. "I'm melll-ting!" Grabbing a napkin, I kissed Joshua, Rose, and then Kate on the top of the head. Kate reached up and held my hand, and I stayed there for a moment with my chin resting on her hair. I had the strangest urge to confide in her about the biopsy, but I knew it would be incredibly wrong to tell her without telling James.

"It's so good to have you here." Kate's voice trembled with emotion.

"It's good to be here." Standing up, I wiped off Rose's oatmeal deposits, feeling gushy and warm like the stuff on my cheeks. "I guess we'd better get going."

Kate seemed a little embarrassed, too. It was the first time we'd shared a hug that wasn't the kiss-kiss, tap-tap kind used by foreign dignitaries and Hollywood stars, the kind that didn't mean anything.

"See you this afternoon," she said. "Maybe today we can finally make it out to see the mermaid pool and the sister sycamores." All week long we'd been trying to find time to go, but I'd been tied up with extra Jumpkids practices, or one of Kate's kids was napping, or supper needed to be cooked. We hadn't yet made it round the mountain.

"That sounds good. I definitely want to take you there before I leave." Time was running short. This was Monday. Next Monday, Jumpkids would be over, and I would be heading home. The biopsy would be behind me, and the cancer question answered.

Kate glanced away, like she didn't want to acknowledge my eventual departure. "All right. Have a good day, you two."

"See you this afternoon."

By afternoon, it was clear that I probably wouldn't make it to the mermaid pool tonight. Our first full rehearsal was looking more like an exercise in firefighting than a musical theater production. Keiler and the other counselors were showing Herculean patience as they tried to herd noisy, excited little bodies to the correct places. I had been elected director because nobody else wanted to be. Shirley usually did the job. She called from the hospital to wish us good luck, and to give me a few pointers.

"Keiler says you're really good," she said. I had a feeling Keiler hadn't really said that, and Shirley was just trying to butter me up.

"I don't know about that, but I'm doing the best I can. Right now it looks like mass chaos."

Shirley laughed. "It always does the first time you put them all together in one room. By the end of the week, you'll be surprised." She didn't say whether it would be a good surprise or a bad surprise.

"I hope so. I'm way out of my league here."

She chuckled again. "I don't know. Keiler thinks you ought to take the job full-time." For just an instant, I thought she was serious.

"Oh, no." I said it so as to make sure she knew we were only joking.

"The counselors say you're really good. . . ." She trailed off on an up note, her voice teasing. She was obviously a woman with a good sense of humor.

"Oh, *no-o-o*," I said, playfully but more emphatically. "I'm a networking consultant, not a pint-sized production manager."

"Hey, I was a thirty-two-year-old lawyer when I started with Jumpkids." She laughed. "Now I'm forty-five years old and pregnant with twins, so anything's possible."

I gave her a sympathetic groan. There was probably a good story behind her transformation from lawyer to Jumpkids director to pregnant with twins at forty-five, but I didn't have time to ask. Onstage, the zebras were running amuck. "I'd better go-o-o-oh-no. The zebras just stampeded and knocked down three wildebeests."

Shirley burst into giggles. "Sounds like things are right on schedule. Hang in there, Karen."

"I am."

"Have fun."

"I am. Take care, Shirley." Setting down Brother Baker's cordless phone, I rushed to the stage to assess the damage to the wildebeest herd.

The counselors had it fairly well under control by the time I got there. Keiler was doing a good job of straightening out the rowdy zebras.

"Somebody needs to whup John Ray's butt," Sherita said from where she was skulking on the stage stairs. "He don't listen, and he keeps takin' his tail and swingin' it at people."

Onstage, Tina was holding the tail in one hand and John Ray in the other, giving him a solid talking-to. "Looks like Tina has it figured out."

"Needs his butt whupped," Sherita grumbled, giving John Ray a murderous look. It was more interest than she'd shown in anything all week, so I decided to go with it.

"Well, we aren't going to whip anybody's butt here, Sherita, but if you'd like to offer a suggestion as to how to control the zebras, please feel free."

"They need their . . ."

"Without whipping any butts," I finished, and she curled her lip at me. I figured the conversation was finished.

"Take their tails off," she said after glaring at the zebras for a minute.

"They have to learn to work with the tails on." Although at the moment, collecting the tails was a tempting thought.

Sherita huffed. "Take John Ray's tail off. Nobody's gonna notice

212 · LISA WINGATE

that. If he ain't gonna behave with it, take it off, and he'll just be a zebra without a tail."

Turning slowly, I pointed a finger at her, trying not to seem too pleased lest she realize she'd accidentally said something constructive, and pull back into her shell. "That's not a bad idea." Stepping onto the stage, I waved at Tina. "Tina, take John Ray's tail off for now." The kids stopped what they were doing and looked at me. A zebra with no tail? What was Miss K thinking? I gave them my best poker face. "A few tails seem to be misbehaving this morning. If any of you are having a problem with your tails swinging around in circles or swatting other people, please raise your hand." There was suddenly a mass dropping of tails, all hands went still, and the room became silent. I felt . . . pleased with myself. "All right, then let's try the opening number again. Any tails caught swinging around will be confiscated and returned to you tomorrow." I stepped off the stage as the kids moved to their places. I'd never seen a group of little bottoms so still.

"Good job, Sherita," I muttered as we waited for the music to cue up.

Sherita crossed her arms and stood up, trying not to look pleased or involved or interested. Leaning against the wall next to me, she tapped her toe as the first notes of music came on and *"Nants ingonyama!"* blared through the auditorium while the monkey medicine man lifted our fake baby Lion King high into the air.

"The baby lion looks stupid," Sherita groused, loud enough for the nearby giraffes to hear. "It's supposed to be a real baby. I read the script."

"We don't have a real baby." Lord, all we needed now was a baby to manage on top of everything else. Although Sherita did have a point. The stuffed one didn't lend much drama to the opening scene.

"Myrone could do it. I could bring him with me tomorrow. I'll watch him real good so he don't mess with anything. We could dress him up and put whiskers and a nose on him." It was more than Sherita had said all week. Suddenly, she looked enthusiastic. She had sparkle.

Unfortunately, there was no way we could keep up with a toddler for the next five days. I shook my head and she crossed her arms again, shoving herself against the wall.

"I'll tell you what," I heard myself say. What was I doing? "Why don't you and Meleka practice with him at home this week, and then bring him on Thursday and we'll try it with the whole group." She straightened, standing away from the wall, her bright hazel-gray eyes searching my face. She wasn't sure if I meant it. She was waiting for the catch, the letdown. The usual rejection. "You don't think he'll be afraid to be out there with all the people and the costumes?"

She gave a confident chin bob. "He ain't afraid of anything."

"Good." *I hope it's good. I might be having a moment of* Lion King *insanity.* "Why don't you take the mother lion's part so you'll be all set when Myrone comes? Kimmy's mom called this morning, and she has the stomach flu. She might be back by the Friday dress rehearsal, and she might not."

"O.K.," she said, and marched onto the stage to show them all how it was done. Despite the fact that she hadn't practiced all week, she was the best one in the group. Dell was right—Sherita knew the production backward and forward.

The church's cordless phone rang at my seat just as the first number was finishing. No one picked up in the church office, so I answered.

Kate was on the other end. "Well, hi there," she said. "I didn't expect you to answer this number. I tried your cell phone, but it just gave me your voice mail, and, by the way, your voice mail is full."

"Huh," I replied. I hadn't had any voice mail all week, and it hadn't even occurred to me to wonder why. That in itself was an anomaly for me. Normally, I couldn't live a day without voice mail. "I haven't been keeping the cell phone on. I guess the voice mail has piled up, but for some reason it's not showing up on the screen. So what's up? Did you need something?"

"Your Internet search turned up a clue." Her voice rose and she stretched the last word with unmistakable excitement. "The search engine found a link to an article from a little St. Louis arts newspaper. It's called 'Eighty Years of Jazz,' and it's about a woman named Sadie Broshier, who was a dancer and a jazz singer back in the twenties and thirties, and up through World War II. The article is about her marrying an old gent named Broshier in some retirement home in St. Louis, but it also talks quite a bit about her life and the things she did—

entertaining in the USO and whatnot. I can't find anyplace where it says Sadie Walker, and the article doesn't mention where she was originally from, but it came up on your search. Do you think it could be our Sadie? The article was written seven years ago, and it says she was eighty-two at the time. That wouldn't really be old enough to be our Sadie, but it could be a misprint."

I thought about that for a minute, trying to decide whether to get my hopes up. I was surprisingly emotionally invested, and obviously Kate was, too. "I don't know. She wouldn't be the first woman to lie about her age." A memory trickled through my mind, and I chuckled. "Grandma Rose used to do that sometimes, remember? Of course, she was usually bumping it up so people would make a big deal about what good shape she was in for her age. Remember the time the church contacted us about having a big eightieth birthday party for her, and she was only seventy-seven?"

Kate laughed. "I had forgotten about that." Rose fussed in the background, and Kate hurried to wind up the conversation. "Well, anyway, I tried to get in touch with the newspaper that had the article, but it doesn't exist anymore. I e-mailed the article to Ben and asked if maybe he could check into it while he's in St. Louis this week. The retirement home wouldn't give me any information over the phone, but if Ben goes there in person, maybe . . ."

"That sounds good." I wondered, suddenly, why she had called instead of waiting until tonight to tell me all this. She hung on the phone like there was more to say. I could hear her moving around, trying to quiet Rose. "Anything else?" Onstage, Dell was just beginning her solo in the waterfall number. She was singing quietly, so timidly I could barely hear her voice. "Dell's singing right now."

"Oh, that's good." Kate's focus seemed to be elsewhere. "Aunt Jeane's coming for our little Memorial Day family gathering."

"That'll be fun. We haven't gotten to visit in a while." I watched as Tina stopped Dell, then leaned down to whisper in her ear. Dell nodded, pressed her lips into a determined line, and straightened her body with a deep breath. When she started to sing again, her voice rang through the sanctuary, pure and sweet and perfect.

"Dad's coming for Memorial Day, too," Kate said, then she sucked in a breath like she was waiting for a bomb to explode.

"O.K.," I heard myself reply, and I suddenly knew I didn't care. I didn't care if Attila the Hun was coming to our family gathering. All I cared about was that Dell, who had been so shy a few days ago that she wouldn't even raise her head and talk to people, was onstage, singing. She hit a long, high note, head falling back, eyes closing, dark hair tumbling around her, arms unfolding into the air, stretching out like wings.

Tears filled my eyes, and I realized I was on my feet. "Listen to this!" I said into the phone, then held it in the air.

At that moment, Dell looked like she could fly.

I barely remembered saying good-bye to Kate. All I could think about when Dell finished her song was getting to the stage to give her a hug. I nearly trampled three gazelles on my way. I was dimly aware that I was interrupting the performance, showing favoritism, and I probably looked ridiculous dashing across the set with my arms flailing at my sides, squealing, "That was great! That was great!"

Dell launched into my arms with a force that knocked me back, and we tumbled onto the floor, landing among the warthogs, who, as warthogs will do, jumped on top of us and created a pig pile.

Pinned underneath the mass of squirming, giggling bodies, I closed my eyes and laughed until I ached, tickling feet and kissing little body parts. It was a moment I knew I would never forget. A moment of the pure and complete joy of childhood.

"This looks more like a scene from *Hair*," Keiler joked from somewhere overhead when the frenzy died down and the warthogs lay exhausted.

"It feels like a visit to the chiropractor."

The kids slowly unpiled, leaving Dell and me to disentangle ourselves and get up. I gave her one more quick hug, and then Keiler called for everyone to hit their marks for the next number. The kids bounded into place with only a modicum of pushing, shoving, and tail swinging. I went back to my place offstage, and Mojo Joe clapped his hands, saying, "Positions, everybody. Positions. Hold it! Where is the rotten log with the gummy bugs in it? We need the rotten log for this one!"

The set crew appeared with the rotten log, which looked suspiciously like an old packing barrel covered with brown paper, and the show went on.

By lunchtime, we had more or less made it through every number. The kids were tired but surprisingly cheerful as they split into core groups for lunch, after which they would spend the rest of the day working on their specific parts. I sprung the news on Keiler that I had an appointment in town and would be gone over lunch, and probably for a half hour or so after that.

He didn't ask any questions, just said, "Take your time. I'll hold down the fort," then continued to the lunchroom with the kids.

I went to Brother Baker's office and took my purse from the closet, searching for an ibuprofen. It had been a great but very noisy morning. I wished James could have been there to see it. He would have been so proud of Dell, and so amazed at how much the kids had accomplished in the week since he left. He would have been astounded to see Sherita perfectly dancing the part of the mother lion.

He would also have been asking why I had an appointment in town, and I wouldn't have had an answer. All the same, I wanted to talk to him, just to hear his voice for a minute before I left. Grabbing my cell phone, I clicked it on, hoping to catch him between flights and deliver an early update on the morning's practice. He'd surprised me by calling the farm almost every evening to see how things were going. It felt good to be interested in something together, even if our conversations were littered with undertones about heading home and tending to the business of unemployment.

When I told him my father was coming for Memorial Day, he would really be worried. He knew that mixing Dad and me was like combining baking soda and vinegar—it was bound to foam up into a mess. We always ended up hashing over the past, who was right, who was wrong, whose fault things were. We never solved anything, which was why I avoided visits with my father. When he heard about my job layoff and the fact that I'd stayed for two weeks at the farm instead of rushing back to pound the pavement in Boston, he'd be all over the issue like a dog on a fresh steak.

James would never believe me when I said I absolutely didn't care. I wasn't interested in dissecting the past or the present with my father anymore. Dad was Dad and I was me. I was all grown up. And that was that. *Hakuna Matata*, as they say in *The Lion King*. No worries.

James would think I'd lost my mind, been possessed by some alter-Karen, who could forgive and forget and accept the fact that nobody's perfect.

The cell phone rang, and I pressed the button without even looking at the screen.

"Hello?" I said, expecting to hear James.

"Where the *bleep* have you been?" It wasn't James. My mind rocketed back to my old reality. It was Brent Giani, from Systems at Lansing Tech.

"Brent?" It seemed like a year, not just a little over a week, since I'd talked to him. "Hey. How are you? How are things there?"

He barely waited for me to finish the sentence. *"Where* are *you?"* He sounded irked, which was unusual. Normally, Brent just slouched and shuffled along in his rumpled khakis and his plaid shirts, moving at his own relaxed pace. He didn't get excited unless the system was down.

"Well, I'm . . ." A line of kids went by in the hall, squealing and making animal sounds, drowning out what I was going to say.

"What was *that*?" he demanded, like he couldn't imagine.

Probably, he couldn't. "Kids making animal sounds." I knew that would really confuse him, so I added, "I'm in Missouri . . . for a . . . visit. Since I didn't have anything *else* to do this week." The bitterness in my voice surprised me. I'd hardly thought about Lansing all week. I hadn't had time. Talking to Brent brought it all back. "How goes it on the *Titanic*?"

Brent didn't laugh, which made me wonder again what was going on. Usually, he was right there with a sarcastic response. "Listen, there's a lot going on. We've been trying to get in touch with you for a week."

"We . . . who?" I stumbled backward, feeling for the side of the desk and sitting down. "What's going on?"

He paused, and the moment seemed to stretch out forever.

"Brent, what's going on?" I pressed, suddenly back in the reality of Lansing and corporate treachery.

When he answered, his voice was lowered. "Some of us are"—another pause, and then—"getting something together. We've got a plan, and we want you in."

I tried to imagine what he meant. "A plan to do what, exactly?"

"Well, let's just say I intercepted a memo last week between Vandever and his henchmen. On the day after Memorial weekend, Lansing is going to send out a memo to our custom-network accounts telling them we're no longer offering custom-network services, and referring them to a third-party vendor. Care to guess who owns the third-party vendor?"

I gasped, everything suddenly clarifying like the pieces of a puzzle falling together—the closing of my department, the quick layoffs of everyone in Custom Networks. It wasn't just a cost-cutting measure. It was part of a plan. "No. You're kidding. Vandever and his bunch own it, don't they? They shut down my department, and now they're going to send the business over to their own little company." My skin went flush and perspiration beaded up on my back, dripping slowly downward in hot streams.

"Ex-actly. Now it makes sense that they're closing down a profitable department and leaving other departments untouched, doesn't it? They're taking this company apart like a junk car, keeping the good pieces for themselves."

"They can't do that!" I fumed, my indignation reverberating through the office. "That's illegal."

Brent groaned. "Technically, who knows? Anyway, it isn't going to matter because we're going to beat them to it."

"How?" My mind revved like a dragster about to take off. "What do you have planned?"

A mad-scientist giggle trickled through the phone. "Heh-heh-heh-heh. Well, say a certain someone had the customer list and sent out a memo to all the customers that same day, offering them the services of a new start-up custom-networking company run by the very people who built their networks in the first place. Wouldn't the customers find that more attractive than using a third-party vendor they've never heard of?"

"Of course they would." The picture crystallized, and I stood there in awe of the possibility. "It's perfect. It's brilliant. We steal back the business Vandever stole from us, and right out from under his nose. Oh, my gosh, that's priceless!" The sweet essence of revenge spiraled through me like wine, leaving me giddy and lighter than air.

"Yes, it is." Brent's voice was low, confident. "We give Vandever and his cronies what they deserve, and our new company starts out with a basis of solid accounts to build on. Almost no risk, and we go from watching the board of directors run our company down the tubes, to running our own company."

Almost no risk. That wasn't exactly true. "But there's some risk for you. You still have a job at Lansing."

"Not as of this coming Friday." He sounded almost gleeful about it. "As of Friday, I'm telling them I'm out of here for good. Next Tuesday, we start up Geo Networking Solutions."

"Geo Networking. Is that what you're calling it?" I liked the sound of the name.

"That's it. You in? We need you here to make this work, Karen."

That heady sense of revenge wafted past, and every inch of my body tingled with excitement. "I'm with you. What do I need to do?"

"Get back here as soon as you can. Yesterday, if possible." In the background, I heard him typing on his computer, and his voice took on a regular cadence that matched the keystrokes. "We're working out all the details with the lawyers this week, and we sign the articles of incorporation next Tuesday, right after the Memorial Day holiday, just in time for the memo to go out to all of our old and dear networking customers."

"I'll be . . ." As if on cue, as if it had been planned by some great, cosmic force, the hallway door opened and I heard the kids at lunch, singing one of *The Lion King* songs.

" '*Hakuna Matata* . . . it means no worries. . . .' "

"Oh, God," I muttered, feeling my breath go out in a great, deflating gust.

"What?" It sounded like Brent thumped the phone. "Are you still there?"

A groan started somewhere in my stomach and wound its way to my throat. It was the sound of being torn in half—half with the kids, and half with Brent and my coworkers. What now?

What now?

"I . . . can't . . ." What should I do? What was the right thing to do? Could I possibly leave the kids just four days before the performance they had worked so hard for? Could I leave Dell, run out on Kate and the family gathering she was counting on?

I took a deep breath, closing my eyes, searching, trying to clear my mind. *Oh, God, tell me what to do. . . .* "I can't leave until after Memorial weekend." The words came from somewhere in the darkness, and I barely even heard them before I was saying them to Brent. "I'm committed to some things here."

He coughed into the phone. "You're kidding, right?"

"No, Brent, I'm not kidding." The determination, the steadiness of my voice surprised me. Inside, my stomach was flip-flopping like a fish on shore.

Brent muttered under his breath and I heard him typing again. "Monday night," he said. "Can you catch a flight Monday night? I can e-mail you the details so you can be ready to sign with us Tuesday morning."

"All right," I heard myself say. My stomach stopped flipping and just lay like cold, silent stone. "I'll be there."

Chapter 20

The week was a strange mixture of *Lion King* rehearsals, corporate espionage, and waiting for biopsy results. I spent the mornings and early afternoons with the Jumpkids, then usually a little while with Dell, playing the church piano or just talking before I took her home. She was frustrated, I could tell. She didn't understand why we couldn't while away our afternoons wading at the river, or learning new tunes on Grandma's old piano, or sitting at the soda shop in town, as we had the first week of camp.

I explained to her that I was doing some computer work, and it was very important—not as important as Jumpkids camp, but important.

"I thought you didn't have that job anymore." She frowned, cocking her head to one side and studying me.

"This is a new job," I told her Thursday afternoon, as we sat in my car outside her house. The windows inside were dark and the TV was on—the windows were always dark and the TV was always on. "I'm starting a brand-new company with some people I work with in Boston."

"Oh." She gave me a resentful look, and for the first time ever I understood the dilemma working parents feel. On the one hand, I was excited about starting Geo Networking, so excited that even struggling along with Kate's lousy Internet service couldn't dampen my spirits. I was practically foaming at the mouth for revenge against Vandever and his cronies. I imagined their smug, unfeeling faces at the board meeting that final Friday, and then I pictured them finding out that Geo had taken the business they were plotting to steal for themselves. The anticipation of perfect justice lifted me a foot off the ground every time I thought about it.

On the other hand, there were Dell and the Jumpkids. When I was with them, I had a sense of something completely new, a warm feeling of accomplishment that came from making someone else's life better. A satisfaction of the soul.

The two were like angel and devil, at war on my shoulders with my head in between.

"Dell, is something wrong?" I looked toward the house, wondering again. All week long, Dell had been quiet and exhausted, with big, dark circles under her eyes. The only time she came alive was when she was onstage. When I asked her about it, she told me she wasn't sleeping well because she was worried about her part in the Jumpkids production. Sometimes, she gave me messages from Grandma Rose, so I knew she must be sleeping some, dreaming.

Still, I knew there were things she wasn't telling me. Uncle Bobby seemed to be out of the picture since the fight with Dell's grandmother, so I surmised that whatever was wrong at home wasn't related to his presence there.

"Huh-uh," she said, giving the front door a narrow-eyed look. Nothing wrong.

I knew if I asked to come in, she'd tell me her granny was sleeping, then she'd bolt from the car before I could follow. For me, Granny was nothing more than a large, shadowy figure occasionally moving past the window inside. Today, I couldn't see her at all.

"When's James coming home?" Dell asked, seeming a little more cheerful.

"Tomorrow morning." I couldn't wait for James to come back, either. All week, we had been talking about the plans for Geo Networking. James liked the idea of the company, but mostly he seemed relieved that I was moving back within the comfortable realm of our normal lives. Like me, he was concerned about the changes in Dell's behavior, but I suspected he thought I was exaggerating.

He'd tried to pacify me on the phone. "Well, you know, she's twelve years old. Maybe she's coming into that moody stage. Remember when Megan was twelve? She about drove her parents nuts." He laughed at the mention of his niece, who was a brilliant girl but a definite drama queen.

"True, but Megan's always been that way," I reminded him. "This seems different with Dell. It's like she's shutting down. She should be happy right now, with all of the Jumpkids excitement. But she's not. She's tired, and . . . I don't know . . . preoccupied."

"Maybe it's the pressure," he suggested, trying to put the situation neatly in a box. "This whole Jumpkids thing is way out of her normal realm. She's probably just nervous about it."

"Probably," I said, because the call-waiting was beeping. "Gotta go, hon. There's a call on the other line. Probably someone from Geo."

We said good-bye and I went back to business, but in the corner of my mind there was a nagging disquiet about Dell. I looked at her now, sitting in the car, seeming reluctant to go into the house, and I felt it again.

There was no point asking her to let me come in, so I went through Friday's schedule, even though we'd already been over it twice. "Now remember, no Jumpkids in the morning. I'll be at church with Keiler and the other counselors, finishing sound checks and getting the costumes and set ready. Your job is to sleep in, relax, get all rested up for the big dress rehearsal tomorrow night. It'll be just like a full performance. We'll have an audience and everything, so everyone needs to be in top shape, all right?"

She nodded, sucking in a quick breath and widening her eyes. " 'K."

"And no staying up late tonight." Shaking a finger at her, I did a pretty good imitation of Grandma Rose. Dell was too nervous to appreciate the joke.

" 'K."

"James or I or Kate will come by for you around four tomorrow, so there's plenty of time to get ready before the curtain at six."

" 'K." She opened the door and slid one foot out. "Is Ben gonna be there tomorrow night, too?"

"No, he won't make it home from St. Louis until Saturday." She looked slightly crestfallen, so I added, "But he'll be here for the big Saturday afternoon performance. All the cousins are coming, too, and my father and Aunt Jeane, so you'll have a whole row right there cheering you on."

She brightened noticeably. "Cool, a family row."

"That's right." I choked on an unexpected lump of emotion. "A family row."

I went home and buried myself in business for Geo so that I wouldn't have to think about Dell's family row. After the weekend, the family row would be back to just Kate and Ben and the kids. James and I would be gone, and with the demands of starting a new company, there was no telling when I would get a chance to come visit. Dell would still be living day to day in the little house across the river, where Granny stayed closeted from the outside world, and Uncle Bobby might show up any minute. Dell would come over to Kate's when she could, looking for attention and love, and someone to support her music. Kate would do her best, give what she had that wasn't already taken by raising two toddlers and caring for the farm. As Dell moved into puberty and her teenage years, would that be enough?

After next week, the Jumpkids crew would pack up and move to another town—Goshen, Missouri, I think Keiler had said. They would set up again and lead a new group of kids through the steps of *The Lion King,* down the path to finding themselves. When summer was over, the counselors would go back to college. Keiler would head for the mountains to become a wandering musician, or else to seminary school. The Jumpkids winter program would continue under a new director, when they finally found someone who'd take on such a demanding job for the salary of only twenty-nine thousand dollars a year.

Life in Missouri would go on just as if I'd never been here at all.

And in Boston, life would go on for James and me. Any day now, Dr. Schmidt would have the results of my biopsy. He'd assure me that everything was all right, and I could put the trauma behind me. Realistically, I'd never need to tell James about the irregular test result at all. The matter would soon be settled, and there would be no more big question marks looming in our future.

It was a comforting theory, but I didn't feel comforted as I went to bed Thursday night. I felt like I was lying to James by trying to protect him from the cancer question. I felt out of place, and I wasn't sure why, because in my mind I had everything planned out: help Kate tomorrow morning with preparations for the weekend guests, go to the church around noon to meet Keiler and the other counselors, finish preparations for the program. James would be in at three. Pick up Dell at four. Get the cast ready for dress rehearsal to begin at six. Perform, go home, and sleep; meet long-lost relatives Saturday morning, assemble family row for the final Jumpkids performance Saturday afternoon, visit with company Sunday, say good-bye to everyone Monday. Leave. Somewhere in the schedule, receive a call from Dr. Schmidt delivering a negative biopsy result.

It all made perfect sense, yet I couldn't squelch the feeling that things wouldn't work out that way. The disturbing sense of something about to go wrong buzzed around my head like a fly, and I tossed and turned all night. I was on edge all morning while helping Kate with the housework. Kate noticed and asked if anything was wrong. I passed it off as opening-day jitters.

"I hope Dell's doing all right," Kate mused as we worked in the kitchen. "I know she must be nervous. She's never done anything like this."

"I told her to stay home and get a good night's sleep," I said. "She's been really tired all week."

"I noticed that. I asked her if there was something wrong at home."

"So did I. She said no, of course."

Kate nodded, frowning toward the kitchen door, as if she wished Dell would show up. There was no sign of her, so both of us went back to work. I was glad when it was time for me to head for the church. The house was too quiet, and I was thinking far too much about the biopsy result. Was that the thing that was about to go wrong? Was some lab technician, even now, holding my future in latex-encased hands, thinking, *This poor woman—this will be a shock. . . .*

When I arrived at the church, I was swept into a frenzy of activity that made me forget about everything. It seemed like only a few minutes passed before it was three o'clock and James was walking in the door. Onstage, we were in the middle of a disaster involving moving clouds and confetti raindrops. Fortunately James jumped in and helped us finish with the set.

"Guess next week will be a picnic compared to this one," he joked as we arranged paper boulders around a waterfall made of Saran Wrap and shiny foil gift paper.

"Oh, no doubt." Both of us knew that next week would be no picnic. It would be fast paced and stress filled. In a way, I wasn't looking forward to that. *You've turned soft over the past couple of weeks,* I told myself. *Need to get back in the game . . .*

James must have sensed the inner dialogue, because he cocked his head back and slanted a questioning glance. "Something wrong? You look . . . different. . . . I don't know, nervous or something."

Smiling, I gave him a belated hello kiss. Our typical kiss, not the kind of romantic, passionate one we had parted with a week ago. He noticed the difference.

"Just opening-night jitters," I said.

He nodded at the explanation. It was easy, logical. He was quick to accept it. A twinge of disappointment went through me. I wanted him to ask what was *really* wrong. But then, I didn't want to tell him.

The back door opened, and Sherita and Meleka came in with Myrone in tow.

"We thought we better come on," Sherita said, trying to conceal a case of real, live enthusiasm. "We didn't wanna be late."

Meleka vibrated in place, then spun around and dashed toward the hallway door, hollering, "I'm gonna go help Mindy." Over the course of the week, she and Mindy had built a strong friendship.

Myrone pointed at Rafiki's tree, which was standing in the corner of the set, waiting to be brought out later. "Twee, twee, twee!" he squealed, and then pointed at the waterfall, "Wooo, wa-wa!"

"Oh, good," I said, glancing over my shoulder at Keiler. "He can tell it's water."

"He ain't dumb," Sherita groused, but she was smiling slightly as she said it. Her bright eyes cut my way for just an instant as she walked down the aisle carrying Myrone. "We're gonna go practice his part." Pausing at the door, she glanced back at me and said, "O.K.?"

"O.K.," I replied. "Yesterday, he was a wonderful baby lion."

Sherita bounced him up and down roughly, looking pleased. "What's a baby lion say, Myrone?"

"Raaarrrr!" Myrone squinted, showing a mouthful of teeth.

"That's right." Sherita turned and started through the door. "And don't mess up today, either."

When they were gone, James glanced around the sanctuary, seeming puzzled. "Where's Dell? I figured she would be here with you. It's you girls' big day."

"I told her to stay home and rest up for tonight." I checked my watch. Four o'clock. "But it's just about time to go get her. Can you go? We've got so much to do here yet, and Kate hasn't shown up. She's probably busy getting the house ready for company tomorrow."

James stood back, clicked his heels together, and saluted me military style. "Ya-vold, Herr General." He sounded like Sergeant Schultz on *Hogan's Heroes*. I had a feeling he was making light of my pointing and ordering the college kids around, but somebody had to instruct them. They were all so nervous, they were practically nonfunctional. I couldn't imagine how they were going to get through next week's Jump-kids camp in Goshen. They were a bunch of free spirits, which made them good at the artistic part of this job and not good at the organizational part.

"Very funny." I was a little sharper than I meant to be. "Sorry." Nervous perspiration beaded on my forehead, and I wiped it away.

"It's all right," he said, obviously disappointed to see me acting like the old humorless Karen. "Relax, Karen. It'll be O.K."

Closing my eyes a minute, I tried to catch a breath. "I can't relax," I admitted. "With the Geo thing and this." I waved a hand vaguely toward the stage. "And I'm worried about Dell." Not to mention the biopsy results. "It's too much at once, that's all."

He kissed me sympathetically on the forehead. "Well, next week, all you'll have to think about is Geo." I knew he said that as an encouragement, but it fell to the pit of my stomach like a rock.

I felt ragged, close to tears. Afraid to speak, I nodded.

"I'll go get Dell." He turned around and left.

Clutching my clipboard to my chest, I sank against the wall. *Get it together, Karen.* What was wrong with me? I felt like I was standing on a live electrical wire and couldn't get off.

Something crashed onstage, jolting me to life. One of the branches of Rafiki's tree had fallen off, and Keiler was desperately trying to keep the now-lopsided structure from toppling over.

"Oh-oh-oh-oh!" I squealed and rushed onto the stage. "Somebody get a hammer!"

In the wings, Sherita was dragging a reluctant Myrone by the arm, saying, "Myrone, I'm gonna whup your butt. I told you to stay with me."

Myrone didn't hear her. He was busy singing a chorus of "Climb da twee, climb da twee!" And then a lion roar or two. "Rrraaarrrr! Rrraaarrrr!"

Keiler and I burst into laughter. "It's always unpredictable," he said, straining to push the tree back into place.

"Yes, it is," I agreed. "That's what I love about it." I hadn't admitted that to anyone, not even to myself. In spite of all the chaos, I loved this. I loved seeing the set come together, watching the production develop, hearing the music and singing. I loved watching kids like Sherita find inner joy and develop a hope that the world had something good to offer. "Maybe I'll come back next summer."

"Maybe I will, too," Keiler said as we held the tree in place while Mojo Joe nailed the branch back on.

Mojo wasn't very good with a hammer. "Hey, I'm an ar-tiste, not a lumberjack," he said in a stage voice with a heavy lisp. The three of us cracked up.

We were standing back, laughing and looking at the lopsided tree, when the back door burst open and James rushed in, his face ashen and his movements quick and angular.

"Where's Dell?" he said as he ran down the aisle. "Is she here? Did her grandmother bring her in? There's nobody at the house. No lights on. Nothing."

229 · The Language of Sycamores

"Are you sure they're not just asleep?" I asked, slowly working up to his level of panic. It wasn't like James to panic.

"I checked inside. There's nobody there. The dog was tied up in the yard with no food and water. It looks like they've been gone a while."

"They don't have a car. Where could they go?" A cacophony of terrible images ran through my mind—images of Uncle Bobby coming to take Dell away someplace where we would never see her again.

"We gotta find Dell." Mojo Joe braced his hands petulantly on his hips. "She's my main girl. She cain't be gone the night of dress rehearsal." He didn't realize that, at the moment, dress rehearsal was the least of our worries. I knew there was no way Dell would miss dress rehearsal—unless something terrible had happened.

"Go see if Brother Baker knows anything," I said to Keiler. "I'm going to go call Kate. Maybe she picked up Dell and her grandmother, or knows who did." *But if someone had picked Dell up, they would be here by now. . . .*

James turned and headed for the door. "I'm going back and talk to a couple of their neighbors. Maybe they know what's happened."

"Maybe," I said, the word a thin, fragile thread of hope.

For the next hour, we searched frantically for Dell. The cast members began arriving one and two at a time until they were all there, getting in costume, completing last-minute run-throughs of their parts.

My hopes sank. If Dell was anywhere in the vicinity, she would have been with us, even if she had to walk. There was no way she would miss her first big show.

James called on my cell to tell us that the neighbors said an ambulance had gone down Mulberry Road in the middle of the night. They didn't know where it stopped. James had talked to Kate, and she remembered that Dell had disappeared once before when her grandmother was suddenly taken to the hospital.

"Kate says she gave Dell strict instructions to call if that ever happened again." James sounded worried and puzzled. "Kate told her to call collect, call the cell phone, anything, just let them know where she was and if she needed help."

"Then where *is* she?" My stomach swirled and I felt sick. If she wasn't calling, it was because she couldn't.

James groaned under his breath, as if he felt things spiraling out of control and the flight captain in him was trying to keep a cool head. "I don't know. I'm on my way into town. I'll be there in a minute."

We hung up, and I walked to the stage, where the kids were taking their places to do a quick rehearsal of the battle scene between the good lions and the evil lions.

Mojo Joe squatted on the edge of the stage with his hands outstretched, palms up. "Where's Dell? Where's my girl? I need her for this scene."

"We can't find her." My throat tightened. "We don't know." I swallowed hard, pressing my fingers to my lips to keep them from trembling. "Have Sherita stand in for now. She knows Dell's part."

Joe looked as crestfallen as I felt. Nodding, he stood up and waved toward Sherita. "Sherita, hon, come here. I need you to stand in for Dell's part for now."

Sherita handed Myrone off to Brother Baker, then walked to the middle of the stage and looked around the sanctuary. "Where's Dell?" She gave me a peeved sneer. "The little Indian girl chicken out?"

"We don't *know* where she is," I replied harshly, not in the mood for Sherita's attitude. "There's no one at her house. The neighbors said there may have been an ambulance there last night. That's all we know."

Realizing the seriousness of the situation, Sherita jerked back. Her eyes met mine for just an instant, with a sympathy and understanding that surprised me. "I'll stand in. I know her part." She headed for Dell's mark, then turned back. "Ya know, when Ma'am Beans had her stroke—that was the foster mom before this las' one—they sent us to that Debuke House foster shelter over by Cainey Creek. Maybe Dell's there. That's where kids get sent when there's an emergency, if they ain't got family." She shrugged noncommittally, then continued on to Dell's mark. "But I hope she ain't there. That's a bad, bad place."

I met Brother Baker at the bottom of the stairs. "Do you think she could be there?"

"I don't know." He handed Myrone to me. "But I'll call and check. I know the director there. We donate bears for their Teddybuddies program."

He disappeared through the door, and I stood there not knowing what to hope for. Seeming to sense my need for comfort, Myrone wrapped his arms around my neck, and I cradled him like a security blanket.

James came in the door, and I explained the situation to him; then we stood impatiently waiting for Brother Baker to come back. Onstage, the rehearsal continued, with Sherita doing an adept job of Dell's part.

Just as the song was ending, Brother Baker returned, his expression grim. "She's at the Debuke House emergency foster shelter. She was taken there this morning. Her grandmother had some sort of attack last night, and is in pretty bad shape. Her liver and kidneys are failing, and they don't expect that she will live very much longer. The foster shelter is trying to get in touch with Dell's uncle, but they haven't been able to contact him, and—"

"We can't let him take her," I blurted. "They don't understand what he's like. There's no way he's fit to take care of a little girl."

Brother Baker nodded with the practiced calm of a man who'd been through it before. "Let me get to work on it." He glanced at the stage and then at his watch. "How long until showtime?"

"Thirty minutes," I admitted glumly, knowing that alone in a strange place, Dell was watching showtime draw closer, too.

Nodding, Brother Baker headed for the door again.

Keiler came to the edge of the stage and squatted down, then looked from me to James and back, perceiving that the news was not good. "The audience is starting to arrive. Is Dell going to be here, or are we sending Sherita on?"

"Send Sherita on. Have Meleka take Sherita's part as the mother lion," I said quietly, feeling my heart strain between excitement for the rest of the kids and an intense ache for Dell. Whatever it took, we were going to have Dell here for tomorrow's performance.

Chapter 21

J ames and I slipped through the choir door and stood in the hallway with the kids as the sanctuary filled to capacity and beyond with family members, churchgoers, and townsfolk. Everyone wanted to see whether a group of hapless college students could really turn ninety-seven children, many from the neediest families in town, into a theater group in two weeks.

The audience murmured at a low hum, admiring the set and catching occasional glimpses of costumed children peeking through the hallway door into the sanctuary. James took charge of the door, keeping things to a dull roar and protecting little fingers.

Kate came out of the church office and stopped beside me, her face knitted with worry. "Brother Baker's been on the phone with the foster shelter and the hospital. He's trying to get Dell out of there, but basically her grandmother has to give permission, or else it has to go through the courts and the foster care system, which could take days or even weeks. Her grandmother is in and out of consciousness. It's hard to tell how much she understands."

I nodded grimly, but not without hope. Brother Baker had been known to work miracles. He had a powerful ally on his side. "Tell him James and I are ready to go get her as soon as he tells us it's all right."

Kate hesitated for a moment, taking in the crowd of expectant animal faces, all looking at me, waiting for instructions. "I could go. . . ." The sentence seemed unfinished.

"You've got Joshua and Rose by yourself tonight with Ben gone, and besides, you shouldn't go to the shelter alone—just in case her uncle Bobby shows up there." It sounded like a logical argument, but the truth was that it seemed right for James and me to go after Dell.

"I'll tell Brother Baker," Kate replied, her face giving little indication of her feelings.

Nearby, Keiler told the kids it was two minutes to showtime, and no more peeking through the door. They hushed and grew amazingly still as he brought me the director's clipboard. "Do you need me to direct, or do you want to do it?"

I looked at my determined, excited cast members, eyes shining behind their costumes—Sherita, Meleka, Myrone, Edwardo dressed as the Lion King cub, John Ray standing perfectly still among the zebras, not daring to swat anyone with his tail. How could I not come through for them now? "I'll get the first number," I whispered to Keiler. "We're still waiting for word about getting Dell from the foster shelter." I pictured Dell alone in an institutional-looking room, like a prisoner in a cell, watching the minutes tick by, and my eyes welled up. Was she wondering if we had forgotten her?

Keiler laid a hand on my shoulder and squeezed lightly. "Two minutes till showtime. Better give them their last-minute reminders."

Nodding, I wiped my eyes and surveyed our African zoo of wildebeests, giraffes, baboons, elephants, gazelles, lions, monkeys, warthogs, and zebras, who were being very good. They stood like statues while I repeated the instructions, all of which they had heard before. Hit their marks, don't run into each other, sing loudly, move near one of the hidden microphones for solos. "All of you are ready," I finished. "You were great yesterday—better than great. Don't worry about the audience. Do it just like you did yesterday when they weren't there. If you mess up or miss your mark, don't get upset and don't start to cry, just catch up as quickly as you can. This is all for fun. If I catch anyone not having fun, then I'll be mad, but other than that, I am proud of all of you. You're all very special. You're Jumpkids. Jumpkids don't give up and they don't quit. Let's get out there and show this whole town what Jumpkids are made of."

The kids raised their hands and twittered them in the air in the silent Jumpkids cheer. Beside me, Sherita raised one hand and held Myrone with the other.

After a moment, Keiler shushed them. "Most of you already know that Dell can't be here tonight, so Sherita will be stepping in for Dell. Before we go out there, why don't we take just a minute to say a prayer for Dell, so that she'll know we're thinking about her? I want you to pray so hard, she'll be able to feel us right there in the room, all right?"

The kids nodded, suddenly solemn, and all of us bowed our heads. Throughout the hallway, small voices muttered simple prayers.

"Please," I heard myself whisper. "Please, God . . ." Emotion choked off the words.

"Send an angel," Sherita's voice finished softly. A hand slipped into mine, and I realized it was hers. I felt a peace that surpassed understanding.

"Yes," was all I could say. I imagined Dell in a room filled with angels. No longer alone and afraid.

Keiler ended the prayer by asking for the success of the performance and the safety of the performers. In the auditorium, the drum chant cued up, and Keiler pushed open the stage door, so that the hallway flooded with sound.

"Hit your marks!" I said, and the stampede began—in a quiet, orderly sort of way. I followed them up the stairs and stood in the wings as they moved into the opening number. Onstage, the monkey medicine man took Myrone from Meleka's lap, carrying him slowly to the front of the stage, then thrusting him high in the air just as the speakers blared *"Nants ingonyama!"*

Onstage, the animals began to dance in a symphony of sound and motion that was filled with energy and pure joy.

It was, I was sure, a moment I would remember forever. I was filled to overflowing with wonder, as if every empty part of me were suddenly complete, every yearning answered. It was like nothing I had ever experienced—a moment of absolute grace.

When the song was over, the kids moved to their new marks, some of them leaving the stage as the on-tape narrator told the next part of the story.

James stuck his head in the door when the tide of kids had gone out. "Let's go. Brother Baker said we need to head for the foster shelter *now*."

I handed the clipboard to Keiler. "Wish us luck."

He hugged me quickly. "Godspeed," he whispered in my ear.

Straightening my shoulders, I turned and hurried after James.

The sounds of the performance followed us out to the parking lot and into our car. Rolling down the window, I listened as long as I could. "They're doing so well."

James smiled, his face dimly lit by the dashboard lights. "You were incredible. I think maybe you should have been a theater director or a music teacher." I had a feeling he was trying to distract me from asking about Dell and I wondered why, since we were supposed to be on our way to pick her up.

"So what did Brother Baker say? Are they going to let us take Dell?"

James winced. "Everything's pretty uncertain. Brother Baker is trying to convince the grandmother to give over temporary guardianship. The shelter faxed a form, and he headed for the hospital fifteen minutes ago. She's more afraid of Dell being in state custody than anything else, so he thinks she'll sign. Now we just hope that she's conscious when he gets there, that she really will agree, and that Uncle Bobby doesn't show up before we get this done, because"—he scratched his forehead roughly, then clamped his hand back on the wheel—"if he does, things could get complicated."

"We can't let that happen." It seemed as if the car wasn't moving fast enough along the dark ribbon of highway. I imagined Uncle Bobby arriving at the shelter before us, taking Dell away. "Hurry."

"I am." James glanced at the speedometer, which was already up to seventy-five. "It isn't going to do her any good if we get in a wreck on the way there." It sounded like something Grandma Rose would have said. For a moment, I felt her in the car with us, leaning forward in the back seat, her old black shoes pushing an invisible accelerator to the floorboard.

Closing my eyes, I leaned against the headrest, trying to breathe. "We have to get there first."

"I know."

Thoughts and ideas began to cycle rapidly through my mind, like the bits of light flashing past, entering for a moment, then disappearing through the windows. In the silence of the car, in the pounding of my heart, and the drumbeat in my ears, there was clarity. Turning toward the window, I let air rush over my face. It smelled of earth and water, new spring growth and blackberry blossoms.

Comfortable things. Things that suddenly seemed so very right. In a sudden burst of emotion, I found the meaning of life. Of my life.

"I don't want to leave." I wondered, at first, if I had said it out loud, but I felt it in my soul like something hard and solid.

"What, hon?" James seemed to be lost in his thoughts. I wondered what they were.

Taking a deep breath, I opened my eyes and sat up, very deliberately closing the window until the rush of wind whistled a mournful soprano, then disappeared. In the quiet that followed, I said it again: "I don't want to leave."

"What do you mean—on Tuesday?" he asked carefully, but his tone said that he knew I meant more than just Tuesday.

Turning slowly to look at him, I painted the picture that was forming in my mind. "No, I mean I want to stay in Missouri for good. I want to take the job as Jumpkids director in Kansas City, and I want to move there. You can fly out of Kansas City as easily as you can fly out of Boston. I want to build a weekend house on the hill above the mermaid creek. I want us to be Dell's foster parents for now—and later, if she's willing, to pursue adoption." I turned to him, slipping my hand over his, trying to communicate through touch. "We should be the ones, James. We were brought here for a reason, and this is it—her, and the others in the Jumpkids program. I feel it in a way I've never felt anything in my life." I paused, but he only sat there in shock, so I went on, desperately trying to explain. "These last two weeks have been . . . like coming alive. I've had a sense of purpose each day, a reason that involved something larger than myself, the next business deal, the next new car, or the next vacation. It's like there's a door inside me that's been closed for years, and all of a sudden it's been thrust wide open, and there's music in every part of me."

"You can play music in Boston," he said quietly. His hand, under mine, didn't move or turn over so that our fingers could intertwine in silent partnership.

"Not this music." How could I make him understand? "Not the music of the heart. In Boston, it would just be music. Time would go by, and I would go back to all the normal things. Even if we could take Dell back there with us, you know how things would be. I'd be working long hours, you'd be gone flying half of every week. We'd put her in school, and after-school programs, and theater arts programs, piano lessons, voice lessons, dance. You wouldn't have time for catfishing with her, or playing guitar on Saturday nights. The three of us would hardly ever be in the same place at the same time. That's how it would turn out for us there. If we move here, we can make a new start. Dell could go to school in Kansas City, where nobody would know her, where nobody teases her and looks down on her because of her family. She could be in a school that has music and theater, maybe even a school that focuses on the arts. She could help me with Jumpkids in the afternoons and the summers. She'd have room to grow. *We'd* have room to grow, to make a whole new life." Suddenly, the idea was clear in my mind, and I realized it had been there all along—James, Dell, me. A family.

He turned away slightly, hiding his emotions, searching the roadway ahead as if the answer might be there. *This is all too fast,* his body language said. "So you're telling me you're not happy in Boston?" Behind the words, there was an undercurrent, a wounded tone that asked, *Am I not enough, is our life together not enough?*

"It's not that," I rushed out. "It's not a case of having been happy or unhappy there. It's just that Boston feels like the past. I feel like there's something different, something new ahead for us. Like Boston was the first half of our life, and now we're moving on to the second half. The last time . . ." The words trembled, and I pressed my lips together, tightening the billowing cords of emotion, wrapping them into a ball so that I could finally say the one thing I'd never said to him or to myself. "I felt this way eight years ago when we found out we were going to have a baby—like our life was about to become something totally new, something we never predicted. I don't know if I was ready for it at the time, if I was ready to give up so much of myself, but I felt something. And when we lost the baby, we let it go and just went on with life as we knew it. I don't want to let it go this time. This time I'm ready."

"Ready?" he repeated quietly.

"Ready to embrace change, I guess. Ready to take a leap of faith and accept the possibility that I don't have to be the one in control all the time, that I'm so afraid of not being perfect, of failure, that I'm not really living. I'm so afraid of sinking that I've been standing on shore all my life with my toe in the water. We've kept each other there. We're over forty years old. We're financially stable. Why not dive in now, together, and see what happens?"

He shook his head slowly, swiveling to look at me as we stopped at a four-way. "Karen, I never in a million years thought I'd hear you say something like that. This just doesn't . . . sound like you." Brows drawing together, he wheeled a hand in the air. "I mean, what about Geo Networking? Geo is just your kind of deal. All week long, you've been talking about the plans, about how you couldn't wait to get back at Vandever and his crowd, how satisfying it was going to be to see Geo take away the business they thought they were going to steal from Lansing Tech. Now all of a sudden you've had a complete change of heart?"

Change of heart. That was a good term for it. "Yes . . . I guess I have," I said thoughtfully. We passed through the intersection, and I sat silent for a moment, examining my thoughts. "I just realized that Geo is all about revenge—at least for me, it is. I'm not looking forward to it because I'm excited about the *work.* It's the same work I've been doing for fifteen years. Same job, different name. I'm into Geo because I want to get back at Vandever and the rest of his cronies for destroying Lansing Tech. But the problem is, when the revenge is done, I'm going to be sorry I made that choice, that I gave up a chance at a new kind of work and a little girl who seems to have been made for us and us for her. This chance is never going to come along again. Shirley at Jumpkids is practically begging me to take the director's job. I know I can do it. I can be good at it. It's not much money, but who cares? We have enough money. It's time to start making a life. A real life."

He acknowledged the idea with a single nod and a contemplative stare into the darkness beyond the headlights. "Maybe," he said, letting out a long breath. "It's an awful big jump."

I held my breath. Was he was coming around, starting to see the life that was painting itself in my mind? "It's not the end of the world. It's only Missouri. Just think how much more you'll get to play with your tractor."

As usual, humor helped to defuse the tension, to bridge the gap between us.

He squinted thoughtfully, testing the idea. "That's a point in Missouri's favor."

"Absolutely." Something heavy sat atop the elation that should have been rising inside me. I knew what it was. "James . . . there's one other thing I need to tell you. Now, before we make any real decisions." I couldn't let things go any further without letting James know that there was a question in our future. "I had an appointment at Dr. Conner's office the day before I came here. . . ." How was he going to feel about this? What was he going to say? Would his fears spoil everything? "My second Pap test came back irregular, and Dr. Conner wanted to do a biopsy. It's probably nothing, but you need to know there is a possibility that . . ."

"That you have cancer again?" he finished.

"It's possible. But it's probably nothing. Dr. Conner said it's probably nothing. He just wanted to be sure, and since I wasn't going back to Boston right away, I had Dr. Schmidt do the biopsy here. I'm still waiting for the results."

"And you didn't tell me?" I could see him struggling with anger, fear, and his own past. "My God, Karen . . ."

"I'm sorry." How could I make him understand? "I just . . . I couldn't face thinking about it at first, with everything that happened at Lansing, and then I came here. Things were so good with the Jump-kids, and so relaxed between you and me. I didn't want to spoil it. I didn't want to worry you. You worry about the cancer too much. I worry about it too much. Let's face it—that's the real reason we never had a family, never made any big future plans. We're living like people on borrowed time, and we shouldn't be. We have to go ahead and . . . I don't know . . . embrace life."

Seeming shocked, he cut a glance sideways, as if he was afraid we might be tempting fate by saying "cancer" out loud.

I rushed on, because I didn't know what else to do. "But that's the thing, James. Don't you see? We can't keep letting our lives be ruled by what could go wrong. Life isn't guaranteed—we know that. This latest scare is probably nothing, but if I were to find out tomorrow that I have cancer, I'd want to be here with you and Dell, working with Jumpkids. That's what I'd want to be doing."

Slowly he turned his hand over so that our fingers interlaced. A team. A pair. "You're right," he said. "You know, you're right. It's time we got on with life."

In that moment, I was reminded of all the reasons I loved him so much. He was steady, careful, rock solid in a way that made even these fledgling ideas seem concrete. I wondered if he was analyzing the details in his mind, calculating the odds of things working out the way I wanted them to. "There's Kate and Ben to consider. They've been practically raising Dell for two years. How are they going to feel about our taking her?"

I hadn't wanted to think about how Kate would feel, and whether this would drive a wedge between us. Kate and Ben loved Dell, too. "I know Kate and Ben would take Dell in, and I know Kate would give what she can, but Kate's energy is taken up with Joshua and Rose. Dell has so many needs, and there isn't much left over for her. She feels like she should be a helpmate to Kate, rather than a kid herself. She needs time to discover who she really is, to figure out who she wants to be other than just a caretaker for her grandmother or Kate's children. She needs someone to take care of her." In my heart I knew it was meant to be, but I also knew that James had a right to make the choice on his own. "We don't have to make any big decisions right now. We can take the weekend to discuss things with Kate and Ben, and to talk to Dell.

But either way, I want to stay here and take the Jumpkids job. It just feels . . . right."

James nodded, and I sensed his thoughts melding into mine, our minds and hearts uniting into a common dream as we slowed and pulled into the parking lot of an old, rambling farmhouse with a state highway sign out front that said DEBUKE HOUSE and a tall security fence in back.

"Uncle Bobby's truck isn't here," I breathed, scanning the parking lot. "Maybe they weren't able to find him."

James surveyed the house as we exited our car. "The sooner we're out of here with Dell, the better."

Hurrying onto the porch, we rang the buzzer. An African-American woman, probably only in her midtwenties, looked out the window, then came to the door and unlocked it, allowing us into the entryway. She locked the door behind herself before saying anything.

"You must be James and Karen." She shook James's hand and then mine. "I'm Twana Stevens. Brother Baker called and said you'd be here any time."

"Is Dell here?" I rushed to say, not able to wait for polite introductions. "Is she O.K.?"

Twana flashed a friendly, understanding smile. "She's fine. She's a little upset about everything that's happened and about missing the play tonight. We haven't been able to convince her to talk much. She didn't want to come in the house. We let her sit on the back steps for a long time, but then we had to bring her inside. The sheriff called and told us to go on lockdown until we can get this thing straightened out. We've had contact from her uncle just a few minutes ago, and he is insisting on picking her up, as he is her next of kin. No word from Brother Baker yet on getting the grandmother to sign over temporary guardianship."

I swallowed the rising swirl of fear in my throat. "Can we see Dell?"

Shaking her head, Twana stepped back, motioning us toward a doorway to an office. "I'm afraid not. Our policy is to keep everyone away from the child until our psychologist can talk to her. We don't want anyone coaching the child on what to say. At Dell's age, it's very valuable to get her input." She followed us into the office. "I know it's hard, but right now we're waiting for the psychologist and for word from Reverend Baker, and, of course, for her uncle to come and present his side of the story."

James stood reluctantly in the office doorway. "There's no way we can at least tell her we're here?"

Twana shook her head. "I'm afraid not, but try not to worry. She's watching TV in a room with a staff member. She's fine."

Nervously, I sat in one of the office chairs, gazing down the hall at several closed doors and a stairway to the second floor where there were more closed doors, any one of which could have been keeping Dell from us. From somewhere not far away, I heard children's voices, but not hers. Twana offered us coffee and magazines, then left the room with an encouraging smile, closing the door behind her.

James and I sat silently in the tiny office, like patients in a doctor's exam room, wondering if we would live or die. Fifteen minutes slowly ticked by, then a half hour. In the corridor outside, we heard muffled adult voices and doors opening and closing.

Exhausted, I let my head fall into my hands, combing my fingers into my hair. "I can't stand this," I said, impatience prodding me to do something, *anything* but sit there trying to look calm. "You'd think someone could come in and tell us what's going on." I imagined Uncle Bobby leading Dell away, no one telling us until it was over. "They could be letting him take her right now. Isn't anybody going to tell us what's going on?"

James stood up, reaching for the door handle. "This is ridiculous. I'm going to see what's happening out there."

"James, don't!" I jumping out of my chair, I grabbed his arm. "We can't afford to come across as hotheaded. We have to be perfect. Our only advantage over Dell's uncle Bobby is that we're not like him."

James let out a long breath, taking his hand off the doorknob. "You're right." Instead of sitting down, he paced the small room, fiddling with pens and paper clips on the desk.

The doorknob finally turned, and James and I stood at attention, frozen. A man with a long gray mustache stepped in and pulled off his cowboy hat, introducing himself as Mick Sewell, the director of De-buke House. We shook his hand, then sat in the guest chairs while he moved behind the desk.

I held my breath, waiting to see what he would say, trying to read the answer on his face. "There is a man across the hall, grieving the impending death of his mother and weeping for love of his niece, and he cannot understand why anyone would contend his right to take custody of her." He expectantly tapped his pen on the desktop, and my body went cold. He was going to take Dell from us and give her to Uncle Bobby.

"You don't . . ." I said, but he silenced me with a wave of his hand.

"I'm not finished yet." His tone warned me not to interrupt again. "However, Brother Baker is a longtime friend of mine, and he has helped this shelter out many a time in dozens of different ways. He is trying, so far without success, to convince Dell's grandmother to sign over temporary guardianship. I have also talked to Dell, who seems very fond of you both, and very determined to participate in the Jumpkids play this weekend. Yet she cannot, or will not, give me any reason why I shouldn't send her with her uncle, pending a hearing. I have only your word and Brother Baker's that he is an unfit custodian and can't be trusted to take her home even for the weekend, pending more formal custody arrangements next week."

Anger flamed in my stomach and rushed hot into my throat. I answered before James had a chance to. "She's afraid." Lifting my hands, I pleaded for the man across the desk to understand. "Why don't you ask Bobby Jordan what he's done to her to *make* her afraid of him? Or ask him about driving to my sister's house, stumbling drunk, to pick her up, or why he calls her his little nigger girl?" My voice reverberated through the room, and I hoped Bobby Jordan heard me across the hall.

James laid a calming hand on my shoulder. "Mr. Sewell, we're very concerned that if Mr. Jordan is allowed to leave with Dell tonight, he'll take her out of state and won't bring her back for formal custody arrangements. If she goes with us this weekend, she will definitely still be here next week, and then the courts can decide what's best in the long run." He looked the older man in the eye—the confident, logical, determined pilot about to smoothly lift a 747 into the air. "We're just asking you to err on the side of caution, that's all."

The director gave James a nod of respect, then focused on me again. "I'm going to my office to check with Brother Baker again. Please wait here." He was gone from the room before we could get any indication of his thoughts.

James slid his hand down my arm, giving my fingers a squeeze and holding on. "I think that went well." He gave me a wry smile. "At this point, he ought to be afraid to tell *you* no."

I covered my face with my hands, feeling stupid. "I lost it, didn't I? You think I scared him?"

"You scared *me*."

Leaning over, I rested my head on his shoulder, closing my eyes. Getting Dell wasn't going to be as easy as just wanting it to happen. "It's such a long way from here to permanent custody. What if they don't even let her come with us temporarily? What if they let Uncle Bobby take her, or what if they keep her here? Sherita said this isn't a good place to be. Dell is so fragile already. . . ."

James stroked dark strands of hair from my face. "One thing at a time, Karen. Just relax."

I sat there watching the minutes tick by on the clock, counting them as the long hand passed eight thirty and started toward nine. Back in Hindsville, the performance, the after party, and the cleanup would be done. The Jumpkids would be heading home.

The clock was nearing nine when the door opened and Mr. Sewell stepped in again. He remained with his hand on the doorknob, even after it was closed. I wondered what that meant. "Things have changed just a bit. After your comment, I put a call in to the DMV, and it does turn out that Bobby Jordan has a record of drunk-driving offenses. And in fact, there is an outstanding warrant for his arrest in Missouri for failure to appear in court, and a parole violation in Oklahoma. The sheriff just came to take him into custody." He looked down at his notepad, concealing his feelings about the news. "In short, he is in quite a bit of trouble, and certainly in no position to assume custody of a minor child, even for the weekend. Brother Baker has conveyed this information to Dell's grandmother, and she has consented under the witness of her doctor." He glanced up, the corners of his mustache twitching as if he couldn't maintain his stern countenance any longer. "Now, if you'll step into the hall, I believe the young lady is more than ready to leave."

Letting out a gasp of joy, I jumped from my chair, hugged James, then hurried with him into the hall.

Dell was standing with Twana Stevens at the foot of the stairs.

"This girl's ready to go home and go to bed," Twana said, fondly laying a hand atop Dell's head. "She's a very lucky girl to have people who love her so much."

"We do." I opened my arms, hoping.

Twana urged Dell forward, and she came, a tentative step at first, as if she were afraid we would disappear like a mirage. Three quick steps, and she was part of our family. Somewhere inside, I knew it wouldn't be just for the weekend. It would be forever.

Chapter 22

Saturday morning dawned bright and clear. I woke in the predawn hush and couldn't remember where I was. In my dream, I'd been in a boardroom in Boston, the new Geo team on one side of the table, Vandever and the Lansing brass on the other. Tempers were high, and my heart was hammering in my throat.

Looking at Vandever I wanted to strangle him, wrap my hands around his neck and squeeze the pasty flesh. . . .

He turned to me and smiled—not his usual false, detached smile, but a real smile that reached all the way to his eyes. Blue eyes, like Grandma Rose's. "I heard a whisper in the sycamores," he said, but the voice wasn't his; it was Grandma Rose's. No one else in the room seemed to hear it. I blinked, and she was standing at the head of the table, smiling, her arms stretched out to me.

Jerking awake, I sat up in bed, looking around, trying to establish where I was and what was real. James stirred next to me, looping an arm over my waist, and everything came back, filling me with contentment. I wasn't in a boardroom in Boston. I was at the farm with James and Dell.

My heart slowed its hurried rhythm, beating in a peaceful hush that matched the morning quiet. I was home. We were home.

Sliding from under James's arm, I walked to the living room and checked on Dell lying on the couch, her dark hair cascading against the old quilt. I thought of the three of us visiting her grandmother at the hospital last night after we left Debuke House.

James and I had waited in the corridor while Dell went into her grandmother's room. Through the glass, I watched her stand a few feet from the bed. Arms crossed, head tilted slightly sideways, she studied the network of wires and tubes. She didn't speak, just stood staring at the hulking form in the bed, the face obscured by machines.

Finally, she turned and left the room, saying to us, "We should go. It's late." I took one last look at the form in the bed, wondering what Dell felt for her and what their life together had been like. Was there love? Cruelty? Neglect? Something in between? Would we ever know? The secrets were locked inside Dell, perhaps forever.

She didn't want to talk about her grandmother's condition as we left the hospital and drove home. She just stared out the window, resting her head against the seat, until she fell asleep. Watching her, I wondered how much damage the last few days had done, and how long it would take for her to come out of herself again, or if she ever would.

When we returned to the farm, we sat together on the sofa—Dell, James, and I, talking about the future. Making plans. Planning to be a family.

My eyes filled with tears as I thought about it now. Leaning down, I pulled the quilt over her sleeping form, and happiness welled up inside me, rising to my lips in a sob of pure emotion. Dell stirred beneath the covering, her brows drawing together, her full lips pursing at the sound.

Stifling the noise with my hand, I hurried to the bathroom to dress so I could go outside and clear my head. I didn't want James or Dell to find me crying on our first morning together.

Slipping into my sweats, I reached into the vanity drawer for a tissue. The box was right where I expected it to be—in the second drawer, where Grandma Rose always kept it. Curlers and hairbrushes in the top drawer, tissues in the middle drawer, towels in the bottom drawer.

I smiled to myself, feeling her in the room like a benevolent spirit. *I wish you were here*, I thought. *I wish you were here to see this.*

The Kleenex clung to the yellowed cellophane, lifting the container out of the drawer. Finally, it pulled loose and landed on the floor, scattering stray hairpins and an envelope that had been stuck to the bottom of the box. Leaning close to the mirror, I dabbed my eyes before picking up the box and then the envelope. The paper felt surprisingly cool in my hand, and I stopped to look at it, reading the name written on the back. *Karen,* it said, and I touched the handwriting, Grandma Rose's handwriting, running downhill, trembling slightly. Why would she leave something for me here, beneath the tissue box in the vanity drawer of the little house, where I might never find it?

Putting on my sweats and shoes, I slipped silently from the house, carrying the letter, testing the glue on the flap with one finger, opening it carefully. Grandma's flowers were all around me as I walked along the path. The air was filled with fragrance, clear and pure, heavy with dew not yet scattered by the morning breeze. I imagined Grandma Rose on her knees by the trellis, pulling weeds and singing "Amazing Grace" in a high, off-key voice that crackled with age.

Smiling at the memory, I sat on the iron bench. Hearing her voice in my mind as I drew the letter out of the envelope, I touched the paper but didn't unfold it. Just marveled at its existence.

A dim shadow fell across me and I glanced up, with the fleeting thought that Grandma Rose would be there, but it was Kate.

"You're up early," she said, and sat on the bench next to me.

"You too." I scooted over to give her some room.

Smiling, Kate rubbed her eyes wearily. "Rose was up early, then back down. Teething again, I think."

"Just in time for company."

She yawned, her words coming in a soft sigh. "Yeah, just in time for company. Everyone should be here by about eleven. Ben just called and said he may be a little late, but he'll arrive by lunchtime, for sure." She narrowed her eyes, giving me a frustrated look.

"Relax." I shoulder butted her, wondering if I should bring up the issue of Dell. We'd come home so late last night that we hadn't talked heart to heart. "It's going to be a great day . . . just because we're all here."

Rescuing a white rose petal from the grass, Kate sat flattening it between her fingers, studying at the intricate spray of pink at the edges. "I'm glad, you know . . . about you and Dell and James. I know I said that last night, but I want you to know I really mean it. I know this is the right thing for her." A tear slipped beneath her dark lashes and trailed down her cheek. "It's strange the way things work out." Sitting up, she wiped her face impatiently and forced a smile. "These are happy tears, I promise."

I knew the tears were born from both joy and loss. "I love you," I said, realizing how truly blessed we were to have each other. How could I have been so self-absorbed for so many years that I failed to realize what a gift my sister was?

"I love you, too," Kate blubbered, and we shared a soppy sister hug.

I forgot about the letter in my hand until I reached up to wipe my eyes.

Kate motioned to it. "What's that?"

I pointed to my name on the envelope. "It looks like a letter from Grandma Rose, but I found it in the vanity drawer, underneath the tissue box. Why would she put something there if she wanted me to have it?"

Tilting her chin to look at the handwriting, Kate shrugged. "There's no telling, Karen. Toward the end, Grandma was doing some pretty strange things—forgetting where she put stuff and forgetting things she'd done, leaving her belongings in odd places. . . ." She trailed off, leaning on the arm of the bench and resting her chin on her hand. "But I'll also tell you that during that time we had a special sort of . . . I don't know . . . spiritual connection. That time together reminded her of so many things she had forgotten about her life. It caused her to think about what really mattered, after ninety years. She wrote about those things in the little journal I sent you, and she left the book lying around for me to find. I think it was her way of getting beyond all the pride and stubbornness and old resentments that kept us apart. I think she would have wanted you to read it, too."

"I'm sorry I didn't read it," I said, turning the letter over and slipping my finger under the flap. "I just wasn't ready. It wasn't time yet."

Kate nodded like she understood.

"It's time now." I breathed the words softly, opening the letter. Four pages, folded neatly around each other. Three from a yellow stationery pad that was crusty with age, and one smaller page in the center, white parchment with watercolor wildflowers along the edge.

I held it open with the small page on top. The writing quivered like Grandma's hands, running downhill across the page.

A breeze stirred the garden around us, carrying the scent of roses as I read out loud.

> *Darling Karen,*
>
> *I cannot say how I know you will find this letter. Sometimes I just know. You'll come for the tissue box, perhaps while you are here for my funeral, or later when you come to help Kate finally clean out the little house. A memory or a hard moment will strike a tear in your eye, and you'll come for the tissue box. You will find this letter and know I am here with you.*
>
> *I feel that the end of my life is coming soon, and there are some things I have not been able to accomplish. I know you will be the one to complete these tasks for me. You are my strong one, my independent, practical girl, and you'll find a way. You always do.*
>
> *First, take care of my babies and Kate and my little Dell. When I look at her, I am ever reminded of you as a girl, and I know somehow that you and she will be special to each other. She hears the melody of the breeze and the music of the sycamores, just as you do.*
>
> *Second, live a good life. Be happy, be content, be silent. Do not waste time. Time is a limited and precious gift. Live in a way that every moment matters. Capture every thought, every scent, every note of music, every glint of sunlight on the water, every chance to help another human soul. Do not yearn, but be content with what God gives you, with who He created you to be. Find your purpose in*

life. Use your gifts. Make a life with no place for fear and no room for regret.

You will find that the only thing that will really matter in your life is the love you have for other people and the love they have for you. Money, career, anything else in life is useless without love.

There will be times when you will think "What's the use? I hate my life. Nothing is turning out the way I want it to be."

I remember when Skip was a baby and I had to stay indoors with her while Grandpa and the hired help went out into the field to work. One day when they had gone back out after lunch, I went upstairs and stood by the window to see what field they were hoeing. I stood there and actually cried because I couldn't be out there with them as I wanted to be.

Now I ask you—wasn't that silly? How thankful I should have been to have a healthy baby, a nice home, and a husband who loved me!

Just the other day, I was driving home, and I somehow looked toward the old farmhouse. I must have stopped the car and sat there for a while, looking at the upstairs window, imagining myself standing there with my baby daughter in my arms. All at once, I realized that was sixty-five years ago, and all those good times were gone in the blinking of an eye, and I'm an old lady now.

If I had it to do over again, I wouldn't shed even a single tear, standing at that window. I would hug my beautiful child, look at my home around me and the fine crop in the fields, and thank God for his wonderful gifts to me.

You have so many gifts, my dear one. Use them all to the fullest, every moment. I will be smiling down from heaven.

There is one last thing I must ask you to do for me, my practical girl. Make amends with your sister. Do not harbor the little grudges of childhood. How I wish I could deliver this message to my own dear sisters: I am sorry. Just that. I was wrong. I held a grudge when I should have forgiven. I criticized when I should have loved. Most people need love much more than they need critics. Remember that, and you will live a good life.

I Love You,
Grandma Rose

Beside me, Kate stretched out a hand and touched the letter, her brown eyes wet with tears, glittering in the amber morning sunlight. "I wish she could be here to see the family coming today."

"Me too," I said, folding the letter and putting it back in the envelope as a breeze whispered through the sycamores. "I think she is here."

Kate gazed into the treetops, standing up. "I think you're right." Her lips lifted into a slight smile. "Because I feel the need to get in there and bake apple pies. That *has* to be Grandma."

Chuckling, I climbed to my feet. "Apple pies sound perfect. I'll peel apples if you'll do the crust."

"Deal," Kate agreed. We headed inside to bake apple pies—something we had never, ever done together.

"Do you actually *know* how to bake an apple pie from scratch?" I asked as we went in the door.

Kate giggled. "No. But we can try the recipe in Grandma's box, and if that doesn't work, we'll toss the whole thing in the trash before anyone wakes up."

"Sounds like a good plan." Linking arms, we went in the door.

By the time everyone else woke up, we had apple pies with sloppily braided crusts baking in the oven. After breakfast, we tried a few more of Grandma's recipes, while James and Dell took baby Rose out for a walk. The house began to smell just the way I remembered it—thick with an aroma of dough and cinnamon and the syrupy drips that burned onto the bottom of the oven. We were just starting a batch of Grandma's banana-oatmeal cookies when Kate glanced at the clock and realized company would be arriving soon.

Joshua came wandering through the kitchen, looking for cookies, and refused to believe that there were no cookies yet, only raw dough. Hopping up and down, he moved along the edge of the counter, trying to catch glimpses into the various bowls and baking sheets, anywhere cookies might be.

"Josh, there are no cookies yet," Kate insisted, putting a tray into the oven, as he reached for a cookie sheet hanging partway off the counter. "No! Josh! Those aren't cookies, that's"—the cookie sheet toppled, just as Kate finished with—"flour!" The room filled with a white cloud, and when it cleared Josh was standing with his hands behind his back, smiling impishly like Casper the Friendly Ghost.

"Ohhh, Josh," Kate groaned, looking at the mess with an astonished, mortified, what-do-we-do-now expression.

Twisting his lips to one side, Josh rolled his eyes upward, flour clinging to his eyelashes. "It's not cookies," he observed. "It's snow. Wotsa snow."

Kate and I burst into a gale of laughter. We didn't even hear the back door open until someone said, "Oh, my gosh, what happened?"

We turned around, and Jenilee was standing there with all of her family. Kate and I looked at each other and laughed harder.

"Come . . . on . . . in," Kate coughed out.

"Jeni-wee!" Josh exclaimed, and ran across the kitchen to give her a big, white hug. He was still clinging to her legs when he noticed that there were children behind her—a boy and a girl not too much older than he—staring at him wide eyed.

Jenilee stepped aside and quickly made the introductions. "Joshua, this is my niece and nephew, Alex and Amber. You guys are cousins."

Alex and Amber gave Joshua uncertain looks, clinging to the hands of their father, a tall, dark-haired man who had Jenilee's broad smile, as he stepped forward to introduce himself. "I'm Drew Lane. This is my wife, Darla." He motioned to an attractive woman with curly brown hair, who put her hand out to shake mine and Kate's. Drew finished the introductions, motioning to a blond high school age kid. "And this is my little brother, Nate."

Kate and I gaped at Nate. He looked like Joshua all grown up and without the flour coating.

Jenilee knew what we were thinking. "I told you he and Joshua look just alike," she said, pulling a photo from her purse and handing it to Kate. "Look how much his baby pictures are like Joshua."

All of us craned to see a small boy struggling to hold up a stringer of fish; then we looked at Joshua.

Shrugging, Nate said, "I've got a better tan," with an impish grin that was exactly like Joshua's.

We laughed again, and an old woman elbowed her way from the back of the crowd, pulling an elderly man behind her. She had Grandma Rose's hawkish nose. "I guess nobody's going to introduce us." Grabbing my hand, she pumped it like she was trying to draw water from a well. "I'm your grandmother's cousin Eudora Gibson . . . I mean Jaans. This is my husband, June." She gave him an adoring look. "We're newlyweds."

June smiled, slightly embarrassed, then shook our hands good-naturedly and said, "Pleased to meet you."

Once the introductions were over, Kate surveyed the flour-covered kitchen. "I'm sorry about the mess. We just had a . . . little . . . culinary disaster. I guess we could go sit on the porch and visit. We're still waiting for everyone else to get here, and for my husband, Ben, to return from St. Louis."

Mrs. Jaans swept into the kitchen with a determined stride that rivaled Grandma Rose's. "Oh, hon, I think before we do anything, we better clean this place up."

Our first act as a family was to rescue the kitchen. By the time James and Dell came back with Rose, things were pretty much back to normal, which was a good thing, because as soon as Mrs. Jaans saw the baby, she wasn't interested in cleaning the kitchen anymore. She sat in one of the chairs playing patty-cake with Rose, while Kate, Darla, Jenilee, and I finished baking the cookies and fixing lunch, just in time for the arrival of my father's sister, Aunt Jeane, and her husband, Uncle Robert.

"Well, your father should be here any minute. He stayed with us in St. Louis last night, but he wanted to drive his own car here today," Aunt Jeane said, whisking a hand through her short gray hair as she moved efficiently into the kitchen.

Uncle Robert trailed behind her, carrying a platter of deviled eggs. "Get ready, Kate," he warned, smiling. "Your dad stopped off for supplies for another one of his junior science experiments. Something involving a wading pool, a hula hoop, glycerin, and dish soap. It'll probably be a little messy."

"Oh, that's all right," Kate said, then quickly made the introductions. Afterward, Aunt Jeane sent Uncle Robert outside to put the eggs on the picnic table. He passed my father in the doorway, and Kate ran through the introductions again as my father came in.

Once the greetings were over, we stood in uncomfortable silence. I waited for Dad to bring up the Lansing business in front of everyone. I didn't doubt that Kate had prepped him on all of that, and it would be like him to start a discussion right there in front of everyone. No doubt he couldn't wait to analyze the events and my possible culpability in the company's demise, and to point out all the ways that I hadn't quite lived up to *perfect*. He'd have things to say about my new plans for my life. He would want to expound on all the reasons why moving to Missouri and taking a twenty-six-thousand-dollar-a-year job was insanity.

I bolstered my defenses when he turned to me. A pulse pounded in my throat, like I was a kid again, standing there with my less-than-stellar report card. "Hi, Dad," I heard myself say flatly.

"Karen." His face gave no indication of his feelings. He raised his arm slightly, then put it back down, as if he were uncertain whether to hug me or shake my hand.

I wanted to reach across the space between us, but I couldn't. He moved again, as if he felt the same.

He cleared his throat. "I hear you and James have some big changes in the works."

"Yes. We do." *Here it comes,* I thought. *The lecture. Right here in front of everyone . . .*

He drew in a breath, and for the first time I could ever remember, stopped and really looked at me.

"We're ready for something new," I said, losing the awareness of anyone in the room but my father and me. "I guess we're just at that point in life where the old things don't satisfy anymore."

His lips fluttered slightly, a hint of some emotion, perhaps a bit of a smile.

Outside, there was the sound of the empty wading pool hitting the sidewalk and Joshua hollering, "Gam-paw! Gam-paw! I gonna get the water hose now. . . ."

Dad laughed, seeming relieved to have the tension broken. "Guess that's my cue." Turning away, he paused to pat me on the shoulder, then added quietly, "Your grandma Rose would be pleased."

I watched him walk out the door and take command of the water hose, filling the blue plastic wading pool, then adding soap and glycerin, while the kids, including Dell, squatted around the edge, chattering with anticipation. Stirring the concoction with a rake handle, he puffed bubbles into the air, laughing as the kids ran to chase them. He wasn't the stiff, serious, ramrod-straight man I remembered. He looked like somebody's grandpa—gray-haired, wrinkled, slightly stooped, and out of fashion in his khaki pants and plaid shirt, completely smitten by the laughter of a younger generation, not the least bit worried about decorum, the house rules, or whether he got his clothes wet.

It occurred to me that he wasn't the man I remembered. Just as life and the passage of time had rewritten me, they had rewritten him. Things could be different now, if only I would let them.

Chapter 23

❧

Ben called just before lunch to say he'd been delayed in St. Louis and couldn't make it back in time for lunch. Kate wasn't happy, considering that the whole family was there and he was the host, but she was even more concerned that he arrive in time for Dell's Jumpkids performance at two o'clock.

Letting out a frustrated sigh, she hung up the phone. "He's on the way. He promises he'll be back in time for the Jumpkids production. He'll meet us in front of the church at one thirty."

I nodded, feeling sorry for Kate. She'd worked so hard planning the get-together, and she didn't want our first family meal to take place without Ben. "It's just one lunch," I said, trying to cheer her up. "We have all weekend."

"I know," she agreed halfheartedly, gazing out the window at the lawn, where my father and Dell were helping the kids create gigantic bubbles using hula hoops. Jenilee's brother Nate fashioned a loop out of a piece of loose wire from the yard fence, dunked it in the soap, and helped baby Rose hold it up, creating a huge bubble. It floated lazily away like an overweight balloon, and Rose reached out her arms. Scooping her up, Nate flew her across the yard like an airplane so that she could pop the bubble.

"I can't believe how much he reminds me of Joshua," I commented.

I'd been staring at Nate all morning, amazed by the resemblance. "There's just no way Jenilee's mother could be adopted. It can't be a coincidence how much Joshua and Nate look alike."

Kate chewed her lip contemplatively. "I guess we may never know. Mrs. Jaans seems sure that Jenilee's grandparents lost their baby and adopted another. But you know, that was a long time ago. Maybe she's mistaken."

"Maybe so," I mused.

The old clock in the living room chimed eleven thirty, and both Kate and I glanced toward the hallway door. "We'd better get lunch on." Kate started for the refrigerator. "Dell has to be at the church by one o'clock."

"Guess we'd better get busy," I agreed, checking my watch as my stomach fluttered, then flipped over, then fluttered again with a sudden case of theater nerves. If nothing else happened according to plan today, I wanted Dell's performance to go perfectly.

We hurried to get the lunch onto trays and take it outside for the picnic. When all of us sat down, we filled the gigantic old stone table, which once had been used to feed farmhands during threshings. The air was alive with voices—the high-pitched laughter of the children, the low, raspy sounds of Mr. and Mrs. Jaans, the clear tenor of James and Jenilee's brothers as they talked cars and guitars, the slight Southern accent of Jenilee telling my father about her chemistry class. Resting my chin on my hands, I just sat listening to the conversation and the laughter, both melody and harmony blending together to create a symphony of family. At the end of the table, Dell stopped talking and looked at me, smiling slightly, her dark eyes warm and content. I knew she heard the music, too.

Beside me, Mrs. Jaans was talking about how this reminded her of the old days when they used to have big family dinners. "Our people didn't have much money, but when we got together, we could sure put on a feed. Many a time, we laid out a picnic on the riverbank, and all us kids swam in the river. The men went upstream and fished, and our mamas sat on the shore and hung their feet in the water." She smiled, her cloudy eyes twinkling above plump, flushed cheeks. "Those were sure enough good times."

Beside her, Mr. Jaans laid his hand over hers. "So are these," he said, and they exchanged a quick kiss.

Nate stood up and snatched the last deviled egg off the platter, where Mr. Jaans had been guarding it. "No PDA," he chided.

Mr. Jaans waved a fork threateningly, watching his egg disappear into Nate's mouth. "You're just sayin' that because you don't have a pretty girl on your arm."

Nate laughed and shook his head.

Mr. Jaans waved the fork at Nate. "I could give ya some pointers, young fella—maybe help you out a bit."

Elbowing her husband, Mrs. Jaans blushed. "Don't you dare, June Jaans. You had too many girls in your day."

James gave me a mischievous look, then turned to Mr. Jaans and said, "That sounds like a story."

"Don't get him started talking about the old days." Mrs. Jaans swatted a hand in the air, batting the question away like a fly. "He was a saxophone player in a jazz band, and he knew a few words of French he learned from his mama, and that was all it took to catch the girls' fancy." She paused, gazing off into the distance, lost in a memory, then said, "I sure wish I could tell y'all more about your grandma Rose and her sisters, though. You know, the family fell on hard times when Sadie was about sixteen. Rose was a couple years younger, and Augustine only about ten then. Their papa fell off a roof and broke a hip, they lost their little crop farm, and they was forced to move into town. Wasn't too long after that Rose hired out as a mother's helper so as to feed the family—there were three brothers younger than Augustine, one of them not much more than a baby. Right about that time, Sadie left home. Nobody ever wanted to talk about why, but rumor was that she run off with a traveling cabaret show. Just up and left without a word to anyone. It was more shame than their poor mama could bear. She'd always had 'spells,' but after Sadie run off, she had a nervous breakdown and had to go to an asylum. After that, no one ever mentioned Sadie's name again."

Kate sighed. "I wish I'd known to ask Grandma Rose about it, but she never talked about her sisters."

Aunt Jeane frowned thoughtfully. "The family feud was one of those taboo subjects with Mother. She didn't want questions about her family and she made that clear, so we didn't ask."

My father nodded in solemn agreement. "If Mother wanted something a certain way, that was the way it was going to be. You knew better than to ask questions."

"Suppose she had her reasons." Mr. Jaans held his wife's hand on one side and Jenilee's hand on the other. "It don't matter what happened in the past. The important thing is that we're all together now."

Drew ruffled his sister's hair fondly, glancing up just in time to see his son sneak a cookie from the platter. "Alex, you leave those cookies alone until after you've finished your sandwich."

Mrs. Jaans scoffed, pushing the cookie plate closer to the kids. "Oh, let him have a cookie. It's a special occasion." She smiled at Alex. "Here, Sweet, have a cookie. They're good for ya. Got bananas in 'em."

Alex was only too happy to oblige.

Kate and I ducked our heads and chuckled, glancing at each other. "Who does that remind you of?" Kate muttered under her breath.

"Grandma Rose," I mouthed.

Aunt Jeane caught my reply and smiled, then lifted the cookie platter and held it above the table. "Cookies all around. They won't be nearly as good tomorrow." It was exactly the kind of thing Grandma Rose would have said.

Joshua grabbed a cookie and examined it carefully. Scratching a streak of unmixed flour with his fingernail, he studied his fingertip with his eyes crossed. "I found snow!" He showed his discovery to Alex and Amber, who gave him confused looks, then began examining their own cookies for snow.

Kate shrugged sheepishly at me. "Guess we'd better mix the dough better next time."

"Guess so, but they're not bad for a first effort." Glancing at my watch, I realized it was twelve thirty. "Dell, I guess we'd better take off if you're going to be at the church on time for Jumpkids."

" 'K." Dell nodded, grabbing a couple of cookies to go. "Is James gonna come with us?" She gave him a beseeching look.

"Wouldn't miss it." James slid from under the table, and the three of us said our good-byes, then headed for town.

By the time we reached the church, the counselors were already at work and the performers were starting to arrive. I opened my door to get out of the car, but in the backseat, Dell didn't move. She sat watching Sherita carrying Myrone upside down, while he hugged his sister's knee, squealing with glee. Or else he was holding on for dear life; it was hard to tell.

"We'd better go in," I said to Dell.

Tipping her head to one side, she studied Sherita thoughtfully. "Did Sherita do good last night?"

"I didn't see too much, but Keiler called and said that she did very well. Why?"

"Maybe she oughta do my part again tonight," Dell rushed out, as if she had been thinking about it on the way to town. "I don't think I oughta do it. I didn't get to practice yesterday. I might do it wrong."

"Dell," I admonished, resting my chin on the seat and reaching out to touch her arm. Her skin was a rash of goose bumps. "You'll be fine. As soon as the music starts, you'll remember everything."

"I think I'll forget it all. I can't remember anything."

"You can do this." I tried to sound positive, but inside I was starting to worry that we were asking too much of her, with everything she'd been through in the past two days. *If she doesn't go onstage, everyone will understand.* "It's up to—"

"If you hurry up and get in there, you'll have some time to practice." James cut me off, like he knew I was about let Dell off the hook.

Dell thought about that for a moment, then opened her door and got out. " 'K," she said with a mixture of worry and resolve. "I guess I better get goin'." She rushed off toward the building before we were even out of the car.

"You're right," I said to James. "It's good that you convinced her to go. She'd never forgive herself if she didn't go on today. She needs to prove to herself that she can do it." I found myself hoping this would be one of the defining events of Dell's life—the moment she stopped being ashamed of who she was and afraid of the world. Her chance to show the whole town that she was someone special.

James closed his door and strutted a few steps toward the building. "I can do this dad stuff . . . I think."

Tucking my arm into his, I hugged close to his shoulder. "You'll be great at the dad stuff."

Stopping, he slipped his arms around me and kissed me right there on the sidewalk, then stood gazing down at me. "Happy?" he asked.

"Yes," I whispered. "I am happy." The words were true, in so many ways.

The church was hopping with activity when we went inside. Keiler was onstage performing repairs to the cellophane waterfall and talking on his cell phone. "Oh, good, she's here," he said, glancing at me as he jumped off the stage in one quick, high-energy bounce. He handed me the phone on his way to the door. "Here, talk to Shirley. I have to go get some duct tape."

I juggled the phone into position while climbing onto the stage. James followed, then went to see what could be done about the waterfall, which had somehow shed its blue cellophane water overnight. Now there was a huge pool, with no water flowing into it.

"Hi, Shirley," I said, taking a wad of cellophane from the pool and observing that it was stuck together like a giant baseball. "It looks like the set has somehow modified itself overnight."

"It always does," she said cheerfully. "So Keiler tells me you called him last night and told him you might be convinced to take the director's job."

"I think so. Crazy, isn't it?"

"Not so." Her voice was warm and reassuring. "O.K. You do have to be a little crazy to do this job, but you're going to be great at it. Keiler says you're a natural."

"I don't even *have* the job yet," I reminded her, balancing the phone on my ear so I could use both hands and feet to untangle the cellophane.

"You will." Shirley seemed confident. "Every one of your summer counselors is writing a letter for you. That's all it'll take to get the board to put you in. Well . . . that, and you have a pulse."

"Thanks." I laughed, straining to hand the cellophane to Keiler, who had returned with duct tape. The phone slipped from my shoulder, and I caught it in a clumsy juggle on the way down. "Sorry about that. We have an ongoing disaster here involving cellophane and duct tape."

Shirley chuckled. "All part of the job description."

"Strange . . . but true." Almost anything could be part of this job description, which was exactly what I liked about it. Life as a Jumpkids director would be nothing if not an adventure. I wondered if I would be able to explain that to Brent Giani when I called to tell him I wasn't joining Geo Networking—I'd consult, I'd help, even call clients or fly to Boston if they needed me, but I was taking another job. A completely different kind of job. Brent would be stunned. All of them would.

On the phone, Shirley was talking about the details of the application process, how the Jumpkids board in New York was structured, and how the foundation worked. She offered to send me a few brochures, some news articles, and a copy of the charter.

"That would be good, thanks," I said, slightly distracted as Limber Linda ran by, frantically searching for her duct tape.

Keiler tore off a few more pieces, stuck them to his frayed jeans, then passed the duct tape across the stage like a football. Linda made the Hail Mary catch, spun around like a dancer, and then headed out the choir door, saying, "Thanks. The darned headdresses won't stay on the giraffes today."

I tried to imagine how she was going to fix loose headdresses with duct tape. "I'd better go," I told Shirley, as she was finishing the explanation of the paperwork. "I think one of the counselors is about to duct tape costumes onto the children."

"Wouldn't be the first time," Shirley assured me. "Good luck, Karen. Or I guess I should say, break a leg, since you're practically official now."

"Thanks." We said good-bye, and I set down the phone, then went after Linda, leaving Keiler and James to finish the waterfall.

Dell was practicing her solo as I passed by the vocal music room.

She sounded shaky and uncertain. Halfway through the song, she stopped. "I can't do it." Her voice trembled with tears.

"She ain't doin' it right," Sherita carped from somewhere in the room.

I stood outside the door, afraid to go in. If Dell saw me there, it would only add to the pressure. She would be afraid of disappointing me.

"What? Don't tell me you've forgotten the Jumpkids secret?" I heard Tina say.

"It ain't workin'," Sherita groused.

"Sherita, that's enough," Tina reprimanded. "You can either be constructive or you can leave the room. Dell just needs a minute to warm up. Everyone gets nerves. It's nothing unusual. Let's try it again, Dell."

The music cued, and Dell started the song from the top. I waited a minute to see if Sherita would come out, but she didn't. Finally, I hurried on to find Linda and the duct tape.

When I entered the costume gallery, the helpers were, indeed, duct taping costumes onto children, but fortunately to clothes, not to skin or hair or skin with hair on it. The giraffes, now halfway dressed and wrapped securely in harnesses of silver duct tape, seemed to think the costume addition was fantastic, sort of superhero-robot-like, and they admired themselves in the row of long mirrors before putting on the rest of their costumes.

By the time we were ten minutes to curtain, we had everybody costumed and lined up backstage. The kids were calm, having been through the performance the night before.

In the orchestra pit, the percussion band started playing the prelude, accompanied by a clear, sweet piano melody. Glancing around the corner, I saw Dell at the keys, dressed as a young lioness, her face painted with shades of tan and gray, decorated with a nose and whiskers. The first bars of music were uncertain, and she glanced toward the crowd, missing a note, then pausing to catch up with the orchestra. When she started again, she closed her eyes, and within one bar, she was lost in the music. In the audience, people murmured in appreciation, stretching in their seats to see who was playing, taking on looks of surprise as they guessed her identity.

I wished she could see their faces. After tonight, none of them would ever look at her the same way again.

In the second row of the audience, Kate grinned. Sandwiched between Aunt Jeane and Mrs. Jaans, she gave me the thumbs-up with tears in her eyes, then twisted in her seat, looking for Ben, who still wasn't there. I knew she wanted to share this moment with him.

Except for the small space saved for Ben, our family row was full, as was the rest of the sanctuary. The ushers were frantically setting up folding chairs in the aisles. They finished just as the kids were hitting their marks for the opening number. Dell left the orchestra pit and hurried to her place on stage.

In the back of the auditorium, the door opened, letting in a slice of light, and I saw Ben there, holding the door open for some latecomers. I motioned to Kate, and she turned around, waving at him and then raising her hands helplessly because someone had just sat down in his seat. He gave her the O.K. sign as he helped one of the latecomers into a folding chair, then stood in the back against the wall.

The music cued for the opening number, and the auditorium blared with sound.

The kids moved into action like professionals.

In her place with the lion pride, Dell looked nervous and unsure. Watching the other cast members she followed in the dance rather than leading, as she usually would have. I wondered again if we should have pushed her into going onstage. She had so much on her mind right now—her grandmother, the short stay at the foster shelter, her future with James and me. No wonder her emotions were on edge.

The lions jumped to a squat, and Dell missed the cue. Sherita gave Dell's costume a yank, and Dell dropped into place, embarrassed.

My heart ached for her. I wanted to run onto the stage, take her in my arms, and stop the whole thing right then. In the family row, James raised his hands helplessly, and Kate bit her lip. Both of them knew that after Myrone's cameo and some narrative on the tape came a scene among the lion pride, during which Dell was supposed to do a solo. Shortly after that would be her big duet with Edwardo at the waterfall. Watching her now, I wondered how she would make it through even the first small solo, a verse of a song called "If You Believe."

The first song finished, and the monkey medicine man lifted Myrone high into the air as the finale. Myrone squirmed and let out a roar, and the crowd burst into spontaneous applause.

Sherita beamed at me as the lions moved into place for the next song. I smiled back, joyous for the other children, aching for Dell.

"She's having a tough time of it," Keiler whispered, leaning close to me.

"I know." Panic began to swell inside me. "I shouldn't have pushed her to go on. She's just not up to it today. Maybe we should find a way to take her off, before . . ."

Keiler motioned to cue the music for the next number. "She'll come through."

The music started, and I held my breath as Dell rose from the lounging lion pride and came forward to sing. Dark eyes wide and white rimmed, she stared into the crowd, frozen. The music for the first verse began, but she remained silent. Behind her, the lion pride exchanged confused shrugs, and Keiler signaled the sound engineer to recue the music. Dell cut a desperate glance our way. I stood there helpless, imagining how she felt—heart pounding, mind racing, nervous perspiration dripping beneath her costume. All alone in front of the people who knew she couldn't do this.

I closed my eyes as the melody before the first verse played again. *Please, please give her courage . . .*

The chorus began and a voice rang into the air, high and sweet.

What do you know of things you can't see? . . .

I opened my eyes, realizing the voice wasn't Dell's. From the lion pride, Sherita was striding forward, her movements lithe and lyrical. To the crowd, I knew it would appear planned. When Sherita reached center stage, she stopped and faced Dell, as if to sing a duet.

Turning from the audience, Dell looked into Sherita's eyes, nodding almost imperceptibly. All of a sudden, she began to sing, as well. Her voice mixed with Sherita's in perfect harmony, filling the sanctuary with music as the lions danced around them in a symphony of movement and color.

My heart swelled with pride and awe, and tears welled in my eyes as I watched Dell and Sherita, two outcasts standing strong within the circle together, no longer willing to bend before the world.

I hugged them both as they came offstage and another group went on, while the narrator talked on tape. "That was great," I whispered.

Dell beamed, and Sherita shrugged away from me, trying to hide a smile. She leaned close to Dell, shaking a finger. "I ain't doin' that again. You gotta sing your own solo next time."

"I will." Dell straightened her body confidently. "Thanks, Sherita."

"It's O.K." Sherita did her best to look gruff. "I guess you probably didn't get much sleep las' night."

"I'm all right now," Dell promised, straightening her costume and intently watching the performers onstage. "I'll be ready for the next one."

And she was. The rest of the performance was pure magic, and by the time it was over, the audience was on its feet, roaring in a standing ovation that called the actors back for four curtain calls.

When the stage lights finally dimmed, Dell couldn't wait to get to our family row. I waited with her impatiently while the tide of audience members flowed out and the ushers moved the folding chairs from the aisles.

Kate grabbed Dell in a gigantic hug as we reached the second row. "That was fantastic! You were amazing."

"Yesh, amazing!" Joshua chimed in. "You looked like a big lion. Do lions sing?"

We laughed as Dell made her way up and down the family row, offering hugs of pure jubilation. "Where's Ben?" she asked, suddenly noticing that someone important was missing.

"In back," Kate answered. "He got here just as the performance was starting."

"But he saw it?" Dell asked, her dark brows rising hopefully.

"I saw every bit of it," Ben answered, making his way up the aisle, following somebody's grandmother, who was doing a fairly determined job of elbowing her way against the tide of outgoing guests. She stopped when she reached us and held her hand out, offering Dell a single pink rose. "This is for you," she said, smiling, her blue eyes twinkling beneath a puff of hair dyed bright red. "A star should always have a rose on her opening night. It's good luck."

"Ummm . . . thank you," Dell said, embarrassed. Taking the rose, she glanced at me uncertainly.

The woman didn't move on, but turned to Ben instead. "I suppose you ought to introduce me," she said, sounding like a spitfire.

Ben jerked into action. "I'm sorry." He glanced up and down the family row, aware that he didn't know all of the names. "This is . . . everyone. Everyone, this is Sadie Walker."

Chapter 24

Even at ninety-three, with her back rounded and her body slightly stooped, Sadie Walker was a tall woman. The puff of deep artificially red hair arranged in a loose twist atop her head made her even taller, so that she seemed formidable standing there in the chapel. Her eyes, robin's egg blue like Grandma Roses's, were acute, and spoke of a clever mind and a good sense of humor. She was wearing a blue lace shirt, slightly transparent, with a camisole underneath, a long denim skirt, chunky red jewelry, and tall cowboy boots with cream-colored bottoms and red tops. She was fashionable, glamorous, larger than life.

Mrs. Jaans recognized her and reacted before the rest of us. "Oh, Sadie! Oh, Sadie!" she exclaimed, so excited that she knocked over a folding chair, tripped, and stumbled into James, who caught her and set her back on her feet. She didn't even notice—she just stretched out her arms and headed for Sadie Walker at a run, crying, "Oh, Sadie, it's cousin Eudora. Don't you remember me?"

Sadie took on a look of recognition and threw open her arms, nearly knocking out a group of bystanders. "Oh, Eudora!" She pushed past an usher who was trying to fold chairs. "Eudora! Eudora!" They locked in an embrace, sobbing and laughing, stopping to look at each other, then hugging again.

Still seated in the second row, Joshua, Alex, and Amber stared with their mouths open, amazed and slightly wary of the histrionics.

When Sadie and Mrs. Jaans were finally finished, we made the rest of the introductions as the sanctuary emptied. Brother Baker came by and reminded us that the after-party potluck dinner was ready in Town Square Park, and they were waiting for Dell and me and the rest of the Jumpkids counselors, as guests of honor. I stood there, torn between celebrating the successful Jumpkids performance and talking to Sadie Walker, at last.

Sadie seemed to be thinking the same thing, but she glanced at Dell, who was fidgeting in place with her rose, and said, "I haven't been to an after party in years!" Clapping her hands together, she looped an arm through Dell's, and they started toward the door together. "Come along, sugar. A star shouldn't be late for her own celebration."

Sadie swept out the door with a confident, regal stride, and the rest of us followed along like dust in the wake of a tornado.

James glanced at me and smiled. "This is something."

"I guess," I agreed, listening as Sadie talked to Dell about crossing the street.

"All right, wait just a minute, love. There's traffic. I don't move as fast as I used to. Here, hold on to my arm. Here we go. A bit like trying to get a three-legged turtle across the highway, isn't it?"

Dell giggled, and Sadie hugged her close. Oddly, Dell didn't seem to mind at all.

Sadie went on talking as Dell helped her onto the opposite curb, while the rest of us trailed across the street. "Your performance was wonderful, especially the dance at the waterfall. Did you know I was a dancer and a singer? I still am, but just at the retirement homes now. A little music helps brighten those old folks' days. But when I was young, I sang and danced at Radio City Music Hall—imagine that. It was quite a life, quite a time back then."

"Really?" Dell asked, and Sadie began giving her a history lesson on Radio City Music Hall and the early days of the musical variety hour.

Behind me, I could hear Kate whispering rapid-fire questions to Ben.

"Ben, why in the world didn't you tell me you found her?" she asked, clearly in awe of Sadie's presence. It was a reality almost too strange to believe—my grandmother's long-lost sister, the only remaining immediate family member of her generation, walking at the front of our line, at ninety-three years old, discussing the history of theater, jazz, and early television variety hours.

Ben chuckled. "I wanted it to be a surprise. I only tracked her down yesterday. That newspaper article was wrong. Her last name is still Walker. She was married to an old gent for a few years, but he passed away. She doesn't live in a retirement home. She *performs* in them. She sings and dances, if you can believe that, and she still lives alone. She's something of a legend."

"Are you sure she's *our* Sadie?"

"I'm sure."

Baby Rose squealed in Kate's arms and babbled, "Da-da, da-da."

Ben paused long enough to take her, and I dropped back with them, joining the conversation as Ben went on. "Wait until you hear her whole story. She's got a scrapbook about a foot thick. She's been on *The Ed Sullivan Show,* the *Firestone Variety Hour,* in several of the old musicals. She sang and danced at Radio City Music Hall, and on Broadway. She's had quite an amazing life. These days, she spends her time on the steps of the state capitol, lobbying for senior citizen rights, Medicare, pollution control. I had to wait for her to picket a state senator's house before she would come today." He grinned sheepishly, glancing from me to Kate. "The next thing I knew, I was walking the picket line with a bunch of old folks. I think I made the noon news."

Kate laughed. "You're kidding."

"Nope. Just wait until you've spent a little time with her. You'll see. You wouldn't believe the stories she told me on the trip down here."

"Did she tell you anything about why she left home—what happened between her and Grandma Rose?" I asked.

Ben shook his head. "She didn't seem to want to talk about that. Maybe she will later." He looked ahead to where Sadie had stopped on the sidewalk to show Dell a dance step. They made quite a pair, Dell in her white T-shirt and denim shorts, with her cinnamon skin and long, dark hair, and Sadie in her blue skirt with her pale olive complexion and red hair swept into a puffy twist. They stood erect with their arms held gracefully in the air like wings, dancing to music only they could hear.

I stopped just to watch them, dimly hearing Ben say, "Getting to know Sadie Walker is quite an adventure." I had a feeling it would be. Sadie Walker had gravitational pull. Already, the family was starting to spin around her like planets around a sun. We stopped to watch as little Amber joined the dance, and Sadie showed her how to hold her arms. The three of them spun together in the golden afternoon sunlight, Sadie slowly, the girls faster. Dell floated past Aunt Jeane and on to Ben, reaching for baby Rose, saying, "Com'ere, Rosie. I'll show you how to dance."

Ben slipped Rose into Dell's arms, and together they twirled away like leaves caught in the whirlwind of Sadie's dance. Rose squealed and leaned back, throwing her tiny hands into the air, fingers outstretched to the wind in a moment of pure exuberance.

Watching them, I realized it didn't matter what had happened in the past. The only thing that mattered now was that my grandmother's only remaining sister was finally home.

When the dance was finished, we continued on to the party, where a potluck supper was waiting and Jumpkids music was playing on a boom box in the old bandstand. The kids followed Sadie through the line, and I paused to talk to Keiler. "Looks like it's going to be an interesting weekend," he said, watching as Sadie went through the line and then took a seat on a bench beside the gazebo. She was telling a story, her face animated and her hands moving as soon as she set down her plate. The Jumpkids began to gather around her, listening.

"I think it will be quite a weekend," I agreed.

He nodded, strands of shaggy hair drifting in the afternoon breeze. "You going to be ready to go to Goshen Tuesday?"

"I'm not sure," I admitted. "I may have to return to Boston and take care of some things, but I'll be back as soon as I can. Shirley said she would speed my application through, so I can be official."

Keiler gave a sly, sideways look. "Who'd have guessed the lady on the plane would end up being my new boss?"

I met his gaze, taking in the wise, patient look behind his continual jokes and boundless energy. "You guessed. You told me this was going to be a trip off the map."

Lowering his lashes, he looked away, a man unwilling to tell his secrets. "I had a feeling"—then he grinned and rapped his head lightly with his knuckles—"but I never know whether those feelings are coming from the full side of my head or the empty side."

I smiled back, pointing to the Les Paul emblem over his heart. "I think those feelings come from here. You know, you really ought to think about seminary school. You have a special gift."

"We all have gifts." He surveyed the kids, now settled in the park with plates of food, and the community volunteers busily serving drinks and desserts, and the Jumpkids counselors moving through the line. "The trick is finding out what they are."

"Sometimes we have to be *reminded* of what they are," I corrected.

"That too."

Limber Linda called to us from the food line. "Come on, you guys. Hurry up and get some food and a glass of tea. We want to make a toast."

Dr. Schmidt was serving lemonade and tea at the end of the table. He leaned close to me as he handed me my glass. "Got your test results via FedEx this afternoon. Nothing to worry about. I'll talk to you more on Monday."

I stood staring at him, shocked, uncertain, afraid to react. "Wh-what?" I breathed. I wanted to hear him repeat the words, to be sure I hadn't imagined them. "Are you sure? It's O.K.? Everything's O.K.?"

"It's fine." He squeezed my arm, his touch making the moment more real, the news more concrete. "There were no abnormal cells on the biopsy. The inflammation that showed up on your tests at Dr. Conner's office could have been caused by a number of things, possibly an infection that has since cleared up. It's hard to say now, but it really doesn't matter. The biopsy was one hundred percent normal."

One hundred percent normal . . . I felt the earth shift beneath my feet, as if everything were moving from slightly off-kilter to level. The colors of the grass and the trees, and the iris blooming around the bandstand suddenly seemed brighter. "Boy, that's a good word," I whispered.

Dr. Schmidt frowned, cocking his head to one side. "Hmmm?"

"Normal," I said, feeling laughter bubble from somewhere deep inside me. "A few weeks ago, *normal* seemed impossibly far away."

His eyes twinkled with the wisdom of a man who had witnessed the turning points of many lives in our small town. "Congratulations on finding your way back. It's not a bad place to be."

"No, it's not. Thanks, Doc," I said, feeling the prickle of joyful tears, feeling lighter than air, as if I could raise my arms and float into the vast blue sky overhead.

Dr. Schmidt glanced up as James, Jenilee, and Aunt Jeane came to the table. "What'll you have to drink?" he asked with a conspiratorial wink that told me he'd leave it to me to share the good news with my family.

"Water," I said, watching as he filled my cup to the rim and handed it to me. The liquid spilled onto my fingers, cool and clear, mineral scented in a way that reminded me of the moment just before I sank below the surface of the mermaid pool.

I waited while the rest of the family took their glasses. When we were finished, the servers filled their own plates and we moved to benches around the park.

Mojo Joe, who turned out to be something of a poet, stood on the bandstand steps and gave an impromptu toast. "To all of us gathered here today, and all those who couldn't be. May every coming day be as good as this one. May we always find the company of friends, the kindness of strangers, and the beauty in ourselves. *Hakuna Matata.*"

A cheer rose from the crowd, young voices mixing with old as together we raised our glasses to good friends, kind strangers, and *The Lion King*.

When the after party finished, our family stood in the church parking lot, trying to figure out who would go in what cars. All of the kids wanted to ride with Sadie, who seemed more than happy to soak up their adoration.

Patting their heads fondly as they gathered around her, she turned to Kate and me. "I'd like to go see Rose. I know she's gone, but there are some things I'd like to say, where she's laid to rest."

"Why don't we all go?" I suggested. "We were going to visit on Memorial Day. Let's do it today instead. We can stop and pick some wildflowers on the way."

Sadie slipped her hand over mine and gave a squeeze. "That would be perfect."

We climbed into our cars and left the church parking lot in an odd caravan, with our car in the lead, Sadie and Ben next, and everyone else following behind. Dell elected to ride with Sadie so she could listen to more stories.

As we drove, I told James about the news from Dr. Schmidt. He let out a long breath, like he'd been holding it for a while. His eyes glistened with moisture, and he reached up to rub the emotions away.

"James," I said softly, laying my hand on his arm, suddenly seeing how afraid he'd been. "Everything's all right."

"I know." He smiled slightly, glancing at our intertwined fingers. "It's just hard to believe everything's finally all right. Seems like it's been a long time since we were all right, you know?"

Squeezing his hand, I laid my head against the seat. "Long trip," I said, using pilot's terms. For eight years, we'd been orbiting our grief, staying far from it, far from each other, looking at life with the detachment of a holding pattern at ten thousand feet. Now, suddenly, here we were, on the ground, together, in a completely new place.

"Rough landing."

Smiling, I watched the sweet pea, primrose, and yellowbonnets drift by. "True, but the pilot knew what he was doing." I knew the pilot wasn't James or me. Neither of us could have imagined the flight path or the destination for this trip. Yet God knew how to land the plane safely, even when James and I were panicking in the passenger seats.

In the golden evening light, the colors seemed brighter, as if I'd removed sunglasses and was seeing the world clearly for the first time. The primrose was deeper pink, the black-eyed Susan like yellow fire, the sweet pea a dash of vibrant magenta, and the trees an explosion of bold spring green. Rolling down my window, I let the breeze blow through the car, carrying the scent of growing things, of grass and water and sky.

The car slowed as we passed over the place on Mulberry Creek where the old wooden bridge had been replaced with a new steel structure, a sign of changing times. I jolted in my seat, almost reaching for the steering wheel. "Oh, stop. Turn in."

James hit the brakes and slowed just in time to pull into our driveway. Behind us, the other cars did the same, brakes squealing and tires rattling on the gravel as we bounced up the drive to the cleared patch of ground where James's tractor kept a lonely vigil.

He gave the machine a look of pure adoration. "I haven't shown your dad my sweetheart yet."

From somewhere behind us, I could heard my father getting out of his car, saying, "Is that a fifty-seven John Deere?"

James was out of his seat before I had a chance to say anything. Shaking my head, I got out and waited for the rest of the family to exit their vehicles.

Nearby, the tractor puffed to life, and Joshua scrambled across Aunt Jeane to exit Kate's car, hollering, "Uncle James, can we take a twak-tow wide?"

Uncle James was only too happy to oblige. Jenilee's brothers held the kids back while James, my father, and Uncle Robert hooked up the wagon. Ben handed baby Rose off to Dell, and she came back to where we were standing. "They're gonna have a full load," she observed. "I think Rose and I better stay here and help pick wildflowers to take to Grandma. It's all *guys* in the wagon, anyway."

"Why don't we girls walk down to the waterfall?" I suggested.

" 'K," Dell said, handing baby Rose to Aunt Jeane. "I'll lead. There's an easier path where you don't have to climb down the rocks."

"That sounds good," I agreed. "I'll help Aunt Sadie." Behind me, Jenilee had already slipped her arm into Sadie's in preparation for our journey.

I backed up a few steps, and Sadie held out her other elbow, smiling mischievously. "You can help me, too. We'll bring up the rear."

Dell started down the path and we followed behind her, first Kate with baby Rose, then Aunt Jeane, Mrs. Jaans, and Darla. Beside her, little Amber stopped to look indecisively at the tractor, which had sputtered to a halt. James, Ben, my father, and Mr. Jaans were under the hood, while Uncle Robert held Joshua and Alex in the wagon.

"C'mon, Amber," Jenilee said. "Let's go before the guys catch us. This is an adventure for just us girls."

"Where we goin'?" Amber asked.

"To a waterfall," I answered. "To a special place where the mermaids used to live."

Amber's five-year-old mind considered the idea behind wide, dark eyes. "Not really?" she said finally.

"No, but we used to *play* mermaids there," I admitted. "But there really is a waterfall and a beautiful pool and the most fantastic wildflowers growing out of the rocks."

Amber gave an excited squeal and trotted ahead to catch up with Dell. Beside me, Sadie tipped her head back, listening as a breeze stirred the sycamores. "I remember this place." The words were little more than a breath exhaled, a whisper of memory. "Oh, I remember this place."

"Grandma Rose used to bring us here," I told her as we walked. Ahead, Dell descended the slight slope to the riverbank, and Amber slipped past her, dashing toward the water. "When we were done swimming, she'd always walk back to the sycamore grove to pick wildflowers alone. I never understood why until we read Augustine's letters about the sister trees. Grandma Rose never stopped thinking about her sisters. She never stopped missing you, even if she was too proud to say so."

"Nor I her," Sadie said softly, turning her ear toward the sound of the waterfall as we descended the riverbank and walked along a deer trail near the water's edge. "I remember that sound. I remember it like it was yesterday." Her blue eyes grew misty, lost in memories. A tear slipped from the corner and ran into the lines on her cheek. "Oh, in my mind I'm a girl again. I could let go of your hands and run along this path, dive into the water, and swim to the bottom." She slipped on a patch of wet, mossy stone, and Jenilee and I paused to steady her. Sadie turned her attention to the trail, choosing her footing more carefully. "How did I come to be in this old body?" she asked wistfully. "And so many years gone by. I should have returned home sooner. Pride is a terrible thing. It's a death of sorts."

"Yes," I agreed, looking ahead at Kate. If not for these past two weeks, we might have traveled the same path as my grandmother and her sisters.

Memories assaulted Sadie as we drew close to the pool below the waterfall. She stopped just before we rounded the last bend. Letting her head fall into her hands, she began to weep in earnest. Jenilee and I stood beside her, not knowing what to do.

"Your initials are still carved in the rocks," I said, hoping to lift her grief. "Yours and Grandma Rose's. Jenilee, your grandma Augustine's initials are there, too."

Sadie's head jerked up and she blinked at Jenilee. "Are you Augustine's granddaughter?"

Jenilee frowned in confusion. "Yes. Augustine's daughter was my mom."

I realized that in our introductions, we must have left that out. Sadie was just now making the connection. She brought a hand to her mouth in amazement, then lowered it again. Then she touched Jenilee's face, whispering, "Oh . . . I just assumed . . . I thought . . . When Kate said you were cousins, I assumed you and your brothers were Eudora's children."

Jenilee's lips formed a silent *O*, and she shook her head. "No, I'm Augustine's granddaughter."

Tears sprung fresh from Sadie's eyes, and she lifted aged hands to cup Jenilee's face, featherlight, as if she were afraid to really touch her. "Then you're mine, too," she breathed. "Oh, I should have realized it when I looked at you. You have your mother's eyes. Where is your mother, child?"

Jenilee blinked, surprised, her brows drawing together. "She passed away several years ago."

Sadie's head fell back as if the words were a physical blow, and she deflated like a balloon losing air. Jenilee and I rushed to catch her.

279 · The Language of Sycamores

"It's all right," I soothed. "Let's go on to the waterfall so you can sit down."

"Yes." Sadie's voice was faint and she was heavy in our arms. "I'd like to sit down."

Jenilee gave me a worried frown and I shrugged, uncertain of what to do but go on.

By the time we rounded the bend, Sadie seemed to have composed herself. "I think I'd like to sit on the ledge and dangle my feet in the water, like old times." She smiled, watching Dell, Amber, and baby Rose splash around in the shallows with Aunt Jeane and Mrs. Jaans, who had rolled up their pants and waded in. On the far shore by the waterfall, Amber's mother was sitting on the mermaid stone, watching the clouds go by.

Kate stopped picking flowers and came over to us. "Everything all right? I was starting to wonder about you three."

"Everything's fine," Sadie answered, struggling to pry off her tall cowboy boots using a forked stick as a makeshift boot jack. Clutching an overhanging branch, she lowered herself to the rock shelf with enthusiasm, her melancholy seemingly forgotten. Kate, Jenilee, and I exchanged surprised glances as Sadie swung her legs around, her feet and the hem of her blue skirt falling into the cool, clear water.

Bracing her hands behind herself, she let her head fall back and gazed up into the sycamores for a long time. "Sit down here," she said finally. "Sit down here, and I'll tell you the story of what really happened."

Kate, Jenilee, and I surrounded her on the rock ledge—Kate and I on one side and Jenilee on the other.

Jenilee kicked off her sandals and dipped her feet in the water beside Sadie's, watching the ripples spread into the pool, then turning her attention to Sadie.

Sadie began her story as she gazed into the water, into the past. "Once, there were three little girls who played here. They didn't have a very good life in some ways, but they had each other, and that was enough. When their work was done, they came here to hide away from the world. The oldest girl was flighty and frail, given to illnesses and fainting spells the doctors couldn't explain. The doctors thought she wouldn't live a long life, and because of that, she was fanciful, with a head full of music and dreams. Sometimes she invented stories about fairies and mermaids, and tried to convince the others those things were true. The middle girl was practical and stern, because she had to be. She was the strong one who carried much of the family burden. She was often cross and tired from her work, from caring for her sisters and the little brothers, who came one right after another, some surviving infancy and some not."

Sadie paused and smiled at Jenilee, stroking Jenilee's shoulder-length blond hair. "The third girl was younger, a tiny child born too early, quiet and sweet, filled with love. But by the time she came, their mother was angry and bitter, sad from the stillbirths of several babies and the struggle to feed and clothe a family. Their father had grown weary as well, given over to drink and depression."

Sadie sighed, shaking her head, the pleated line of her lips trembling. I thought of my grandma Rose, stern, practical Grandma Rose, the middle girl of the three, the one who protected the other two even though she was a child herself. In all the years I knew her, she kept that part of herself hidden from us, yet it explained so many things about her.

Kate didn't seem surprised by what Sadie was saying, only saddened. *Grandma Rose must have told her,* I thought, and I was envious again of their time together before Grandma died. I wished it had been me. As soon as I had the chance to go back to Boston, I would read the little book of life lessons that Grandma had written for Kate. . . .

Beside me, Sadie went on. "When the oldest girl grew into a young woman, and she began to have her monthly time, her fainting spells ended, but she kept that secret to herself. She knew that if she told, she'd be sent away to work, to help support the family, and that would be the end of her singing and dancing. In her dreams, she became wealthy on the stage and she took her brothers and sisters far away from that little white house. In her dreams, she saved them all." She shook her head with a wan, trembling smile. "What a silly, foolish girl. She didn't tell, even when her middle sister was sent away, only fourteen years old, to be a mother's helper for a wealthy woman in the city. This oldest girl kept silent, even though she knew it should have been her who went away, so that her sister, who was very bright, could finish school."

Sadie's cloudy blue gaze settled on Kate and me, apologetic, sad, filled with regret. "As often happens, her wrongs came back to haunt her. It wasn't long before her father, whose drinking had run the family into impossible debt, made plans for her to marry an older man who had survived one wife and wanted another. There was no choice about it—the paperwork was already signed, her suitcase packed by her mother. Her father took her that day after school to the man's house in town. That night this stranger, this old man, took her as his wife, and she felt herself disappearing."

Tears glittered in Sadie's eyes and dripped unheeded down her cheeks as she remembered her painful past. "In the morning, the girl woke and cleaned herself and packed her bag. She didn't leave a note, just slipped from the house with what she could carry. There was a traveling cabaret show in town—it had been the talk of all the decent folk, so she knew about it. She went to them and she begged them to take her in, and there among the forgotten and the unloved, she found a family. That night, she danced onstage for the very first time, awkward and ashamed but alive again. She danced the dance of Salome, with seven veils."

Sadie tipped her head back, drinking in air, moving her hands gracefully in front of herself like a Salome laying down the veils. "She went on and made a good life after that. Oh, she was never very famous or wealthy, but she lived and she laughed and she grabbed at her dreams. She tried to send money home, but it came back with her sister's angry letter telling her she was dead to her family. So she stayed away. She went on with life, and some years later, she fell in love with a man while working on a film production in California. Oh, he was handsome, and successful, and she fell for him so blindly." Sadie's face glowed with the memory. "They shared such a passion together in their little cottage by the sea. They talked of the moon and the stars, of marrying and setting sail on a boat to the far corners of the world."

282 · LISA WINGATE

Drawing in a long breath, she shrugged helplessly, her eyes becoming clear again. "Then she became pregnant, and he left. She went away where no one would know, and she had a beautiful amber-haired baby girl." She laid her hand on Jenilee's knee, smiling sadly. Jenilee's eyes brimmed with tears, and Sadie wiped them away with trembling fingers. "She knew she couldn't keep her baby, and that broke her heart, as the doctors told her she must never have another. This one beautiful little angel was all there would ever be. She wanted her baby to have a home, a mother and a father, so when the baby was just four weeks old, she searched out her sister Augustine. She knew that Augustine had married a good man, and that they would take the baby in and raise her with care and never tell anyone she was a love child."

Sadie held out her arms as if she were cradling a baby. "The swaddling blanket was wet with tears when she knocked on the door. She found Augustine crying on the other side, grieving the loss of a newborn child. And then she knew. She knew there was a reason for all of this. Her sadness fell away, and she felt a peace that helped her place the baby in Augustine's barren cradle. She gave the baby one last kiss, and she promised never to come back, never to bring shame to her daughter.

"And she never did. She kept that baby only in her heart all those many years . . . and in here." Reaching into her blouse, she pulled out a heart-shaped locket, dented at the tip and worn smooth by years close to her skin. Her fingers trembled as she opened it. "This one picture was taken the week her daughter was born. That was all there was, until today." Letting the locket fall, she slipped her hands over ours. "Who knew that she would one day sit in this place with her sister's children, and with her very own granddaughter? Who could have imagined such a wonderful circle of life?"

The question went unanswered, though we each knew the answer. Some things are so far beyond human explanation that they can only belong to God.

God, who took the child of one woman and gave her to another, and now brought her back. Who saw sisters parted for a lifetime and finally reunited through a new generation. Who sent the years that asked and the years that answered.

It was His fingertip that charted the winding course of the river, His hand that hollowed out the pool where the mermaids once again swam, His brushstrokes that painted the twilight hues in the blue Missouri sky.

His breath that now whispered overhead among the sycamores.

LISA WINGATE

&

The Language of Sycamores

This Conversation Guide is intended to enrich the
individual reading experience, as well as encourage us
to explore these topics together—because books,
and life, are meant for sharing.

A CONVERSATION WITH LISA WINGATE

Q. *What is your "typical" day? How do you fit writing in with being a wife and mother?*

A. My typical day begins with getting the boys off to school, which is a change for me in the last few years. My typical day used to be entertaining a toddler while hurrying to write during naptimes. Now that everyone is in school, I usually sit down to write while drinking my tea first thing in the morning. I hear the cadence of the words like music, and when I'm really into a story everything else fades away. It's sometimes hard for me to remember that the people and events in the stories aren't real—which, actually, may mean I need some kind of therapy. It has occurred to me that I spend a great deal of time listening to the voices in my head and talking to imaginary people!

On a good writing day, I may find myself still in my pajamas with my keyboard in my lap at eleven a.m., all of which is fine, unless neighbors stop by, and I end up answering the door with a bad case of bed head, sheepishly saying, "No, really, I didn't just get up. I've been working for hours."

Q. *How do you develop your characters? Is there some of you in each of them?*

A. My characters tend to be based on people I have known and sometimes people I have crossed paths with for only a moment or two in life.

There are also aspects of the characters that come from my imagination, from the process of discovering a story and the people in it.

I meet my characters the way you would meet any new person in life. I do not invent them all at once; rather, they invent themselves as the story develops. In the beginning, I know only the obvious things about them. I know how they look, how they talk, how they react to other people and situations around them. I discover the deeper aspects of each character as the story goes along, and many of those things surprise me. Characters will say, do, or think things that cause me to deeply ponder their motivations, their desires, and the events in their pasts that have shaped them into who they are. Eventually, they become real to me, with quirks, and feelings, and histories all their own.

Q. *How do you choose titles for your books? Does this title have a special meaning?*

A. Usually, sometime during the process of writing a book, the "perfect" title will come to me. Sometimes, this happens at the beginning, along with the book idea, as in *Texas Cooking*, which I knew was to have that title from the very start. In other cases it takes longer. *Tending Roses, Good Hope Road,* and *Lone Star Café* were cases in which I searched and agonized over titles all the way through writing the book (it's a little like having a baby with no name), until finally the right title came along.

In the case of *The Language of Sycamores*, I'd written about one-fourth of the book before the right title became apparent. I went out walking on a breezy evening, and the sound of sycamore leaves fluttering in the wind transported my mind, just for an instant, to the old family farm, twenty years ago. I realized that memories can be tied to anything, even such an everyday sound as leaves combing the wind. Each type of tree has its own particular language. For me, the whisper of sycamores takes me back to the old farm, the popping sound of cottonwood leaves, to the house I grew up in, to the swish of wind in the aspens to my first married year in the mountains of New Mexico, and to the hush of palms to my early childhood on the Florida coast.

I knew that Karen was having much the same experience on her return visit to Grandma Rose's farm. The familiar sights and sounds carried her back to the past and back to herself. Among these, of course, were those lofty sycamores, which whispered the secrets of mermaids and fairies and sisterhood and finally shared their wisdom with new generations.

Q. *How do the humor and the deep, dark emotions coexist in your books?*

A. As they do in life. Laughter and tears are often close cousins. There is an old saying that there are times when you can either laugh or cry, and it's better to laugh. I think a book needs a balance of humor and serious emotion to make it work. There is nothing more endearing than a character (or a person) who can laugh at him- or herself, who is determined to smile in the face of adversity, who has an imperfect, silly side. If you know that a person loves to laugh, it is only that much more powerful when you see that person cry.

As a writer, I try to write the kind of stories I like to read. I like writing that celebrates the good in the world and in people, that leaves me feeling uplifted and hopeful. I like stories and characters that cause me to think about the world in a new way, to look beyond the surface of things and people. I love a story that makes me laugh, cry, then laugh again. When I turn the final page of a book, I want to feel as if I've just eaten the last bite of Thanksgiving dinner and I'm ready to sit back in my chair, let out a long, slow sigh, and tell everyone else how good the food was.

CONVERSATION GUIDE

Q. What kind of writer do you consider yourself? What literary label are you comfortable with?

A. I think I would consider myself a mainstream fiction novelist, an inspirational writer, and in some ways, just an old-fashioned storyteller, though I don't think the labels really matter. I write the stories that are in my head and heart, which is all that I can do. For me, writing is much like being a child again, playing in the backyard, where we built pretend houses from sticks, pine needles, rocks, or piles of grass clippings. We created imaginary characters and began living out the lives of those characters, getting to know them as we went along. The stories developed from there. They were God-given treasures from our imaginations. We didn't chart our plotlines ahead of time. We just discovered them as we went along, and I still do. The only difference now is that my mom no longer makes me come in at dark.

In terms of historical writers, I very much admire Mark Twain, who wrote about everyday things, spoke in language you didn't need a dictionary to read, and often made use of humor. His stories sought to answer timeless human questions by considering the events of everyday life and the wisdom of ordinary people.

Q. How would you describe yourself?

A. Mother, wife, author, true believer, imperfect person, hopefully a good friend. I try to show up for my friends and family when they need me. One of my greatest Mother's Day gifts was a card from my son, which contained all the normal things kids say in Mother's Day cards. The final sentence said: "You always keep your promises." I know that isn't true one hundred percent of the time, but I think my little fellow has figured out one of the timeless axioms of life: If you tell people they are what you want them to be, they will try that much harder to live up to your expectations.

Q. *The character of Grandma Rose is based on your own grandmother. What kind of grandmother do you think you'll be?*

A. I think I will be a good grandmother. I hope I'll be the type who is more interested in going on picnics than in worrying about mud on the floor or dishes in the sink. I hope I'll bake cookies and trundle off to school and baseball games with my basket full and force them on people who are on a diet. I hope I'll be one of those grandmothers who goes around adopting every kid in town—who knows that my grandchildren are just slightly superior to any other children ever born, but is too polite to say so. I hope I'll dump bubble bath in the wading pool, rather than making the kids go inside for a bath. I hope I'll wake up sleeping babies so that I can sit and cuddle them, show them shooting stars and sunrises, sneak chocolates to them behind their parents' backs, and tiptoe into their rooms after bedtime to tell them stories. I hope, when my children tell me they'll be arriving for a visit on Wednesday afternoon, I'll start cooking on Monday morning, and by noon Monday, I'll call asking why they're late.

Q. *If someone wanted to find more information about your books or write you a note, how could they do that?*

A. Through my Web site, www.lisawingate.com. One of the most wonderful things about the publication of the books has been the chance, through e-mail and speaking engagements, to talk with so many people from so many different walks of life. Writing as a career is an odd paradox, in that it is a solitary profession in which you spend your time trying to communicate thoughts, feelings, emotions, or experiences to other people. What you find, after talking to enough people (real and imaginary), is that the human condition changes very little from life to life, from generation to generation. We all want happiness, contentment, a sense of belonging, to love and be loved. We all struggle with common choices, challenges, and sacrifices, and there is comfort in knowing just that. On any given road, you're never the only traveler. There are always people ahead, there are always people behind. The trick is to learn what you can from those you pass along the way and to remember that the builder of the road knew what He was doing.

Q. *Where did you grow up? Was your childhood like or unlike those of the characters in the book?*

A. I was actually born in Germany, and my family moved several times after that when I was very young, due to my father's job advancements. He was in the computer industry very early on, and his opportunities were always changing. I was a naturally shy kid, so moving and switching schools and friends was hard for me. We finally settled in Tulsa, Oklahoma, when I was still in elementary school, so I am more or less a native Tulsan.

I grew up in a typical busy suburban household, with two parents into careers and no extended family nearby. We kids spent our time roaming the neighborhood, scaring up games of tag and touch football. As long as we were home by the time the streetlights came on, no one worried about us. We had a kind of freedom kids don't have today. Even though we lived in a neighborhood, we had space to be and pretend, to create and wander. We had no concept of private property rights. Any tree was ours to climb, and every field was crisscrossed with bike trails. We had grand names for every patch of trees—names like Sherwood Forest and Peaceful Forest—and every kid in the neighborhood knew which forest was which. It was a long, lazy kind of childhood, not filled with all the carefully scheduled activities kids have today. I wish every kid could have that time to wander and create imaginary worlds. These days, kids don't like to be bored. They don't expect to be, and that is a shame. Some of our greatest childhood moments grew out of lack of stuff to do. We learned to invent our own imaginary adventures because there were no videos and video games to invent them for us. Necessity may be the mother of invention for adults, but boredom is the mother of childhood invention.

QUESTIONS FOR DISCUSSION

1. In what ways do the characters in the book measure success? How are their values reflective of, or a reaction to, today's society? How have expectations changed in the last fifty years in terms of the typical American family?

2. Do you agree with Brother Baker's assessment that it is our scars—our little nicks, dents, and imperfections—that make us able to relate to other people? Have you seen evidence of this in your own life?

3. Karen defends her career change by saying that, after years of pursuing the outward symbols of success, she now desires a job that will give her satisfaction of the soul. In what ways do you seek satisfaction of the soul?

4. Karen's journey home causes her to rediscover lost parts of herself. Do you think it is possible to rediscover lost interests and passions? What lost passions would you like to rediscover?

5. Karen describes the moment of childhood's end, in Mrs. Klopfleish's class, when she suddenly became conscious of her own imperfections. After that, everything was different for her. Do you think everyone has such a moment of moving from the innocent self-acceptance of childhood to the self-criticism and self-consciousness of adulthood?

6. Karen asks, at one point, why God would give Dell such an amazing talent, yet put her in such an oppressive, destructive environment. What are some possible answers to that question, or is there an answer?

7. In what ways has the decision to have or not to have children become an invisible barrier between Kate and Karen? Have you seen instances in which this issue has divided friends and family members?

8. Which sister, Kate or Karen, did you relate to more easily?

9. On the plane, Keiler notes that it is the tragedies in our life that bring us back to the foundations of family and faith, the things that do not change when everything else does. What have been the foundations in your own life? What events have taken you away from them, and brought you back again?

10. The sound of sycamore leaves is a touch point that takes Karen's mind back to her childhood visits to the farm. Are there similar touch points in your own life?

11. Karen jokingly says that, if there were anyone, anywhere stubborn enough to manipulate other people's lives from beyond the grave, it would be Grandma Rose. In what ways is Grandma Rose still a presence in the family, even though she is gone?

12. James finally confesses to Karen that one of his reasons for not wanting children was his own fear of being left alone to raise a family, as his father was after his mother's death. In what ways do we let fear rule our lives? In what ways does fear keep us from really living?

13. What does the river symbolize in the story? In what ways are Karen's plunge into the mermaid pool and the eventual return of the new generation to the riverside symbolic?